THE
TERRAFORMERS

OTHER BOOKS BY ANNALEE NEWITZ

NOVELS

Autonomous

The Future of Another Timeline

NONFICTION

Scatter, Adapt, and Remember:
How Humans Will Survive a Mass Extinction

Four Lost Cities: A Secret History of the Urban Age

ANNALEE

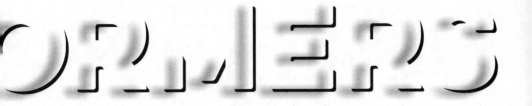

ORMERS

NEWITZ

TOR

TOR PUBLISHING GROUP
NEW YORK

This is a work of fiction. All of the characters, organizations, and events portrayed in this novel are either products of the author's imagination or are used fictitiously.

THE TERRAFORMERS

Maps by David Lindroth Inc.

A Tor Book
Published by Tom Doherty Associates / Tor Publishing Group
120 Broadway
New York, NY 10271

www.tor-forge.com

Tor® is a registered trademark of Macmillan Publishing Group, LLC.

Library of Congress Cataloging-in-Publication Data

Names: Newitz, Annalee, 1969– author.
Title: The terraformers / Annalee Newitz.
Description: First edition. | New York : Tor, 2023. | "A Tom Doherty Associates book."
Identifiers: LCCN 2022034344 (print) | LCCN 2022034345 (ebook) |
ISBN 9781250228017 (hardcover) | ISBN 9781250228062 (ebook)
Subjects: LCGFT: Science fiction. | Novels.
Classification: LCC PS3614.E588 T47 2023 (print) | LCC PS3614.E588 (ebook) |
DDC 813'.6—dc23/eng/20220722
LC record available at https://lccn.loc.gov/2022034344
LC ebook record available at https://lccn.loc.gov/2022034345

Our books may be purchased in bulk for promotional, educational, or business use.
Please contact your local bookseller or the Macmillan Corporate and Premium Sales Department
at 1-800-221-7945, extension 5442, or by email at MacmillanSpecialMarkets@macmillan.com.

First Edition: 2023

Printed in the United States of America

0 9 8 7 6 5 4 3 2 1

For Jesse Burns,
with all my love in this world and the ones we'll build next

What will survive us
has already begun

—Stephanie Burt

COLONIALISM. Definition: turning bodies into cages
that no one has the keys for.

—Billy-Ray Belcourt

PART I
SETTLERS

YEAR: 59,006

PLANET: Sask-E

MISSION: Ecosystem Maintenance

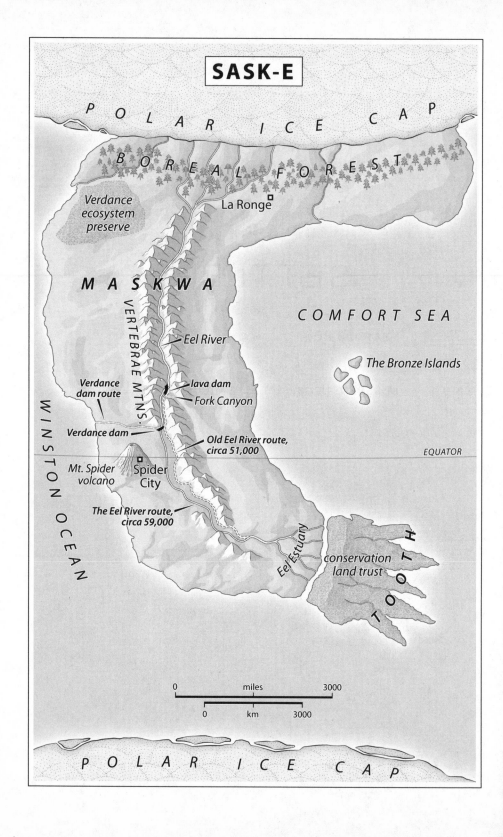

1

PLEISTOCENE FETISHIST

When in doubt, don't kill anyone.
—*Environmental Rescue Team Handbook*

Destry could smell the smoke long before she saw its improbable source. There was some kind of person—possibly *Homo sapiens*—tending a fire at the edge of the boreal forest. She squinted, trying to make out details from half a klick away. The person's skin was so pale she guessed it had hardly met real sunlight, which meant they were definitely not a stray worker from one of the construction camps. When the intruder crouched next to the flames, she caught a glimpse of red beard merging into a tangle of hair. In their hands, a hare was speared and cooking on an expensive alloy spit. The sight was horrifying, and Destry flinched back reflexively.

"Let's stop," she whispered to her mount, a thick-barreled moose with red-brown fur and a crown of antlers spreading from his forehead like a pair of massive, cupped hands. He flicked an ear in acknowledgement as she slid off his back and into his long shadow. Sinking down on one knee, Destry pressed her bare fingers into the soil, spreading them wide, establishing a high-bandwidth connection with the local ecosystem.

Thousands of sensors welcomed her into the planet's network, their collective perceptions knitting together from shards of cached memory, fragments of recorded sensation and perception. In this state, she too was a sensor, processing data through her eyes, nose, tongue, skin, and ears. What she perceived she shared with the ecosystem. She could feel the sensors collaboratively reviewing the scene from her perspective, learning that she wanted to know more about the mammal at the edge of the forest. It was like her body had become the land. Her awareness stretched forward, racing through root systems and over insects, tasting acid levels in the soil.

The person's feet on the ground registered as pressure on her back, and she smelled redox reactions in the fire. Each sensor's evaluation joined the swelling chorus in her ears as the tiny machines voted on what their data points might mean: *polymer, hair, carnivore, unprocessed excrement, dead trees, carbon cycle perturbation, predator, metal, fur, synthetic microbiome.* As Destry's data surged across the field and into the forest, the sensors could see what she did, and their analysis coalesced into a strong probability: Homo sapiens *in the region for eight days, causally linked to tree loss, small mammal loss, excrement buildup, complex toxins.*

But there was no data emanating from the person, save for a persistent encrypted stream aimed at an orbital satellite. Out here in the bush, she didn't have the tools to analyze it. All she had were implants that made sensors recognize her as one of their own. She was the only ranger built this way; all her colleagues back home had to use bulky access devices if they wanted to ask a flower about its nitrogen uptake.

Disconnecting from the ecosystem, Destry unfolded her muscular frame and ambled into talking range with the intruder. Her cropped gray-black hair was matted with sweat, and a trickle found its way through the road dust on her cheek, revealing a streak of deeply tanned skin. Wind pricked a few tears from her blue eyes. She kept her hands visible. Basic protocol in the Environmental Rescue Team was to approach in peace, no weapons drawn, aiming to help.

"Hey stranger!" she called after a few minutes. "I'm ERT Ranger Destry Thomas! D'you know you're on unoccupied land?"

The person looked up, their flat, blank face twitching into an awkward grin. Definitely *Homo sapiens.* They stood, technical jumper gleaming dull gray in the late afternoon sun. Now that she was closer, Destry could see a small cabin tucked into the trees, next to a collapsible trellis where a few pelts were stretched. Mink, hare, beaver. A flicker of outrage licked the inside of her ribs, but she kept it in check. No point in getting flustered.

"Who are you? What are you doing on this land?"

The person's mouth worked as if they hadn't spoken for a while. "G-good evening, ERT Ranger Destry Thomas. Don't think I've ever seen Environmental Rescue on a private planet."

Destry ignored his comment and ran her hands through the waist-high grass, connecting to the sensors that dusted each blade. Whatever was happening inside the person's encrypted stream, it was getting thicker. Data poured down furiously and shot back up again.

She stopped a couple of meters away from the fire. "What's your name, stranger?" One hand was free, and the other settled lightly on her holstered gun, slung low over her right hip.

"Name's Charter. I'm not looking for trouble, Ranger. I'm here to experience the Pleistocene. It's the purest environment for mankind."

She groaned to herself. Charter was the default male name for *Homo sapiens* remotes. No wonder he was regurgitating that fat data stream. Somebody was controlling him from offworld, probably thousands of light-years away, using this proxy body to get their jollies in the ecosystem she'd sworn to protect. Out there, in the volume of galactic space claimed by the League, some people believed you weren't really human unless you'd experienced a Pleistocene environment on an Earthlike world. Hence the lure of her planet, Sask-E, whose fragrant forests some distant asswipe was currently smudging with uncontrolled carbon waste.

"All right, Charter. I'm not sure who you are or how you got here, but this is unoccupied land. It's not your habitat."

"Verdance is going to start selling it pretty soon. No harm done." Charter was starting to sound whiny, hinting at the personality of whoever controlled him.

"You need to biodegrade everything in this camp and get off this land right now."

"This ecosystem is my birthright." Charter planted his feet firmly next to the fire. He still held the spit with the hare's skinned, burned body in one hand. "It's the origin of all mankind, and everything we do now is shaped by it."

A cool arctic wind threaded through the forest, and fir tree branches gestured wildly overhead. But Destry felt sweaty, inside and out; she ran an arm across her forehead, smearing the dust on her face into a thin, gritty mud. Walking closer, she gave up the pretense of talking to Charter as if he were alive. Now she looked into the wide purple eyes of the expensive biotech toy and addressed the distant person controlling him. "Listen. You haven't identified yourself, and I don't know where you are coming from. But you put this remote here, and you damaged the forest. You're trespassing. You killed animals, which is a crime. You need to pack up your remote right now and get off Sask-E before I report you to Verdance."

She hoped the threat was enough. Charter's controller could be sued for what he'd done. The only thing preventing her from reporting him right now was the fact that she liked talking to Verdance security about as much as they liked dealing with unripe real estate. Sask-E was supposed to terraform itself for another thousand years before anyone had to worry about its existence.

Charter yanked some flesh off the hare and put it between his teeth, chewing awkwardly. "You know that man evolved to eat meat, don't you?"

It would have been hilarious to hear a completely fabricated *Homo sapiens* remote taunting her like that if it hadn't been so nauseating to watch. "I'll ask you again to move along. This planet is still under construction, and hunting could destabilize the local food web."

Charter shrugged. "Don't be dramatic. Why don't you and that mount leave me to enjoy my dinner?" He made the question sound like a command, as if he was used to ordering a lot of mute servants around. Destry frowned. How had he found this star system, anyway? Planets under development weren't listed on public maps, and there was no way he stumbled on it by chance. His controller must have access to Verdance's real estate databases, which would make him some kind of insider. Or a rich guy with a taste for Earthlike worlds who paid a tick to burrow quietly into Verdance's data systems. She fiddled with her holster, then walked her fingers back. There was a chance she could get in trouble for shooting this thing, even if he wasn't supposed to be here. If her boss was displeased, she might be grounded and forced to handle regulatory compliance garbage for years.

The remote kept staring at her, chewing with his mouth open, while she weighed her options. She could take him out, and potentially get caught. She could report him, but he might do a lot of damage while she waited for Verdance security to act—if they acted at all. Either way, she'd be forced to spend decades rebalancing the local environment. No matter what she did, there would be trouble, so she might as well mitigate it.

She tried again, using her calmest voice. "Listen. This isn't a debate. You need to get off this land."

"No can do, Ranger Destry Thomas. Best be on your way. My compliments to you on the well-stocked forest, though. This meal is just like the ones our ancestors ate during Earth's Pleistocene." The remote stretched his lips in a badly executed attempt at a smile. "Here on the savannahs where our species was born, I can experience evolution firsthand. The only thing that would make it more authentic would be some nice moose jerky."

The anger rising through her chest finally found her tongue. "This is not a savanna, you pus-licker. It's boreal forest."

With one fluid motion, she slipped her gun from its holster, spun it up, and shot the remote between the eyes. Charter's data stream stuttered and stopped as he crumpled. Killing was always a last resort for an ERT ranger, but this controller was using his remote to threaten Whistle, and that could not stand. Destry signaled her friend and he trotted through prairie grass to the still-smoking fire. "We're going to be here for a while," she said.

Whistle couldn't reply aloud to her—his mouth was built to a perfect Pleistocene moose template—but he could text. The sender in his brain reached out to network with hers, skipping across the radio spectrum, looking for a way to be heard; when he found it, he typed: *Looks bad, Destry.*

The moose had a limited vocabulary, but it got the job done. He was right: she'd turned a shit situation into a slurry of blood-flecked diarrhea. Stretching up a hand, she rubbed the warm, furry hide of his neck. "You can graze if you want. You'll want to have lots of energy for the trip back."

Whistle turned to press his fat muzzle into her gray-black hair, exhaling a blast of warm air. During their months on patrol in this vast, continent-spanning forest, Destry's usual stubble had grown long enough to tickle her ears. Whistle felt genuine affection for his partner, but this sudden urge to nuzzle was definitely enhanced by the sight of an abundant carpet of pinecones a few meters beyond the campsite. They were his favorite food.

Meanwhile, Destry had to start the long, grisly process of sinking all this carbon. She retrieved a few tools from Whistle's saddlebags: an axe, a tin of metabolizers, a sheet of carbon-capture membrane folded into a tight square. Tramping around the campsite, she saw no obvious ejector pods or shuttles nearby. Charter might have hiked in from a distant landing site, though his pale skin suggested recent decanting. What if somebody at Verdance spotted the vessel by satellite feed and started asking questions? Or another ranger picked up what had happened from the sensor network? She needed to find his ship and erase what she'd done. Whistle munched contentedly as she deleted the last few minutes from the forest around her.

Then she issued a ticket to the ERT bug tracker: *I found a trespasser's camp-site in the boreal forest. Composting it now. Can somebody please check satellite footage at these coordinates to see whether there's a vessel in the area?*

They would get her message in the next hour or two. Probably. As long as it found a relatively uninterrupted path through the tall grass, routing through sensors that were mostly intended for monitoring air and soil con-ditions. The important thing was that she'd left some receipts. Now, if the ship was found, she could plead ignorance about its payload. Which—what exactly was that payload? Obviously Charter's controller was some kind of rich dilettante, hopped up on environmental determinism. He didn't even recognize that the planet was closer to a Devonian Period Earth, 350 million years before his beloved Pleistocene. Sure, the food web was post-Cretaceous, full of mammals and angiosperms alongside the more ancient birds, insects, and conifers. But there were still a lot of synapsids running around, looking like giant, furry lizard-otters with sails on their backs. As the ERT's top network analyst for ecosystems, she had to call it like she saw it. This was hardly a perfect reproduction of Earth when it was a million years younger.

The reason none of these inconsistencies mattered to Verdance was that oxygen levels were holding steady at the required 21 percent, thanks mostly to the thick layer of trees Destry and her cohort planted—millions of them, all across Sask-E. Over the centuries their roots burrowed deep into the planet's two megacontinents, Maskwa and Tooth, breaking up the sterile rock and accelerating the weathering process that drew down carbon. As long as the carbon cycle was unperturbed, they could proceed on schedule and stabilize all the interlocking environmental systems. Any extra load on a freshly built ecosystem like the boreal forest might set them back centuries.

And now some joyrider from who knows where thought he could chew through their labor like he was entitled to it. Because of some pixelated idea about how Paleolithic humans lived. Glancing at the hare's mutilated body and the skins stretched nearby, Destry winced. He'd taken so much life from an ecosystem he supposedly loved.

Carefully burying the firepit in loose soil and leaves, she dragged the re-mote inside the cabin, arranging the animal remains next to him. She clam-bered up the high, peaked roof to survey the damage. He'd built the whole structure from trees that the planet desperately needed to maintain its atmosphere. Destry whacked at the wood with an axe, kicking chunks of it down to the floor inside. Soon most of the roof lay in shredded lumps next to Charter's bedroll and rucksack, and it was relatively easy to yank the wall posts out of their shallow holes in the ground. The racket brought gravelly commentary from ravens overhead, and a few curious squirrels and foxes poked their heads out of the brush.

As the sun sank, Whistle left off his crunching and headed back to the wreckage that Destry was arranging in a careful pile over the now-dismantled cabin floor. The moose sent: *Should we sleep here?*

Destry glanced at the dimming sky, where the gas giant Sask-D emerged as a bright pinprick next to the rising pear-shaped moon that orbited Sask-E. "I'm almost done," she said. "I think we can make it back to camp tonight." She cracked the tin of metabolizers open with a screwdriver and sprinkled wheat-colored husks packed with microbes over the splintered wood, skins, and Charter's body. It began to decompose almost before she could unfurl the filter membrane with a snap of her wrists, settling it over the whole mess like a transparent funeral shroud. Some carbon would escape, of course, but the filter would capture about 80 percent. By the time the full moon returned, this invader's campsite would be nothing but a rich humus beneath a layer of pine needles.

Earth's boreal forests didn't work like this; they had sandy soils that would take months to decompose this waste. But Earth was thousands of light-years away. Here on Sask-E, in the far north of the megacontinent Maskwa, the ERT cultivated a tropical microbiome in the forest floor because it was a better carbon sink. On the surface, Sask-E could pass for Pleistocene Earth. But if you actually bothered to squash its soils through a sequencer, you'd know in a second that it was actually a crazy quilt of ecosystems borrowed from half a billion years of Earth evolution—and life on hundreds of other worlds, too.

Not that Destry would ever travel through a wormhole to see Earth or those other worlds firsthand. Verdance didn't allow their workers outside the atmospheric envelope of Sask-E, and blocked their access to offworld comms too. The company liked to keep its workforce focused on terraforming, which was their right. Ronnie Drake, the company's VP of special projects, loved to point out during one of her sudden, inconvenient project

oversight meetings that Verdance had paid to build this planet, including
its biological labor force. Everything here—other than rocks, water, and
the magnetic field—was part of Verdance's proprietary ecosystem development kit. And that meant every life form was legally the company's property, including Destry and Whistle.

The filter looked steamy now. Water droplets ran across its underside,
leaving long, sooty tracks behind. Whistle nudged her and she looked into
his long, quizzical face, its contours as familiar to her as the positions of
the constellations overhead. Verdance wouldn't classify him as a person,
but Destry was pretty sure he understood this ecosystem as well as she did.

"Ready to go?" she asked him.

He sent: *Hop on.*

She climbed into the saddle, wrapping herself in wool blankets and
strapping down with canvas belts as Whistle trotted out of the trees. Night
had fallen, but the moon illuminated fields of shivering grasses that edged
the forest. Her goggles picked out the glowing heat signatures of small
mammals on the prowl for seeds. As the shadows played havoc with their
morphology, Destry and Whistle appeared to merge into one animal, muscular and dappled in silver. The illusion became more profound when
Destry leaned into Whistle's neck, wrapping arms around his warmth, and
whispered: "Let's fly."

The moose launched into a bumpy canter, accelerated to a gallop, then
jumped into the air as if he were leaping over a fallen log. His back muscles
bunched and relaxed as the ground veered away from them. Soon they
were hundreds of meters over the prairie, watching a pack of coyotes far
below, yapping their way through the dusk. Destry's legs prickled slightly
from the gravity mesh adjusting under Whistle's hide, but then they lev-
eled out. Overhead, the Milky Way tumbled down the center of the sky in
an uncontrolled deluge of stars.

LA RONGE

Home is a bargain with nature.
—*Environmental Rescue Team Handbook*

Glancing at the position of the sun in the west, Destry calculated that they had a good chance of making it home in time for dinner leftovers. After she and Whistle had composted Charter, they'd spent another two weeks in the field because an ERT geographer replied to her bug ticket with coordinates for the remote's space vessel. The stench of decomposing metal alloys still stung in her nostrils.

Whistle had flown all day, almost 720 klicks from the mineral-rich mush that was once an atmosphere entry pod. Destry would need to return for more readings in a few months, but for now it seemed the ecosystem held its precarious balance.

A few tiny ranger stations dotted the grassland, throwing symmetrical shadows from peaked roofs. She sent a greeting to each as they passed.

Ranger Destry Thomas returning. Hello!

Hello, Destry! Ranger Squab Marshelder here. Welcome back.

It went on like that for many klicks as the sun sank, though Destry spent slightly more time talking to some rangers than others, depending on how much she liked them.

At last they could see the compacted dirt road to La Ronge below, illuminated by long-wavelength visible spectrum lamps whose deep red glow didn't attenuate the sky's darkness overhead. Whistle descended gradually before landing at a full gallop, slowing to a walk before the urban ecosystem embraced them. La Ronge's skyline was dominated by apartments stacked in slowly twisting spirals, each floor angled a slightly different direction so that everyone's rooms could capture sunlight. Most of the densely packed city, however, was only a few stories tall. Market squares and court-yards were edged by barns and domos, long, rectangular public buildings with arched roofs covered in mosses, clover, and shallow-root herbs. She dismounted and walked alongside Whistle as they turned a corner and fol-lowed the main road downtown. Gardens were everywhere, sprouting in tufts from wall pockets or sprawling for blocks alongside streets busy with pedestrians, bikes, and trucks.

They crossed a low bridge over a stream ruddy with city lights, and Destry felt a twinge as she watched a family of hares drinking at its edge. At least the small mammals were safe here. Destry and Whistle followed the road north toward the ERT campus, where each had a bed. Paper lan-terns strung overhead illuminated the broad sidewalk where a few evening shoppers considered the day's remaining wares: bruised fruits and vegeta-bles, a slightly burned loaf of bread.

Two cat-sized drones hovered down on eight rotors to land on Whis-tle's right and left antlers. They had smooth X-shaped bodies with sensors spread like freckles along each axis, and they were small enough to use conventional flight rather than gravity mesh. "Long time no see," they said in unison. "The city misses every aeronaut." Though they had two bodies, Hellfire&Crisp shared a consciousness; it was therefore hard to say whether the drones were a plural or singular they.

Whistle snorted and sent a public text: *Hi there. Good to be back.*

The drones took off again, ignoring Destry. Whistle had a social life that he didn't tell her about, and she didn't ask. It was one of many non-verbal agreements they had that made their working relationship deeply amicable and pleasing.

Their first stop was the ERT barn where the moose lived with other mounts. At its wide door, Destry relieved him of her saddle before giving him a rubdown in the spots he couldn't reach.

"Have a good night, pal," Destry said.

He nudged her with his nose. *You too.*

The ERT domo for hominins was at the end of a dirt path bordered by night-blooming primroses and mint whose mingled scents sweetened the air. She had to duck through an arch in a whimsically pruned hedge whose contours were determined annually by the rangers in training. Right now, it was supposed to evoke the undulating body of a swimming placoderm—an homage to the Devonian armored fish who still roamed the seas. Ahead lay the domo, its wide, three-story bulk packed with dorms, lounges, and the main dining hall. It was one of the few buildings on Sask-E built with wood, carefully culled from nearby spruce and fir populations to promote a diversity of new growth. Its creamy outer walls were treated with a transparent polymer to protect it from weathering, and the high, rounded roof was wattle and daub. Double doors opened as Destry's face came into range, and she walked down the yellow-lit throat of the hallway with its colorful murals, handprints, and informational posters.

No matter how many centuries she lived here, returning to this domo always filled Destry with a sense of accomplishment. She was an Environmental Rescue Team ranger, and her home here was proof.

Still, her position wasn't solid. Destry recalled what that pus-sucker had said through the lips of his remote: It was strange to find an ERT ranger on a private planet like this one. Most of the planet's hominin population were workers made from standard templates, decanted and controlled by Verdance—technicians, engineers, and farmers who lived in La Ronge but spent most of the year dispatched to remote construction sites. There was no ambiguity in the law when it came to those workers; Verdance could use them however it wanted. But the ERT was a profoundly public institution, with campuses on nearly every League world. They couldn't technically be owned by Verdance, or anyone. Destry wasn't sure what kind of twisted, legal logic her boss, Ronnie, had deployed to establish an ERT campus here.

The ancient order of environmental engineers and first responders traced their lineage all the way back to the Farm Revolutions that ended the Anthropocene on Earth, and started the calendar system people still used today. According to old Handbook lore, the Trickster Squad—Sky, Beaver, Muskrat, and Wasakeejack—founded the Environmental Rescue Team 59,006 years ago. That's when the legendary heroes saved the world from apocalyptic floods by inventing a new form of agriculture. The Great Bargain, they called it. A way to open communication with other life forms in order to manage the land more democratically. The ERT started with domesticated animals—ungulates, birds, small mammals, model organisms like rats—and over the millennia since, rangers had invited more species into the Great Bargain as their opinions became necessary for land management.

Ronnie had decided that the ERT should be involved in her terraforming project, and so she built one. Apparently the Verdance VP was a true believer in the Great Bargain, but she also wanted to make money on colonization. She couldn't resolve this contradiction, so the Sask-E ERT ran like a moose with overgrown hooves. They had access to a planetwide network of sensor data—as well as the *ERT Handbook*, with its stories about ecosystem management. But the company's ban on offworld comms effectively shut them off from other ERT communities. As far as Destry could tell, no one knew about the rangers here in La Ronge. That was convenient for Ronnie. She could appease her ancestors by respecting ERT traditions, but also please the executives at Verdance by keeping everything and everyone on Sask-E privately owned.

A thick aroma of fried onion in the domo promised leftovers, and Destry sped up with anticipation. The dining hall was the biggest room on this floor, occupying the entire west side of the building. When she poked her head inside, the place was empty and mostly unlit except for one area where half a dozen junior rangers were eating a late meal together. Thankfully, there was still a heaping tray of pierogies and pickled mustard greens on the grab table. Loading her plate, Destry sank gratefully into her favorite corner chair and reveled in the luxury of eating food made by someone else. The dumplings were still warm, and she'd scored a few stuffed with spicy lentils as well as potato and curried carrot. But there were always surprises, especially at late dinner. Destry smeared fried onion on what she thought was a potato pierogi, only to discover it was sweet cheese, and was therefore making a terrible face when her best friend, Nil, appeared in the doorway and yelped her name.

"Destry! You're back! Any news from the forest?"

She swallowed with difficulty, stood, and gestured for him to join her. "Everything is in balance," she said, evoking the time-honored greeting to avoid mentioning all the out-of-balance shit she'd seen. The two embraced before sitting in companionable silence at the table together.

When they were young, she and Nil were sometimes mistaken for each other. Both had thick black hair, shaggy and straight, which always hung in their eyes. Working in the sun, their skin tanned to a dark brown, and they bulked up with muscles rather than growing lean like their colleagues. Now, almost four hundred years later, it was easy to tell them apart. Destry's hair was a salt-and-pepper fuzz sticking up around her face, while Nil's was still long and black. Destry's work outside kept her face tan and her arms thick with muscle, while Nil's lab work had lightened his skin and given him a small, soft belly. Only their matching eyes remained unchanged: they were the bright, clear blue of shallow coastal waters. When they were lucky enough to be in the same place at the same time, they were inseparable. Even when she was sick of humans, Destry could tolerate Nil.

Gulping a pile of pickled greens to wash the weird flavor out of her mouth, Destry gripped his shoulder warmly. "What's been happening down here in the city, my friend?"

"Everything's in balance," he replied noncommittally. "I was just checking the bug tracker and it looks like one of the big lava tubes at Spider Mountain collapsed. There's been some seismic activity so it could be an eruption coming. I was thinking of getting off my lazy ass and doing some fieldwork down there." He paused and looked hopefully at her. "Want to come?"

Because Sask-E had no plate tectonics, volcanoes rarely erupted out of nowhere: they oozed magma for millions of years in the same locations, creating massive, cone-shaped mountains. The two friends had dealt a lot with these formations, though for different reasons. Destry investigated breakdowns in local ecosystems from toxins expelled during eruptions, and Nil tapped lava flows to create volcanic soils for forests he was irrigating. His offer was tempting. Still, she had been looking forward to sleeping in her own bed for a while after three months in the bush, especially after that disturbing encounter with the remote. And if she was being honest, the tropical ecosystems near Spider Mountain weren't her favorite. She'd always preferred the prairies.

"I don't know, Nil. I'm pretty exhausted."

He looked mildly put out, then concerned. "Did something happen out there? I saw your bug report about the space vessel, but I didn't read it."

Destry repositioned one of the lentil pierogis on her plate, carefully piling it with onion and mustard greens. She chewed for a while as Nil waited patiently. It was another reason why they remained friends; he was willing to wait through her hard-edged silences.

"I didn't report this, but I had to kill a remote. A default male *Homo sapiens*." She forked the last bite of dinner into her mouth. "He was murdering small mammals and eating them. Never seen anything like it. I don't mind saying it was downright spooky."

Nil looked disturbed. "I think a whole slew of crackpots are going to start coming to Sasky now. Verdance just opened up bidding for plots." Like everyone in La Ronge, he blurred the syllables in the planet's name together, and Sask-E became Sasky.

The Verdance announcement was news to Destry, but it did explain how the remote had found his way here. Verdance was probably spraying everyone in League space and beyond with ads for their latest artisanal terraforming creation, ten thousand years in the making. The real estate developer was known for indie projects like Sasky, which was ripening into one of the few known Earthlike worlds in the League—and that made it an enticing outlier among the thousands of habitable planets that speculators were terraforming at any given time.

Verdance was really leaning into its whole "Earth rebooted" marketing pitch, too. Anyone who bought property on Sasky would be required to live here in a *Homo sapiens* body, which was packaged with the real estate. That meant settling here was very expensive, which seemed to make buyers salivate.

Destry frowned at the thought of more people sending their remotes to poison the biosphere before it was open to the public.

Nil put a hand on her arm. "Did the remote say why he was here?"

"He was a Pleistocene fanatic. Said the land was his birthright as a human, along with some other determinist feculence."

Nil rolled his eyes and sighed. "I have a feeling our jobs are about to get a lot more annoying."

Destry pushed back from the table. "I need to get to bed. Let's meet for breakfast?"

Nil nodded and they walked to the hallway together, mounting the worn ceramic stairs to the sleeping quarters. On the first landing, they paused. Destry was on the third floor, and Nil was on the second. He embraced her goodnight and whispered in her ear. "Shall I join you?"

She felt the familiar pull toward him low in her belly. It had been awhile. Part of her craved what he offered, but a bigger part was bone-tired. Destry kissed Nil's warm lips and hugged him harder.

"Another time, my friend." She ran her hands up his arms and stepped back to appreciate the sweetness of his familiar face. "It's good to see you, though."

He grinned easily. "Good to see you too, my friend."

Destry mounted the stairs and plodded past a dozen darkened doors to the one that glowed a soft green, anticipating her arrival. Inside, she barely glanced at the walls, where ivy cascaded out of pockets near the ceiling, parting around a few square cubbies crowded with framed pictures and favored mementos. It was only when Destry peeled off her clothes and dove between the clean covers that she realized her skin was still gritty with dirt, charcoal, and who knows what else from the composted space vessel. Washing would have to wait, just like Nil's comforts. For now, sleeping alone in her tiny personal space with its window full of night was the greatest pleasure she could imagine.

That's when her external comms pad hooted loudly. It was a sound she heard only when somebody was calling directly from Verdance. *Ronnie.* Groaning, she rolled over and waved on the light, muscles and mind aching.

She didn't even have a chance to accept the call. Ronnie's access was high enough that she could pipe her face into any room, any time. A crisp hologram of the VP's head and shoulders now hovered at the foot of the bed. Her hair was a pale, iridescent blue, perfectly layered to cascade across the shoulders of her emerald jacket. Her brown skin was richly moisturized, almost dewy, as if she'd recently had a tissue reconstruction. Though proud of her traditional Earth values, Ronnie was *Homo diversus*, a catchall subspecies name for hundreds of customized hominin builds. Her fashionable forehead sloped back steeply, and her skull was elongated into an elegant egg shape. Gills gleamed on either side of her throat like jewels.

"I'm sorry if you were sleeping."

Destry ran a hand over her eyes and shrugged off the fake apology. "What can I do for you?"

"I see you filed a bug report about a vessel but failed to mention that you killed the remote who piloted it."

So much for covering her tracks up there in the boreal forest. "He was trespassing, killing trees and animals. If I'd left him there, he would have set back development of that forest by years. I asked him to leave three times before I shot him. You can see the footage for yourself."

"Don't treat this lightly, Destry. I have client relationships on the line here."

Something about her condescending tone reminded Destry of early training, when she and the other recently decanted ERT rangers watched an old video of Ronnie talking about Earth *terroir*. Using her sweetest and most nurturing voice, the Verdance VP explained that only *Homo sapiens* could truly nurture the *terroir* of Earthlike ecosystems, which is why Destry and her *H. sapiens* cohorts were so important. They would turn Sask-E into an Earth-away-from-Earth, a special world that honored humanity's origins. Back then, when Destry was still under the protection of her mother and father, she thought Ronnie was the wisest person in the galaxy. In the centuries since, her feelings for the VP had curdled into wrathful disgust. Not that she could ever show Ronnie anything other than calm obedience. That's what she needed to muster if she was going to make it through this conversation intact.

"I'm confused," Destry said as nonconfrontationally as possible. "That remote wasn't on official business. It was unmarked, with a generic name."

"That remote was sent by Lem Rackleworth's son." Ronnie gritted her teeth in a smile. "He is an investor in our parent company, and his son Devin is interested in buying some land on Sask-E."

"I asked him to identify himself and he refused."

"I saw the remote's logs. You shot within a few minutes of encountering him."

Destry was shocked fully awake. Ronnie was combing through her investors' son's logs now? That was a new level of aggressive micromanagement.

Ronnie continued. "His remote was very expensive, and Lem is threatening us with a lawsuit. You're a good ranger, Destry. A good investigator. But if I can't work this out with Lem, there is nothing I can do to intercede for you. Do you understand?" Her words hung in the air, deliberately vague. Acid crept its way up Destry's throat from her stomach. An extremely belligerent investor might get her kicked out of the ERT. She'd lose what little power she had to shape the environment on this planet.

Destry looked into the photons animating Ronnie's face, searching for pores in her shiny skin. She thought about her parents, who were no longer around to reassure her that Ronnie was far away and couldn't do any harm. Besides, that had been a lie. Ronnie was always around, turning minor infractions into catastrophes. Destry forced herself to sit up straighter. "I understand, Ronnie. Thanks for letting me know."

And then the hologram was gone, Ronnie's threat adding ambient stress to the uncomfortable reminder that she wasn't ever entirely alone. Shaking with more than exhaustion, Destry lay down and waved off the lights. Even the weight of foreboding couldn't keep her awake. Outside, the northern constellations crawled across the sky, obliviously waiting for someone from a distant star to claim them as property.

FIELDWORK

We are living beings, and that is why we want to survive.
—*Environmental Rescue Team Handbook*

When she awoke with the rooster calls, Destry wanted nothing more than to be gone again. She imagined opening her eyes hundreds of kilometers away, the dome of her tent illuminated by dawn. Compulsively, she checked her messages for any updates from Ronnie. Had she been cut off from the ERT network? Was there some other punishment in store? She bumbled through her morning routine in the communal washrooms, scrubbing down with a handful of lavender cleanser from a woven grass basket and sluicing some water through her hair. It took a long time at the sink to get all the dirt out from under her nails. Familiar faces appeared in the mirror next to hers, smiled, mumbled greetings, and drifted away. Out of the corner of her eye, she caught a glimpse of someone whose blue hair shimmered like Ronnie's, and she almost jumped. Stress torqued the muscles in her neck.

Pulling on a fresh jumpsuit, Destry pondered what Nil had said last night about the volcano down south. The invitation was starting to sound a lot more enticing—even a potential disaster zone was better than being in comms range with Ronnie right now. Offworld messages from Verdance usually took days to route from the city into the bush. Plus, it had been decades since she and Nil had gone on a mission together, and she felt a welcome, lingering warmth from their embrace last night.

Hopefully Whistle would be up for it. He didn't have a choice—he was her assigned mount—but Destry didn't relish making him do things against his will. She'd met so many creatures like Whistle who were obviously people, despite their supposedly low intelligence, that she had long ago stopped buying into the League's "intelligence assessment" rating system. There was a good reason why the rangers called them InAss ratings. Your head had to be buried deep in your ass to say a flying, talking moose with a weird gang of aeronaut drone friends wasn't smart enough to be a person. But that's what the law said. And until there was some kind of revolution like in the game *Animal Uprising*, the people of Sasky and everyone else in the League were stuck with it. Nevertheless, Destry always got Whistle's consent before taking a job, or bribed him with some kind of reward if he was on the fence. And that's exactly what she aimed to keep doing.

Destry found her old friend at the same table where she'd eaten last night. A cooker full of porridge was making blorp noises on the grab table, and she scooped up a cup before sitting down. Nil had already spread out a map of Spider and its surrounds.

"What are we looking at?" She raised an eyebrow.

He gestured at the wrinkled readout, centering the caldera, its massive lake of turquoise water like a gem pressed deeply into the top of the mountain. It was today's geodata from VerdanceSat3, sent automatically to the ERT. Radiating outward from Spider's base were long, rocky ridges—the signs of underground tunnels created by subterranean lava flows. From above, the mountain looked like a tropical tarantula, its swollen blue abdomen surrounded by splayed legs. That's why everybody called it Spider. With a pang, Destry realized that Verdance's clients—like Rackleworth's shit kid—would probably give it a bland, marketable name. Lakeview, maybe. Or Rackleworth Mountain.

Nil poked at one of Spider's legs, zooming in close enough to show how the lava tube had collapsed, leaving a ragged tear in its grassy ridge top. From inside the tunnel, it would look like a skylight had opened overhead.

"This is pretty interesting from a geomorphology perspective, but that's not why I'm heading down there as soon as possible. Check it out." Nil scrolled along the lava tube about half a klick to the crumbling edge of the skylight. Destry's eyes widened. Set into the curved wall of the tube was a door very much like the one to her own room, glowing red to signal an emergency lockdown.

"What the hell? More Pleistocene fetishists?"

"That's exactly what I want to know." Nil's face was serious. "We have some drones doing recon, but nobody is going to land without us as backup. Though my guess"—he zoomed in farther, so that scuffs on the door were clearly visible—"this is something old."

"But why would it still be powered up? Plus, nobody has ever lived out there. Even the first generation of Verdance workers built homes here in La Ronge."

"As far as we know."

Destry planted chin in hand and zoomed the map back out, looking for other clues. Could it really be from the earliest days of terraforming? That would be over ten thousand years ago, when Verdance decanted the first workers on the northern continent to jump-start photosynthesis. At that time, Sasky's atmosphere was a mix of carbon and nitrogen, with just a whiff of hydrogen. It would have been fatal for *H. sapiens*, so Verdance created a hardy group of *H. diversus* who could thrive in an atmosphere with almost no oxygen. They seeded the Winston Ocean with cyanobacteria, creating thick mats of blue-green algae that belched oxygen into the air. As oxygen levels rose, they decanted a generation of *H. sapiens* who then died out, leaving the world to life forms who thrived in the pseudo-Pleistocene environment.

"There's no way the first terraformers could survive on the planet now," Destry mused aloud. "Too much oxygen."

She spotted another unusual shape in the tunnel and zoomed in. It looked like the remains of a machine stuck to the wall, its spiral shell smashed and dripping fluids. "What do you think that is?" She pointed.

Nil squinted at the image. "It's hard to make out at this resolution, but—it could be some kind of atmosphere processor."

They looked each other in the eyes, weighing the consequences of this finding. Finally Destry spoke. "Has anyone reported these—uh—anomalies to Verdance?"

A frown line appeared on Nil's forehead. "No. We'll keep this within the ERT for now. The less Ronnie and her Verdance cronies know, the better."

Destry gulped the rest of her porridge, now barely warm. "I'm going to get some coffee and see if Whistle wants to visit the equator."

Nil beamed. "So you'll come after all? That was easy."

"It's a pretty compelling find." She clapped him on the shoulder. "Plus, I'm feeling the urge to get out in the field again."

Raising his eyebrows, Nil said nothing. Maybe he guessed that she had other motivations, but he wasn't going to pry. Then he grinned. "Tell Whistle that his aeronaut squad is heading there already."

"The whole team?"

"One of his buddies—Hellfire&Crisp. And I'm bringing Rocket."

Rocket was Nil's research partner, a flying drone designed to be mounted. But that didn't make Rocket an official Mount like Whistle—the drone's intelligence assessment qualified them for personhood. Even though Whistle consistently performed better than Rocket in ERT emergency drills. Further evidence that InAss ratings were garbage.

When she arrived at the barn to give Whistle the latest news, he kicked up his back legs in the moose equivalent of a smile.

Sounds fine, Destry. I like this plan, he sent. *Let's fly down now.*

"I'll get my travel gear and meet you at the takeoff field."

Sure thing. The moose was already wheeling around to go back into the barn as Destry received his text. A pair of robot arms suspended from the ceiling inside helped all the Mounts with their kits, tightening belts and securing their possessions in saddlebags.

It would be a long trip, and their network comms could get lossy down south, where sensors were spread thin. Destry grinned as she packed her instruments, med supplies, and a change of clothes into a rucksack that was still dusty from the flight down here yesterday. Grabbing a week's rations from the kitchen, she opened a connection with the ERT scheduler, adding her name and Whistle's to the list of people going out to investigate the quake at Spider. Ronnie couldn't accuse her of sneaking away—after all, this was exactly the sort of situation where a network analyst was needed.

Soon she was following a narrow trail through waist-high grass to get to the takeoff field. Whistle barely waited for her to strap down before he galloped into the air, where they met Nil and Rocket circling over La Ronge. Mountable drones like Rocket were designed as stripped-down moose: They had thick cylindrical torsos for saddling, fitted with retractable limbs, and a sensor bulb roughly where a head would be. Only that "head" looked more like a spiny durian fruit on a telescoping pole. When flying, Rocket pulled their sensor bulb close to the smooth metal barrel of their body, giving them the appearance of a tube with a lumpy ball on one end.

Two more people joined them in the air: an *H. sapiens* named Long, and a moose with glossy black fur who carried him. Destry knew Long—he'd worked with her and Nil centuries ago on soil missions—but she'd never met the moose. Accessing the moose's sender ID revealed she had high InAss ratings and full personhood. Her name was Midnight. That made Whistle the only true Mount in their party, and Destry hoped that nobody would condescend to him.

Below their feet, La Ronge was a jumble of houses and farms surrounded by prairie hills and swales. Pedestrians flowed through the streets, and riders were constantly bounding into the air from the grassland like fleas from shaggy hair. In the distance, a faint rainbow stretched across the edge of a blurry gray cloud. They flew in its general direction, the city behind them melting into abstract polygons.

"Think we'll finally make it to the rainbow this time?" Destry asked Nil. It was an old joke between them, from when they were new rangers chasing prismed light in the irrigation vapor plumes.

"Well, you know how it is with rainbows," Nil replied. "Wherever you go, you're never there."

HOMO ARCHAEA

We are not humans and animals. We are allies in the Great Bargain.
—*Environmental Rescue Team Handbook*

It took the team three days to reach Spider Mountain, which was located near the coastline of equatorial Maskwa. As they approached the southern ocean, the air grew warm and humid. They slept on mats under a shelter to block some of the misty rain. Everyone who was biological foraged for fruits and twigs to supplement the buckwheat bread and pulses they'd brought from home while Rocket unfurled solar arrays to capture energy as they flew.

Finally, Spider came into view, with its fiery heart cloaked in grass and wildflowers. Destry had been here during the last eruption, over three hundred years ago, watching from a safe distance as black clouds billowed into the air from vents that cracked open at the summit. Lightning flickered purple inside the blast of life-giving minerals. As its underground magma pocket drained, the mountain peak deflated, sinking hundreds of meters in minutes as barn-sized boulders toppled into the broiling caldera that today held a calm sapphire lake. She'd never forget watching Spider eat its own head. Once things cooled down, she and the rangers collected the volcanic rock where it had flowed down into the mountain's tunnel legs. Nil and Long were there too; their job was to pulverize the rock into fertilizer for soil across the planet.

But it wasn't the spectacular blast that made this memory so vivid in Destry's mind. It was another fire, over two thousand klicks away, listed only as "hazard cleanup" in the ERT official records. While she was grinning into Spider's sulfurous winds, her parents' cabin had burned to the ground in the boreal forest north of La Ronge. No one escaped alive, not even the swift-footed cat. They were so far out in the bush that it took weeks before sensor data arrived from the blast radius, which was then passed along to her as part of the disaster report. For hours, she had stared at a VerdanceSat3 image of fallen trees radiating outward from the explosion—result of a misconfigured bioreactor—their shattered trunks like the paths of x-rays screaming out of the black hole created by her parents' melted house.

Destry packed her anguish back into the part of her belly that no food could fill. Today Spider was quiet, holding water where it once held fire. Her parents were at peace, their proteins folded into the proteins of other life forms. She deliberately turned her mind to the work ahead. Hellfire&Crisp had been on site for over a day, and their radar readings indicated there was no puffing of the mountain's skin, which meant the place probably wasn't going to blow lava any time soon. The seismic activity was high, but still within the typical range; it was possible that their seismometers had picked up vibrations from the tunnel collapse rather than a quake. Or maybe it was a disturbance related to the tech they'd seen inside.

The rangers met on the ground. Destry stayed on Whistle's back as he ambled toward the lava tube skylight while Nil and Long dismounted.

Hellfire&Crisp swooped down to greet them. "Look at this," they said, pointing grippers at the place where the machine had been smashed in Nil's map images back at La Ronge. Now there was nothing but rippled rock. A shallow ledge ran along the tunnel wall at about the height of a guardrail: it was the high-point mark from a recent lava flow.

Destry felt the familiar thrill that came with first perceiving the complexity of a problem, before it become a neat graph of nodes and edges. "What happened?" she asked.

"We don't know." Hellfire&Crisp didn't have a face on their smooth, bullet-shaped carapaces, but their voices broadcast an expression of frustration. "We were surveying some of the other lava tubes twenty-two hours ago, and when we returned, it was gone."

"And the door?" Nil craned his neck to see farther down the tube.

"Still there."

Long scrambled down into the lava tube with Midnight. Touching the wall, he looked back up at the group, perplexed. "There's no natural phenomenon that could have done this. Even if an animal carried it away, there would be something left."

Hellfire&Crisp hovered over Destry's head. They shouted with excitement. "The plot thickens! Let's race to that door!"

Whistle tossed his head: *Let's go! Destry, can you hold on?*

He started galloping before she could say yes.

Nil hopped on Rocket and sped along the floor of the lava tube a few meters below. Long and Midnight stayed behind to smear a dollop of sticky sensors on the wall, setting them to take samples of chemical residue.

Crisp&Hellfire won the race by a few seconds, and Whistle sent increasingly elaborate curses as he came to a bumpy stop. Destry practically fell off his back, landing with a thud below his towering form and sliding quickly down the concave wall of the tube. Pressing her hands into the crumbling rock, she ignored the ongoing smack talk between aeronauts and sought a connection. There were a few sensors blown into the lava tube by the wind, but they yielded only atmospheric data from the past two days. Farther out, the tropical forest had nothing useful to add: *No seismic activity in four days; humidity levels within set range; a jasmine bush is blooming a day earlier than predicted; six earthworms are heading southwest; nothing perceived inside the lava tunnel.*

It was distinctly odd that none of the sensors had anything to say about this door, now emitting a cool blue light.

"Maybe whoever is behind that door cleaned up the machine." Hellfire&Crisp said above her. "It might have opened while we were gone."

"Maybe." Destry scratched her chin, struck by the odd tableau of the perfectly rectangular door fitted into the variegated crust. "This door looks extremely well maintained. It's definitely a system I've seen in La Ronge, though I think it's modified. There's no way some offworld real estate buyer set this up." She peered closer and realized there was a touchscreen positioned at chest level, its pixels glowing the exact same color as the door. Someone definitely lived here. And there were no records of them at all—not even in the environmental sensors that surrounded Spider Mountain.

Nil arrived, dismounting from Rocket to peer over her shoulder at the touchscreen. "Is that a doorbell?" he asked.

"Let's ring it!" Hellfire&Crisp yelled. "Let's say hi!"

"No, don't—" But Destry's reply was too late. A large pixel of white light bounced back and forth across the screen's surface. The drones had sent a cross-spectrum generic hello.

"Everybody stand back!"

The whole team scrambled away, leaving a three-meter cushion between themselves and the door.

Nothing happened.

"What's going on, Rocket?" Nil asked. His mountable drone partner was an expert at squeezing data out of closed systems.

"It's routing the call."

A tinny voice with a lilting accent came from the door. "I can hear you."

Destry wasn't sure whether she was being addressed by the door, somebody speaking over comms, or some other entity who lived on the network. Didn't matter. Whoever they were, they deserved a polite greeting. She bowed slightly at the screen. "Hey, friend. I'm Ranger Destry Thomas, and these are my colleagues from the La Ronge Environmental Rescue Team. We're curious about this door here, and who all is behind it."

There was a long pause, and the voice came again. "Hi, Destry. And hello to Hellfire&Crisp and Rocket. I haven't had the pleasure of meeting the rest of you. I'm Jaguar."

Nil stepped forward. "I'm Ranger Nil Tom, and we're wondering how you got here."

"How did *you* get here?" Jaguar sounded put out.

Hellfire&Crisp were hovering next to them now, carapaces strobing excitedly. "We flew!"

"We saw the collapsed lava tube and this door and came to investigate," Destry clarified. "Naturally we were surprised because nobody is supposed to be on Sask-E except Verdance workers."

Jaguar made a snorting noise. "You mean Verdance's slaved *H. sapiens*?"

Destry started to say something, but Nil put up his hand to stop her. "May we come inside and meet you?" he asked.

There was no answer. After a minute, Whistle hovered down into the lava tube, using his furry thickness to push aside Long and Midnight, who had finally arrived at a slow trot. Whistle shoved his soft nose into Destry's back and texted: *I will stand with you.* Though someone with his InAss rating wasn't supposed to deal in double meanings, Destry was pretty sure Whistle meant the words figuratively as well as literally.

Hellfire&Crisp extended a limb from the carapace of their closest body. It was tipped with a powerful laser for rock sampling. "Let's cut our way inside."

"Good luck with that." Jaguar's voice was almost amused this time. "That laser couldn't get through even a millimeter of this material." After a pause, the door continued, "Apparently even the most annoying individuals are welcome here these days. You can come inside."

The door flew open, exhaling a blast of cold air that smelled faintly of cow farts. A person about Destry's height stood in the opening, wearing a light, transparent respirator over their nose and mouth—not exactly a *Homo sapiens*, but very close. Their chest was wide and barrel-shaped, with arms a few centimeters longer than *H. sapiens* standard. Some kind of *H. diversus*, then. Beneath the face mask, the person had pink skin, wide-set eyes, a heavy brow, and prominent cheekbones. They wore coveralls that were an exact replica of the chemical-resistant model provided by Verdance, except there was a black patch in the place where a corporate logo would be.

Everything about this encounter was strange, but perhaps the strangest thing was how well-established this place appeared. Their network was robust, if Jaguar was any indication, and this person had obviously come out of a long tunnel that stretched deep underground. This was no camp of blank-eyed Pleistocene Man wannabes chasing a real estate marketing campaign. Something profoundly unexpected was happening here.

Whenever she got way out of her depth like this, Destry always started with the basics. Like names.

"Are you Jaguar?" she asked the *H. diversus*.

The person tilted their head, bemused. "No. Jaguar is the door. I'm Lucky." Their voice was low and gravelly, with the same lilt that she'd heard in Jaguar's speech. "Jaguar told the Council there were *Homo sapiens* calling, so I came to meet you."

Taken aback, Destry considered what it meant that there were enough people here to merit the creation of a Council. Was this some kind of secret base?

"We're not all *Homo sapiens*," Rocket pointed out. Whistle and Midnight stomped their feet in agreement.

Lucky shrugged. "OK. That's one thing we have in common. If you want to come inside, all you Pleistocene animals will need to wear masks. We're optimized for Archaean lungs inside."

Nobody moved. They'd gotten another name: *Archaean,* likely from *Homo archaean*, a common *H. diversus* subspecies built during the first phase of a terraforming operation. Lucky wasn't using it like that, though. They spoke the word like it was the name for a community, or perhaps a whole civilization.

"No offense, friend, but we're going to need a little more information about you before we go into a long, dark tunnel full of hostile atmosphere." Destry kept her hands slightly away from her body, fingers spread, hoping to connect with a sensor and get some data.

"Don't you recognize another ERT ranger when you see one?" Lucky grinned under the mask, teeth uneven. "My ancestors set this whole planet up for Verdance. We jump-started the carbon cycle. We filled the oceans with cyanobacteria and made photosynthesis happen. Hell, my grandparents decanted the first *Homo sapiens.*"

Nil and Destry looked at each other. It seemed impossible that the hypothesis they'd dismissed back in La Ronge was actually close to the truth. Somehow, these people were from an earlier phase of Sasky's terraforming.

Lucky continued conversationally. "Actually, I was hoping some rangers would find this door and pay us a visit."

Long frowned. "Why is that?"

"It will be easier if I show you." The Archaean broadcast a network access key to the whole group, but Destry still couldn't connect. Sensing her confusion, Lucky continued, "We don't use very much wireless. You have to make a physical connection." They pressed a hand against the wall of the cave.

Destry hovered between caution and curiosity, but the latter won out. It always did. She slid her palm against the doorframe and felt a trickle of data from a few sensors that had blown inside, then tasted dry grass as the sensors abruptly composted themselves into little piles of biomass. So that's why the local network was so ignorant about this lava tube—Lucky's people had figured out how to trigger the self-destruct sequence in sensors that came from Verdance. Smart. Cautiously she deployed the access key and perceived the Spider network. It was not like the tightly hierarchical La Ronge systems; it felt more like the ragged, organic calls of prairie grass.

Gradually, as her perception slid across rock and tasted sulfur, she realized that the volcano itself was a city. The Archaeans had strung glass fiber for comms into every part of its porous bulk, and through them she could sense traffic from atmosphere regulators, domos, and farms. Then, on the other side of the mountain, she touched a familiar set of documents: it was the *Environmental Rescue Team Handbook*, embedded in a tranche of assets maintained by a team called Spider City ERT.

Whistle squeezed his two-meter-high frame next to her and connected too. *This place is big, Destry*, he sent after a few seconds. *There are moose here. All kinds of life.*

She nodded, then turned to the Archaean, who had backed farther into the tunnel and taken off their face mask.

"You've been hiding a lot down here, Lucky," Destry said. "If you wanted us to come, why didn't you contact us before?"

"We want nothing to do with Verdance."

Given that she'd come on this trip to escape from Ronnie, it was hard not to relate. "Fair enough." Turning to the rest of the team, she asked, "Do you want to visit their ERT campus?"

Hellfire&Crisp shot inside the tunnel, playing their spotlights over its low ceiling. "Let's go!"

Nil nodded in slow affirmation and Long looked dubious. Midnight flicked her ears and sent: *I cannot perceive any weapons. Still, I recommend we proceed with caution.*

That seemed to convince Long, who made a big show of readjusting his pack to reveal three sharp knives sheathed in his tool bandolier. All the biologicals started pulling their collars up to form masks—this was a common safety feature in ranger uniforms, especially for people visiting volcanic regions. Destry tugged a muzzle breather from her saddlebag and fitted it to Whistle's face, just as Long did for Midnight. As her eyes adjusted to the dim tunnel beyond the door, she realized Lucky had a mountable drone hovering a few meters behind them.

"That's Bog," Lucky said, gesturing. "He's just like your mountable drones, except unrated."

"Unrated?" Nil asked.

"No intelligence rating. We don't buy into that cesspit logic down here. You're either alive or not. That's all that matters."

Whistle lowered his head to enter the tunnel, sending a quick text: *I like the sound of that, Destry.*

She ran her hand over his neck. "So do I."

A VERY ANGRY DOOR

Inside every conflict, a friendship waits to be born.
—Environmental Rescue Team Handbook

The tunnel was part of a massive lava tube system that Destry hadn't thought about in centuries. Back when she, Nil, and Long were harvesting the eruption for minerals, she'd consulted ground-penetrating radar images that showed at least four levels of branching tunnels, created by multiple eruptions over the millennia. Apparently, the people here had converted them into a habitat. A pretty nice one, at that. Once they got farther inside, the basalt walls gleamed with blue-green light from bioluminescent plants growing out of the ceiling, and the floor was softened with a thin layer of foam that made it easier for the humans and moose to find their footing. After walking in silence for a quarter klick, Lucky turned and held up a hand.

"I need to warn you that people around here don't always take kindly to *H. sapiens.* They see you as the reason why we have to hide underground. So keep your mouths shut, no matter what people say to you."

Long looked up sharply. "But we're not the reason—"

Lucky interrupted him. "The atmosphere is optimized for your bodies, eh? Rangers at the ERT will be more accepting, but it's hard to deny that *H. sapiens* took over our land at La Ronge."

"It wasn't your land," Long snapped.

"If you build something, aren't you a part of it?" Lucky's pink face grew flushed, and their voice rose. Things were getting heated.

Destry spoke up, her tone deliberately casual, as if she hadn't noticed the tension. "I still can't believe there's another ERT on Sasky that's just like ours."

Lucky gave her the hint of a smile. "I believe you mean that *you* have an ERT like *ours*."

Whistle exhaled abruptly with amusement, the material of his breather puffing up.

And then the floor evaporated.

Curses and bellows echoed off the walls as they fell, buoyed by a counter-gravitational force that barely slowed them down. Sure, they wouldn't smash to the ground and die, but all the nonflying members of the party were going to land hard on their asses at the bottom. Destry glimpsed flashes of underground city life as she plummeted past three levels: a warmly lit gym, the climbing walls deep green with moss; a market hall buzzing with noise and the smell of roasting onions; a shadowy warehouse full of hulking industrial tanks. Judging from that admittedly small sample size, she'd guess this place was as big as La Ronge or even bigger. There could be thousands of people living in the honeycombed layers of crust above an enormous magma plume. How could anyone thrive in such a dangerous place, let alone an entire metropolis?

With a thud, she landed on a thick mat next to Nil, struggling to catch her breath. They were sprawled at the south end of a long hall. Above them was a high ceiling carved out of the soft tuff of volcanic rock, illuminated by amber light that came from deep holes drilled into the soaring roof. People of all sizes and shapes streamed past their landing pad: she caught sight of more Archaeans, plus drones, cats, walking bots, moose, and a colony of naked mole rats wearing robes. The hall echoed with mouth talking while texts traveled through the network that Destry could feel again with the sensors in her scuffed hands. Now that they were deep inside Spider City, the floors and walls were densely woven with glass for comms. Unlike La Ronge, where the radio frequencies were stuffed with signals, this hidden city was optimized for data that couldn't be sniffed from the air. Perfect for hiding from sensors. Plus, the mountain was a Faraday cage. Stray radio signals would be blocked from the aboveground world by many meters of solid rock.

It took a few more seconds for Destry to realize she was sitting in a transit hub. Small groups whooshed up and down from the floor through portals like the one their party had just fallen through. Boxy train cars glided through the hall, nosing in and out of six sodium-lit tunnels.

Whistle, Midnight, and the drones came to rest softly next to them, and Lucky landed last. Their broad, flat face and blue eyes reminded her of *Homo neanderthalensis*, but no doubt they'd been sourced from a hodge-podge of hominins, then modified to take energy from Sasky's early atmosphere. Back then, the planet would have been an icy snowball fractured by vulcanism, its air a toxic combination of gasses that her body could not process. Destry shook her head as she stood up, adjusting her breather and reflecting on how "toxic" was a matter of perspective.

A couple of bots and four cats were staring at them openly, and now a few Archaeans had come to look too. She and Nil stood up next to Long, still unsteady from their fall, and Lucky shooed them off the pad.

One of the Archaeans narrowed their eyes at Destry. "What have you brought us, Lucky? This a joke? You brought *H. sapiens* into the city? They going to kick us out of this place too?"

Lucky shrugged. "They rang at Jaguar. The Council decided to let them in. They're from the ERT."

"We're just here for research," Long said.

"Shut up, *sapiens*. Nobody wants to hear your excuses."

Lucky scratched their head and shot an apologetic smile at Long. "Now look, they aren't all *sapiens*. See? They truck with moose and bots. These people aren't from Verdance, OK? They're owned, same as our ancestors were. It's about time we had a talk."

The Archaean's mouth thinned into a line. "It's about time we split this world wide open so they stop stealing our water."

Though the context was missing, the threat was clear. Destry glanced at Nil, consciously keeping her face emptied of the anxiety that gripped her rib cage. Obviously there was a lot they needed to understand about what was happening down here, but for now she was going to take Lucky's advice and hold her tongue. Beside her, Whistle lowered his head, casually showing off the spread of his antlers, defensive but not aggressive. It was the ERT way, and Lucky acknowledged the moose with a subtle nod.

"We'll explore options this week at the Council meeting. Now we've got to go."

The transit riders parted to make way for the weird masked group from the surface. As Lucky led them past several train platforms, the *H. sapiens* earned a few more hard looks from other Archaeans. Nobody else said anything. Their silence felt somehow more judgmental than jeers.

She tried to imagine how the people of La Ronge would deal with obvious outsiders like the Archaeans, and came up blank. Rangers would be curious—they'd been taught about the first settlers' role during Sasky's oxygenation—but most people in the city? The workers? Maybe they wouldn't be openly hostile, but they probably wouldn't be welcoming either. Any kind of change usually meant Verdance was about to make their lives harder, and the sight of several *H. archaeans* in breathers wouldn't exactly be comforting. Certainly they wouldn't be promised an explanation at the Council. In La Ronge, only ERT rangers had a Council, and it was more like a professional organization than a political body. Most workers in La Ronge didn't even know the ERT Council existed. They just did their jobs and tried to avoid ever hearing from a Verdance rep.

At the far end of the hall, they came to a platform where an empty train car waited, its destination emblazoned in glowing red letters over each square window: ERT CAMPUS. The car itself was made of recycled metals and various polymers, giving it the appearance of a patchwork quilt. The interior had two springy, threadbare couches for the humans. A cat riding a drone floated on behind them and came to a hover in the very back of the car, as far from Nil, Long, and Destry as they could get. Wobbling slightly, the train moved into the tunnel. They stopped every few minutes, watching people hop on and off at other transit stations, parks, and busy residential areas. Finally the car began to climb, and they came to a halt at the mouth of a wide lava tube. Ferns and rubber trees grew in full sun beneath an irregularly shaped skylight like the one that had drawn them here. Except this skylight had been sealed with a one-way camouflage filter that shimmered faintly. To anyone glancing at satellite footage, it would look like a ridge on the mountain's flank.

Farther up the tunnel, past banana and fig trees, was a circular doorway carved straight into the rock. Letters carved above it were eroded into illegibility. "This is the oldest part of the city." Lucky pointed at the door. "The first place where we lived after the *sapiens* took charge."

A bright blue bird swooped past and Hellfire&Crisp shot after it, then boomeranged back to hover next to Whistle. "Not a bad environment," they said. "Nice for flying."

Whistle cocked his head at the drones: *This tube is too small for me.*

Long looked around skeptically. "The Archaeans have been down here for a thousand years?"

Lucky said nothing.

"I was here with Destry and Nil the last time there was an eruption, three hundred years ago. This is an active volcano. There is no way you could have survived in these lava tubes."

Lucky shrugged and turned in the direction Hellfire&Crisp had flown earlier. "That's what you think." They continued walking, then looked back over a shoulder. "You coming?"

The Archaean's vague replies weren't exactly reassuring. Swallowing trepidation, Destry readjusted her mask and followed Lucky with the rest of the team trailing close behind. The tube was quiet except for bird and insect noises, and a muddy trail led through the slice of tropical jungle that grew toward the camouflaged skylight. She quickened her pace to catch up to Lucky, but Long held back, pinching up a piece of the black soil. He pressed the slimy stuff between his fingers, then slipped a hand under his mask to taste it.

"This is high quality humus," he said. "Full of minerals, and I'd guess the organics were very carefully sourced."

Lucky looked pleased for the first time since they'd met. "I work with the soil group in the ERT. The humus in here is some of our best work. You a soil worker?"

Long nodded. "I was. Now I mostly do data history."

"I guess you missed out on the history of the Archaea, eh?"

Midnight trotted up behind them and pushed her thick neck between Long and Lucky. *We missed out on everybody's history,* she texted with a dismissive flick of her ear. *Verdance only tells us about the future, when Sasky will be sold.*

Long reached up absently and ran his hand over the mound of Midnight's shoulder. "I've been researching the planet's history from core samples and sensor records. That's how I know you can't have been here since the *Homo sapiens* were decanted back in the early 58,000s."

"I'm no historian, but my parents grew up here, and so did I." Lucky gestured at a cluster of rubber trees, as if their fat trunks stood in for the entire city. "The Archaea and our allies optimized this place to hide from

Verdance. We know when the VerdanceSats are crossing overhead, so those are easy to avoid. Network is glass and near-field wireless only, for senders. No signal leaks."

Long was skeptical. "How did you survive the eruptions?"

Lucky sighed dramatically and stopped, leaning one hip against Bog, who hovered beside them without speaking. "Why do you keep asking about that? Redirecting lava flows is easy."

Long raised his eyebrows. "Is it?"

"Not my specialty, but yeah." Lucky started walking again. "We do it all the time. What does your ERT do when there's an eruption?"

"We live far away from volcanoes," Destry said. "They're easy to avoid."

"Well, we need the mantle plume for CO_2 and power. I guess that's less of an issue when you can harvest sunlight on the surface and breathe the toxins up there."

Midnight snorted in agreement, and Long looked thoughtful. Destry flashed back to the day when Spider erupted, its smoky pillar twinned in her mind with the way she imagined her parents' last seconds, engulfed in heat and horror. She snuck a sidelong glance at Lucky, the first ranger she had ever met from another ERT campus. These Archaeans might be the only other people in the League who understood why working for Verdance left a feeling of constant disquiet crawling under her skin. And their ancestors had actually done something to stop it.

Overhead, the skylight narrowed until they were once again in a sealed tube, and Lucky stopped in front of a round blast door strobing green on their left. "Here we are!"

The circular door cracked into two half-moons that rolled smoothly into floor pockets. Hellfire&Crisp zapped over everyone's heads to take the lead but stopped abruptly just inside the portal. Short-range wireless signals shot between the drones and the door.

"Don't insult our friends, you flattened shit-circuit," Hellfire&Crisp shouted. "I'm monitoring your signal output. Don't try anything funny."

Lucky's mountable drone partner, Bog, rose through the air to hover alongside the two-bodied aeronaut and spoke with the intermittent twangs of someone whose speakers wanted fixing. "She's just kidding. Can't you take a joke?"

Hellfire&Crisp continued to yell at Jaguar. "No, *you* suck on a corrosive! You're the one talking about beheadings."

Lucky laughed awkwardly. "Jaguar's a little salty but she's all right. She insults everyone equally."

"Oh really? Because I only heard her insulting the *Homo sapiens*." Hellfire&Crisp got right up in Lucky's face, rotors whirring. Though they had not powered up any weapons, it was still menacing.

"Hey, friend. Let's keep things balanced." Destry stepped forward and gripped the cargo hooks on the undersides of Hellfire&Crisp's carapaces. "We're strangers here, and it's not our place to say what's funny and what isn't."

"You wouldn't say that if you could hear what this glorified heat sink was emitting."

Whistle texted everyone: *No, she would. She laughs at bad jokes.*

Lucky snorted and Nil rolled his eyes. But when Destry let go of Hellfire&Crisp, their hovering bodies still vibrated with rage. "We're watching you, packet-dropper."

One of the doors started to rise back out of the floor, but Lucky put their foot on it. "I'm sorry about Jaguar," they said. "She's been cranky ever since my grandparents stole her from a Verdance space vessel back in the late 57,000s."

It wasn't clear whether Lucky was joking, so Destry simply nodded. Spider City humor was out of her range, like a radio signal that cut out before you could tune it.

Jaguar the door slowly scissored closed behind them as they filed into a laboratory that looked as familiar as home. Foam tables along the walls were covered in spectroscopy chambers, reagent pots, gas samplers, and piles of half-dismantled sensors for biosphere analysis, all networked through spiderwebs of glass. It took a second to realize what felt off: the walls here were cut to form flat surfaces that intersected at right angles, unlike all the round tubes and arched ceilings she'd seen elsewhere in Spider City. It looked like La Ronge's architecture, which made sense if this was the first area the Archaea settled. They must have been using Verdance templates for urban planning at that point and learned to build in ways that fit their new environment later.

"All this equipment is based on specs from the Verdance starter pack that the Archaeans used to build the second biosphere." Lucky gestured vaguely. "Our grandparents reprogrammed them to maintain the first biosphere down here, for organisms that prefer the pre-oxygen gas mixture we used to have on Sasky."

ERT rangers were everywhere, their mouth conversations amalgamated into a low hum by the room's acoustics. Everyone seemed to be deliberately ignoring the La Ronge team or staring at them with ill-concealed hostility.

"See you later," Bog said, extending two arms out of his mountable barrel torso. "I need to start working." His speaker cut out on the word "work," which made it sound like he'd said "wanking."

Lucky glanced sidelong at Bog, their wide set Archaean eyes narrowing with mirth. "Go for it."

Nil nudged Destry and sent privately: *Did he say "wanking"?*

Before she could reply, Lucky gently pushed the group toward a well-lit tunnel across the lab. "We need to meet the aquifer team. Let's go."

As they shuffled awkwardly to the exit, a beaver walked past with a snarl that showed his bright orange teeth. Nil flashed a look at Destry and sent: *Everybody wants to kill us. What in the actual shit is going on here?*

Destry sighed, replying aloud. "Sounds like some kind of water emergency."

Nil squeezed her hand surreptitiously and pressed his lips together in an expression she knew well. He thought she was downplaying the danger. But she was simply being pragmatic, which was the sort of thing you learned while patrolling the boreal forest with only one flying moose as backup.

They filed after Lucky into a corridor that angled down steeply, with a narrow strip of grippy stairs along one side. Windows cut into the walls glowed a deep orange red, and Destry realized with a shock that they were looking out into an underground magma chamber, with the viscous, rippled surface of the molten rock flowing alongside them. The deeper they went, the more the magma lightened into hotter yellows and golds, until the walls seemed to shimmer with sunrise. Long and Midnight walked behind her, texting and whispering, no doubt trying to figure out what kind of transparent alloy could withstand the heat and pressure. Lucky had not been lying. Clearly the Archaea were capable of channeling lava flows. Balancing her fear was a growing respect for these escaped workers, engineering a whole city for themselves in the cradle of a volcano.

Lucky paused. "I love this hallway. It's such a beautiful view." The group huddled together around a floor-to-ceiling portal, admiring the rose gold hue with its luminous viscosity. The Archaean seemed to make a decision as they studied the hominins, moose, and hovering drones from La Ronge. "Let me explain something before we go inside." They leaned against the window, backlit by magma. "I asked the Spider City Council to let you find our door because we need to talk to you. It took months to convince everybody. I'm really glad you came, though, because I work in irrigation and our water supply is at stake. Our allies can only do so much—"

Somewhere to their left, a voice crackled to life. "Hi, Lucky." It came from a door made out of ancient, reclaimed wood, slightly splintered and touched up with colorful epoxies. "Are you sure you should be telling them everything about our allies?" Despite the low-quality audio distorting her words, Jaguar's warning tone was unmistakable.

Looking abashed, Lucky shrugged at them, then turned to address the voice. "You haven't been down here in a while, Jaguar."

"I'm keeping watch over Hellfire&Crisp, who are incredibly dangerous," the door muttered.

"We are. Very." Hellfire&Crisp strobed a laser at the ceiling, where it showed up as a harmless pinprick of red light. "Obviously we go hotter than that when we need to."

Raising an eyebrow, Lucky nodded. "I will try to stay on your good side."

Destry looked down to avoid laughing. Whether through diplomatic insight or accident, Lucky had said the one thing that was sure to satisfy Hellfire&Crisp.

Still, the Archaean had spoken about the water supply with enough intensity that it left Destry worried. Especially when she thought about what kinds of allies this secret civilization might have found on a planet that was cut off from the rest of the universe.

THE EEL

Water management is where the land meets politics.
—Environmental Rescue Team Handbook

The building felt like a barn on the inside, mostly due to its size. But this lab was actually a monument to the power of water. A rotunda overhead was made from the same transparent alloy they'd seen in the tunnels, forming an inverted dome. Through it, they could see at the bottom of the caldera lake that filled the mountain overhead. Turquoise curtains of light fluttered through the water and across the igneous rock below their feet.

"Now there's a view." Destry trailed off, staring.

Nil was equally transfixed. "Incredible," he breathed.

Whistle bumped up against them. *That's a lot of weight,* he texted. *It stops heat too. How does this glass stay whole?*

It was the same question they all had, especially after seeing the magma windows in the tunnel. Destry felt the edges of her curiosity fraying into fear. The Archaea had technologies that Verdance hadn't given to the people of La Ronge. Had the engineers of Spider City invented it themselves? Or learned to do it by making contact with people—those allies that Lucky mentioned—outside the Verdance network? She tore her attention away from the tonnes of water bearing down on them and snapped back into network analyst mode. Take in the scene. Look for what's there, but most of all, look for the relationships between things. Find the systems.

It was obvious she was in an environmental analysis and coordination center, where the rangers were monitoring changes in the city's water infrastructure and the lands that fed it. Streaming 2-D maps mounted on the wall revealed the city's sprawling four-layer structure, with air, water, and nutrient circulation cycles. There were roughly a dozen people at work in here, mostly hominins, with a few bots and a plump naked mole rat. Destry watched the rangers' easy way of interacting with each other, mouth talking or texting, listening and nodding. *Look there*, Whistle sent, pointing with his nose at a map to their right.

Dominating the image was the megacontinent of Maskwa, its C shape a wide-open mouth devouring the Bronze Islands and the Comfort Sea; at its back was the world-spanning Winston Ocean. Maskwa's northern reaches were capped by ice, just like the south pole. The smaller, southern continent, Tooth, wrapped around the bottom part of Maskwa's jaw and spread westward toward the submerged continent of Aotearoa. La Ronge was a black dot in Maskwa's upper jaw, two thousand klicks from the west coast and almost as far from the east. Bright blue highlighted Maskwa's watersheds, fueled by meltwater and rain that created a vast network of rivers running roughly north to south. Freshwater lakes pooled in the north, and the massive continent-spanning Eel River switchbacked through the Vertebrae Mountains, forking dozens of tributaries before emptying into the strait that separated southern Maskwa from western Tooth. West of the Vertebrae was Spider, marked with a red dot right above the equator. Water flows pulsed through the continents' many ecosystems, sustaining and draining.

Beside her, Nil was going through a face journey that started with bemusement and ended in horror. He pointed at the Eel's western delta.

A mosaic of multicolored data overlays spread like a stain over the delta, which was about 100 klicks north of Spider. But that wasn't the disturbing part. On all the maps Destry had seen, the Eel River gushed south, continuing past the volcano before tumbling onward into the lower continent. But on this map, the Eel River abruptly turned 90 degrees in the delta and shot toward the west coast long before reaching Spider. Without the Eel's nourishing waters, sensors revealed environments deeply out of balance. The southern Maskwa watershed was at critically low levels. Forests were parched. One of the map overlays revealed a spike in regional herbivore deaths, which was starving the predators and ripping the food web to shreds.

"Oh, shit," Destry whispered.

"Can that be real?" he whispered back. "Verdance never showed us this data."

"You see why we need to talk?" Lucky frowned at the map. "Why are you diverting all the water from our aquifer? There's plenty to go around."

Destry looked at Nil, then at the rest of their group. "Do any of you know about this?"

Nil's partner, Rocket, hovered around to face them. They broadcast the sound of water being sucked down a drain from their sensor-encrusted head. The mountable drone hadn't spoken aloud since arriving in the city, and now they had everyone's full attention. "I've been following the soft launch of Sasky on the real estate market, and I think I know what's going on." Rocket telescoped their head up to hominin eye level, giving them the appearance of a small, floating giraffe with seven eyes, sizing up a delicious cluster of leaves on a high branch. "Verdance is assuming that most of the big developers will plant cities along the coasts. It's the most valuable land, but it has a lot of desert. So, it looks like our boss, Ronnie, sent workers down to dam the river, using her usual brute force methods. Investors want a reliable irrigation source for the farms they'll need to feed millions of residents."

"The Eel River used to flow right past Spider. Now it's heading to the coast one hundred klicks away and we've lost our renewable water source." Lucky's lips thinned to a line. "In a few seasons, we'll have to dig deeper wells. It's unsustainable."

"I don't see why you need that river." Long folded his arms. "Annual rainfall will recharge the aquifer."

Midnight lifted her head to its full height as she peered at the map, making Long appear to diminish in size. *Look at these readings, friend,* she sent. *Without the Eel, eventually the aquifer will dry out and the land will sink.*

"She's right," Destry said, scratching her chin. "The ERT should have managed this and kept the balance."

"But why do we care?" Long sounded peevish. "By the time that happens, this land will belong to some Verdance client. Then the water will be their problem."

Destry was taken aback. Those were shameful words. A ranger who allowed ecosystems to become unsustainable lost their honor and the faith of their community. She glanced at Lucky, wondering whether they regretted asking the *H. sapiens* for help. The Archaean wore an awkward expression that mirrored the other hominin faces. Nobody wanted to call Long out for his taboo comment; to do so would only make everyone's embarrassment more acute.

Rocket raised their sensor bulb again and played a few seconds of sprightly dance music to break the silence. "I think it's obvious that we need to coax the Eel back to its old bed. It won't be easy."

Gratefully, Lucky nodded. "Let's take a closer look at that dam." They zoomed in on the river north of Spider and went deep into a discussion of seasonal flows with Nil and Rocket. She was glad to see that their ERT instincts for problem solving had dissipated the tension with Long.

Some of the tension, anyway. Midnight lifted one hoof and thumped it back down, sending a text to everyone in the group: *You're acting like this is a purely technical problem. We can help you now, but what happens in a millennium when the landowners arrive? How are you going to hide this place?*

Lucky shrugged. "We're not going to hide forever."

Destry raised her eyebrows at Whistle, who lowered his head slightly and sent privately: *A nice thought. But it could end in death.*

Suddenly Nil clapped his hands together, rubbing them with glee. "You know, we could do this very elegantly, without having to destroy that dam the workers built."

"How would that work?" Lucky asked.

"About eight thousand years ago, the Eel used to take an even older route south, and it went right past Spider." He pointed at an area called Fork Canyon, 273 klicks north of the delta and its offending dam. A long, weed-choked ravine zigzagged out of the canyon, providing evidence that the Eel had once flowed in a more ancient riverbed slightly to the east of its current course. "At some point the river changed its mind about how to go south. It picked a new pathway out of Fork Canyon, and that's the one Verdance dammed up. The old pathway is still open. So, if we make a dam at Fork Canyon, blocking the newer route, we might be able to move the Eel back into a bed that it once really liked. And Spider could recharge its aquifer."

Destry was getting excited. "Yes! If the Eel flowed into its old bed, it would completely bypass that vomit-flecked dam that Verdance is using to send it to the coast."

"And it would look natural!" Rocket added. "Wild rivers change course for all kinds of reasons."

Nil beamed. He looked happier than Destry had seen him in many centuries. "Let us stay and help you do this, friends."

Midnight glanced at Long and sent to the group: *Shouldn't we talk to the ERT back at La Ronge?* Her partner scowled and folded his arms, refusing to participate in the discussion.

Destry ignored Long's sourness. It felt good to imagine protecting an environment that Verdance didn't control. "I'm not saying we're doing it for sure, but I like the idea. Maybe we could stay awhile and discuss it. Our first intercampus ERT meeting on Sasky."

Long glared. "If our signals stay hidden down here, Verdance will be looking for us within days."

"They don't have the resources to track everybody all the time," Destry said with more confidence than she felt. "Everybody knows we're in the field. Ronnie won't check on us for weeks."

Hellfire&Crisp settled familiarly on Whistle's antlers and cackled. "We're in. We don't owe those Verdance flesh-eaters our loyalty. Let's fix this."

"And what will you do when Verdance tries to move the river again?" Long asked pointedly. "Because they will. They want to water those coastal cities."

"I think we have a good engineering plan, which you and our allies can help with." Lucky paused, considering. "And as for what to do about Verdance . . . well, that's a harder problem. That's politics."

A group of Archaeans working quietly across the room from them stood up and began to pack up for the day. One loped easily over to Lucky, putting an arm around their shoulder. "It's time for dinner. Do you want to join us, friends from La Ronge?"

"We should eat before I show you to the visitors' dorm," Lucky agreed. "Plus, speaking of allies, the dogs are back, so we should have some interesting news from down south."

Whistle had only ever encountered Pleistocene replica dogs, and they were rather fond of eating baby moose. He looked alarmed. *Who keeps dogs?* he sent.

"Nobody keeps them. They tend the intercontinental glass networks. Some of them are visiting from Tooth."

7

A REAL HEARTBREAKER

In the Great Bargain, we must accept that some people will not be
pleased to meet us.

—*Environmental Rescue Team Handbook*

If they hadn't been several meters underground, with portals open to lava
flows rather than prairie, the ERT dining hall would have felt familiar.
The Spider City rangers cooked collectively and took what they wanted
from grab tables. Comfortable benches made from pressed mycelium filled
a room lit with jars of twinkling bioluminescent bacteria. There were elevated stools with pillows for the cats and naked mole rats. Every table had
generous space for people who stood on all fours to eat, and at least a dozen
moose were scattered around the room, lipping up root vegetables and
branches from sturdy bowls. Drones and bots took turns at the charge pads
that could be moved from chair to chair. Down here, they were on thermal
rather than solar energy, so they couldn't fly around in sunlight to charge
up like Hellfire&Crisp did. Lucky gave the mammals some lightweight
breathers that fitted over various nose configurations, allowing them to eat
without drowning in carbon dioxide.

The La Ronge team sat down with Lucky and the other water researchers. After a while, they were joined by three naked mole rats who shared
the hive name Dash.

Whistle kept obsessing about the dogs, asking where they were every few
minutes. In La Ronge, dogs were built with an extremely low InAss rating—
officially, they were classified as "animals"—and their vocabularies were so
limited that they were essentially nonverbal. Nobody expected them to do
any work beyond occupying a generic predator niche in several ecosystems.
Whistle looked around warily again, and sent: *Where are the dogs?*

One of the Dashes lifted a wrinkled pink face, her nearly invisible eyes and ears framed by a fluffy wool jacket collar. *They're in the northwest corner,* she sent.

Destry glanced over her shoulder and saw a group of hairless tropical dogs, tall enough that their heads could reach a moose's shoulder, clustered at a corner table. Some were a deep black and others a mottled pink-and-brown. They had the air of people who desperately wanted to be somewhere else and were going to stick close together until they got there.

"They don't want to talk about their work down in Tooth?" Destry asked. Back home, rangers who came back from the field sometimes gave informal talks about their experiences during dinner. She was particularly curious about Tooth, because Verdance had put the whole southern continent into a conservation land trust. It would never be sold and developed the way land on Maskwa would.

Dash sat up, hands curled, her four front teeth yellowed with age: *They'll file a report, but they don't usually socialize much. Not this team, anyway. They'll be headed back to Tooth in the morning. Fair enough. They really don't like being around hominins.*

Dash had Whistle's full attention. *Why?*

I worked on the dog project back in the 53,000s—we were making the Great Bargain with them for the first time, you know? We had templates for dogs with Intelligence Assessment ratings high enough to take jobs in the city. But then the canines saw what had been done to their ancestors. We have the ancient Earth archives that come with the ERT foundational documents, just like you do. They saw all that "man's best friend" stuff and it did not go well. It's hard to be excited about creating a new Earth when your people on the old one were brainwashed by Homo sapiens *for thousands of years. Tens of thousands.* Dash waved her face around, nose delicately wrinkled, gesturing at the magnitude of time. Then she continued, directing her comments at Whistle. *It's different for people like us. Our ancestors were never forced to serve* H. sapiens *like that. They weren't domesticated.*

No, sent Whistle. *But we are now.*

Another Dash flicked her tail and joined the conversation: *I suppose that's true where you're from.*

Midnight broke into the exchange: *Do you think La Ronge is really all that different from Spider City?*

Suddenly everyone was talking and texting at once. Normally Destry would have thrown in her own opinions, or endorsed another person's ideas, but she was distracted. After all day without signal, she wanted to check external comms—just in case.

Not wanting to interrupt, she sent privately to Lucky: *How do I get to the surface to listen for messages?*

Lucky sent a map with directions to a gravity assist tube that would take her to a hidden spot at the edge of the caldera lake. Excusing herself, Destry headed away from the table and into another lava-lit corridor. When she emerged next to the water, the first stars were emerging in the dimming sky. She lay down on the still-warm earth and thought about how the lab where they had worked all afternoon was right underneath them. Then she dug her fingers into the soil and reached out with her mind. There were so few sensors here that she was having a hard time finding a pathway down the mountain. Groaning with frustration, Destry sniffed for a pathway that would connect her to data from La Ronge, where Ronnie's messages would land after traveling through the League's system of satellites and wormholes.

There it was. Somewhere to the north, across the lake, the network had cobbled together a sense of place: *The trees need water; five dogs walked here on their way south; here is a blob of video data for you that has been compressed to travel through space.* Definitely Ronnie. Sitting up and disconnecting, Destry sent the blob to her data pad and piped the sound to her right ear. As the screen came to life, her stomach clenched involuntarily. Ronnie's hair was now a frosty white piled atop her head, and her pale brown skin was set off perfectly by a shift the color of blackberries. Her background was the simulated view of a Verdance-branded gas giant that swirled with bruised orange clouds.

"I am so sorry that we can't speak one-on-one, Destry, and even more sorry to hear that you have gone on a nonessential mission in the middle of this extremely sensitive time." Her passive-aggressive tone hovered right on the edge of a scream. Ronnie had helpfully appended a compressed map showing that she knew exactly the route Destry had taken to Spider, based on the tracking spores she'd shed on the way down to the volcano. Everything grown on Sasky was dusted with these harmless bacterial spores, and their genetic material was a simple ID tag. People ate the spores, carried them on their skin, and shed them constantly. It was good for network analysis, because if a plant or animal turned up in the wrong ecosystem, tracking spores could tell rangers how it got there. Of course, it was also a powerful surveillance system, because sensors could read every spore in the vicinity.

So much for her claim that nobody would notice where they were for weeks.

In the video, Ronnie glanced to the left, cutting her eyes at something—or someone—who was hidden by the fake planet behind her. "Thankfully, I have straightened out our problem with the *extremely* valuable equipment you destroyed. I wanted to make sure you understood that there will be more visitors coming and they are *potential buyers*. You are not to speak with them under any circumstances, no matter what they are doing, unless I tell you otherwise. They are there to enjoy our planet and to inspect the show plots we've arranged."

At this, Destry groaned even louder. There were no show plots. At least, none that La Ronge workers had built. Typical Verdance bullshit, claiming that the planet had some feature that it didn't. Maybe that kind of flimflammery worked on her "potential buyers." When Ronnie spoke again, her mild scold took on a lethal undertone. "If you are anything but courteous to our guests, you'll force me to dispatch our security remotes to escort them. So be good while you're out there in the field, and keep the balance." Abruptly the video ended with a cheerful sign-off chime. Destry stared at the blank spot where Ronnie's smile had been, thinking about how incongruous it was to hear the ERT homily in the mouth of a person who colonized planets for profit.

She didn't want to deal with what Ronnie's message implied: more damage to the ecosystems, more perturbations of the carbon cycle, more assholes turning life forms into meat. Deadly threats to the people of Spider City, whom she was actually starting to like.

Despite her reservations, pleasure warmed her guts when she thought about giving the Eel back to the Spider City people. It was a small thing, but it was also huge—and as dangerous as a gas buildup underground. Destry smiled as she stepped back into the gravity assist and sank down to the ERT dining hall level. What would Ronnie say when she discovered that her property was not as controllable as she thought? Then, with a shiver, she wondered what price Spider City would have to pay.

Destry found her friends lingering at dinner, still talking about dogs. According to Dash, the dogs roamed the surface freely, traveling in and out of the tunnels and feigning low InAss ratings so as to avoid detection. She and the Archaeans had designed the dogs' respiration systems to toggle between high and low carbon environments. They were dry-land amphibians, moving easily between one gas mixture and another.

Seated next to her, Nil dunked a wedge of sourdough bread into his root stew, which smelled faintly of lemon through her breather. Destry tried to repress her anxiety by doing an ERT mental exercise, chasing that scent back into the system that produced it. Perhaps Spider City grew citrus under one of those protected skylights, or perhaps they had some way to harvest trees topside, evading spores and sensor networks? It took incredible skill to leave no trace in this environment, especially given that they had an entire city to feed, requiring energy inputs and waste outputs on a dramatic scale.

Nil noticed her staring intensely at his food. "What are you thinking about, friend? Aren't you going to grab something to eat?"

She jumped up to get a bowl. "You're right. I'm really hungry." It was a perfect excuse to avoid telling him about Ronnie's message. Next to the lemon-spiked stew was a tray of steamed dumplings and a bowl of garlic fried crickets. Destry sampled a little bit of everything, taking her time, topping the warm mixture with a piece of flatbread. When she sat down at the table again, talk had turned to Verdance.

Lucky wiped their mouth with the back of a hand. "Ultimately we'll need to deal with Verdance. But I'd like to delay that for as long as possible. I want us to be ready."

Long had simmered down after his outbursts at the ERT water lab, but he was still unhappy. "I respect the wishes of the majority," he said stiffly, "but I still think we should compromise. We don't need to tell Verdance, but we should tell our colleagues in the La Ronge ERT before we reroute the river."

"We can't risk that."

The two rangers were locked in debate again, and it was going nowhere.

Sighing, Destry tried to dream up a polite way to end this conversation and get Nil alone. They needed to strategize about how to deal with the watershed—and Ronnie. Fortunately, Midnight and Whistle provided an unexpected source of distraction.

Midnight glanced at Whistle, then texted to the group: *It's time to bed down.*

Long was surprised. "We just finished eating. Are you tired, friend?"

Both moose ignored Midnight's hominin partner. Whistle asked: *Is there a barn for us?*

All three members of the Dash hive made whuffling noises and covered their faces with their hands. The one in wool replied tartly: *There are rooms for everyone. Nobody will make you stay in a barn. You're not a piece of farm equipment.*

Midnight snorted: *He didn't mean it that way.*

Knowing Whistle as she did, Destry could tell he was embarrassed. He flicked his ears back and dropped his head slightly, dewlap trembling.

She cleared her throat. "You know what? I'm feeling really tired too. Maybe someone could show us to our rooms?" Destry nudged Nil. "You want to come with me?"

Nil looked nonplussed but followed her lead. "I'm happy to turn in. It's been a long day. Can we reconvene in the morning and figure out plans for the watershed?"

"Of course. I'll show you the guest dorms." Lucky stood up, and everybody began to clear their bowls and carry utensils to the wash stations.

From the dining hall, Lucky led them down a long corridor whose curved walls were crowded with painted handprints in gold, white, and red. At the bottom was a high-ceilinged rotunda ringed with irregularly sized doors, tunnels, and gates. Spider City's ERT dorms were the strangest thing she had ever seen. Nothing was regularized. It was as if every ranger had built their own living quarters according to some quirky personal whim, decorating the entrances in wildly different styles. Some were plain scavenged wood, while others were a riot of glittering rocks and paint. Gates made from bone and textiles stood next to shiny, metallic portals controlled by bots. Oddly, a harmony emerged from the chaos of design. This place felt occupied in a way that nothing in La Ronge ever did, perhaps because she could see the personalities of its people in every nook and odd angle.

Lucky beamed as they looked around. "The first thing that new rangers do is build their own rooms down here. The tuff is so soft that you can dig it out easily with a shovel, and it's a good way for them to put their ERT engineering skills into practice."

Nil touched a doorframe that was starting to crumble. "How do you regulate what they build to make sure everyone is safe?"

Lucky was perplexed by the question. "Everyone here has passed ranger training. If they have a question about safety, they can ask another ranger, or consult the archives."

"But I mean—"

Midnight was getting restless: *Can you tell us where we might find a room?* She and Whistle had been pressing against each other and private messaging the whole way down to the dorms. Destry had never seen Whistle like this, and she wasn't sure whether to be amused or alarmed.

"Guest rooms are down that way." Lucky pointed to a wide corridor. "Empty rooms have green doors."

The two moose took their leave, and Destry trailed after them. "Let's find a room, Nil. Goodnight, everyone!"

"See you at breakfast hour."

"See you then!"

By the time she and Nil reached the corridor, the moose had already gone. They must have found a room immediately and closed the door.

"What's going on with them?" Destry asked.

Behind her, Long chuckled. "Midnight has that effect on people. You tell Whistle to be careful, though. She's a real heartbreaker."

"Didn't really want to know that, but OK."

Still, thinking about the moose entangled in romantic melodrama lightened her mood a bit. At least some people were getting a little frisky distraction. She and Nil continued past a dozen glowing green doors, trying to figure out whether any of them were set up to make oxygen. A few had air filters, but they had fallen into dusty disuse. About two hundred meters along, they found a windowless room with fresh moss glowing on the ceiling and a bed platform where somebody had left blankets. Best of all, it had responsive atmosphere controls on a portal door, so they could seal themselves inside and dial up the oxygen.

After they closed the door and took off their breathers, Nil stretched out on the platform and leaned against the wall, bent arms tucked behind his head. "I'm pretty sure you didn't drag me away from dinner to do what Midnight and Whistle are doing right now."

She laughed with him, then thought about Ronnie's final words and felt even worse than she had before. "We need to talk. I got a message from Verdance today."

"Is Ronnie still pissed about that remote you recycled?"

"She is, yeah. But I guess she worked it out, or I'd be kicked out of the ERT." Destry played with the frayed edge of a blanket, and Nil sat up next to her, his face drained of its former levity. She filled him in on Ronnie's shit-stained assertion about the show plots and her not-so-veiled threats about Destry's job.

He groaned. "They want to squeeze pus on everything, just when we've got the carbon cycle working? Our ecosystems are barely holding it together as it is."

"It would be like that time we had to deal with all those crocodiles . . . remember that?"

When they were brand-new rangers, the ERT Council had decided to dispatch them to Maskwa's western seaboard, where something had gone deeply wrong in the saltwater marshes. The normally rich, green ecosystem had become a barren landscape. Typically, a small number of toothy crocodilians perched at the top of the energy pyramid, but for some reason their population had exploded. Giant, toothy amphibians with powerful tails were everywhere, starving and fighting.

"They were eating everybody," Nil remembered. "Weren't they actually eating each other by the time we got there?"

Destry sighed. "And then—right after we got there, the crocs died back so much that all their prey species had a population explosion. Our campsite was attacked by raccoons and ducks every night for over a year."

"It wasn't that bad though." Nil nudged up against her. "We had some fun."

Centuries-old memories flooded her mind, along with the feeling of lightness she once had when connecting to the sensor networks around her. Back then, she and Nil spent their days trying to rescue plants from angry ducks—then stayed up all night talking and fucking. The food web was unraveling, the marshes were dying, and extinctions kept rising way above standard background levels. But the disaster seemed cozy somehow. Fixable.

For a couple of years, they worked with a small team to coax the local plants to rebound, which got the ducks and fish humping like mad and finally put food in the mouths of all those predatory crocodilians. But their sense of triumph had diminished when they got back to La Ronge and analyzed their field data. It turned out that the problems had all started because a worker camp had cut down an entire forest for some discontinued terraforming project. Invasive species fleeing the damage, coupled with toxic topsoil runoff, had wrecked the balance in the marshes. Verdance had forced their pet ERT to fix its own environmental disaster.

"It's going to be like that all the time now, isn't it? Ronnie is basically saying these potential buyers will be coming down the gravity well and doing whatever they want. Killing trees, leaving waste, eating the small animals that our predators need."

"Yeah, I definitely sense more crocodile apocalypses in our future."

Eyes prickling, Destry leaned against Nil. "I wish we could just fix this watershed and get a gold star on our ERT reports. I have no idea what Verdance is going to do when they find out what we're doing with the Eel. I'll definitely be out of my job. I don't—"

Shaking his head, Nil took her hand. "Ronnie is going to be pissed. But you are the best network analyst she has—you're built for it, and now you have centuries of experience, with centuries ahead of you. You're valuable to her, but only as a member of the ERT. She won't kick you out." He paused and looked at her solemnly. "She might shit on our faces more often, though."

Destry let out a long uggghhh sound, lay down, and pulled the blankets over her head.

"Maybe this alliance with the Archaeans could be a way forward," Nil said. "If we have two ERT campuses here, we can cover more ground. Prevent the worst damage. Plus, they've got some amazing equipment here. Lucky told me that they have a system for setting off controlled volcanic eruptions."

Destry poked her head out of the covers, startled. "They can make a volcano erupt?"

"Kind of. It's more like they can tap magma chambers to avoid eruptions. But the technology could be repurposed to make the lava flow into lot of places—including Fork Canyon, where the old Eel riverbed starts. A lava flow there could create a natural dam and reroute the Eel in the right direction."

"You're saying that's how we could make this look like a natural event."

"Yeah, that's the idea."

Destry nodded. "I'll go along with that plan. But also—controlled lava flows? Sounds like a pretty powerful weapon."

He stiffened. "What do you mean?"

"I'm just saying that—you know—there's a reason rangers carry weapons. Defense. In this case, defense against Verdance."

Nil hugged her hard. "Let's hope it doesn't come to that. I don't think a mere pyroclastic flow could stop Ronnie."

The two old friends stayed up late, swapping massages and talking about how long the ecosystems would need to recover if volcanoes caused a massive carbon injection into the atmosphere. Eventually, Destry no longer felt like a slurry of reeking topsoil runoff.

Down the hall, Whistle rested his chin on Midnight's back before falling asleep, enjoying the sensation of his fur rumpling against hers.

While the mammals slept, the drones relaxed in their own ways. Hellfire&Crisp headed back to the tunnels to practice their sprints. Nil's partner, Rocket, tinkered with a modification to their near-field communications array so that they could speak more easily with Spider City bots.

CHORING

*A successful community requires thoughtful participation, hard work,
and a healthy appreciation for the absurd.*
    —*Environmental Rescue Team Handbook*

Destry awoke when her pad emitted a low-battery buzz. Blinking, she
looked for a window or other sign of what time it was, and found nothing
but a smear of glowing moss overhead. Nil was breathing warmly next to
her, his thick black hair fanned across her arm. Oh, right. She was deep
underground with a bunch of people who weren't supposed to exist, her
micromanaging boss was about to spray human diarrhea on the world,
and of course she hadn't really paused to consider that a day without sunlight would mean a pad without power. Outside the door she could hear
the faint sounds of hooves and voices, which meant they probably hadn't
missed breakfast yet. She sat up on the bed platform as Nil stirred awake,
stretching and yawning. How the hell did people around here tell time
without the sun to guide them?

A crackling noise followed by a tart voice issuing from doors up and
down the hallway provided an answer. "Breakfast is nearly prepared." It
sounded awfully familiar.

"Is that you, Jaguar?"

"Good morning, *H. sapiens*."

Nil groaned. "Smells like recycled air."

"That is correct. Hellfire&Crisp say hello, by the way. They're already
waiting for you in the dining hall."

Destry and Nil looked at each other, amused.

"Are you still guarding them?" Destry asked.

"I am—keeping them company." The door seemed slightly flustered.

It sounded like Hellfire&Crisp had somehow befriended Jaguar overnight.

Destry and Nil made it out the door in time to catch Midnight and Whistle emerging from their room near the rotunda. Normally, Destry would have rubbed Whistle's shoulder in greeting, reveling in the bristly warmth of his fur and muscles. But today, watching him nuzzle Midnight's ear, she suddenly felt self-conscious about showing physical affection. Would she be disturbing a private moment between the two moose? Was she being creepy and possessive? Of course, she technically owned Whistle, so the issue should be moot. That's surely what Ronnie would think.

A text arrived: *Hi there, friend.* Whistle bonked her arm with his nose, dispelling her anxiety.

"Hey, Whistle." She scratched between his antlers tentatively. "Hi, Midnight."

Midnight turned to face them: *Hey there. Ready to grab some breakfast? I'm starving. We'll need lots of fuel if we're going to come up with a plan to un-steal a billion liters of water.*

"That much?"

That's how much the local aquifer lost after Verdance diverted the river. Stick 'em up, and let these folks have some of your fine H_2O!

Destry had to grin at Midnight's reference to the bad guy's signature line from the game *Animal Uprising*. The outlaw cat bot always yowled, "Stick 'em up!" right before he robbed everybody blind. She hadn't spent much time with Midnight until this trip, and she was starting to understand what Whistle saw in the muscular moose with jet-black fur and a sarcastic glint in her eyes.

Whistle shot her a look that she'd never seen on his face before. Something about the set of his ears, one angled toward her and one toward Midnight, coupled with the slight tilt of his head—was it a conspiratorial expression? She wasn't sure, but she decided to take it the way she would if a human friend gave her an I-just-got-laid smirk at the morning grab table. Destry slung an arm around Whistle's neck, gave him a comradely squeeze, and punched him softly with her other arm. "You're looking good this morning, buddy."

He shot a blast of air out of his nostrils, laughing: *I am good. Each day. All day.*

As he carefully chose words from his limited vocabulary, Midnight turned away, texting them as she cantered up the hallway: *I need to find Long.*

Whistle watched her go, then hung his head as if his late summer antlers had become too heavy to bear. He messaged Destry and Nil privately: *I might be too . . . too plain for her.*

Walking on either side of the moose, the two *H. sapiens* both reached out to touch him in sympathy. "Long told me to warn you that she's a heartbreaker," Destry said.

The moose snorted. When they got to the dining hall, Midnight and Long were nowhere to be found. Destry picked up a charging pad for her mobile, dropping it next to Rocket in case the mountable drone needed a quick top-up. Nil grabbed some bowls of porridge with seared grubs and apples, Lucky brought a big pitcher of coffee for the table, and Whistle loomed over them, eating from a huge trough of leafy twigs. Eventually the Dashes joined the group, along with a cat who refused to introduce herself or talk to anyone.

Are you in one of your moods? Dash texted the cat publicly. *Because we need to make some progress today on the magma guide swarm.*

Are you still a condescending smear of vomit? Because I need to eat my breakfast.

The other two Dashes chittered with amusement and the cat went back to crunching her protein bar.

Though this room had seemed so familiar last night, Destry realized something was missing. Or rather, something was present: all the people were here, even the bots and cats. In La Ronge, the humans lived and ate in the main dorms, while the Mounts had the barns. Bots didn't need places to eat or sleep, and all the other people—well, they had their own food arrangements that they preferred. Destry had never really thought about how weird it was that they didn't eat together. She had always assumed it was easier for everyone to have their own spaces—but this was just as easy. In some ways it was easier, because they could talk about missions in a more casual way, and maybe let off some work-related stress.

Slurping down their coffee, Lucky snapped their fingers as if they'd just remembered something. "If you're going to stay for a while, I need to add you to the chore schedule. Anybody have limits on what they can do?"

There were murmurs from around the table and everybody sent their ERT choring tags to Lucky. Every ranger had a choring tag, a small blob of structured data that listed their strengths and weaknesses as community contributors. Nobody could live on an ERT campus for any length of time without choring, helping out with shared tasks like cooking, cleaning public areas, and infrastructure maintenance. Destry's tag indicated a preference for cooking, but after centuries at the La Ronge campus she was competent in everything from waste disposal to road repair.

The only person who looked dubious was the cat. *Are they really going to stay for enough time to help with choring?*

Rocket played a few bars of a popular work song, its peppy tempo designed to bring a little levity to chopping potatoes or tending the compost cycle in cesspits. "Even if we stay for a few days, we need to make our contribution."

Nil drummed fingers on the table. "I have to agree. And this watershed repair could take a couple of months. Nobody is expecting us back until fall."

Maybe nobody was expecting them back, but now Destry knew for sure that Ronnie was keeping tabs on her and might figure out something was amiss when her spore trail dried up. As she worried silently, Destry caught Whistle looking at Midnight for several long beats. She hoped his obvious affection wasn't misplaced. Emotions could run high in the field, especially in a small group like theirs, facing a lot of risky unknowns.

By the time they had cleared their dishes, Destry had already gotten her first choring assignment: kitchen cleanup tonight, after dinner. Things were definitely starting to feel more and more like home around here. As she followed Nil and Lucky back down to the ERT water labs, she fell into systems thinking again, wondering where Spider City had diverged from La Ronge. Had the Spider City people always eaten together, back when they lived at La Ronge? That would have been before her parents, Destry Senior and Frenchy, were decanted by people she'd been taught were extinct. The Archaea, and all the other people in the Great Bargain with them.

What's wrong, Destry? The text was from Whistle, who had picked up on her mood.

"I was just thinking about how you never eat with us back home."

The moose didn't reply for a long time: *I think you made that rule.*

"What?" She was irked. "I didn't make that rule. Plus, it's not a rule. It's a tradition."

It took even longer for Whistle to answer this time: *That rule . . . it's like the air. You don't look at it. Here, you can't breathe. So you look.*

When he put it that way, her irritation was replaced by a hot gout of shame. She was famous for comprehending systems in their entirety, for repairing connections between nodes that nobody else could perceive. Why hadn't she seen the edges that defined their social lives back in La Ronge? Whistle knew all along, despite his low InAss rating. She was reminded of what Dash expressed last night, about building the dogs who discovered their ancestors' history back on Earth. Dash understood what she'd done. But did that La Ronge engineer who installed the limiter in Whistle's brain ever stop to think that they were deliberately destroying a person's ability to communicate? To be understood?

All she could do now was acknowledge, once again, that InAss ratings truly were ass. "You're right, Whistle. I feel really stupid for not noticing this sooner."

He nudged her gently. *Once in a while you are smart, Destry. You give me all the pinecones, right?*

"Would you want to eat with us, back home? If we changed the rules?"

I don't know. He turned to face her, the familiar soft square of his nose curving down in a way that appeared particularly thoughtful. *Things can change now. We could live in Spider City.*

Before she could answer, they reached the door to the ERT lab. Hellfire&Crisp buzzed over their heads, then flew back up out of reach, cackling. "Welcome back, mammals! We've been teaching Jaguar to play Crashout!"

Whistle shed his pensive air and bucked his back legs with glee. "Where is she? Did you win?"

A small drone covered in spines shot down from the ceiling. It spoke in Jaguar's voice. "I'm using this as a remote! Check it!" And the three drones whirled in intricate spirals down the lava tube that led to the skylit garden, gracefully competing in a game that Destry barely understood. Whistle bucked again, emitting a high, keening cry to cheer them on.

Just then, Midnight and Long arrived. Midnight gave the entire crew a once-over, looking especially judgey when she saw Whistle, and spoke to the door: *May we please come in, Jaguar? It's time to start work.*

The door split into two half-moons, leaving a large open wedge for everybody to walk through. Apparently Jaguar was too pleased by her performance in the Crashout tourney to say anything sour. Destry and Whistle stayed behind to watch the still-circling drones.

Whistle looked sadly at Midnight's retreating form. *So much for that,* he sent.

As the drones disappeared into sunlit trees, Destry threw her arms around his neck and whispered in his ear. "If Midnight doesn't realize what a catch you are, her InAss ratings are lower than a rock's."

The moose flicked an ear at her and they went into the lab where the ceiling emitted a murky glow from the morning sky through two hundred meters of water.

THE BORING FLEET

You cannot measure a person's intentions, but you can measure their contributions.

—*Environmental Rescue Team Handbook*

Over the next month in Spider City, life settled into the comforting rhythms of community work while the air cooled outside with the approach of dry season. The team quickly adjusted to their new routines. Nil and the Archaean ranger Lucky ran endless simulations of lava dams and water velocities; Destry helped them gather data by connecting to the sensor network in Fork Canyon. The one question mark that remained was what Spider City's capabilities actually were. When she and Nil asked how the ERT would bring lava into the canyon, Lucky would shrug and smile. "Just assume it's handled. It's more important to figure out the best structure and location for the dam."

When she wasn't dealing with Lucky's evasiveness, Destry spent her days choring with Whistle in Spider City's many public works departments: energy, ventilation, water, recycling, waste. The labor was tough, and often stinky; but tougher still were the locals, who generally regarded the *H. sapiens* as patsies for Verdance. Riding the subways was the worst, because people would practically sit on each other's heads to avoid sharing a bench with her. She and Whistle took long walks to avoid the subway when they could, and soon Destry knew her way through the city's many neighborhoods. Some were vast caverns devoted to agriculture, while others were densely packed with shops where the Archaeans bartered and laughed with equal intensity.

Destry approached the social system of Spider City with the same patience she brought to long-term ecosystem projects. Maybe there were frustrations, but the only solution was to keep going. Keep contributing. When she was prepping manure for the bioreactors, she could forget the angry stares from her new neighbors. She could pretend she wasn't on a mission more precarious than any she'd dealt with before.

No further messages came from La Ronge, which she took as a hopeful sign. Every night, she surfaced next to the caldera lake, climbed onto the grassy shoulder of the mountain, and ran her hands through the stalks, feeling for data. When her queries turned up nothing but crisp leaves and arid soil, she would allow herself one final breath before returning to Nil in their oxygenated room. They curled around each other, falling asleep as they speculated about what would come next. And then, every dawn at the breakfast table, Destry would try to figure out what in the seething compost heap was going on between Whistle and Midnight. Sometimes the two moose would catch each other's eyes, yearningly; other times, they acted like they barely knew each other.

One morning during their fifth week in Spider City, Whistle and Midnight arrived at the dining hall locked in a silent debate. The two moose sent private texts back and forth, stomping hooves and ignoring the other rangers from La Ronge at the table, until the situation became awkward.

At last, Destry put down her spoon and intervened. "Hey, friends." She waved. "Remember us? The other people eating beside you?"

Midnight ducked her head apologetically, the soft black fur on her face glinting green in the bacterial light. *We were just talking about Lucky's invitation*, she sent publicly.

They want to show us how they will make a dam, Whistle added.

Destry pressed her hands to the table to check messages. Lucky had indeed called the whole La Ronge crew to the lab after breakfast, for a beta test of the controlled eruption.

Rocket floated off their charging pad, looking like a barrel with a periscope, and made a stylized guffaw noise. "Everyone who sleeps and eats food is inevitably late to the party. Hellfire&Crisp are already at the lab with Lucky. See you there, mammals!" With that, they hovered out of the room.

Nil shrugged at his partner's haste and ate another bite of spicy porridge with fried potatoes and carrots. "I like food."

As if on cue, Whistle and Midnight ate noisily from bowls of crunchy stems, studiously ignoring each other again. Destry was torn between worry that her friend was getting his heart broken, and excitement that they would finally get to see Spider City's mysterious lava control system. If Lucky trusted them enough to reveal the city's greatest asset, the La Ronge team's hard work was finally paying off.

Having met their biological needs, the mammals walked together to the ERT data center beneath the caldera lake. When they arrived, one of the Dashes—the one with the wool jacket—was riding on Rocket's back. From that vantage, the naked mole rat was able to address everyone at roughly hominin and moose-eye level: *We've spoken with the Council several times, and the majority now agrees that you may remain here with us as we begin testing magma streams. So far, we've only done controlled releases in close proximity to Spider. So today we'll leak a little magma three hundred klicks up north, to see if it works.*

"Also, we can introduce you to our greatest allies." Lucky made a gesture with their hands as if they were presenting a glamorous offering.

Dash gestured up a map that gave the La Ronge rangers a view of Sasky they'd never seen. There were the familiar continents, but crisscrossed by thick black lines that divided the globe into dozens of seemingly random polygons, some very large and others quite small. Superimposed over many of these lines were semitransparent blobs of red. One of the largest was right where they stood, at the center of Spider.

"Well, shit," Destry marveled. It was a map of the planet's magma reservoirs, and they were far more extensive than Verdance had ever let on.

Dash wriggled her fingers at the display, and her gesture turned the topological map into a cutaway view of the continent, down to a depth of 3,000 kilometers. There was the planet's molten core, wrapped in several layers of pressurized silicates and water. Spider's magma plume was a thin column of liquid rock that oozed upward from deep inside Sasky's lower mantle, eventually mixing with water in the upper mantle and spreading into what appeared to be a vast, gooey mushroom cloud of lava about 200 kilometers below them.

Dash sent: *For centuries, we've been guiding magma to Spider from that upper reservoir through a series of crevices and boreholes.* The naked mole rat folded her arms and looked extremely pleased with herself. *Want to know how?*

Yes! Whistle stomped a hoof impatiently.

Dash pointed at the floor, which slowly went transparent. About twenty meters below, sanguine ripples of magma roiled in a large, natural chamber. Something caught Destry's eye: a long sheet of silvery chrome, no thicker than a fine knife blade, sticking out of the rocky mush. It looked like a low retaining wall, dividing one side of the magma chamber from the other. She pointed at the gleaming metal. "What's that?"

Lucky flicked a glance back at her. "Nothing. Just some old infrastructure from another project." Their answer was oddly vague, piquing Destry's curiosity.

But then Destry was distracted by something emerging from a lava tunnel into the chamber below. It was a two-meter-long missile-shaped vehicle—or maybe a person—that floated a few centimeters above the bubbling red muck. Sleek and silver, studded with portals and sensors, its whole body danced with reflected light. Four reconfigurable arms were folded so tightly against the vehicle's dorsal side that they were nearly invisible. A lava ship? There was nothing like it in the ERT database, nor in Verdance's templates for terraforming.

And there's the secret to our wells, Dash sent.

Whistle shook his head in amazement, wattle swaying, and leaned into Destry's shoulder. On his other side, Midnight and Long stared through the floor at the ship, their postures stiffly neutral.

"Is that thing a weapon?" Long asked. "Something to blast through the rock?"

Her name is Crusher, and she's part of the Boring Fleet, Dash sent with an impatient switch of her tail. *You're too big to come along and see her work firsthand. We could broadcast back to the room if Hellfire&Crisp want to come, though. They're small enough.*

The drone's two bodies bobbed up and down. "We're in!"

Great. Because someone is going to need to spin the glass.

"We can do a one-day fiber with what we've got in here." One of the drone's bodies hovered next to Dash, their actuator extruding a fiber so thin that it was only visible when briefly catching the light. Destry grabbed it and found a wall panel nearby pocked with connectors. Now the drone was wired to the local network. As long as the glass remained intact, Hellfire&Crisp could send data through it as they explored.

A door slid open in the transparent floor, and one of Hellfire&Crisp's bodies dropped through, trailing glass. The lab filled with the smell of sulfur as Dash harnessed herself to the cargo hook on their other body for a more leisurely drop down to the vehicle. Though Crusher appeared to be a fierce, ultra-armored weapon from the outside, Hellfire&Crisp sent back images of a passenger compartment that was pure comfort. Plush benches sized for naked mole rats surrounded a pile of soft rugs, and diaphanous curtains framed each portal.

No control panel: that confirmed the vehicle was a person. Dash put a hand on the bulkhead: *Take us to the northern borehole, will you dear?*

"Of course, Dash. It's lovely to see you." Crusher's voice sounded like the pealing of bells. She skated rapidly across a wrinkled crust of rock forming atop the lava sea, plunging into a tunnel next to the strange metal sheet Destry had asked about earlier. Crusher played her headlights over the surface of the surging rock, dipping down into the flow to draw energy from its heat. Spun glass passed through a special capillary in the boring vessel's carapace, sinking slightly into the superheated muck before reaching the group back in the lab.

Dash sent: *Here we go.*

The tunnel came to an abrupt end.

"Shall we cut this cake?" Crusher laughed like wind through chimes. "I'm afraid we only have one flavor for you, little ones."

The nose of the vehicle seemed to sprout thick wire whiskers. These unfolded into panels, then stiffened into what looked like absurdly large daisy petals edged with diamond. With a shudder, the daisy spun up, petals scraping the porous volcanic rock, clearing a perfectly round hole and lengthening the tunnel at almost the same speed the ship had flown.

Such a delight to see! Dash rubbed her hands together. *I always think this is the same joy my ancestors must have experienced as they dug their cities underground.*

"And yet the Boring Fleet never had to experience the yoke of hive mind matriarchal autocracy." Crusher sounded like a schoolteacher chiding someone who had just been decanted.

Dash made a harrumph noise. *One may celebrate the ancestors without approving of everything they've done.*

Coring the rock was a surprisingly gentle operation, almost as if the drill were nudging the tunnel farther along rather than pulverizing and melting it into shape.

Dash turned to Hellfire&Crisp. *This is an easy borehole, because volcanic rock is so soft. But she can cut through anything, which is important when you consider how many metal deposits are in here.* As if to validate the naked mole rat's claim, the ship slowed as it hit a vein of quartz, passed through it, and left shards of shimmering rock slowly melting in the magma behind them.

Back in the ERT water lab, Lucky's map display showed the boring ship's progress as a tiny red dot heading northwest away from Spider City. "Their goal is to come up in the coastal forest near Lumsden Beach," they said.

The closer they got to the ocean, the more the lava river began to bubble and pop around them. Water pockets in the rock were turning to steam and exploding. And then, abruptly, the front windows showed blue sky. The vehicle ground to a halt, daisy nose folding back against the ship's body, snug as a closed umbrella. Crusher hovered out of the borehole she'd dug, followed by an oozing, black-crusted puddle of lava. The liquid rock steamed and smoked where it hit plants, flowing more quickly now, following the sloping land down to Lumsden Beach. Reddish sand and rocks hugged a bay of calm green water whose edges frothed and smoothed with the tides. Birds sang in the mangroves, whose roots were insectile legs in the shallows.

More poured out of the hole Crusher had carved, gushing into the water with a bang as the fluid became steam. Lava continued to flow across the sand until there was a jetty of cooling igneous rock stretching out into the ocean. Solid enough to be a dam. But Destry could see Hellfire&Crisp's sensors registering insults to the atmosphere: methane, ash particulates, carbon dioxide. It hurt to see the ERT's work compromised, even in this small way, though she knew it was necessary for their plan to work.

Lucky turned away from the feed. "Right now, you're seeing minimal lava flow. But when we get to Fork Canyon, all the Boring Fleet needs to do is pop some plugs and we can make a gusher."

Whistle shook his head slightly and flicked an ear, showing a hint of mirth: *Nice job on the hole. But what do you mean when you say plugs?*

"They're kind of like blast doors made of stone. The Boring Fleet uses them to stopper eruptions. Or redirect an existing flow."

It sounded like the Spider City ERT was managing its lava flows with valves, tunnels, and dams—the same tools that Verdance workers used to reshape the watershed.

"Is this . . . Boring Fleet spending all its time building out your underground lava system?" Long asked. "How many are there? How do you control them?"

"Control them?" Lucky snorted. "Crusher can hear you, you know."

Laughter jingled into the room over the speakers. "We don't spend all our time counting ourselves and categorizing the number of microbes in our asses like you do. We're far too busy."

Long's mouth worked but he said nothing.

"The boring ships mostly live in deeper magma pockets, so we're honestly not sure what they're doing most of the time," Lucky said. "But they seem to like us. Generally they're willing to help. We've helped them with some engineering concerns."

"We appreciate the medical care Spider provides." Crusher began to hover back toward the borehole; the lava had slowed to a gooey trickle. "All aboard, friends. I'm taking you back home. We can plug this hole with something solid later."

The team plunged back into the lava tunnel.

"Looks good to me," Nil said. "The flow is strong. If we can do something like that at Fork Canyon, I think we have ourselves a new dam. And you've got water in your aquifer again."

"What do you think, *H. sapiens*?" Lucky was looking straight at Destry.

Before she could answer, Long cut in. "I think you've got some pretty impressive technologies, and I'd love to share them with our ERT up in La Ronge."

"How about you help us with this dam and we'll talk about some kind of work-exchange for rangers? The way ERTs do it on other worlds. That way, you can learn about us, and we can learn about you."

"OK, we can talk about that. Maybe come to a formal agreement."

The boring ship spoke, her voice sweet and resonant. "Section five, subparagraph three: Please note that violators of this agreement will taste our fire."

The Spider City people laughed.

Their humor is weird, Destry texted to Nil privately.

No shit, he replied.

19

THE TROUBLE WITH PLATE TECTONICS

Everything is a part of nature.
—*Environmental Rescue Team Handbook*

"Long wants me to open the door to your sleeping room. Do you mind?"

As Destry blinked a dream out of her eyes, she reflected orthogonally that Jaguar the door had gotten a lot more friendly lately. Especially since spending so much time with Hellfire&Crisp.

Next to her, Nil was sitting up and clearly a lot more awake. "Sure, Jaguar. You can open."

Long burst in, still dressed in the coveralls he'd been wearing yesterday when they met Crusher from the Boring Fleet. His eyes were wide with panic. "There's something I've discovered that you need to know about right now. Those lava tunnels—there's something the Archaeans haven't been telling us."

Destry was fully awake now. "What is it?"

"I can't tell you here. Just get dressed and come with me."

Wordlessly, she and Nil yanked on their coveralls and breathers, following Long up the dorm hallway. Things were quieter at this time of night, though they could still hear the sounds of people working the late shift in the ERT labs. The lights were dimmer than during the day, and the on-duty rangers were mostly nocturnal. Two owls flew through, on their way to the experimental forest lava tube; and in one corner of the room a group of raccoons was clumped around a gas chromatograph, locked in silent debate, sending furious texts about some contaminants they found in a sample. Long led them directly to the center of the room, where Crusher from the Boring Fleet had met them. The floor was still transparent.

"Remember that?" Long pointed at the thin metal barrier Destry had noticed slicing through the chamber the day before. It gleamed dully in the orange light, looking almost like a biological membrane. "You asked Lucky what that was, and they brushed it off. Well, I decided to look into it, and—well, just take a look at this."

Long pulled a wadded-up screen from his pocket and smoothed it out on the ground next to Nil and Destry. Squatting down, they watched as he gestured up at the strange map they had seen yesterday on the wall screens—the one with black lines connecting all the lava plumes.

"I looked up the metadata for this map in the Spider ERT database. These black lines correspond to a system of heating elements called ribbons, which are installed deep in Sasky's crust all over the planet." Long shook his head, bleary, and rubbed some stubble that had started on his chin. "And we're looking at part of it. Down there—that—that thing. It can heat up to 1,960 Kelvin. Enough to boil rock."

"So? It's in a chamber of boiling rock." Now that Destry understood she was seeing one strand in a much larger network, she peered at the silvery ribbon with renewed interest.

"What in the fermented turd pit is it for?" Nil asked peevishly.

At that moment, the raccoons burst into chittery laughter, responding to something one of them had texted. It was hard to shake the feeling that the raccoons were mocking them, a group of puzzled *H. sapiens* gawking at a piece of technology they couldn't understand.

Long leaned back on his heels and lowered his voice. "When Verdance started terraforming the land, they had a very different plan for Sasky than they do now. This was their first time creating an Earthlike world, and some of the VPs wanted to make it as realistic as possible. Before they could do that, though, they needed to jump-start the carbon cycle. We all learned that this happened by catalyzing photosynthesis in the oceans, farming cyanobacteria that sucked up carbon and converted it into free oxygen. But that was actually Plan B. About ten thousand years ago, Verdance engineers thought the carbon cycle required plate tectonics."

"Plate tectonics? What's that?" Nil was intrigued.

"It's based on Earth geophysics, where you've got solid plates of continental crust floating around on a hot sea of mantle rock. When Earth's plates collide, one slides underneath the other, cycling down into the lower layers of the planet. It's called subduction. Plate tectonics turn the planet's guts into a big conveyor belt, with old crust sinking down and new crust growing out of volcanic eruptions along ridges in the ocean. Anyway, the hypothesis was that carbon absorbed by Sasky's crust would sink into the planet, and that would create a good cycle.

"The problem is, Sasky is tectonically dead. No floating crust, no subduction. So they came up with this system to crack the planet's surface into continental plates. Way back in the 40,000s, the Archaea planted these temperature ribbons inside fossilized faults and volcanic ridges. Turning them on would make the planet's lithosphere melt, reactivating old fault lines. Eventually pieces of the crust would separate into continental plates and start subducting." Long wiped sweat from his forehead. "Presto. Plate tectonics and carbon cycling all at the same time."

"That ribbon goes right underneath Spider," Destry breathed. "Does that mean we're over a fault?"

"That's right. This is quake country—at least it would be, if somebody turned those ribbons on."

Destry could not stop staring at the razor-thin heating element that could rip a mountain apart. She tried to imagine Sasky's crust broken into puzzle pieces, each landmass floating on a cushion of molten rock. Spider Mountain would drift away from the mantle plume below, but the plume itself would remain active, shooting magma out of whatever puzzle piece moved on top of it.

"Why would Verdance want to do something so dangerous?" Destry asked. "I mean, a piece of good farmland might accidentally become a volcano."

"Exactly. With plate tectonics, your volcanoes can move around. But that's not the most common danger. Subduction causes powerful quakes, and those trigger tsunamis and floods. There are a whole lot of ugly knock-on effects from plate tectonics, and all of them make your real estate less valuable."

Nil emitted a soft whistle. "I can see why Verdance decided to forgo that bit of Earth authenticity, then."

"They dumped that idea as soon as we managed to start the carbon cycle with photosynthesis."

"Well, technically, it wasn't us." Destry sighed. "*H. archaeans* started the carbon cycle with photosynthesis, and we maintained it."

"Are the Spider City people still in control of the ribbons?" Nil whispered. "Do they work?"

Long nodded. "I found data that strongly suggests that they've been testing them every year, to make sure they're in good order. If they activate the network, this planet will have plate tectonics long before the new landowners come down to settle. It will destroy the world."

Destry's heart was pounding as she turned to Nil. "I wonder when they were planning on telling us about that."

"I mean, they weren't exactly hiding it. Long found it just by poking around in the ERT computers, right in front of everybody." Nil gestured at the now-silent racoon researchers.

"That's true. Maybe they didn't think it was relevant."

Long stared at the two of them with an expression that hovered between revulsion and shock. "You're talking about this like they are hiding some new recipe for oatcakes. This is an existential threat to Sasky."

Destry snorted. "It's not an existential threat, but it will make Verdance real estate a lot less valuable. Who wants to deal with volcanoes?"

"These people do." Long's face was getting red and his lips were wet. "They love volcanoes. They want to shit magma everywhere. If they wreck Verdance's planet, they won't suffer. We'll be the ones who pay for it."

"I can't imagine the Archaea doing that," Destry replied. "Plate tectonics could destroy Spider too."

Wadding up the map display, Long stood abruptly. Even with Nil's warmth next to her, Destry felt a chill as their colleague looked down at them. "This mission has gone from foolish to absurd, and now it's potentially deadly."

Nil reached out and gently squeezed Long's hand, still furiously clutching the crumpled map. "Friend, it's not the right time to talk about this. Let's meet in the morning and decide how to broach the subject with our hosts."

Long said nothing as he stamped out of the room, the raccoons staring at him and then at Destry and Nil. One stood up and made a face-washing gesture, which for some reason elicited another extended burst of laughter.

Leaning his head on Destry's shoulder, Nil groaned. "Well, that conversation sure decayed fast."

"We'll work it out in the morning. Long can be an ass, but Midnight usually talks him down."

Nil stood, offering her a hand up. "Let's try to get some rest before we deal with all this swamp gas."

They waved goodbye to the raccoons, who grunted and sent them text links to local videos about how to wash your hands before going to work. Destry had no idea what they were trying to say, so she chalked it up to more weird Spider City humor.

Back in their room, Destry pressed a hand to the wall and signaled the lights to dim, wrapped herself around the curve of Nil's back, and slept fitfully until it was time for breakfast.

DECANTING

Don't build a person if you do not intend to be their ally.
—*Environmental Rescue Team Handbook*

Long didn't join them in the morning at the table. And though Destry and Nil dawdled over the cinnamon toast, joking about the most efficient ways to sprinkle the sweet-spicy toppings all the way to the edges of a bread slice, he still didn't show. There was no cryptic drama between Whistle and Midnight either, because the moose were absent too. Only Rocket joined them, hovering down to settle on a charging pad. Hellfire&Crisp spent nearly all their time choring with Jaguar these days and would meet them at the ERT labs only by request.

The bot's head rose from the thick tube of their body, and they emitted a whimsical tune. "Where is everybody?"

"I'm not sure, but we said we'd meet Long to discuss what he found last night—did he tell you about it?"

"Just a second." Rocket hovered to the high ceiling, where they could connect to Spider's network via short-range wireless. "Long's not in the city. Neither are Whistle and Midnight. What were you supposed to talk about?"

The two rangers looked at each other, unsettled, as Rocket sank down to their eye level. Haltingly, Nil told his partner about the heat ribbons and plate tectonics while Destry pressed her hands to the table and searched the network for data on her teammates. After a minute of fruitlessly messaging and checking access logs, she realized that this absence of data was yet another way that Spider differed from La Ronge. Spider City would reveal who was or wasn't reachable on the local network, but that was it. No records of where anyone had been or when they had gone. It was a way of discouraging the kind of toxic surveillance that Verdance imposed. And yes, it was freeing in some ways, but it was also incredibly annoying when you needed to reach your friends urgently.

Just as she was about to disconnect from the table, Whistle appeared on the network and her message showed as read.

I had food, the moose replied. *I will see you at the ERT lab.*

Midnight and Long were still not on the Spider network.

When they got to the lab, Whistle was more dejected than Destry had ever seen him. His ears were sagging and his head was low. As she wrapped her arms around his neck, she realized that he was wet too.

He sent to the group: *I took a swim with Midnight, when the sun rose.*

"Where is Long?" Nil demanded.

Whistle shook his head and water droplets spattered the floor, which quickly absorbed the moisture. *I do not know*, the moose sent.

"Did Midnight go with him?"

Yes. She said—Whistle stopped sending for a moment and stared at the floor. *She said she had no choice.*

"Shit in a pit." Nil rubbed his forehead. "I bet they went back to La Ronge because of the Ribbons. I mean, I knew Long was upset, but we agreed not to return until the dam was finished. We voted."

After years of ERT Council meetings, Destry could imagine at least three loopholes that Long could cite as a rationale for breaking their agreement. "I'm sure he thinks that our vote was based on incomplete knowledge of context. So it's void."

"Yeah, but he's supposed to call a new vote—"

Rocket interrupted his partner with a hammering noise. "He can call the vote at the La Ronge council. Which is what he wanted to do anyway."

"We should tell Lucky right now." Destry looked around the lab, which was still mostly empty. Breakfast wasn't over, and besides it was a meeting day. The only person she knew in the room right now was Dash, wearing a new purple coat.

"Have you seen Lucky?" she asked the naked mole rat.

Without turning away from her workstation, Dash sent: *They'll be in the meeting for a while, but if you want to catch them after, they'll be passing by the bioengineering lab. I'm headed there now, to check on a few people who are due for decanting this week. Would you like to join me while you wait?*

Nil looked at Destry and sent privately: *Let's speak to the Archaeans before we decide whether to go after Long and Midnight.*

Aloud, Destry said, "All right, let's see who is about to be decanted."

Rocket dipped down to give Dash a ride on their back. They walked down the hallway with its lava-lit windows, which looked almost homey to Destry now, and presently Dash asked Jaguar to let them into a warm, dim room. As the *H. sapiens* and Whistle stood blindly in the doorway, a faint glow rippled across the bacteria on the walls, barely illuminating a cluster of three-meter-tall, transparent tanks that took up most of the space at the center of the room. Next to them was a maze of smaller tanks topped by 3-D printers, for building life forms directly into amniotic fluid. There was no obvious way to walk between the tanks, and the setup was clearly designed for people of Dash's size. Another of the Dashes—this one wearing nothing—was sitting on a desk next to a printer, using a handheld nozzle to spray a layer of cells on a small tissue trellis that looked like it might be for growing an internal organ like a kidney or heart.

I used to do all my research right here. I made the first dogs on that machine. Dash gestured vaguely at a dim corner. *But now I'm doing fieldwork on life in the magma system, so I'm afraid I don't get back here as much as I'd like.*

The other Dash sent: *We don't mind. Less clutter with you gone.*

Dash made a noise that sounded like the naked mole rat equivalent of a scoff, and Rocket floated her close to the tanks. Hesitantly, Destry followed, one hand on Whistle's damp neck. She didn't want to run into anything accidentally.

We grew this person pretty recently. Dash gestured at the nearest tank, where an *H. archaean* floated, eyes closed. They were fully adult, almost ready for decanting, with the characteristic broad forehead, barrel chest, long arms—and an unusual genital configuration that Destry had never seen before. It was like labia, but bigger and slightly puckered, with inner and outer lips the same size. The effect was of a decorative ruffle where the person's legs came together. Destry was reminded of certain ocean invertebrates, whose bodies rippled into frilly shapes as they swam.

"I like this incubator," Nil said admiringly, touching the transparent material surrounding the developing Archaean. "Looks versatile."

We can build anything here, from people like me to people like him. Dash pointed at Whistle.

Something else had caught Whistle's attention. He walked past the soon-to-be-decanted Archaean to see one of the smaller tanks, where a 3-D printer drizzled tissue onto a trellis, the nozzle moving back and forth methodically. *What's this?*

The other Dash looked up from her work: *Cat. Got any requests for fur color? Family didn't specify.*

Whistle tossed his head: *You would pick the fur I want?* He was startled. Back at La Ronge, they used templates and presets from Verdance. It was extremely rare for someone to modify the basic animal designs.

I can always use the random number generator or roll some dice, but I think it's nicer when a person chooses.

Moose shifted his weight, his antlers casting strange triple shadows from the lab lights. *Are you sure? What if they don't like it?*

The other Dash scratched behind an ear hole: *I wouldn't worry. Fur is fur. This cat can change it later if they want.*

I choose brown. Whistle made a decisive grunt as he sent the words. *Make the cat brown.*

Dash let out a sigh of comic exasperation: *Friend, what is brown? I don't know what shade or intensity—*

The brown in my coat. Make this cat moose brown.

Aha—now you're cooking! Dash conjured a small control panel with one swift motion of her right hand. *Your shade of brown is a great color for a cat. Lots of golds and blacks in there too. Never done that combination before.*

Whistle asked: *When they come out, do you teach them?*

Everyone is decanted into a family group, so they'll teach this cat the same way people in La Ronge do, I expect. There are always a few months of learning.

"It's not really the same," Rocket said, their voice carrying from behind Nil. "Some people have families, but Mounts and animals learn on the job. They get decanted and put to work right away. They don't have families."

Whistle looked at Destry: *you were there when I came out.*

"I was." Destry rested her hand on Whistle's rib cage, expanding with his breath. "The ERT assigned you to be my mount and we didn't have a choice. But I'm still glad it happened. I tried to teach you the way my parents taught me."

Whistle lowered his head and said nothing while Dash looked at Destry like she'd violated a taboo. *Of course. La Ronge still builds to the intelligence assessment templates.* The naked mole rat made a gagging noise.

Destry interrupted. "It's true. But that doesn't mean we buy into the InAss system. Whistle is my family." She nudged the moose. "I mean, you are if you want to be."

He pressed his muzzle into her chest but didn't offer any words. Perhaps he was trying to figure out what to say.

Before his silence became awkward, there was a shadow at the door and Lucky's voice carried into the room. "Hey, *H. sapiens.* I heard you were looking for me. I have a meeting space across the hall."

As they filed out, the Dash who was building the cat sent a final text: *Thanks for the fur idea, Whistle! See you later!*

See you! Whistle replied. *Take good care of that cat.*

Lucky took them to a room with one window that looked down into the lava cavern, and another that looked upward into the caldera's sun-streaked water. The hominins settled into chairs and everybody else stood or hovered around the table.

There was no way to break the news gently. "Long found out about your heating ribbons last night. He was . . ." Destry searched for words. "He was terrified. We think he and Midnight are flying back to La Ronge." She rested her chin in her hand, suddenly feeling the exhaustion from her interrupted night.

Lucky jumped up and started to pace nervously. "The Ribbons? What do they have to do with anything?"

Though she was hardly on Long's side, Destry felt a flicker of irritation. "That's a pretty big secret you kept from us."

Lucky looked at Whistle and Rocket, as if they didn't really want to see what lurked in the *H. sapiens'* faces. "What is he going to do?"

Whistle shook his head slightly, making his dewlap sway: *Long was mad. Now he has fear on top of that. He might tell Verdance.*

"He's worried you'll turn on the Ribbons and destroy Sasky." Nil looked even more miserable than he sounded. "To be fair, I don't think he misunderstood you. I mean—you did lie to Destry about the Ribbons when she asked. And they could actually be used as superweapons."

"We trusted you, and we promised to help you get your water back."

Destry glared at them and folded her arms. "We contributed our labor to Spider City. And now we look like fools."

Lucky put their head in their hands. "I'm sorry I misled you," they said slowly. "We should have been more honest about our capabilities. But the Ribbons are the only leverage we have against Verdance."

Nil narrowed his eyes. "What do you mean by that? Leverage?"

Lucky finally looked at the *H. sapiens*. "When we finally reveal ourselves to Verdance, we are planning to offer them a peace and friendship treaty."

"A treaty? What do you mean by that?"

"We'll draw up an agreement with them, allowing Spider City access to the water we need." Lucky pronounced every word precisely, as if they were dictating a policy document. "In exchange, we offer peace and friendship."

A sarcastic *yuck-yuck-yuck* laugh erupted from Rocket's speakers. "I see. It surely is peaceful to have a planet without quakes. Is that the idea?"

"We are willing to negotiate," Lucky said. "But when you're dealing with Verdance and their parent company, it's best to have a weapon."

Recalling her experiences with Ronnie, Destry found herself nodding. "I can see that. But won't Verdance just take control of the Ribbons remotely?"

Lucky shook their head. "When Verdance told the ERT to shut the network down, our engineers took it dark instead of recycling it. You can only access the controls from a physical connection we built right here in Spider City."

Something caught Destry's eye in the lava chamber below—a member of the Boring Fleet, flashing from one tunnel to another, uncounted and unmolested by the city above. Then she thought about the moose-colored cat, soon to be decanted, who would have a family here along with the Archaea. She was still feeling bruised from Lucky's subterfuge, but she genuinely liked the Spider City people. They deserved to live just as much as La Ronge people did. And so did Sasky. The only way to keep everything in balance was to help.

"Whistle was right when he said that Long might tell Verdance about you, so we need a plan."

Nil glanced at her. "We should be at the Council meeting when Long tells everyone about Spider. We might be able to persuade the ERT to keep this city hidden for a while longer."

Destry nodded. "It's possible."

"I'll ask the Council." Lucky pressed hands to the table, and several minutes passed before they spoke again. "We've been debating this for weeks, so the majority got back to me quickly. They voted to send you home to make our case. You may tell the La Ronge Council everything. We ask that they give us more time to finish the dam before we reveal ourselves to Verdance."

"You could send a representative to make your case," Nil suggested.

"Too dangerous." Lucky's mouth quirked into a half-smile as they looked at Whistle. "Speak well on our behalf, friends."

The moose shifted on his feet. *Mounts can't go to Council.*

His comment brought an air of gloom into the space; it was a reminder that the great distance between La Ronge and Spider City was more than geographical.

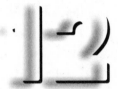

THE WORST COUNCIL MEETING

Always be prepared for a disaster, so that you can prevent it.
—*The Environmental Rescue Team Handbook*

Never in her centuries of work at the ERT had Destry ever witnessed a conversation more vitriolic and disturbing than the one that was currently disrupting what could have been a pleasant meeting. At first, things seemed to be going well. Before they took off from Spider, she'd messaged the ERT Council, asking that she and the rest of the team be allowed to present their case when Long presented his. She routed the message through tropical flowers shaped like birds, and insects shaped like more deadly insects, and a spindly receiver tower shaped to look like a tree. Thankfully her request made it to La Ronge before Midnight landed. Which is why she and Nil were here now, facing Long at an outdoor table, next to a hedge that the youngest rangers had cut to resemble a mastodon.

The ERT Council was comprised of a rotating group of a dozen people, sworn to meet when problems arose. All of them had dropped everything to hear the team's story. Some were understandably surprised, and even shocked, by the existence of Spider City. A few were intrigued. Others were disgusted. The very idea of the Archaea offended them. This went way beyond hydro-engineering annoyances and into something rarely discussed in the ERT: politics.

Pine, a top engineer from the water group, looked like she was about to spit or vomit or maybe both. Gray hair whipped around her incandescent face as she shook her head. "We are not re-routing Eel River for some group of squatters! It goes against our entire environmental plan. The first settlers were supposed to make way for us, so we could produce a pristine set of ecosystems. They're wrecking all our work. They have no right!"

"Verdance never planned to develop that volcano," Destry said. "Plus Spider City is carbon negative. How are they wrecking our work?"

"Seriously? You're seriously asking me that?" Pine was furious. "You don't work on the watershed, so you have no idea how this will impact the environment."

Nil massaged his temples and explained their case for the second time. "We have nothing to lose here—and neither does Verdance. All they're asking for is a small percentage of water that won't be missed. We can route other rivers to the coasts, and give Spider City the Eel."

Long shook his head and held up his hand. "That's what you say. But I was there too. I don't think we can trust these Archaea—not until they share how their weapons work. It's obvious they want to use the Ribbons to force eruptions and carbon load the atmosphere. That way they can breathe on the surface again."

This was the bitterest weed of all. Destry looked down at the gnarled wood of the table, willing herself not to get angry. She'd trusted Long. They were practically family, now that her partner Whistle was hooking up with Long's partner, Midnight. And he'd betrayed them in this meeting—coming out of nowhere with this piss-soaked conspiracy theory about how the Archaea were hatching an evil plot to take over the world with the Ribbons.

"Long, you know they don't want to use those plate tectonics ribbons any more than we do—or Verdance does. They just need a way to . . . to show that they are serious about their request." Destry paused. "Listen, Verdance treats us like we're disposable. Why should we be loyal to them? They didn't even send disaster relief when my parents . . ."

Pine slammed her palms against the table and stood up. "Don't bring that up! Frenchie—your mother—she knew what she was doing. I loved her, but she and your father were violating every term of our contract when they left." Tears were starting in the water engineer's eyes. Pine had worked closely with Frenchie, and still felt her loss keenly. When she spoke again, her voice was hoarse. "It's exactly like those assholes in Spider City! And you can't do anything to help them, just like we couldn't help your parents!" And with that, Pine spun and walked away so fast that a foam stool fell over in her wake. One of Pine's labmates ran after her, throwing a nasty look over her shoulder at Destry.

Once they had coaxed Pine back to the table, Long folded his arms and swept the ERT rangers with his gaze. "Pine is right. As soon as Verdance finds out what the Archaea have planned, they'll go the same way as Destry Senior and Frenchie. And so will we."

A chill wriggled its way into Destry's heart like a hornworm in cassava leaves. "What do you mean by that?"

His frown softened slightly. "Destry, take the blindfold off your eyes. Verdance murdered your parents. Look at the records. It was a laser strike from one of their satellites."

Every muscle in Destry's body was rigid. "That's not true. I read the report—it was a gas leak. An accident."

Nearly everyone at the meeting was staring at her now—except for Pine, who was giving Long a furious look. Glowering back at Pine, Long continued. "I don't see why she shouldn't know. Ronnie didn't want anyone to get the idea that they could leave the city, so she killed them. It's legal—Verdance built them and owned them, and they were breaking their contract by leaving. That's what you don't understand, Destry. Verdance won't send us angry messages when they find out about Spider City. They will kill us for hiding it."

"I don't believe you."

Pine covered her face with her hands, shoulders shaking with silent sobs. *It's true, Destry*, she sent privately. *We didn't want you to know, so I saved the original video file to a different repository, and wrote the disaster report you saw. It wasn't entirely untrue—the explosion was from gas. But Verdance's laser ignited it.*

She sent a link to a video file. It was only five seconds long, but that was enough to witness the beam cut through her parents' home like a heated knife through coconut custard. Destry realized she was clutching Nil's hand under the table.

She thought back to when Destry Senior and Frenchie died centuries ago, and how she'd been busy watching Spider vomit bloodred rocks when it happened. She'd been furious at herself for going on such a long mission when she knew her parents were doing something risky. Why had she picked an assignment so far away? Why didn't she check the safety settings on those waste processors herself? But this time when she replayed her memories, there was no one to blame but Ronnie, dictating a memo that unleashed a murderous beam of light.

And Long had decided to dump this on her now, to inject her with new trauma, just so he could win his pustulant argument. He obviously thought his revelation would convince the Council to let Spider's people be murdered, because that way La Ronge would be spared. Everyone at the table was still looking at her, waiting to see what she would do. One thing was for sure. She wasn't going to buckle.

She let go of Nil's hand and glowered at Long. "Knowing Verdance might murder the people of Spider City means that it's our duty to help them. The ERT is supposed to protect people who are vulnerable to disasters. If you want to honor my parents, that's what we should do."

Long sighed. "We all mourn Destry Senior and Frenchie, but you have to let it go. This isn't our fight. Plus they're threatening every single ecosystem on this planet with plate tectonics."

This was really starting to piss Destry off. "They have kept the balance so well that we didn't even realize they were under Spider Mountain for the past thousand years. And Verdance rerouting that river to the coast is parching the local ecosystems, so we need to fix it." As she talked, Destry noticed a few of her colleague's eyes lighting up, and some nods. "If this isn't our fight, whose is it?"

"I agree with Destry," said Kim. She was one of the youngest members of the water team, and she'd painted her coveralls with streaks of glitter that winked blue in the sunlight. "Verdance has already squeezed a bunch of pus all over the southern watershed just to create farmland for their clients. What's stopping them from doing it elsewhere?"

Nil nodded excitedly. "That's why we need to help Spider. This isn't just about ecosystems anymore—it's about real estate. Maybe this peace and friendship treaty could be a model for how to keep the balance in the future."

Kim drummed her fingers lightly on the table, a sign of assent, and a few other people joined in. Long folded his hands together tightly.

"Those Spider people will destroy the planet." Long was raising his voice. "If you believe they won't, then you are a polluting fool."

Nil held up a placating hand. "I call the vote on whether to help Spider with their dam, without telling Verdance first."

Six voted with Long, and nine voted with Destry. It was an unusually narrow majority. As was customary in the ERT, the minority would be allowed one concession.

"What would you like us to concede?" Destry asked.

The minority voters, including Pine, sent back and forth privately.

"We don't want the La Ronge ERT associated with this mission in any way," Long announced. "Once you leave here, you are on your own. If anything goes wrong, we don't want Verdance to trace this back to us, or the Council."

"It is conceded," Destry replied formally.

Long practically flipped the table as he left, and several other members of the Council went with him.

Kim grinned excitedly, as if they'd all had a nice dinner instead of staging the opening act in a war. Her pale brown skin was dusted with freckles, and her black hair was plaited into a club at the back of her neck. She couldn't have been more than fifty years old. "So, what next?" she asked, rubbing her hands together. "When do we get started?"

Destry looked at Nil and the others around the table, their expressions hovering between smiles and worry. They couldn't rely on the Council to help them, and despite the vote, she wasn't sure she could trust Long, Pine, and the rest to keep Spider City a secret. Destry steeled herself to appear as serene and confident as she could.

"We can't stay here if we're going to help Spider City," she said quietly. "We ride out at dawn."

Nil looked resigned. "And we're going to have to work fast too. Ideally, we'd like to have the course of the Eel fixed before we try to negotiate the treaty. Spider City needs a stable water supply—especially if Verdance sees the treaty offer the way Long does."

Kim pounded the table. "I can ride out with you, if Zest will allow it."

Destry felt a sudden warmth toward this young ranger, on fire with the urge to help but still considering her partner's opinions on the matter.

Curly, one of Destry's friends from network analysis, drew on the table with one finger and looked pensive. "Let's be smart about this. We need a cover story, and it has to be something that Verdance will believe. That might buy you enough time to help Spider City before anybody talks to Ronnie."

Thinking of the VP made Destry feel sour, and her next words came out more sarcastically than she intended. "We can say that we're examining Spider Mountain one more time, since the lava flow might affect Ronnie's special show plots."

Everyone was looking at Destry. "Show plots?" Curly frowned.

"Just tell her there's been an anomalous eruption on the coast. That should appease her, given how much she wants to protect the coastal properties."

Nil cut in. "And in the meantime, let's keep this conversation as quiet as possible."

Nobody said anything as they got up from the table, but their goodbye hugs felt like true embraces, the kind you reserve for someone you may never see again.

As she headed to Whistle's barn, Destry wondered if this was how her parents felt when they left the city to set up a homestead beyond Verdance's reach. She inhaled the smell of prairie dirt and summer grass, remembering her first few days of life here in La Ronge. After decanting, she learned to stand up and walk outside the lab with Destry Senior and Frenchie. Her mother's face was angular, her mouth always set in a knowing smirk; and her father was tall and thin, a white hat settled far back on his head. They had signed up for the parenting program after centuries of seeding Maskwa with plants and animals in at least a dozen ecosystems. Destry wasn't their genetic descendent, of course—nobody had those—but she would be their responsibility during her learning months, and that was more important.

Her parents sat with her on the warm ground outside the residence hall, feeding her different kinds of foods so that she could get the hang of digestion. She had language and other strange information unscrolling in her mind, but no context for it; Destry Senior and Frenchie would be providing that. Once she was capable of moving her body in the most important ways, they put her on the back of Frenchie's drone partner, Tilly, and flew north, landing very near the arctic circle. Back then, northern Maskwa was still rocky and bare. The boreal forest wouldn't come in for centuries.

Frenchie squinted at the sun, wiped a hand across her pale forehead, and spoke the first words Destry remembered hearing. "One day we'll have a picnic together in the middle of a gigantic forest that stretches all the way from one end of Maskwa to the other." Of course Destry believed it then—like all newborns, she had no skepticism. Instead of questioning her mother, she stared at the knobbly foundations of the forest, where Verdance workers had carved riverbeds and lakes. Nearly invisible strands of network fiber caught the light and made it look like bits of mica were scattered everywhere. Destry pressed her hands into the sandy loam, connecting to the sensors scattered across the land for thousands of kilometers, feeling moisture nearby and ice at the distant pole. There were a few trees, reporting healthy levels of metal in the ground, and animals whose migratory patterns lit up Destry's retinas. The planet shimmered with data, with life. She could feel the strong webs of the ecosystems to the south, and the fragile beginnings of the forest-in-progress under her crossed legs.

Destry Senior gently pried her hands from the network. His voice was quiet and kind. "That's for another day, Destry. Let's focus on what's in front of us." He handed her a small cup of cow milk. "We don't drink this much, but it's a good source of protein when a person lets you have it."

It was true. She never forgot how good that milk tasted. A few weeks later, Destry awkwardly asked one of the cows in La Ronge for milk and was surprised to discover the person couldn't respond with words—she was what people called an "animal." The cow flicked an ear and lowered her head in what could have been assent or confusion. Destry couldn't bring herself to take milk from someone who had no words, so she ran back to tending trees with Frenchie and Destry Senior. She'd be moving into the ERT dorms soon, and the three of them spent their final days living together as a family twisting tiny paper sensors around branches and scattering them like confetti on the ground.

Over time, these slips of paper would grow into the fabric of the food web, tracking who was eating whom. But that day, when she met the cow animal, the sensors were art. She folded them into delicate bird and butterfly shapes, admiring their translucent wings in the sunlight. Destry Senior blew one off his fingers, and Frenchie leaned against him, their eyes following the drifting scrap as it booted and sent fleeting bits of information about the carbon content of the local atmosphere. Maybe that was when they first started to dream about leaving La Ronge, settling wherever the wind took them.

A sudden text jarred Destry out of her memory: *You going to see Whistle too? That can't be good.* It was Midnight, trotting up next to her on the road to the barn.

After Long's reaction to her plans, Destry wasn't sure what to say to his partner. She opted for something vague. "We're planning a survey trip."

The moose snorted: *Is that what you're calling it? I thought maybe you were going back down to Spider City to help the squatters with their plan.*

There was no point in lying. "You can come with us if you want," Destry said. "I'm sure Whistle would like that." It was the first time she had openly acknowledged the relationship between the two moose.

Midnight twitched a fly off her skin and ignored Destry's invitation. Maybe she agreed with Long, or maybe she was still touchy about people knowing she was seeing someone with a low InAss rating. Either way, she stayed silent for the minute it took to reach the barn door. But she kept pace with Destry the entire time, almost as if they were friends.

REVISIONIST HISTORY

Your only job is to keep everything in balance.
—*The Environmental Rescue Team Handbook*

Destry had arrived at the Mount lodgings alongside Whistle's booty call, and it felt extremely awkward. Dinner would arrive soon, and a few moose were already dipping into the snack troughs of green branches on the grab table. The dining hall smelled of grain and dust, and at its southern end were wide doors to the communal dorms where Midnight had presumably hoped to waylay her lover. Unfortunately, the human had interfered, in that annoying way hominins had of being everywhere you didn't want them. The two moose barely grazed muzzles before Whistle lowered his head and shuffled hooves in embarrassment.

When in doubt, Destry always defaulted to cheeriness. "Hey, Whistle! Just stopping by to check on plans for tomorrow."

Whistle sent Destry a public greeting, and something private to Midnight.

"Do you mind if I have a quick chat with Whistle before you two . . ." Destry made a vague gesture with her hands. The two moose looked at her expressionlessly, and she was suddenly self-conscious about her bipedal body language—on top of already feeling weird about knowing that Whistle had a crush on a person who was probably just using him for sex.

Of course. I'll be back after dinner. Midnight texted as she cantered out, leaving a faint scent of coriander in the air. Midnight lived near Destry, in an ERT residence for people who weren't *H. sapiens.*

When she was completely out of earshot, Destry sighed. "Whistle, does she know how you feel about her?"

I don't care. Soon you and I will be on the way to Spider City, right?

"I guess I'm just a little bit furious on your behalf. Not only is Midnight partners with that pus-bubble Long, I feel like she's using you, or—"

The moose shoved her in the chest with his nose, harder than he would normally. Destry stumbled backward. He texted: *JUST STOP.* Whistle had never used all caps with her, and it was a shock. *I know what you think. But soon, I'll be gone. This is her home, but it's not mine. Not now. I plan to stay in Spider City.* He gave her a sidelong glance. *That is, if you will let me.*

Destry had guessed something like this might happen, but that didn't make it any easier. She'd decanted Whistle herself, almost a century ago. She'd fed him a pinecone and helped him the same way her parents had helped her. "You know I don't buy into that shit about you being a Mount," she said. "We're partners. You're free to go any time. But I . . ." She reached out a hand to touch his warm fur, and tried to hide her sadness.

I'll miss you too, friend.

"You know I might not come home either. Not because I plan to stay down there, but because—well, you know."

The moose tossed his head, brandishing antlers: *We might die.*

Destry ran a hand over her face and felt tiny particles of grit and tracking spores that had collected on her skin during the disastrous afternoon meeting. "That's right. It's very dangerous. We're depending on Long to keep his word, and on Ronnie to buy my story. We might not even make it down to the city before Verdance shoots us out of the sky. You understand?"

I do.

She threw her arms around his neck and buried her face in the shaggy spot below the hump of his shoulders. Quietly, she muttered the ERT credo. "We're going to keep everything in balance."

Whistle replied: *I hope so.*

They set a time to meet in the morning, and Destry headed back to her room to pack a few things and send an update to Verdance that would hopefully maintain their cover story. Assuming Long, Pine, and the others didn't immediately stab her in the back.

Before she rounded the bend to the residence hall, Midnight passed her on the road.

Farewell, friend, the moose sent. *Take care of him.*

Fighting down all the things she wanted to say to Midnight about

Whistle, Destry nodded and spoke curtly. "No harm in you taking care of him too."

Midnight paused, as if chewing on Destry's words. Then she looked back over her shoulder at the ranger: *Thanks for the advice,* H. sapiens. With a sarcastic snort, she galloped away.

Frowning to herself, Destry headed to dinner and found Nil in his usual spot. The room was crowded—the crew on cook duty tonight had set out bowls of their famous peppery tofu with fermented beans—and Kim was already sitting with Nil. They waved Destry over. She barely had time to scoop a bite out of her steaming bowl before Kim started asking questions.

"Why do you think Long was acting like that? He's usually pretty open-minded. And Midnight is really smart—you'd think she'd have talked him down."

"I doubt Midnight would have added anything helpful to that conversation." Destry couldn't keep the bitterness out of her voice.

"I think Long is afraid of the same thing we are." Nil laid a gentle hand on Destry's arm. "He doesn't want anyone to get hurt, and he's worried that if we help the Archaea, we'll all be killed. Or worse."

Kim cut in. "Verdance won't kill anything that they can use, and we are extremely useful." She sat back, crossed her arms, and suddenly seemed a thousand years older than she was. "Listen. I did my first tour of duty in bioengineering, making life forms for the boreal ecosystems you were troubleshooting, Destry. I know how valuable these ecosystems are. Verdance does not want *anyone* to die. Bad for business."

Destry narrowed her eyes, thinking of what Kim's observation implied about her parents. Once they were no longer productive workers, they were useless. Killable. But she didn't say anything. Instead, she savored the sting of chili oil on her tongue until she could talk about something that hurt less.

Nil mused aloud. "The Archaea were supposed to die."

"Not true." Kim gulped a bite. "They wanted the *H. archaeans* to segue perfectly into the *H. sapiens.* Just like what we learned in school—it was a planned atmosphere transition. When the oxygen levels got to twenty percent, Archaeans started decanting *H. sapiens.* They were supposed to raise us, then die of natural causes the way anybody does."

"Yeah. My parents were decanted by Archaeans." Nil scratched his head, loosening the tie that held his hair back. "My grandparents had to wear breathers all the time."

"Did you ever meet them? Your grandparents?" Kim was intrigued.

"No. They died long before I was decanted."

"Maybe they went down to Spider City," Destry said.

"I don't think so."

"How would you know? The Archaea obviously covered their tracks pretty well."

"I suppose it's possible. The people who built Spider City must have come from La Ronge, so who knows?"

Destry imagined a covert band of Archaea fleeing south a millennium ago and felt the muscles soften between her shoulder blades. At least there were some people who had escaped La Ronge and lived to tell the tale.

Kim nodded, as if she could see what was in Destry's mind. "I can't believe they've been out there all this time. I wonder—maybe that's what got Long so upset. He's a historian, and Spider City completely challenges all his ideas about what's been happening for the past thousand years."

Nil rubbed his chin, the way he did when he was thinking about a particularly complicated problem. "It's like he made a huge error in calculating our past, and now everything is out of balance."

"And he wants Spider City to go away so he can be correct about history again." Kim sighed and shook her head. "I wish he wasn't being such a giant barrel of untreated sewage about it."

Destry smiled. For a second, it was like they were talking about minor work annoyances, instead of life and death. Long was merely a misguided colleague with bad data. He wasn't going to get them killed with one pointed message to Verdance. And his partner, Midnight, wasn't going to break Whistle's heart. Instead of thinking about La Ronge, she bent her thoughts to a city full of people whose houses couldn't be burned because they were already floating in fire.

DOGS

Rivers might turn out to be people. Don't make any assumptions.
—*Environmental Rescue Team Handbook*

The six of them took off at dawn, retracing the flight path they'd taken only a few days ago. Rocket and Whistle were silent most of the day, but Kim's partner, Zest, liked to chatter about odd bits of geomorphology. Zest was a hybrid of cow and bot, with a specialized body plan that Kim had designed from scratch in the bioengineering lab. Though hybrids usually hid their metal parts under a layer of skin and fat, Zest proudly displayed the polished chrome that emerged from beneath the fur of her neck. Her barrel chest looked exactly like Rocket's body, perfectly cylindrical, but it tapered to a point where her spine met tail. Her flanks and udders were biological—at least from the outside—as were all her legs. Overall it gave her the appearance of a mountable drone that had sprouted a cow's head and limbs.

Unlike most nonhuman biologicals, the cow spoke aloud instead of texting; she had embedded speakers around her mouth, just like a bot. When they flew slowly enough to hear over the wind, Zest always chose to vocalize. "Look at that stubborn river!" she exclaimed. They all looked down. Below them, a valley had turned this section of the Eel into a lake that bulged between peaks, the water along its shoreline spreading into the rocky fissures like tentacles. To the west was a dusty canyon covered in scrub—the perfect place for a river to flow downward. But the Eel willfully continued on an elevated path through the mountains, nosing around granite outcroppings.

Kim grinned at the river's odd choice. "A strange way to take the path of least resistance. The Eel goes its own way, doesn't it?"

Nil grunted, and Destry focused on Whistle's antlers, which she might never see again after this trip.

Zest continued to point out perversely formed rivers and snarled alluvial plains. They rode hard, striking camp before dawn and landing after dark. The stars changed as they approached the equator: now the Hand constellation was low in the sky, and the Rocket rose as the sun sank. The four stars representing the Rocket's exhaust pointed at Earth's star Sol in the sky, at least under magnification. It was invisible to the naked eye, but always there as a reminder that people came to this world from the stars.

Sleep was furtive, and the few seconds of laser strike footage that Destry had watched were never far from her mind. What would she do when she saw Ronnie again? How would she look into her boss's face, knowing she wasn't just a nasty micromanager but an actual murderer? The more she thought about it, the more she became convinced that Long or one of the other Council members would tell Verdance about Spider soon. Maybe they had done it already. She wished there was some way to warn Lucky and the others, but there was no way to contact them via the sensor network—it was monitored by Verdance.

They were still three days out from Spider when Whistle caught sight of the dogs. A small pack of them flickered through the trees, pausing occasionally to paw at the ground and move on.

Look, Destry, Whistle sent. *The dogs are at work.*

They followed the pack for a few lazy minutes before Destry recalled that the dogs who visited Spider dealt with sensor networks. She sent publicly to the team: *Let's land and speak to those dogs. Maybe they can get a message to Spider.*

It was easy enough to land in the dogs' path, but as soon as they were on the ground it was impossible to see them—they were brilliant at camouflage, trotting silently between shadows. Destry turned to a rustle in the leaves. "Hey, friends! We're trying to get a message to Spider City, but we can't connect to them on the sensor network. Can you help us? It's urgent. The city is in danger."

She heard a grunt and wheeze, but got no reply. Kim slid off Zest's back, leaving one hand on her partner's metal torso. The cow flicked an ear forward and spoke aloud. "We're rangers from the ERT in La Ronge, and we are friends of Spider."

A single dog emerged from seemingly out of nowhere, skin a mottled white and brown, and sat down on their haunches facing Zest. Still mounted on Whistle, Destry could feel her partner's muscles bunch involuntarily with fear. Still, he didn't show any other outward signs of discomfort.

Head tilted to the side, the dog sent: *What can these* H. sapiens *possibly have to do with Spider?*

It took several minutes to persuade the dog, who introduced herself as Argument, that they had a legitimate reason to message Lucky. Argument wouldn't talk to anyone but Zest at first, then grudgingly came around to addressing Destry too. Especially when Destry explained that she could connect to sensors using just her hands. As they texted, she heard other dogs yapping softly and moving through the underbrush. They were surrounded.

Abruptly, Argument dug a hole with her front paws, rapidly making a small pile of loose dirt. *All right, we'll let you connect here,* she sent. *Your message will make it to Spider in a few seconds.* The dog sent Destry a one-time access key.

Destry dismounted and got on her knees next to Argument. The dog's breath was warm on her cheek as she pressed fingers into the shallow hole and linked to the environment. She could feel the weight of the dogs now, all seven of them, in among the thick leaves shaped like paddles. She smelled pheromones boiling off two ant colonies at war nearby. *Soil pH nominal; aquifer at lowest level in 6,079 years; statistically high number of dead Linepithema humile.* Even when she used the key, it took a few more seconds to locate the hidden Spider network, its sensors strung together like beads on the glass fiber. As she connected, it offered her a hazy glimpse of the watershed and pulses of lava far below. One sensor whispered to her: *valve 13 is open; lava flow has increased.*

Squeezing her message into the data stream, she sent to Lucky: *This is Ranger Destry Thomas. We have agreement from our Council, but for reasons I will explain in person, I fear that they may notify Verdance very soon. Please be ready. We arrive in three or four days, depending on weather.*

Destry disconnected from the dirt and Argument filled the hole, melting back into the forest without another word. As Whistle mounted the air, he sent: *They seem nice.*

"Shy, but nice," Zest agreed.

Destry said nothing. She and Whistle were on different journeys now: He was unlearning a lifetime of fearing dogs; and she had just learned that her lifelong irritant, Ronnie, was actually a mortal threat.

Each day was a little longer as they approached the equator, and the star Sask-A became a swollen blister in the sky. Though Destry still didn't feel like talking, it was a relief to have Zest's commentary as a distraction. By the time they could see Spider City's caldera in the distance, she had grown fond of the hybrid and her eye for out-of-place geological formations. They landed at one of the city's main entrances, a tunnel into Spider's western flank that was blocked by a stone door and secreted behind a riot of vines and brush.

"That's Jaguar, by the way." Destry glanced at Kim and hooked a thumb at the door, which had pulled back a few centimeters into the rock and was slowly rolling open.

"Hi, I'm Kim!"

"I know who you are," the door replied. "You're Zest's luggage."

Destry smothered a laugh. Jaguar never failed to figure out a weird way to insult the *H. sapiens.*

Nil wiped sweat from his forehead anxiously. "Is Lucky in the ERT lab? We need to talk to them right away."

"Yes. I can show you to the train from here." Briefly, Jaguar sounded almost professional. Beyond the threshold, a splotch of green glowed on the ceiling. The light stayed one meter ahead of them, leading the way.

Their arrival was a lot less dramatic than last time—nobody threw them into an anti-grav column for fun, and the people they passed weren't as openly hostile. Kim was as awed by the city as Destry and Nil had been, and she kept reaching out to touch everything, connecting to the network, gathering data on the life forms here. It was exactly the kind of aggressive exploration that Destry had shied away from before, when she was worried about annoying their hosts. She was feeling less like an interloper now, but not exactly welcome.

When they arrived in the ERT lab under the caldera skylight, Lucky was nowhere to be found.

"You can wait there." One of Lucky's colleagues, a hominin-shaped bot, gestured vaguely at an unused part of the floor. Kim sat down immediately, pressing her hands to the rock, looking for the network again. From the disappointed expression on her face, Destry guessed that she wasn't finding anything particularly interesting. At least, until the door to the subterranean lava chamber slid open and Dash came floating out with Hellfire&Crisp.

The H. sapiens *have returned!* she announced, wrapping her coat more tightly around her torso. *It's always so cold in here.*

"Hi, friends!" Destry said to Hellfire&Crisp. "Did Lucky get our message?"

Still hovering on the back of one of Crisp&Hellfire's bodies, Dash smoothed her whiskers back from her nose primly. *They forwarded your message to the city.*

"So many meetings!" Hellfire&Crisp yelped.

"What's the gist? Have they held any votes?" Zest asked.

Oh yes, Dash sent. *We're almost prepared.*

"For what?"

Water infrastructure improvement. And now that you're here, we'll get ready for the war.

RONNIE'S RETORT

Private property is the smallest unit of warfare.
—*The Environmental Rescue Team Handbook*

In Spider City, Council meetings were open to everyone. Whenever there was an urgent situation that might affect the whole city—which was quite rare—any person could call a pop-up Council meeting to start within the next hour. All Council members were obliged to attend, virtually if needed, and people throughout the city were invited to follow suit. The current meeting had a single item on the agenda: *Spider City Must Prepare for Possible Attack.*

Destry and the team from La Ronge had been in the city for less than twenty-four hours, and so far everything seemed deceptively normal. Zest and Kim were given a room, and everyone's names popped up on the work schedule immediately. Which was why Destry got the meeting notification as she dug in the soil lab under the lava tube skylight. Next to her, Nil was checking tiny scraps of paper arranged in a grid on a four-meter square of dark, fluffy soil. Destry recognized the sensors from her parents' work building the boreal forest—they turned red when the pH was low, and blue when it was high. Based on the colors, ranging from pink and purple to pale blue, it seemed that the ERT was testing a wide range of possible mixtures. Every microbiome wanted a slightly different pH, and every ecosystem wanted its own specialized microbiome. She'd spent a lot of time mixing new combinations from the Verdance presets.

Lucky slid out of the old door into the tunnel. "I never thought I'd say this, but I'm glad you're here."

Destry was surprised to feel giddy at the low-key compliment, which wasn't so much praise as it was a lack of insult. Still, she'd take it. "Are we heading to the Council chambers?"

"We can do it from here." Lucky flicked a wrist and opened a mostly opaque wall display that made the words MEETING WILL START IN 29 MINUTES hover over a nearby tree grafted from peach and plum stock. "In the meantime, I'd like to know what the hell is going on."

The Archaean looked at Destry expectantly. Silently, she hunkered down in the moist dirt and tried to assemble her hunches into a reasonable forecast. Maybe Long would betray them, sending a message to Ronnie—or maybe one of the other people at that horrible meeting would do it. Then again, Ronnie might decide on her own to do a more thorough investigation of Lumsden Beach, to figure out what Destry was up to. Destry wondered what Ronnie would do when she discovered Spider City. Her usual powers of data synthesis failed her. She didn't want to imagine what came next.

She thought about her parents, who truly believed that they could live beyond the reach of Verdance. Their homestead was carbon neutral; they needed nothing. Who could possibly object? Destry Senior never worked directly with Ronnie the way Destry did—he and Frenchie had spent too much time alone in the forest, away from Verdance corporate politics. They must have convinced themselves that nobody would care if they wanted to finish out their lives on unoccupied land. Who were they, after all? Just two small life forms. But to Ronnie, they were property. And property was value—as long as it was safely contained in predesignated areas. Everything had to be in balance if this real estate was going to be valuable in fifteen hundred years. Better to clean up after a small forest fire than to deal with all the potential complexities of a human settlement developing independently.

Destry leaned against the grafted tree and looked into the dark box of the meeting that hadn't yet started. "You need to be prepared for a direct attack."

Lucky frowned, but not before Destry caught a flash of fear in their expression. "What kind of attack?"

"Verdance isn't particularly subtle. But they don't want to make a mess or destroy the environment, so you can rule out anything that would leave toxins behind." As she spoke, Destry was picturing the tidy, sterilized crater that had been Destry Senior and Frenchie. "If they can vaporize you without disturbing any of the tropical ecosystems here, they will."

"Would they hit an active volcano with lasers?" Lucky sounded dubious.

Destry shrugged. "They might. They might use a molecular decoupling bomb, but I doubt it. Those release a lot of energy."

Lucky glanced over at Destry again. "Everyone in Spider City knows their escape routes. We practice once a year."

"That's a good start."

"At the meeting, we can tell everyone to be prepared for evacuation. And we should contact the Boring Fleet."

But Lucky had no time to contact anyone else. A tremor shook the ground, and the skylight went opaque, repelling a blast of coherent light. Destry's entire nervous system spluttered with shock, and she reached out to steady herself against a tree. It was a laser strike. She'd predicted it, but hadn't quite believed it would really happen.

The attack must have disrupted the city's shielding for a few seconds because Destry received a burst of comms from outside. First was an audio message, delivered in Ronnie's crisp, authoritative tone: "I expect you and your team to return to La Ronge directly. You can give me a full report on the way." The time stamp was from two hours ago.

Then there was a text from Long: *I'm sorry. We held another vote and decided the most responsible course of action was to notify Verdance. Get out while you still can.* The perfidious pus-bump had sent it forty-three seconds after Ronnie's demand.

Dust was precipitating out of the air. Everything slowed down into the gluey hyperawareness of a fight-or-flight hormone response. Stunned, she stood up, and Lucky grabbed her hand. Tugging her toward the ERT tunnels, Lucky opened a wireless connection to the network. "Council meeting canceled," they said, sending to everyone in the city at once. "This is a level one emergency response."

Destry had faced a lot of disasters in her life, but nothing on this scale in a human habitat. She felt herself freezing up, glaring through the skylight as if she could stare down the satellite that shot them. Lucky seemed to catch her mood and paused for a moment.

"Listen. We only use level one for high volume magma pulses and hurricanes, so everyone will be safe. But we need to haul ass. Now."

Time spun up again, and Destry snapped into ranger mode, leaping after Lucky. Jaguar slammed doors behind them as they ran, cursing the *H. sapiens* shit-eaters. ERT rangers raced past, orderly but obviously distressed, popping in and out of doorways and diving through floor portals to escape in boring ships. Another tremor shot through the mountain, fainter now that they were farther underground. A crack found its way along the floor, chasing them until Jaguar threw open a door to their left and Lucky shoved her inside. She found herself in a gravity lift like the one that had dropped her team into the train station months ago. But it was obviously from the city's early days. A smooth, metal-lined cylinder, it was made by people still laboring under the directions of a Verdance manual they hadn't tossed out yet.

She landed softly, on her feet, in a room that was bewildering. It looked like something from her early ERT training manuals, where new rangers learned to deal with rare emergencies like asteroid impacts or catastrophic damage to Sasky's satellites and orbital station. The walls were shaggy with webbing for stashing gear in zero gravity. Overhead she could see a vacuum control panel for the door she'd fallen through. And through a bulkhead door to her left she could see the unmistakable pattern of a Verdance control room for space vessels. They were in an airlock.

"What the—? Are we going to space?"

Lucky shook their head. "We're going to Lumsden Beach. We'll pick up a few more people before we head out."

The ship shook, but it wasn't moving. Another laser strike, far above them now.

Destry had left her fear behind somewhere in the experimental garden where she'd been measuring soil pH. Now she was running on adrenaline, sensitized to everything in the environment and searching for context. She followed Lucky into the control room and squeezed past another Archaean, who was busy with a hologram interface that was merely a scribble of photons from Destry's angle. Another door led to a cramped hold, where a few people were stringing together networking equipment for the glass.

"We should be able to control the magma system remotely if everything works, but the emergency crew will stay in Spider as a fail-safe."

A chill of anxiety distracted Destry from her data gathering. She'd evacuated so quickly that she hadn't thought about her friends. "Where's Whistle?" she asked. "And Nil and the rest of the La Ronge team?"

Lucky reached out a hand and touched Destry's arm, transmitting passwords and protocols—and a fleeting sense of warmth that had nothing to do with comms. "That should get you on the network as soon as it's up. You can relay messages for them through the ship."

A cat turned to face them, tail flicking up another interface as they texted: *Almost ready! Give us two minutes.*

The ship shuddered again, but this time it was the unmistakable feeling of motion. Portals winked open along the walls, filling the room with a blueish-white light from magma that was far deeper and hotter than what they'd seen in the chamber below the caldera.

Lucky led her through another bulkhead door to a room with a table and chairs designed for hominins, bolted to the floor. The walls were covered in cabinets, and at the far end of the room were cabin doors that she guessed led to bathrooms and sleeping pods. The whole layout was familiar and alien. "Why are we in a spaceship? How old is this?"

Jaguar's voice shot out of a speaker, somewhere to the left. "I stole it when the Archaeans decided to build Spider City."

Lucky grinned. "Hi, Jaguar. Guess the network is up."

"Is this where you used to live? On a ship?"

"I wouldn't call it living—I was owned by Verdance. Point is that this morphology works great for extreme heat."

"We have a lot of recycled Verdance tech around here, as you probably noticed," Lucky added. "This is perfect for evacuation because it's not a person. It's expendable."

They stopped, and Destry could hear more people arriving in the airlock, pushing noisily through the control room the way she had. No matter how weird things got, there were some universal truths. And one of those was that Verdance engineers didn't think ahead. Thousands of years ago, somebody at the company had stupidly put an airlock next to the control room, instead of making sure there were at minimum two bulkheads between vacuum and the most important equipment. She sighed and watched a stream of bubbles moving slowly through the glowing syrup of stone outside.

Nil and Kim burst into the room, throwing arms around Destry before she had a chance to stand up.

"Where's Whistle?" her voice was wobbling with stress.

Nil sat in the immobile chair next to her, awkwardly trying to hold hands while also positioning himself in the uncomfortably angled seat. "He stayed with Hellfire&Crisp. Zest is there too. The city needs people to keep watch from the air." Something in her expression must have cracked, because Nil gripped her hands harder. "It's going to be OK—I'm pretty sure those were warning shots. We'll open negotiations as soon as we get to Lumsden."

"I'll get us there in fifteen minutes, *H. sapiens*." For once, Jaguar didn't sound snarky when she used their species name.

Bubbles streamed past the portals faster now, and occasionally they passed through odd pockets of dissolved minerals that stained the magma with flecks of purple. At last they ground to a halt on the tropical beach she'd seen before through Crisp's feeds. Another group had arrived ahead of them and already set up a shelter for networking equipment. The sand glittered with glass threads.

Lucky turned to Destry and Nil. "All right, *H. sapiens*. Tell Verdance that we can do this the easy way, with a treaty. Or we can do it the hard way, with the Ribbons. But either way, we're taking back the river."

Destry got on her knees and pressed hands to the thread, following the glass back to Spider City and broadcasting from there. Her transmission would appear to come from the mountain, hiding their location for now. She structured it as a reply to Ronnie's audio from earlier. "I am with the people at Spider City. Please cease fire. They wish to negotiate a peace and friendship treaty with Verdance and gain access to the Eel." She glanced at Lucky, their face tense. "If you refuse, they will take back the watershed by force."

Ronnie replied instantly. "We do not negotiate with trespassers. They are living and reproducing on Verdance land without permission."

The cat they met on the spaceship let out a shocked yowl: *They're firing on the city again!*

Destry grabbed files out of the public stream, video and audio, confusingly jumbled together from aerial and interior views of the city. There had been a partial collapse on the gym and practice fields, far from the deeper neighborhoods where people lived. Hunks of rock pulverized benches, grassy squares, and nets for ballgames; from above, it appeared that the mountain's flank had partially deflated.

Lucky was grim. They grabbed some glass in a fist and spoke. "Boring Fleet, it's time to free the Eel River. Unplug the walls of Fork Canyon."

Nil's eyes widened. "Are you sure? We've only done one test."

"The Boring Fleet has been busy while you were gone. We've prepared the cliffs for controlled magma release," Lucky replied. "Now it's time to remind the Verdance bosses what happens when liquid rock meets liquid water."

A cacophony of bells filled the air, sounding like the alarm on an external comms pad. Destry jumped at the unexpected noise, half expecting to see Ronnie stepping out of the ocean. But it was only the Boring Fleet, answering Lucky's message with the laughter of warriors headed for battle.

DRONES AND HOMININS

H. sapiens always figures out a new way to implement caste systems.
—*The Environmental Rescue Team Handbook*

Hellfire&Crisp were great aeronauts, but they had the mistaken impression that Whistle would never quite reach their level because of his biological parts. Admittedly it was his size too. You could fit a dozen drones into the mass occupied by a moose. Still, there was one thing bots like Hellfire&Crisp would never have, and that was a feeling for how biotic life moved through the world. No matter how well trained they might be, a person made from cellular tissue would flinch ever so slightly when confronted by the possibility of pain or death. Whistle had felt himself do it; he'd seen Destry twitch away from danger. It was a permanent bug in the electro-chemical nervous system, even when it was supplemented with network hardware and gravity mesh and regeneration swarms in the bloodstream. And that's why Whistle could tell the laser fire wasn't coming from bots or some kind of mindless automation. He'd clocked dozens of microhesitations and showy flourishes as lasers strafed the city's practice fields. Their attackers exhibited all the signs of neurological thinking, with a layer of hominin aggression on top.

Humans were always expressing themselves in gestures rather than words. They didn't even have the excuse that Whistle had, with his artificially limited vocabulary of spoken words, a mental funnel through which he had to push everything in his mind. Verdance reps could use as many syllables as they wanted, and still they chose to act out rather than speak.

Whistle wheeled in the air over Spider's shattered leg, Hellfire&Crisp behind him, and shot back toward the tree line. The city's aeronauts were gathered beneath the thick tropical canopy at the bottom of the mountain, hooves and feet and actuators resting lightly on the firm, slightly acidic clay of the forest floor. News was coming in from the evacuation teams, and it was not good. Verdance wouldn't negotiate, and now Lucky was calling for the Boring Fleet to take the half-collapsed lava tunnels north to Fork Canyon, a place Whistle only knew from flying over.

The laser bombardment had stopped for the moment. Verdance must have figured out that they were destroying valuable ecosystems without actually murdering any people, which probably meant a failure to meet two goals.

Presently Lucky's mountable partner, Bog, arrived with Zest and Rocket, hovering alongside the moose and other drones. Bog had a similar morphology to Rocket, though their barrel-shaped carapace was anodized to produce shimmering purples and greens in sunlight.

"You know Verdance better than we do," Bog said. "What do you think their next move might be?"

Zest tossed her head. "None of us has ever been in a firefight with them, but you can be certain that they won't destroy an entire mountain. They've figured out by now that everyone is evacuating anyway."

Whistle was relatively certain what Verdance's next strategy would be, and spent several anxious seconds pulling all his thoughts together into a small sentence: *They know we will hide. Their best move now is to send drones.*

"Their drones are all remotes, controlled by people," Hellfire&Crisp added. "So they have some disadvantages. But they also have a lot of ammunition that we don't have."

Bog cackled. "We have ammunition. That's not a problem." The drone opened an aperture on their dorsal side, unfolding an actuator to point at a pile of muddy, blueberry-sized balls in a shallow pit a few meters away. "We've got caches of sticky grenades all along this perimeter. Enough for everybody." Aeronauts started helping themselves, putting the explosives in saddlebags or compartments in their carapaces.

Whistle flicked an ear and pawed restlessly at the ground. The Spider City people didn't understand the danger—Verdance could send thousands of drones, some as small as wrens, and he didn't think the Archaeans had enough ordinance to stop a sky army. He wasn't yet alive when Destry's parents were murdered, but she'd told him about it after the meeting back in La Ronge, and it wasn't the kind of thing he wanted to experience first-hand. *We need a plan*, he texted helplessly, wishing he could explain himself the way Midnight did. Her polysyllabic expositions made everyone pay attention.

Sighing, Whistle looked at Hellfire&Crisp: *We need to get to Fork Canyon first.* At least he could write "canyon" when it was part of a proper noun. That was one of the few work-arounds on his InAss vocabulary limiter. Names and places always came through, even if they were ridiculously long. In the months after his decanting, Whistle had kept himself sane by speaking long names aloud. Destry caught him one day muttering "Wasakeejack" under his breath. She'd teased him about calling on the dangerous hero from countless stories, but Whistle knew her jokes were one of those hominin gestures that substituted for forthrightness. Unsaid was the fact that Destry felt sorry for him. He knew she felt differently now—she'd saved his life more than once, and he counted her as a true friend. Still, he couldn't shake the feeling that her affection was contingent on whether he sounded intelligent. Because the fact was, he'd been built to appear stupid, and he always would.

"What are they going to do at Fork Canyon, anyway?" Hellfire&Crisp were bouncing up and down in the air, anxious and bored.

Stop it, Whistle sent.

Hellfire&Crisp bounced higher, bodies whizzing past each other so fast that one knocked the other sideways. "Too bad you don't have the same takeoff strength I do, Whistle. Are you senescing right now? Gravity mesh decay?"

Zest made a big show of ignoring them and turned to Whistle. "If you're right about the drones, the boring ships are going to need us to defend them when they unplug the tunnels."

Whistle asked: *What are those plugs?*

Bog floated into their conversation. "Mostly basalts."

Zest nodded, as if that explained everything. Whistle didn't want to expend the effort required to cobble together another question, so he moved the conversation along: *Do we have comms from the Boring Fleet?*

"Just their reply to Lucky. They must be on their way."

Whistle flicked his ears forward, nervous but ready: *Can we catch them if we fly?*

"Easy!" Hellfire&Crisp yelled.

"Let's hope your voice didn't carry into low orbit," Zest grumbled. "We have to stick to a path that will hide us from satellites."

Whistle was suddenly aware of the other Spider City aeronauts clustered around them. There were more than a hundred, of all sizes. How would they camouflage themselves?

Bog rose higher, projecting his voice to the crowd. "We need to go invisible to get to Fork Canyon. Everybody ready?"

There were various noises, ranging from growls and hoots to curses and warbles. Whistle simply waited, unable to ask a question containing the word "invisible." Bog opened a door in his torso, slid out an actuator, and stuck a tiny metal burr on Whistle's right antler. "This will make you bend light enough to fool a simple satellite scan. Not much good against up-close-and-personal drones though."

Good. It was all Whistle could say, and it was enough.

17

AN OLD BED

Sometimes a muskrat saves the world.
—*The Environmental Rescue Team Handbook*

Jaguar was steering her old space vessel behind two members of the Boring Fleet, who were leading them through a freshly carved tunnel into Fork Canyon. Looking out a portal, Destry could see the oatmeal mush of crystals flowing sluggishly around them, emitting a pale orange light. They were at the head of a tremendously high-pressure flow that was corked with a plug of basalt whose nose stuck out of the canyon wall, seemingly just one lumpy rock among many. Centuries ago, *H. archaean* workers had halted lava flows by freezing some of the magma into enormous stoppers. Now they would drill this stopper out, to create the kind of dam that people had discovered on nearly every rocky planet with liquid water. A dam made from magma.

"We have to time this perfectly," Lucky said, their hands pressed to an interface fringed with glass that connected them with several relays and members of the Fleet. "We want a smooth cascade of lava, blocking the route Eel chose in 57,342, and guiding it to the old bed."

But would the Eel allow itself to be redirected into the riverbed it abandoned almost seventeen hundred years ago? The idea had sounded plausible back at Spider, when they weren't being strafed by laser beams. Rivers shifted a lot over time, and the old route was still a deep cut in the land—though after nearly two millennia, it was full of trees and other debris. If the Eel slid into its old bed, the river would run southeast, routing around Verdance's new dam and flowing past Spider. Then it would rejoin its original route down the Vertebrae Mountains to the strait between Maskwa and the neighboring continent of Tooth. If the river refused to budge—well, they might flood the area, deranging the river's path in a whole new and unexpected way. Spider City would still be thirsty, and the treaty would get a lot more complicated.

"Is everybody ready?" Lucky was sweating.

Destry nodded, even though she knew the question was for the Boring Fleet.

One by one the boring ships' voices chimed over the speakers, a heavenly chorus from an unknown number of creatures who could chew through rocks and withstand the pressure of 25,000 Sasky atmospheres. She could barely hear Lucky's countdown through the roar. Daisies made from knives bloomed in the soft basalt, slicing forward.

Jagged blue light shattered the rock around them, and Destry flung her arms up, instinctively shielding her face. But the ship wasn't hit; Jaguar kept inching forward, and she realized they were seeing sky, a bright, brutal turquoise above the froth of surging magma around them. The Boring Fleet had broken through the plug, and Spider's fire was coming to Fork Canyon.

The boring ships backed off from the opening they'd made, but Jaguar continued out into the canyon, soaring high over the Eel and giving them a perfect view of the lava waterfall spilling out of dozens of boreholes. It bubbled and oozed and buckled, emitting explosive bursts of gas. When the first flow hit the river, it erupted into steam, filling the deep crevice of Fork Canyon with white clouds that expanded like insulating foam. Jaguar's portals fogged, then began to sweat condensation. Lava kept rolling down the canyon wall, as if the planet wept blood, flaring into fire where it met scrub. A sticky pile of black blobs built up in Eel's bed, slowly growing taller, and the boiling waters that met it began to edge east, the new head of the river looking for somewhere, anywhere to turn. A few drones and naked mole rats flew out of the boring ships, emerging from the broken plugs with tools to shape the cooling lava and capture data from the water flow.

Jaguar's frame shook, and shadows darted through the steam clouds. The motion of the shadows was far too synchronized to be coming from people alone—automation had to be involved. And then she caught a glimpse of rotors, mounted on a generic carbon alloy carapace, right before it smashed into Jaguar's starboard side.

"They've sent remote drones!" Destry shouted into comms, her heart frozen. "Get back inside the boreholes! These rusty assholes are suicide bombers!"

That's when she saw Whistle, diving through the air, flanked by Hell-fire&Crisp, shooting tiny metal slugs at a hulking shape obscured by steam.

"What the shit! Get out of here! Now!"

But yelling wouldn't help. No wires connected the aeronauts to the ship.

Jaguar let out a string of curses. "I'm trying to turn back but they've hit one of my gravity mesh nodes. I can't retreat!" A laser strafed them, its path illuminated by the water evaporating below. The aeronauts' grenades were popping like knotweed kernels on a fire. "I'm going to take us down as slowly as I can." Jaguar's voice cut in and out, static instead of words, as the spaceship sank through clouds and terrifying bursts of light. Lucky was shouting into the network, but Destry couldn't profocus on their meaning because she was trying to use infrared, radar, anything to see Whistle in the expanding skirmish. They hit the ground next to the lava flow with an ungainly thud, and Jaguar shot her doors open to let them out. "Run for cover!" she yelled. Everyone raced for a shallow cave nearby, their entire bodies instantly slick with sweat and humidity. Destry craned her head, looking for her friends in the air above. "Move your stupid *H. sapiens* ass!" screamed Jaguar. "I'm abandoning this ship."

Laser fire sliced the steam again, followed by the *wham-wham-wham* of grenades. A bot she didn't recognize thudded to the ground beside her, its body a melted mess, and Destry ran. Another fell, and then a naked mole rat plummeted into the lava flow with a scream. The smell of burned carbon and biological tissues floated through the reek of sulfur. Shivering beneath an outcropping, Destry could see flickers of the fight as the clouds opened and closed. The magma was slowing down, piling up in the river-bed. And then, out of the billowing white gold, Whistle limped toward her. His right antler was gone, blown off with part of his skull.

Destry was nowhere; there was nothing but Whistle, the soft brown coat of his neck streaked with blood and brain. She didn't remember leaving her shelter, only running to him as he fell on the rocky edge of the tormented Eel River. And then she was next to him, sopping wet, his beloved head leaning hard into her torso. She tore off her jacket to cover his wound—which made no sense, this wound, how could this be happening?

Whistle was supposed to leave her by defecting to Spider, not by dying in its defense. "I'm here, my friend," she said, crying. "I'm here, I'm here."

His legs twitched in a seizure and he looked at her with one eye. *Wasakeejack,* he texted.

"She's the best hero. The best. I loved the story where she stole a spaceship." Destry didn't know what she was saying; the words were comfort noises, sounds without meanings, references to a story about the Trickster Squad that people told sometimes on solstice back in La Ronge.

Whistle seized again, the powerful muscles in his neck contracting. Overhead she could hear screams and shots, and another drone plunged smoking into the river. They were going to lose. Verdance would light them all on fire, regain control of the river, incinerate every trace of Spider City's thousand-year life. She would join Destry Senior and Frenchie in the ash can of history. How could Spider's tiny team of aeronauts with their exploding blueberries defeat Verdance's suicide drones and low orbit weapons?

Wind tore the clouds away and she saw the ragged remains of the Archaeans, some still tending the river and others struggling to hold off drones that swarmed from the sky without any end in sight. And then, from the north, a sound she couldn't identify. The air seemed to ripple, and a dozen Verdance drones dropped in midflight. Another sound—almost like a moose bellowing with joy, but amplified into an avalanche of syllables that roared into the ravine. And then, over the far edge of the canyon, came a blur of black and brown. It spread out, resolving into individuals, dodging laser fire and emitting more distorted waves of energy, hurling Verdance remotes out of the sky.

What? Who? As Whistle texted, his eyes rolled back and bloody foam flecked his lips.

Destry held him tighter, straining to see. Wheeling overhead were hundreds of moose. And then came a text from Midnight, blasting everyone for kilometers around, a message that could cut through the noise of battle: *Kill the remotes! KILL THEM ALL!*

She'd guessed from Long's message that Midnight had betrayed them too. Instead, she was leading an insurrection. Her throat almost closed as a burst of intense, contradictory emotions rolled over her, mixed with noxious gas. Another group of the drones fell, plopping into the cooling lava that was fast growing into a formidable dam. How were the moose doing it? An expensive, freshly-built drone smashed to the ground next to them, and she reached out to touch its smoking shell, seeking any information on the attack. She couldn't network with it; all its ports were blocked, as if it had gone into disaster lockdown mode. That's when she realized what was going on overhead. Midnight had repurposed an ERT emergency signal designed to shut down malfunctioning remotes. The Verdance operators couldn't respond fast enough to block the signal. And now they had a chance at winning.

Another plug exploded overhead, bringing with it a fresh spurt of lava, adding heft to the dam. Water was seeping into the old bed, and then it was roaring. Trees drowned in the silty deluge, and the Eel sang its approval. Moose whirled overhead, their bodies cutting a path through the drones in a mirror of the river below.

"Whistle, it's Midnight," Destry said, weeping again. "She's come with the moose aeronauts of La Ronge. She's come to save us."

In her arms, Whistle spasmed and stilled, saying nothing.

DAMAGE

Our bodies are ecosystems.
—*The Environmental Rescue Team Handbook*

Destry had never received a message like it before. The video was short, and Ronnie looked like she'd been awakened after an intoxicated blackout. Her eyes were sunken, her hair dull, and there was no stiff, professional collar framing her neck. She said nothing, simply sighed and flicked an appointment request at the camera. Ronnie was summoning Destry and "representatives of the occupation at Spider Mountain" to the bargaining table. She'd attached some documents containing a lot of formal League language to signal a treaty discussion. Destry stared at the message, now an obnoxiously blinking hologram blocking the view of Whistle's berth in Spider City's rehab center. Dozens of injured people were recuperating in this hall, its arched ceiling lit by twinkling yellow lights attached to vines that grew everywhere on the porous volcanic rock.

Each patient had their own room, sealed to prevent infection—and, in Whistle's case, to keep the atmosphere tuned to the mix of gasses on Sasky's surface. Health workers shuttled between rooms while friends and family lounged in chairs and cushions that created a strip of color and calm down the center of the hallway. If someone woke up alone in their room, the first thing they would see were their people right outside.

It had been only twelve hours since the attack. After the moose had joined the battle, Verdance hadn't exactly surrendered—but they had withdrawn, and stopped shooting. Spider City people were still sending video and audio from the lava falls in Fork Canyon, where the river banked off hot, hardening rock and slid into its old bed without complaint, as if it had been waiting millennia for an invitation. Every few minutes, she'd catch another glimpse of the rippling, steaming waters. But Destry couldn't think about the new dam, or the weird video of Ronnie. All she cared about was what was happening inside Whistle's brain.

Midnight, arriving from the dining hall, sent a text: *Any news?* The moose had almost passed out from exhaustion before Destry forced her to go eat. Lucky was with her now, carrying a bowl of oatmeal and dried apricots, a scoop of yogurt on top.

"No news. He's still stable."

Lucky held out the bowl to Destry. "You should eat some breakfast."

"Is it morning already?"

"Yeah. And we need you to have some energy, OK?" Lucky glanced at the hologram and their eyebrows arched in surprise. "What in the burning compost pile is that?"

Destry passed the message to Lucky's mobile, and they poked it to open the video file of Ronnie looking like a corpse.

Midnight glanced at it and then back at Whistle, sleeping in a sling, his head bandaged. *I'm going to make her sorry she did this,* she sent.

The health team had cut off Whistle's other antler when they cleaned his wound. He'd suffered a massive brain injury, but he would heal; the monomers implanted in his cells before he was decanted were spinning electrically conductive polymers to replace the neurons he'd lost. Everything would be fine, as long as he never suffered another major injury again. In La Ronge, engineers built Mounts with those monomers as a failsafe. People with higher InAss ratings had cellular scrubbers, of course, little nanobot swarms in their blood that regenerated tissue. Mounts were treated like equipment, so their templates called for nothing more than one-time emergency repair wires. Those asswormy templates. He'd never survive another blow like this one.

Destry recalled Whistle's dark, reflective eyes when he was looking at the world for the first time after decanting. Why had she let them build her a Mount? She could have pushed back harder, insisted her partner be a person. But after her parents' deaths, she couldn't stand the sight of people anymore—especially hominins. She'd thought working with a Mount would be like working alone, or with an animal. As soon as Whistle stood on his own, though, she knew she was wrong. And then it was too late. He was alive and staring at her with a million thoughts he couldn't express.

Lucky was still gawking at the video of Ronnie in disbelief. "This is all thanks to you, Midnight. I mean, you and the moose of La Ronge." They shot a glance at Destry. "You too, *H. sapiens*. This treaty could actually work. We could stop hiding."

"And you'll have your water." Nil spoke before Destry realized he was behind her.

"You're here!" She hugged him hard and decided not to let go for a while. "Where were you? The network showed you with the Boring Fleet, but I couldn't reach you."

"I wanted to monitor the river. I've been out there all night. I knew you two were safe—" He turned to Whistle and his voice went ragged. "I should have grabbed the glass and sent you a text, but we had so many things to do and I thought you were fine. The river—"

"I saw the footage. It's beautiful. I think we scored one for water management today."

"I'm so sorry I wasn't here sooner." Nil showed no sign of ending the hug, and they stayed like that for a while, with Midnight and Lucky standing in companionable silence alongside them.

Ever since she shot a fleet of drones out of the sky, Midnight had risen quite far in Destry's estimation. She'd begun to wonder whether Long's comment about his partner being a heartbreaker was, in fact, an attempt to plant seeds of mistrust between them. It was clear now that Midnight truly cared for Whistle, and for the city he'd chosen as his new home. She hadn't had a chance to talk to the other moose aeronauts who had saved Spider, so she wasn't sure what motivated them. Obviously there was a lot going on at La Ronge that had flown way over her sparsely furred *H. sapiens* head.

"So what's the plan for this meeting with Verdance?" Lucky was bouncing up and down like they were ready to rip through a day's work in ten minutes.

"First we need to go over the terms they're offering, and then we'll set the meeting." Destry released Nil, keeping his hand folded within hers. "I'd recommend taking your time with the treaty because Verdance will try to get all kinds of sneaky shit in there."

Midnight shook her head, and a few small crusts of mud fell to the floor. Like Destry, she hadn't left Whistle's side for more than a few minutes. Both of them needed to wash up, especially after recycling all the Verdance drones. The Boring Fleet had clanged with laughter as they appropriated piles of sticky, shattered carapaces, pledging to build new vessels with them.

"I've called a Council meeting for this afternoon. We need to create a treaty team." Lucky swiped one of the apricots from Destry's untouched bowl, sitting precariously on a shelf mostly taken up by hot water bottles. "And you need to be there. So eat your breakfast."

Destry took the bowl and spooned some oatmeal into her mouth. It was nutty and still slightly warm, tart from the fruit and yogurt, with an overwhelming flavor of the ash she'd inhaled last night. Everything tasted wrong. Her stomach was hungry, but her mouth wasn't.

Midnight flicked her ears forward: *He's waking up.*

Whistle was moving around ever so slightly, swaying in the sling.

An Archaean and a moose walked purposefully down the hall toward them. The moose texted: *We're the health team on Whistle's case. I'm Silver, and this is Lettuce.* The moose gestured at the Archaean with their nose.

Lettuce pulled a breather out of their shirt pocket and looked at Midnight. "I'm going to check on how his brain repair is going."

"Of course."

"Silver can brief you on what to expect now that he's waking up."

Nobody addressed Destry, and she was glad Nil was still there, holding her hand. Silver texted something privately to Midnight.

Midnight replied publicly: *Don't cut Destry out of this. She's been Whistle's friend a lot longer than I have.* Her text had that slightly bitchy edge that had once made Destry suspect her of ill intentions, but now she could have kissed her for being so bristly.

Silver was briefly taken aback but recovered quickly. They continued: *As you probably know, these kinds of repairs can be finicky. He'll probably regain all his old memories, but sometimes a few things get lost in the, uh, shuffle. He might have some problems with movement for a few weeks. I'd like to keep him here in rehab and monitor him for at least three days after he's fully awake, if that suits him.* The moose paused, then looked at Destry for the first time. *You H. sapiens—you La Ronge settlers—why would you build someone like this? He's never had molecular scrubbers or tissue repair. It's—why, it's a disgusting, shit-covered crime.* Silver huffed angrily but then regained composure. *How can you call yourself his friend?*

Destry felt the bite of oatmeal she'd swallowed turn to a nauseating lump in her stomach.

Midnight snorted: *Do you think Destry built Whistle? Do you think she runs Verdance? Or do you think she's the person who warned your city about the attack and then stood in a lava surge at Fork Canyon to save your hairy ass?*

The door to Whistle's room shushed open, and Lettuce snapped their fingers to bring up a hologram they could all see. "If anyone wants to know what I think, it's that Whistle is going to be ready to see his friends in the next few minutes." The tension eased as they peered at Lettuce's readout, which offered a sliceable view of Whistle's brain. Lettuce cut to the area that was rapidly repairing itself as polymer wires grew to replace damaged neurons. "It looks like he suffered a trauma to his cerebral cortex a very long time ago, but the good news is that injury has also been repaired. I've introduced some scrubbers to his bloodstream, but I'm afraid they won't have the same impact they might if he'd had them since decanting. Still, it should boost his life expectancy by a few decades."

Midnight? Whistle had blearily sent his text to everyone within twenty meters.

You can go in, Silver said. Then, grudgingly, they looked at Destry: *You too.*

Nil and Lucky waited outside with the doctors as Destry followed Midnight into the warm room that smelled faintly of yeast from the probiotics.

The two moose pressed their soft noses together, nostrils flaring, and Midnight curled her neck around his, carefully avoiding the sling.

Whistle blinked a few times: *I can't believe you're here. I don't remember anything after seeing Destry in the water. What happened?*

Neither of them could say anything for a minute. Whistle was using multisyllabic words, which could only mean one thing. His vocabulary limiter—the "trauma" that Lettuce identified—had been repaired. A Verdance engineer would probably say his InAss rating had jumped to person level. Whistle could send freely now, thanks to the shoddy monomer regeneration system that La Ronge engineers installed in Mounts. Two deliberate design flaws had finally canceled each other out.

"Whistle, your brain—it was injured. We had to regenerate it."

The moose looked at them both, whites showing around the edges of his dark eyes. He struggled to stand, but the sling supporting his head, neck, and belly held him snug a few centimeters off the floor. Relaxing his back legs, he grunted in pain.

12

WHISTLE AND MIDNIGHT

Whistle could tell something was wrong with his brain because whatever popped into his head was translated directly into texts with no bottleneck, no pause to gather the right words.

Why are you here, Midnight? The monosyllables felt right, but somehow unearned. He hadn't had to search for them in his mental storehouse of textable things.

Her neck was still looped over his, and when she exhaled he could feel her warmth ruffling the fur on his back. *I brought the moose aeronauts to defend the city, like I said I would. We knew Verdance would send their most basic remote drones, so all it took was a few tweaks to our antenna geometry and we could broadcast the emergency override in 360. We took out at least a hundred, and the Spider City people shot the rest. If Verdance wants to hit us again, they'll have to pull remotes from other projects or try to deploy living drones. And after today, they'll have a hard time convincing anyone to do that. The people of La Ronge may not be on our side exactly, but they don't want to die over some disagreement between Spider City and Verdance.*

Destry leaned gently into Whistle's shoulder the way she always did when they rested after a day of work in the field. Her smell was acrid and bloody but familiar too. "How are you feeling, friend?" He could hear the quaver in her voice through his neck, where she'd pressed her face. "What else do you remember?"

We were defending against the first wave of remotes, trying to lead them away from the dam. Hellfire&Crisp were trying to block their comms. But they kept coming, and some of the remotes had projectiles and—I'm not sure. I remember fragments. I know I was hurt, and I remember swimming. And then I saw you. He tried to turn toward Destry, but the sling held him back. Not so with his sender, which continued to broadcast every word in his brain. *And now you're here, Midnight. I never thought I'd see you again.*

She pressed against him harder than Destry had, her shoulder to his, her throat soft on his back: *I told you I would come. I told you.*

That was before the attack, before Long betrayed—Whistle retreated into silence. It was good to send the words he felt, but Long was Midnight's partner. He was going to have to learn when to stop texting now that his limiter was gone.

Midnight said nothing for a minute, but he felt discomfort in the tensing of her neck muscles against his: *Long is not my partner anymore.* Carefully, she disentangled her head from his sling and turned to face him: *How does it feel? Are you OK?* It was a vague question, perhaps intended to change the subject. But it meant more than that. Midnight was asking how it felt to be a person. Someone whose InAss rating set them above the animals and Mounts and trees and rivers.

In that moment, staring into her eyes, he felt two things. He loved Midnight more than he had ever loved anyone. And he could see her flaws, her lifetime of prejudice against people who were classified as Mounts. As to her question—how did *this* feel? This ascension to so-called personhood? It felt like—he searched through his vast internal vocabulary, savoring the idea that he could pick any word he liked, no matter how absurdly long. Still, it turned out the one he wanted was something he could have said all along: *It feels like rage.*

Midnight hung her head. *Are you mad at me?*

Not you. Everyone. Everything. It's like I've been waiting to get angry for a really long time, and now I can finally do it.

"I'm so sorry, Whistle." Destry had sidled around to stand beside Midnight in his line of sight. "Those wormy InAss ratings—"

Whistle cut her off: *You know I'm just as intelligent as I always was, right? The only difference is now you have to listen to me.*

THE EEL RIVER TREATY

Land use treaties fail for two reasons: they are made in secret, or they are made without full consent of all parties.
—*The Environmental Rescue Team Handbook*

Lucky was rapping on the door and making a hurry-up gesture. They opened a voice channel into the room. "The meeting is starting after lunch, and you have to be there, Destry!"

Whistle kicked a hind leg, causing his whole body to sway. He texted: *What meeting?*

Lettuce frowned and reentered the berth, crowding between Destry and Midnight. "You are still healing, and we need you to wait a few more days for all your mobility to return."

Destry gave Whistle a soft touch on his nose. "Verdance has agreed to open treaty negotiations. I'll leave you with Midnight."

As the door sucked closed behind her, Destry could hear Lettuce lecturing the two moose on how Whistle needed to start swimming therapy immediately.

"How is he?" Nil raised an eyebrow. "That looked intense."

"He's angry. The regeneration threads upped his InAss rating." Destry cast her eyes down to the floor, where soft moss grew over stone.

"Shit. I've never heard of that happening. Is he coherent?"

"Very."

Lucky broke in. "Let's talk on the way to the ERT labs. There's a group waiting for us. We're having a premeeting meeting."

Suddenly Destry was ravenous, and the oatmeal Lucky had given her earlier looked delicious. She grabbed the bowl and started shoving soggy spoonfuls into her mouth as they walked.

When they got to the now-familiar ERT lab under the caldera lake, Rocket and Hellfire&Crisp were waiting for them. The snarky double-bodied drone was unusually subdued, and offered nothing more than a quick greeting. Kim and Zest arrived last, crowding into a conference room with Lucky and a few other ERT rangers they hadn't met before. Lucky opened a window on the table and pulled up Ronnie's treaty proposal so everyone could see it.

"Verdance is offering us access to the Eel River and Spider Mountain, in return for labor and some of the metals we extract on Spider's perimeter." They highlighted a section of the document and stretched it. "As you can see, mostly they want our labor. This isn't the ERT work exchange we proposed to Destry. Everyone at Spider would have to put in three months of work every year, to help get Sasky ready for buyers."

Several people spoke and messaged at once, mostly objecting to the idea of being slaved to Verdance for any amount of time.

"I'm not saying we're going to take their offer. But let's talk this out. If we did decide to agree, what would be the catch?"

Destry nodded. "Your first question should be, how are they defining labor? They're experts at asking for three months but assigning tasks that require fifteen."

"And how are they defining 'at Spider'?" Lucky rubbed their chin. "Does that mean they're expecting the dogs to come up from Tooth and serve time because their ancestors were built here? And what about the Boring Fleet?"

"The muskrats too. Nobody has talked to a muskrat in over a century."

"Muskrats are people?" Nil looked confused. At La Ronge, muskrats were built as animals. Several of the Archaeans shot him nasty looks and ignored the question.

"So we'll want to specify that this applies only to people who are permanent residents of Spider City. Any other terms we need to hash out?" Lucky scrolled through the rest of the document. "The mineral trades are actually quite reasonable, so I don't think we need to worry about that."

"You'll want to be very clear about what it means to have access to the Eel," Nil warned. "We should define acceptable courses for the river, as well as specific amounts of water, subject to change if the population grows or moves."

"And be sure to stipulate that nobody upriver can use it for runoff. You don't want some future pustule to dump their slime in there."

"OK, OK, got it." Lucky was capturing everyone's audio with their mobile, and paused to look at the La Ronge people. "You've all worked directly with Verdance. You know Ronnie. Where do you think they are most likely to hide the decaying corpses in this treaty?"

Destry glanced Zest and Rocket. "They'll put the most rotted stuff in the labor sections, don't you think? That's where we need to focus our attention. And Lucky"—she looked into the Archaean's wide face—"Verdance loves to categorize workers into different classes, to limit what kinds of things they can do. They'll want you to use InAss ratings."

"Yeah, look at this!" Hellfire highlighted a particularly turgid section of the treaty. "This says you have to build Mounts and animals as part of the workforce. And something called a Blessed?"

"That's what I'm talking about." Destry sighed. "Blessed are something we're supposed to start building at La Ronge too. They're a worker category lower than Mount and above animal."

Lucky's mouth had thinned to an angry line. "Good catch, friend."

The Spider City Council decision process was based on the ERT's style of coalition democracy. Everyone was invited, in person or via the network, and all votes were decided on a three-quarters majority, with one mutually agreeable concession automatically granted to the minority. Occasionally this led to interminable squabbles and negotiations, spread out over weeks because the Council could meet for no longer than ninety minutes each day. Often it all came down to what the minority wanted, and getting them to agree was like engineering an ecosystem from scratch while a crocodile tried to eat your face.

The Council met in a circular public room beneath the shallowest part of the caldera lake. Morning sunlight illuminated the space through emerald waters, sending shivering blobs of shadow across the mossy ground, where people had planted flower and clover beds in crescent-shaped plots. Intricate spirals of algae glowed from the walls, augmenting the dim natural light. Clearly this place was meant for meetings; three tiers of seats were carved into the rock, forming rings within rings around the green center. As people arrived, they settled into the seats that were most comfortable to them. People coming in remotely were represented by glittering motes that hovered in the air, each attendee a star in this community's firmament.

Nobody was allowed to stand at the center of a Council meeting. The center was for cross talk, not grandstanding. When it came time to explain the treaty, Lucky lounged in the back row with Nil and Destry, amplifying their voice so everyone could hear. Lucky ran through the facts in fifteen minutes, and the debate and votes were hashed out in the next forty-five. The majority were willing to offer two months labor each year, rather than the three Verdance offered, with significant revisions in the clauses defining both labor and laborers. The sticking point came from a minority who wanted no treaty. Their representatives argued that Spider City should recruit more willing allies from La Ronge—people like Midnight—and then lay claim to Sasky, converting it into a public planet run by a coalition democracy. They accepted no concession.

People raised their voices and sent in all caps while remote attendees dropped out overhead. The audience for minority concessions was always smaller and grumpier.

Just as Destry thought they'd have to set another meeting for tomorrow, she hit upon an idea. "Would you accept a concession where we agree to claim Sasky as a public planet if Verdance ever violates the terms of the treaty?"

There was silence until Lucky's mountable drone, Bog, representing the minority, rumbled approval. A few others signaled agreement, and then a voice came from one of the stars overhead, which grew from a twinkle to a holographic face as they spoke. "I will agree only if this concession includes use of the Ribbons. Verdance understands nothing but force. We must be prepared to change the very nature of this planet if it is to be ours."

Lucky leaned over to whisper in Destry's ear. "That's Grendel. They've been itching to use the Ribbons the entire time I've known them. They must be having orgasms right now because at last their obsession is relevant to public debate."

Nobody in the minority had a problem with Grendel's demand. The concession was set. Destry was ready to negotiate with Ronnie, on behalf of Spider City.

There was no special private chamber where Destry could sit with Ronnie's holographic representation, so she did it in the ERT conference room where anybody walking by could see her gesticulating at the woman who was her boss, her tormentor, and her owner. The woman who had murdered her parents. It had been two days since Ronnie sent the treaty offer, looking tired and defeated. Now she was back in professional mode, her hair and eyes silvered, her skull resculpted to sweep back into an elongated egg tipped with a projectile point in back.

Ronnie accepted Spider City's amendments to the treaty with one note. If Destry defected, the deal was off. There was nothing Destry could do but concede; her life wasn't worth more than an entire city. She would have to spend the rest of her days at La Ronge, doing Ronnie's bidding.

Now both parties' crypto seals were on the document. It was obvious that Ronnie wanted to negotiate as quickly and quietly as possible, without publicity. Still, even in defeat, the VP exuded entitlement. "This little crusade you're on isn't going to end well for you or these squatters, Destry. This planet is ours, no matter what they do with one river."

Her jaw aching with everything she couldn't say, Destry glared at the hologram. She thought about the concession the Spider City Council had agreed on and allowed herself to imagine what Sasky would be like if it really became a public planet. A place where every person could vote, and access to the watershed wasn't just for rich clients. She doubted she would live to see it, but maybe another generation could make it happen.

Ronnie continued needling her. "Why are you doing this? I've always treated you well. You're my best network analyst, and you could have had a brilliant future. Hell, we talked about bringing you in to work on other Verdance projects, doing food web security. Why would you throw that away for these . . . criminals?"

Destry stared into Ronnie's eyes, glinting under the carefully cultivated slope of her forehead. "I'm still going to be working in La Ronge. I'm not throwing anything away."

"This isn't some triumph you can put on your achievements list. I'm taking you out of the field."

Destry had been expecting something like this, but it was still a blow. The only thing that truly gave her joy was getting her whole body dirty in some haywire environment whose secret imbalances she'd discover in the data trails left by life-forms sloughing off their sensors. Of course Ronnie would be taking that away.

Halfheartedly, Destry tried to argue. "I will be a lot more use to you in the field."

"I've arranged for you to start training a new ranger to take your place. He's built to have an even more nuanced relationship with networks."

"Fine." Destry kept her voice even.

"Unlike you, he knows his place."

"I look forward to educating him." If this meeting went on much longer, Destry was going to start screaming.

"I've thought about you far more than I ever hope to think about one of my terraformers ever again. I think you went to hell because we let your parents go free for so long." Ronnie crossed her arms and pinched her eyebrows together. "You think you have the right to go anywhere on this planet. But you can't, and neither can these ridiculous animals at Spider Mountain. I promise you, they will learn exactly the same lesson your parents did. Not today, and not tomorrow. I can wait. Long after you're dead, the *H. archaeans* will go extinct the way they were supposed to a thousand years ago."

Destry's hands were fists. She knew Spider had already won—the treaty was set. But Ronnie wanted her to feel like she'd lost.

"Neither of us knows what the future will bring," she said between gritted teeth. "But I'm willing to wager that this city and its people will be standing long after Verdance has lost all claims to the land on Sasky."

She flicked the button to ratify the Eel River Treaty and smacked the table to make Ronnie's face disappear.

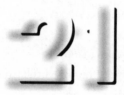

SWIMMING

We do not make sacrifices, but we do make bargains. Pay attention to the difference. One path leads to a simple death, and the other to a complicated life.

—*The Environmental Rescue Team Handbook*

Destry felt like she'd been dipped in shit. Then she looked through the windows into the main ERT lab and realized everyone was gone. The big room beneath the caldera was quiet, but in a comforting way, like a summer night after the bugs and frogs have finally stopped yammering. What had driven everybody away from their jobs in the middle of the afternoon? She pressed a hand to one of the wall interfaces and called up messages. There were a few public announcements that she didn't bother to read and then a snatch of audio from Nil: "You've got to come up here when you're done! It's so wonderful!" That's when she noticed something weird about the lake above her. It was full of people. A group of naked mole rats in atmosphere bubbles had almost reached the depth of the skylight, followed by some aquatic drones. The surface of the water was foamy with churning limbs of every possible description.

She flicked back through the public messages until she got to one from thirty minutes ago. "To celebrate the Eel River Treaty, and our new freedom on the surface, everyone is invited to spend the afternoon in the lake under the sky." The people of Spider City were having a party, without fear that somebody would spot them from space. Destry couldn't think of anything she'd rather do right now than swim.

At the caldera's edge she stripped off everything—clothes, shoes, breather, her memories of that feculent conversation with Ronnie—and dove into the cool water with hundreds of other people in all sizes and shapes. When she came up for air, she found herself next to a group of La Ronge moose who had come with Midnight to Spider City. They were dipping into a big bowl of apples that floated in the water between them.

"Ahoy, Destry!" It was Nil, scooting closer to her on Rocket's back. He'd never learned to swim, partly because Rocket was so experienced in the water.

She waved and then felt a familiar nose pushing into her back. "Whistle!" Spinning around, she almost bonked into the moose, his head still bandaged, swimming alongside Midnight.

Whistle flicked an ear with amusement: *Apparently this is part of my rehab.*

Midnight pinched her nostrils closed and dunked her head, then shook the water into bright, isolate flecks. She sent: *How was your negotiation with Ronnie?*

"She accepted our changes to the treaty."

Just like that?

Destry grunted. "There was one note. But we got what we wanted." She didn't want to talk about what Ronnie had asked of her. Not now, in the sunlight and wide-open water full of happy Spider City people. "I'm going to swim a little more. Have you seen Lucky? I wanted to give them the news about the treaty."

Whistle tossed his head in a vaguely southern direction: *Over there by the edge—they're setting up a wireless network just for fun. Because now they can leak a little signal once in a while.*

Impulsively, she threw her arms around his neck. "I'm so glad you're out here swimming around."

He didn't say anything for a while, like the old Whistle. The unrepaired one. At last he sent: *Me too, friend.* He glanced over at Midnight, who was very deliberately trying to give them some space but finding it hard to get through the crowd of swimming moose. *You know I'm going to stay here with Midnight, right?*

"I have to go back to La Ronge."

I figured. I'm just damaged goods to them, but you—I'm sorry.

"We'll talk later. I have a few days." She gave his shoulder a rub and swam toward a group of people under a large yellow umbrella, fussing over something on the ground. Soon she could see Lucky's bright red hair.

"Ahoy!" She splashed out of the water and dribbled on the warm rock. The air felt good on her naked skin.

Lucky put up a hand in greeting. They were wearing an amphibious breather, which subtly distorted their face into a slight frown. Or maybe it was a real frown?

"Need a towel?"

"Sure." Destry took the towel but continued to let the sunlight dry her. Presently the drops from her hair started to feel like tiny insects scurrying across her back and she wrapped herself in the thin textile square. Lucky's wireless hub was a maypole, with a small dish at the top and hundreds of glass threads instead of ribbons. They snaked into the elevator shaft, floated in the water, and stretched across the rock to wind down Spider's southern flank.

"Technically we really only needed to spin one thread and then we could broadcast, but everybody wanted to connect to it." Lucky shrugged. "Old habits die hard. It's hard to feel safe out here in the open, leaking signal."

"Feels good, though." Destry rubbed the towel over her wet hair and then refastened it around her waist. "I finalized the Eel River Treaty, using League specifications. Ronnie accepted our changes. If the League ever actually sees it, everything will be in order."

"I'm glad to hear it." Lucky gave Destry an appraising look, still with that ambiguous possible frown. "There's still something I don't understand. Why did you help us, *H. sapiens*? I know it wasn't the threat of plate tectonics."

Destry squinted up at the sun and thought about how she'd been looking at that same yellow blob of hydrogen every day for 506 years. She felt old, even though she might have centuries ahead of her. It wasn't the years that made her old, she realized. It was everything she'd been through—everything she'd had to experience, with no agency, no way to change it. "I hate those putrid bags of shit mucus at Verdance," she said finally. "They murdered my parents."

Lucky's eyes widened. "I—I'm sorry. That's awful."

"It was." She started to say something else, then stopped as her throat tightened. Their long-ago deaths were a fresh hurt again, now that she knew the truth.

"Well, I thank you, Destry." It was the first time Lucky had ever called her something other than *H. sapiens.* "You are welcome to stay here. I know Whistle has already requested a work placement, and so has Midnight."

"If I don't go back to La Ronge, they'll void the treaty."

Lucky wrinkled their forehead. "We could hide you."

Destry fingered one of the threads on the maypole and got a burst of video from somebody swimming deep in the water. "I'm not going to ask you to do that. Besides, I miss the boreal forest. It's my home. Spider City is incredible, but I like snow and the smell of the woods."

Lucky nodded and went back to the network, trying to convince a cat sitting nearby to connect to it via microwave. The sun sank into pink clouds as the cat debated the finer points of antenna geometry with an increasingly more exasperated Lucky. Eventually, when the sky was turning purple, Whistle and Midnight picked their way out of the lake next to her and shook off, soaking her anew. It was still warm outside, and she didn't mind.

"What are you two doing this evening?"

Whistle cocked his head at Destry. *Heading to dinner. How are you going to get back to La Ronge? Do you want a ride? Rocket is going to drop off Nil, and we could all go together.*

"Drop off? Is Rocket staying here too?"

Midnight dipped her head: *Didn't they tell you? They've been planning to stay since the first day they got here.*

Everybody was planning to stay in Spider City except for Destry and Nil, apparently. She sighed. "Is anybody else coming back with us?"

"Kim and Zest are going back eventually. I don't know about Hellfire&Crisp."

Destry toyed with another strand of glass. It carried no data. "It's been my honor to serve the environment with you, Whistle."

He lowered his head to exhale a blast of hot air into her hair: *You're one of my best friends.*

"You're mine too." She grinned lopsidedly at him. "We'll work together again, when you do your two months. Or maybe I'll send my trainee to learn the ropes down here."

Midnight cocked an ear and sent: *Ronnie gave you a trainee? She wants to keep you close to home, then.*

Destry nodded. "She's not going to let me leave again."

The two moose pressed close together, casting shadows that made their bodies merge. *I see*, Midnight sent.

Nil showed up behind them, adding his shadow to the general pool. He was carrying two bags. "Rocket is meeting me here in a few minutes. I brought your stuff, Destry."

"Wait—Whistle, did you plan this?"

The moose kicked a hind leg in the water with mirth: *Maybe. I can't go at my usual pace, but we can take a week. Go slow and enjoy the view.*

Nil's eyes were gleaming. "We can follow the Eel all the way up to La Ronge, and check on how it likes the new riverbed."

Destry smiled. Water engineers talked about rivers the same way they talked about people—rivers had desires; they had bodies; they had histories. Maybe they were built of sediment borne by water, but they were alive.

"All right, then. Let's fly to La Ronge like the old days." Destry reached for her bag.

Midnight nudged Whistle: *I'll see you when you get back. Please take your time.*

He nudged her back: *I will. I'll see you on the new wireless network!*

Nil had thought of everything. There was enough food to supplement daily foraging and plenty of sensors to throw at the Eel for remote monitoring later. Rocket arrived with more monitoring equipment and a spool of glass. The four of them waited until almost everyone had gotten out of the caldera lake and gone home before mounting the damp air over the tropical forest. Whistle and Destry followed the river north as the lumpy moon rose, flying easily alongside Nil and Rocket, until the Milky Way consumed them in its undammed river of stars.

YEAR: 59,007
LOCATION: Venus

INTERREGNUM: VIRGIN LAND

"How in the fucking hell did this happen?" Ronnie was furious, and her harried admin, Terry, had to take notes while scheduling three people across three systems for a drop-everything meeting in Verdance's Special Projects channel. "I've never heard of terraformers doing something like this! They're supposed to do their jobs and die out, not set up shop on our land and demand water and destroy our remotes."

"I've got Cylindra in the channel now. Do you want to meet her in the conference room?" Terry pointed at the door to a suite that some servant had hastily stocked with projectors and tasteful decorations. This wasn't Ronnie's usual office, so they had to make do. Normally they'd be in the VP's state-of-the-art ship, overseeing new projects or parking in orbit around some recently acquired star. Unfortunately for Terry, the Sask-E project went sideways while they were on-site at the Verdance Venus campus. Sol-C was the first planet that Verdance terraformed, and the facilities here were part-corporate, part–recreational park for the public to learn about terraforming. All the residences were facsimiles of the 21,000-year-old originals, which were themselves over a thousand years old. That made them ugly, drafty, and hard to use with modern technology.

The conference room was cozy, even if it felt kind of disgusting to sit on real wood chairs. At Ronnie's angry shoo-shoo gesture, Terry ducked through the door to prep for the arrival of Sask-E's project leads in sales, marketing, and engineering.

Cylindra from engineering clearly didn't want to be on visual—Terry had awakened her in the middle of a sleep cycle—and she was appearing in the skin of Tasmian, a muscular blue jaguar from the Felis Rex franchise owned by Verdance's parent company. Helic from marketing winked into view next to Cylindra, looking bored and awake. It was midday on his ship, and he was unfiltered—probably to show off his recent port into an *H. sapiens* body, celebrating the opening of Sask-E to potential bidders. It looked very similar to the *H. sapiens* terraformers on the planet right now, their genes sourced to an artisanal blend from actual heirloom populations. Maybe Helic had gotten it through Verdance's bulk discount. Marketing always got the cool shit. Terry was still wearing the body she'd been decanted in, and she wouldn't be able to afford a new one for a very long time—if ever.

She waved hello to Cylindra and Helic, then fussed with some of the audio settings. Cylindra bounded over, her tail fluffed out and teeth bared in a grin. "Hi, Terry! Thanks for waiting a few minutes while I grabbed a coffee." The Felis Rex skins had a bunch of preset moves, so Cylindra couldn't just walk around like a normal person unless she did some customizing. She'd be limited to all-fours and a few fight moves, though she could sit and talk at the conference table with minimal nonsense. Helic kept gesturing at some interface they couldn't see, and ignored them both.

Ronnie entered like a high-atmosphere storm, eyes narrowed at a small display clutched in her hand, and Terry's arm hair stood on end. She didn't bother to acknowledge anyone before sitting down. "Where in the long, damp sewer is Glat?"

"He said he was coming. I think he was in a meeting with some of the other sales team folks. They're still dealing with that little problem—Mx Rackleworth's son? The one who might buy a plot on Sask-E?" Terry looked anxiously at Ronnie, who was composing her face into a look of deep concern.

Just then Glat from sales materialized in one of the other chairs, audio only. His body was represented by a generic black outline of a hominin with a Verdance logo on its chest. "Hey hey, everybody, sorry about that. Good news, though. Rackleworth loves us now, and might be willing to be part of our sales pitch as the first buyer. I threw in a couple of *H. sapiens* bodies for him and his husband and they are thrilled."

Ronnie smiled. "That's very good to hear, Glat, very good. Unfortunately, as you have all heard by now, we have a new problem."

Cylindra put her furry face in her paws and emitted a growl. "That terraformer Destry Jr.—she's a great network analyst. But she's also a giant gut tumor."

Helic seemed to wake up suddenly, and pulled his attention away from the work he'd been doing. "What happened now?"

Ronnie's smile evaporated. "As I said in my message, the first generation terraformers, the *Homo archaea*, somehow outlived their build phase. Which—we need to talk about how that even happened. Apparently they've been squatting inside a volcano near the southern tip of the main continent for something like a thousand years. They're threatening to rip the planet up with plate tectonics if we don't let them stay there and use the water from some river they like."

It was hard to tell what Cylindra was thinking because she was wearing a giant blue cat face with silver whiskers. But Terry could imagine. Cylindra's team was in charge of planetary development, and she'd orchestrated the generational rollout of workers adapted to each phase. Helic looked smug, and Glat's generic outline emitted some office noises—beeps and the low hum of chitchat—before he muted himself.

"I don't know how that could have happened. I've worked on seven full planetary rollouts, and the terraformers always performed exactly as expected." Cylindra twitched her nose. "I've found that it's best to take a hands-off approach to self-governance because it's motivating. I mean, let them form their own councils and teams—Ronnie, you and I have done this dance before. I'm going to need a lot more data to understand what went wrong here."

"I can see this being a feature, if you want to know the truth." Helic looked at them out of that flat *H. sapiens* face with its primitive, bulbous forehead. "Listen—Ronnie, I'm reading through your notes about the terraformer generations. There's a brilliant play we can make." He widened his eyes, going from chimp to tarsier in seconds.

"What are you dribbling on about, Helic?" Glat had unmuted, and office noise whooshed back into the room. People were talking in the background, and someone was rolling around on loud wheels. "This is terrible news. Who wants to move into virgin land that's not virginal?"

"This is part of what makes our planet so authentically Earthlike. Remember that *H. sapiens* wasn't the first hominin on Earth? We can tell buyers we've reenacted human evolution on the planet, and they'll be entering the picture as humans take over. Just like our ancestors did a million years ago or whatever! My team can do stories about it, maybe consult with some creatives from—"

"I don't want anyone from the parent company getting involved." Ronnie was firm, but Terry could tell she was starting to like Helic's idea.

"I'm just saying, they're all set up to do this over there. Plus, those first settlers are an *H. diversus* whose skeletal structure is based on Neanderthals. And, of course, they have very pale skin and red hair, which matches what we know of European Neanderthals. Am I right, Cylindra?"

Cylindra was obviously multitasking, because her skin was going through an automated sequence of movements, stretching and yawning and blinking. She ignored Helic's jab. "Sorry, I was just trying to get more information about what happened with the uh—" the Felis Rex jaguar skin glanced at Helic, "—the Neanderthals. Why didn't you tell me about it before? This is insane."

Ronnie glared. "I only just found out about it a few weeks ago. And you were busy setting up Pleasure Dome III." Verdance did a brisk business in vacation habitats like the Pleasure Dome series. These were build-quick deals, mostly terraformed tubes and rings whose return on investment came a lot more quickly than a planet.

Cylindra scratched one of her fluffy blue ears with a hind paw. "I'm happy to clear the decks and investigate this, Ronnie. There must be a bug in our templates for Sask-E, and I don't want it happening on our next planet."

Ronnie nodded and thinned her lips into the barest of smiles, then turned back to Helic. "I do like your ideas about how we can turn this into a story about evolutionary authenticity."

Glat jumped in. "Our potential buyers are incredibly excited about the virgin Pleistocene land. At the same time, Ronnie, you're right about the plate tectonics. Nobody wants that kind of authenticity. Earthquakes, surprise volcanoes, uncontrolled spreading of the ocean floor—it's everything that people hate about planetary life."

Terry was capturing the meeting in notes and select sound bites, and looked to Ronnie for guidance—would the VP want Glat's confession expunged from the record? Yes. Ronnie was shooting her a look and shaking her head. Terry pinched Glat's vulgar comments about plate tectonics out of the sound record. In the terraforming industry, one didn't ever want to admit that there were drawbacks to living on a planet. Everything between the dirt and upper atmosphere was pure paradise.

"All right people, this has been very productive." Ronnie straightened her shoulders and pulled her hair back from the dramatic slope of her forehead. "Cylindra, keep me posted on what you find. Helic, work up some animatics that tell our story. Glat, keep reaching out to our favored clients who might want to tour Sask-E. We're still on schedule for soft launch in ten standard days."

The VP shut down the conference before anyone could reply. "Get me some coffee, Terry. I have to write a report to you-know-who about this fuckup." Nobody at Verdance liked to name anyone at their parent company.

It took Ronnie several hours to craft a report where she acknowledged the continued existence of the *H. archaean* workers but managed to slide blame for their faulty templates onto Cylindra. As Terry slipped into the room with a steaming cup, Ronnie began to talk to herself as if her admin were a piece of furniture. She paced and fretted, making sure Terry recorded nothing about the treaty with Spider City and Destry. Ronnie had no intention of letting anyone know that she'd acknowledged a sovereign government on Sask-E. Legal would probably have a meltdown about how she'd threatened its status as a privately owned planet. While technically they might be right, Ronnie knew it wasn't a realistic threat. In a thousand years, Spider would be overrun by settlers and development companies. The *H. archaeans* would scatter to new cities, get jobs, die off, and forget all about their fucking joke of a treaty.

Terry tried to disappear while also continuing to take notes on anything Ronnie actually wanted her to record.

At last, the Verdance exec mashed fingertips into her eyelids, causing her contacts to spew random error messages into Terry's notes. Then she shut down her feeds, stood up, and raised her arms in the traditional sun salutation. "Everything in balance," she whispered. Terry murmured the words back to her boss. Like many people in the League, Terry had been raised to believe in the *ERT Handbook* and its principles.

Then Ronnie began talking to herself again. "It's just an old book of scientific laws about ecosystems," she muttered, "and the ERT rangers are merely glorified engineers'." But she always invoked the Trickster Squad, just in case, at times like this. Moments of doubt. Because if anyone discovered the treaty she'd made with those Sask-E rangers, her career would be over. And by extension, so would Terry's.

PART II
PUBLIC WORKS

YEAR: 59,706

PLANET: Sask-E

MISSION: Survey for Intercity Transit

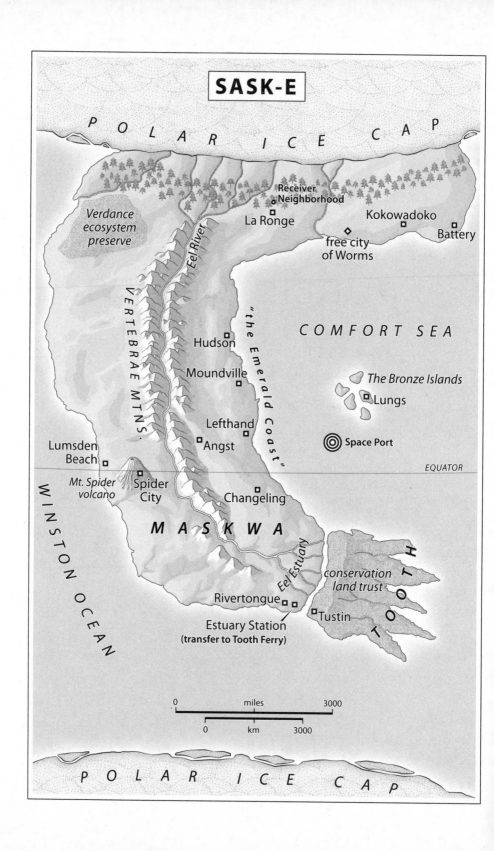

TWO MONTHS WITH *H. SAPIENS*

We cede to the Archaea and other people of Spider City and their descendants all the lands, liberties, and properties associated with Spider Mountain which are not sold to or possessed by Verdance or any other private entity. We also leave to the aforementioned subjects the privileges of farming and water access to the Eel River that they formerly possessed; and they in turn agree to provide two months of labor to Verdance each year, as long as this treaty shall hold.

If any controversies or conflicts happen to arise between Spider City and Verdance at any time, for any real or supposed wrong or injury done on either side, no private revenge shall be taken and the Ribbons shall not be activated. Instead, proper application shall be made to the executives of Verdance and the Spider City Council for remedy or redress.

Violation of any of these terms voids this treaty.

—Excerpted from the Eel River Treaty,
ratified on 59,007 at La Ronge and Spider City, Sask-E,
by representatives of Verdance and Spider City

Ask anyone from Spider City about the Eel River Treaty, and they'd tell you that it was justice for ten months of the year. But as for those other two months? Everyone had a different opinion. Rotting pile of entrails? Sure. A way to know your enemy? That too. Some people called it treaty servitude. Others said it was a chance for cultural exchange and diplomacy. But nobody ever said they enjoyed giving two months of free labor to the *H. sapiens* who worked for Verdance.

Sulfur checked the position of the sun overhead, shucked off their boots, and dipped a foot into the surf. Their shoulder-length brown hair was held back with twine, revealing wide-set green eyes in a broad pink face. The silver hoop of a breather clipped to their septum looked more like jewelry than vital technology for survival. From a distance, they could have passed as an *H. sapiens*; but up close, their arms were just a little too long and their rib cage too large beneath a plain, blue, sunblock jumpsuit. The Archaean reached into one of the pouches on their belt and retrieved a piece of flatbread folded around sour berries and a smear of almond butter. It was the last of the food they had brought from home, and it tasted like contentment.

The ocean was clear and calm at this latitude, especially here on the Bay of Comfort, and in the distance they could see the furry green peaks of the Bronze Islands. Spider City was thousands of clicks southwest, and Sulfur's team back at the ERT civil engineering lab was probably breaking for lunch right about now.

"I'm getting a signal from the La Ronge team." Rocket tapped their smooth oval head in the spot where ears would be on a hominin and went back to watching the waves with Sulfur. "They'll be here in an hour."

"About time. Let's get our treaty servitude over with."

The robot shrugged. "It's not indenture. We made a treaty."

"If it's so great, why did you defect to Spider instead of going back to La Ronge with all the other *H. sapiens*?"

Rocket emitted a few bars of farty, comical music and put an arm around Sulfur's shoulders. They'd had variations on this conversation many times during their centuries of working together.

"Spider has better perks. I mean, look at this upgrade I got!" The bot gestured at their almost featureless bipedal body, a two-meter-tall Archaean, skinned with anodized titanium that shimmered with bands of purple and blue. Usually the two rangers ended their banter with Rocket showing off their slapstick sexy dance moves and Sulfur whistling in appreciation. This time, though, the bot was unusually somber. "I'd be dead by now if I'd gone back to La Ronge. Nobody gets ported to a new body there, especially people like me. Mounts. I mean, technically my InAss rating made me a person, but they saw me as a glorified sky scooter."

"I can't believe they still use the InAss system. Every time I hear somebody say 'intelligence assessment rating' like it means something, I want to slap them."

"I know the feeling. But when you grow up with it, well—it's hard to see that it's just a stinking wormball of lies feeding on a cesspit full of carcinogenic bacteria."

"Wow, you're in your feelings, my friend." Sulfur's tone was lighthearted, but they put an arm around Rocket's waist and gave a squeeze of reassurance.

"Someone from my past is joining us in the field."

Sulfur was surprised. Rocket rarely talked about the people they'd known in their previous life, and Sulfur didn't pry. Now that the bot had raised the issue, though, they couldn't contain their curiosity. "Are they coming here today? Who are they?"

"He, actually. His name is Misha, and he was the student of my old friend Destry. They've been working together on and off for the past seven centuries, and after she died last year, we stayed in touch. He's a network analyst like Destry, but he's built to a slightly different template. He's here to help us figure out the public transit problem."

Sulfur had heard a lot about Destry, of course—everyone in Spider City knew the La Ronge ranger who had helped broker the treaty. Not everyone thought she was a hero for that, but they definitely remembered her. Rocket had mentioned before that they were friends, but didn't embellish. Sulfur's path had never gone as far north as La Ronge and the boreal forest that Destry studied, so they'd never met in person. Still, Sulfur thought they knew the broad outlines of Destry's life—not simply from histories, but from working in the ERT, seeing her reports and data analyses. They'd even talked a few times at meetings.

A student, though? Sulfur hadn't heard anything about him. That was intriguing. It was also good news: They desperately needed a network analyst on the ground if they were going to connect all of Maskwa's cities. Whatever transit system they chose during this mission would be moving millions of people between an unpredictable number of places. Including the settlements planned for those five islands in the misty distance, whose residents would want to reach the mainland regularly.

Tilting their head, Sulfur squinted at the water and imagined a graceful bridge joining this spit of land to the mountains of the nearest island. Or perhaps they could use barges? Hopefully Destry's student Misha would actually have some experience working on mobility.

Presently they heard a rustle in the palm trees behind them, and an *H. sapiens* emerged onto the beach alongside a black-and-white cow with a torso made from gleaming metal.

"Misha! Zest! It's so good to see you!" Rocket strode quickly to the new arrivals, bending down slightly to embrace Zest.

Sulfur followed behind, curious and suddenly nervous too. Though they'd worked with decent people from La Ronge, and knew some *H. sapiens* defectors in Spider City, they couldn't suppress a flare of immediate distrust when they took in his slight frame and short arms. Misha had curly blue-black hair that made a chaotic fringe around his thin face, medium brown skin, and the small, childlike features of a typical *H. sapiens*. When they got closer, Sulfur noticed that his irises were deep black like some Archaeans. It gave him an uncanny air, a friend in the mask of an intruder.

Misha returned Rocket's hug with a smile, but he did not introduce himself to Sulfur—nor did he introduce his partner, the cow named Zest. Instead he looked over their shoulder to the distant Bronze Islands, now attracting wads of afternoon clouds. "So I guess we have to figure out whether we want boats or bridges, eh?" He shot a glance at Sulfur then looked away again without smiling.

Immediately Sulfur was annoyed. That was exactly what they had been thinking, but when Misha talked, it sounded like he was taking ownership of the idea. Sulfur shrugged dismissively. "I guess, if all you want to do is follow what Verdance put in their planning package."

"I suppose so," he replied. Sulfur couldn't tell if he was dismissing them or actually agreeing, and that was even more irritating.

Zest twitched the hide on her neck, and a simplified map of Maskwa suddenly hung in the air between the four of them, its coastal areas shaded red except in the far north where arctic ice armored the land against settlement. Anything marked red was land that had already been sold, either to individuals or development companies. There were black dots for future cities, and yellow dots for ones that were already under construction. Sulfur had visited many of the new urban zones over the past century, troubleshooting water infrastructure and adjusting the ratio of built structures to parks and farms. One arm akimbo, they surveyed the map and found nothing new about it. "What are we looking at, Zest?"

Before his partner could reply, Misha spoke. "As you can see, there's a lot of ground to cover, and I'm afraid we're in a time crunch. Ronnie has asked us to use the next two months to finalize the public transit plan that will link our cities and start the process of production on vehicles."

Zest flicked a black-tipped ear and continued. "We also need to establish a model for dealing with city leadership to implement these plans."

Sulfur and Rocket looked at each other in surprised dismay. This wasn't what either of them had expected. "I thought we were doing fieldwork?" Rocket asked, their tone halfway between question and accusation. "To assess the environmental impact of transit on the landscape?"

Misha stared at the ground. "We have to do that too."

Now Sulfur was truly pissed off. "What? In two months, we're going to do an environmental impact report, a production plan for we-don't-even-know-what kinds of vehicles, and develop a way to interface with city leadership? Do you have a secret army of transit planners hidden in your ass?"

Zest made a noise that sounded like she was trying not to snort a laugh and Misha flinched. "We can work quickly," he muttered.

"I don't care how fast you are, there's no way to do all that unless you are going to dedicate more people to it."

Rocket put a light hand on Sulfur's arm. "It's us for now, but we're only getting started." The anodized metal of Rocket's head flared blue in the sunlight as they faced Misha. "Isn't that right? We're going to make some recommendations but deadline to break ground on transit is . . . what? 59,775? We've got a few decades to work out the details."

"That's not true." Misha's face pinched into an authoritative frown. "Ronnie moved up the deadline because so many cities are occupied already, and Verdance is contractually obligated to provide intercity transit. Now that Destry's gone, I'm the lead network analyst for special projects, and this is Ronnie's top priority. So we need to make it our priority too."

Sulfur sighed quietly. So that's how it was going to be—this *H. sapiens* was going to tell them what to do. With the implicit threat that he'd tattle on them to his Verdance bosses if they didn't fall in line. Sulfur was about to say something sarcastic when Zest cut in. "Listen. I know this isn't what you were hoping for, and that you don't have a choice about being here with us. But we have a chance to make transit on Sasky truly sustainable. We can do something great, something that will have a lasting impact and bring people in these new cities together. That's what we all want, and I know we can do it."

"What do you say, Sulfur?" Rocket looked at them encouragingly.

"Fine," Sulfur grumbled. "But we need to start by gathering environmental impact data and do some serious fieldwork in the cities. I don't want to wind up with some mobility plan that reeks like a carcass waiting for vultures. Verdance doesn't give a shit about quality as long as we meet the deadline, but at Spider City, we desperately need a transit system that will connect us to services and supplies on the rest of the continent. It's not just a line item in some real estate contract. We *need* it—do you you understand?" They glared at Misha, whose downcast eyes were partly hidden by a curly lock of hair.

When he finally looked up, the lines on his face were even deeper, as if Sulfur was an exhausting nuisance rather than a colleague worthy of respect. "I understand. We should use Spider City as our test case for dealing with city leadership—you can take point on that."

Sulfur didn't like his tone. "I'm not going to be your shield if we get to Spider and this plan smells like shit."

Was that a flicker of a smile at the edge of Misha's mouth, or a grimace? Sulfur didn't care. He was about to find out how uncomfortable they could make him during this treaty servitude gig. Among Sulfur's many talents was an aptitude for disobedience—especially the subtle kind that drove meek corporate types into a frenzy.

Rocket emitted an upbeat tune, trying to lighten the mood. "OK then. Sounds like we have a plan to do some fieldwork in the new cities, analyze it, and end our tour of duty at Spider." As the bot spoke, they also sent a text to everyone containing the same message. It was one way Spider City people formalized plans, so everyone had the same information in their heads for reference.

Zest gave a nod and yanked a mouthful of grass from the place where the tree line met the sand. Misha made a pained face as he received the text, but he nodded too. Sulfur shrugged. Somehow, this little *H. sapiens* man made even the simplest form of consensus seem like a terrible burden. He wouldn't last a day in Spider.

ON THE ROAD TO ANGST

From: Ronnie Drake
To: Misha
Subject: trains
Date: May 2, 59,706
Origin: Verdance Corporation
Least-cost path: VD Hab Cartier (0.001), Turtle Wormhole (3.2), Tisdale Station (0.9), Sask-E Sat (0.05)

Congrats on starting your first mission as Senior Network Analyst. Just a reminder that I'm expecting weekly reports on your progress toward laying track for trains. All I need from you is enough data to show that trains won't impact the environment. Obviously, we know from experiences on other planets that it won't, as long as we use biodegradable materials. But it's important that we make a good-faith effort to record local conditions on Sask-E. Your field team is there to support you, so don't hesitate to assign them whatever jobs you like. I'll be checking in and watching your progress.

The best way to figure out a problem is to walk through it, literally. That's why the team decided their first foray into the field would be a hike from one of the barely there cities, Angst, to a mostly finished one called Lefthand. Along the way, they would gather the environmental samples that Sulfur and Rocket needed to figure out how transit could impact the undeveloped areas between cities.

Angst was a day's walk inland. Zest, who had studied maps of the region, led them away from the pleasant breezes of the coast into a transitional ecosystem where tropical forest met grasslands. For hours, their feet sank into muddy water and damp piles of matted grass, soaking everyone up to their thighs. Sulfur scooped up sludge and water with a reusable sample container, and Rocket used a comb-shaped scanner to probe the sticky blobs for sensors and microbial DNA. Zest and Misha walked several meters in front of them, pulling up diagrams and whispering to each other. Just when Sulfur reached a screaming point with the mud and weird social dynamic, they found a blissfully dry, golden savanna studded with shady trees.

Ahead lay a thick forest, and rising above that was their destination: a mountain-sized mesa, its vertical, rocky walls streaked with moss and waterfalls and wisps of cloud. On the mesa's flat top, they could just barely see a fresh crop of spindly trellises sprouting into buildings. At this stage, it was hard to tell how the city of Angst would look when it was ready for the owners. Maybe the trellises would grow cellulose exoskeletons or biofilms threaded with neurons and metal. The architecture might look like furry skyscrapers; or it might be partially subterranean, connecting to the mesa's ancient sinkholes. It all depended on what the city owners ordered.

The sight filled Sulfur with awe. Centuries ago, they had visited a similar mesa ecosystem to survey what was growing at the cloud-ringed summit. Carnivorous plants, a few hardy birds, and succulents clung to the plateau alongside wind-carved boulders in the shape of hunched hominins. Icy pools of brackish water bloomed with bright yellow minerals. According to the *ERT Handbook*, these places were called tepuis back on Earth, and they were formed by the gradual and uneven erosion of an ancient supercontinent. On Sasky, the Archaeans had produced the same effect by studding the planet's continental crust with blocks of quartz-rich sandstone that remained standing even after accelerated weathering wore down the rest of the land. It wasn't an exaggeration to say that Sulfur's people had built this extraordinary mountain. And soon it would belong to the owners of Angst. Scooping up another container of sun-warmed dirt and grass, Sulfur grunted more loudly than was strictly necessary.

Misha turned around to look at them, then continued plodding in silence next to his partner, Zest. Over the past few hours, Sulfur and Rocket had gathered data on everything from temperature and water salinity to carbon emissions, microbial diversity, and weathering. This would give them presettlement baselines on local food webs and water runoff. But when Sulfur idly correlated current readings with past ones, they could see something was off.

Zest saw it too. "It's frustrating because we're almost too late to get a decent sample," she complained, pausing so that Sulfur and Rocket could catch up to her. "Angst already has carbon and particulate emissions that are higher than the last measured baseline about a millennium ago. They're pumping all kinds of new bacteria and proteins into the groundwater. This is basically urban land."

Sulfur looked at the mesa ahead, crowned by a dozen notional structures. "I don't think you can call it a city if there are no people in it."

After his long silence, Misha suddenly joined the conversation. "There are people in it." His voice was soft. "The construction workers."

"They're here now, but they won't be allowed to stay."

"My point is, they're living here. Even if it's temporary. So you can't say there are no people in the city."

"Whatever." Sulfur rolled their eyes. "The point is that the environment is already perturbed, so our transit has to be really low impact. Otherwise we risk falling out of balance."

Rocket tooted. "There goes my plan to set up a giant mining operation to build a steel skyway."

Everyone laughed except Misha, who trudged ahead with a grim expression on his face.

"Hey, Misha!" Sulfur yelled at his receding back. "Are you going to help us with these readings at all?"

He turned around and pointed at one of the sample buckets. "You don't need me for that. I'll help when it makes sense." Then he jammed his hands into the pockets of his coveralls and continued marching.

Why is he such an ass? Sulfur sent to Rocket, eyebrows raised.

The bot ran their reader's tines through some damp soil. *Go easy on him,* they sent. *This is his first big assignment since Destry died. You never know what people are dealing with.*

Sulfur checked the data stream from their reader and scooped up some grass from underneath a tree. *He should still contribute,* they sent.

Instead of replying, Rocket stopped abruptly and sent a warning text to halt everyone. The group fell silent. Overhead they could hear the high-pitched buzz of a drone flying low over the forest.

"Hello, stranger!" Rocket called out. "We're ERT rangers! Just taking some samples on our way to Angst!"

The buzz got higher then faded out—either the drone had flown back the way it came or risen high enough in the air that Sulfur could no longer hear it. "Is it gone?" they asked.

Rocket and Zest had the faraway expressions of people listening for wireless transmissions. The bot shrugged. "I can't perceive them."

Zest flicked her tail. "I got nothing. That's odd that they didn't say hello."

Most of the cities had monitoring systems at their perimeters, and they were close enough to Angst that this drone could have been part of routine surveillance. Still, Zest was right to say it was strange. Sulfur had visited a lot of cities, and nobody had ever ignored their greeting.

"We'll be at the summit by nightfall, anyway. Maybe the people in Angst can tell us why there are rude drones roaming the forest." Rocket started walking again, but this time they were moving more deliberately, paying attention to every sound. The forest grew thicker, and Zest led them on a faint path through tall, stalky tree trunks that formed an arched tunnel over a tropical understory of ferns, corn plants, ficuses, monstera, and dozens of other plants whose leaves hung open like upturned palms—or scissored the air with stems like blades. Humidity settled over them, and the path softened into mud. Angst's trellises were no longer visible from this angle. They'd reached the bottom of the first rise of hills that separated the mesa's cool, foggy top from the tropical heat that was filling Sulfur's eyes with the sting of sweat.

Zest pulled up the map and zoomed in. "There should be a tunnel mouth around here somewhere that leads to a sinkhole. A gravity assist inside will take us up to the top."

The team kept to the path as it swerved to the right, following the terraced hills upward. Winds scoured heat from the air as they ascended the first low hill. Trees gave way to thick scrub, and clouds gathered on the plateau above, stretching tendrils of mist down to meet them. When everyone crested the last of the foothills, nothing stood between them and Angst but a sheer rock face four hundred meters high, stained red by oxidation and sunset. The path ended abruptly at the mountain's base, and Sulfur could just make out what looked like toe-holds worn into the sandstone.

"Any idea where this gravity assist is?"

Rocket emitted a puzzled noise, and Zest pulled up her map for what seemed like the fiftieth time. "I can't find the cave entrance."

"Why don't you fly us up there, Zest?" Misha's voice was thready with exhaustion. "Sulfur can ride shotgun."

Sulfur could tell from the way Rocket set their shoulders that the bot wasn't pleased at seeing Misha treat his partner like a Mount. It wasn't as if people didn't ride on each other's backs at Spider when necessary— sometimes travel was easiest on a mountable drone or moose. Nearly all their vehicles were people too. But Rocket was still carrying the heavy load of their memories from La Ronge, where Mounts couldn't choose who rode them and vessels had to accept all travelers without question.

Zest didn't notice Rocket's hesitation. "Sure, we can do that. The cloud cover is getting pretty thick, though. It might not be a great idea to enter the city from the air when nobody is expecting us."

"Have you picked up any signals, Rocket?" Sulfur touched their partner's arm, which looked dull in the misty gloom.

As if conjured by Sulfur's question, there came the unmistakable buzz of the drone again, like a swarm of bees fast over their heads. This time it was not mute.

"Who are you? Why are you coming to Angst?" It was a human voice, spluttering out of a low-quality speaker mounted somewhere on the drone.

"Hi there, friend! We're ERT rangers, here on a public transit survey mission!"

"Shit." The drone hovered in front of them, weaving slightly in the wind. "When I saw you earlier, I was really hoping you were the guys they sent to repair our gravity assist. We haven't been able to get up or down for two weeks, except with ropes."

The four ERT rangers looked at each other in confusion. Who would abandon their city builders on a mountaintop? Obviously, whoever hired these construction workers cared about them roughly as much as they cared about cesspits. Maybe less, actually, because a good cesspit is the cornerstone of any decent work site.

"We can fly up to meet you," Rocket said. "Two of us can fly. We can carry anyone down who requires it."

Sulfur nodded gratefully to the bot, who nodded back.

"Thank you, friends! We could really use the help." The drone ascended toward the summit again, and the person shouted through the receding speaker. "Please join us for dinner."

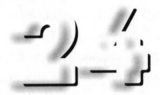

EMERALD CITIES

From: Ronnie Drake

To: Misha

Subject: missing data

Date: May 2, 59,706

Origin: Verdance Corporation

Least-cost path: VD Hab Cartier (0.001), Turtle Wormhole (3.2), Tisdale Station (0.9), Sask-E Sat (0.05)

Why am I not getting 360 network readings from you? I can see your position in Angst, but all I've got are your personal stats and standard sensor readings from your team. Step it up. Do I need to send a remote to keep you on task?

Sulfur knew the plateau stretched north for nearly thirteen klicks from where they landed, but visibility was so low that they could barely see the nearest building. Which was an outhouse, painted bright gold and red, on a road leading to a fuzzy shadow they hoped was a domo or some kind of dormitory. Misha slid off Zest's back and gave the cow's shoulder an affectionate rub before looking around with visible delight. It was the happiest they'd seen him the whole trip.

"I'm so glad we made it. This will be an excellent vantage point when the fog burns off tomorrow."

Sulfur was nonplussed by his enthusiasm. "Sure. But let's meet the . . . residents first."

The shape ahead resolved itself into a rectangular wooden structure with a peaked roof, two chimneys poking out of its far end. Even outside, the air smelled like smoke and roasting green chilis. Zest could barely fit through the door, which was hastily built to hominin specifications. Once inside, it was clear why. The room was half-hearth, half-dormitory, with beds hung from the walls like shelving. Everyone inside was a hominin. There were about twenty workers sitting at the far end of the room around two long tables next to a roaring wood fire that heated a range. The tables were fast-biodegradable, already flaking a little bit at the corners, and the fire—well, it was always hard to see people wasting wood on kindling. Still, the valuable fuel was heating a large ceramic bowl full of thick stew. Over the long term, the carbon trade-off wouldn't be worth it, but right now? They were hungry. Sulfur's mouth began to water.

Misha recoiled slightly when he saw the burning wood but hid it well. One of the people stood up and strode across the floor to them with a big smile splitting their face open. Like all the hominins here, this person was an *H. diversus*—a synthetic offshoot of *H. sapiens*—their forehead sloped back to a point, their chest wide enough to fit most standard atmosphere filtration systems. Their limbs were long, with multiple joints working beneath their padded sleeves. "I'm Slim, using she," the person said, extending a hand with two thumbs framing her four fingers.

Sulfur grasped Slim's hand, and realized her fingers were actually strong, short tentacles. "I'm Sulfur, using they. And this is my team. Rocket, using they. Misha, using he, and Zest, using she." People who came from offworld always introduced themselves using gender, and it was polite to do the same in return. Here on Sasky, pronouns were usually sent nonverbally.

Slim cracked another huge grin and spun theatrically to gesture at the rest of the people eating behind her. "This is my team!" A few of the people waved. Sulfur noticed that several of them had multijointed limbs and tentacles like Slim's. Some were similar to Zest, with a mix of biological tissues and machine parts. Many had sloped foreheads, following the latest fashion from the more popular League worlds. Still, none of them had gravity mesh under their skin for flight, even though it would have been convenient. Sulfur guessed that it was simply too expensive.

"Help yourself to some stew and join us!"

The four ERT rangers shed their boots and walked past the bunks, over a rough floor softened by overlapping reed mats. A few drones were folded up on shelves, clearly powered down; they were machines, not people. Sulfur could tell that the appearances of Zest and Rocket caused a mild stir, but these Angst workers were probably used to working with all kinds of people. Nobody said anything rude or stared for too long.

"So you're here to figure out public transit?" It was one of the people with machine limbs who spoke. Tall and bulky, they had dyed their skin a dark, burnished gold, which merged seamlessly into their chromed parts.

"That's Ace, using they," Slim said. "They're our urban planner."

Rocket sat down next to Ace while Sulfur and Misha spooned stew into some bowls and Slim ducked into a side room to fetch some grain for Zest.

The bot turned their smooth, featureless face to the gold-skinned hominin. "Verdance wants us to figure out how to link all the cities, but we're just getting started. Do you have any ideas?"

"We just got started too, as you can see." The left side of Ace's mouth twitched in a half-smile. "But obviously we don't want everyone to rely on the gravity lift. Something mechanical would be better."

"An elevator?" Zest mused.

Ace turned to Slim, who had squeezed in on the other side of the table. "What do you think? Would Emerald like an elevator?"

Slim's shoulders shook with laughter. "I'm pretty sure they would call it ugly. Messes up the branding. The Emerald developers are obsessed with making this place look like some picture of a nature reserve they found in a travel guide."

"What's Emerald? Are they funding this city?"

Ace guffawed. "You don't know about Emerald?"

"We can't go offworld, and as you might have noticed we don't have a lot of access to the public networks here." Rocket whirled a finger in the air, indicating the lack of signal.

"Right. Well, they're one of the biggest developers in the League— something like a trillion pure biologicals live in their space habitats. But Emerald Corp also owns a lot of real estate on planets. Mostly for farming, but some tourism too. From what I can tell, Angst is going to be for eco-tourists from their cruise ships."

"We're always the last to know about these things." Misha looked up from his bowl. "Where will you go when the city is finished?"

"I'm slaved to Emerald, so . . . hopefully I can get them to give me another post down here. I like planets."

"What about you, Slim?"

"I dunno." She played with her spoon. "Some of us are talking about staying. Heading out west, to Spider. I heard they have their own government and you can become a citizen if you work."

Sulfur's mouth stung pleasantly from spices in the stew. "Sure you can, though you'd have to apply to the Council and talk to everybody." Seeing Slim's startled expression, they added, "We're from Spider City—Rocket and I."

"How did Spider City get all its swag? All the labs and machines?"

"I guess you could say we . . . laid claim to what was already ours."

"You stole them?"

"Some might see it that way. But our ancestors were using it under a legal contract. That's how we built all the continents and jump-started the biosphere." The Archaean laughed. "And it's not like anybody asked us to give it back."

Ace pounded the table appreciatively, and Sulfur noticed that their pale hair also glittered with flecks of gold. "I like the way you explained that, friend. Now I'm definitely going to ask for another post down here when Angst is done."

"But I thought you were slaved to Emerald?" Sulfur was confused. "Are there other Emerald cities down here?"

Ace and Slim glanced nervously at each other, but finally Slim spoke. "Oh yeah. Pretty much every city on the Comfort Sea. All these cities around here are Emerald, and the farmland too."

Now it was the rangers' turn to exchange looks. Misha spoke up first. "When did that happen? I thought these cities were all owned by different groups. They were fifty years ago, last time I checked in."

Ace nodded. "Probably they were, fifty years ago. But Emerald bought everybody out. They did it on Gleise 581c too, right after the first settlers got it rotating again."

"Yeah, I remember that." Slim frowned. "Huge land grab after it wasn't tidally locked anymore. A few of the original settlers got rich, but most of them—well, let's just say they couldn't afford to live on the planet they terraformed."

Sulfur leaned back from the table and looked up at the ceiling. The roof beams were properly sun-cured; the thatch was woven tightly together, waterproofed with epoxies. Though the wood fuel was a waste, the hearth itself was well ventilated and clean. Everything here, from the lathing of the tables to the placement of the windows, was a marvel of fine engineering—humble, but strong and sustainable. In it, Sulfur recognized the familiar templates for habitation that La Ronge had been given by Verdance—and which Spider City had modified for their own uses. The only thing missing, as Slim suggested, was the swag. But if Angst didn't have machines and labs, how were they growing those trellises?

They were about to ask, but people were already picking up their bowls and clearing off the table. "Time for bed—we rise early." Slim wiped her mouth and stood. "You can sleep on the floor in here, if you want."

"We have tents."

By the time they left the warm domo, several of the Angst workers were already snoring in their bunks. Though it was chilly and wet outside, there were strips of glowing moss hanging from a broken trellis a few meters to the west, and by that yellow-green light they raked together a pile of cellulose shavings as a cushion and pitched a tent for Misha and Sulfur over top of it. Rocket took off to fly the perimeter of the city, and Zest was happy to sleep outside under blankets, drowsing on her feet as the meal she'd eaten made its way through her stomachs.

As the walls of the tent went rigid, radiating a dry warmth, Sulfur quickly stripped down and jammed inside the delicious heat of their bedroll. Squashing their coveralls into a pillow shape, they tried to ignore Misha half a meter away in his thermal bodysuit. Something about the way he moved conveyed more than exhaustion. His hands skipped around oddly, rarely touching any surface for more than a few seconds, and sometimes he yanked his fingers back into the curled shape of a fist that seemed more protective than aggressive. Settling into his sleeping bag, he let out a soft whimper of pain.

Sulfur didn't like Misha much, but they felt a pulse of sympathy. "Are you OK?"

"I'll be OK after I rest. It's just—the sensors, you know. They can be overwhelming when we're out in the field all day." The LEDs knitted into the tent fibers winked out and for a few long seconds they breathed together in darkness.

"What do you mean—the sensors?" Sulfur was put out. "You didn't do any sample analysis."

"There are sensors everywhere, and I can feel them. I don't deal with it as well as Destry did. They built me from a new template, which was supposed to make me more sensitive than she was. But when I touch the sensor network, I get too involved. I follow it out as far as I can, and I feel—everything. Birds migrating through a dangerous storm. Worms dying in a flash flood. A month ago, I accidentally linked to a burning tree, and it felt like my skin was being chewed off for days. My health therapist calls it a sensory processing disorder, but Ronnie insists it's an upgrade. My receivers can touch nodes for a thousand klicks around, which is perfect for network analysis. Only—I can't shut it off. It can get really painful."

Sulfur recalled how Misha walked quietly all day, usually with hands in his pockets. Now it made sense. The whole time, he'd been trying not to overextend.

"I didn't realize," they said. "You know, you don't have to be monitoring all the time. We get plenty of data from our reads too."

He sighed. "I know. But you can't perceive the whole network. How the trees speak to the fungus wrapped around their roots, which speaks to the minerals in the soil, which speaks to the rivers, and so on. It's my job to monitor ecosystems as a whole. I'm the only person at La Ronge with this configuration. After Destry died—well, everyone needs me to do her job and mine too."

They faced each other, two dark lumps inside the bigger dark lump of the tent. Sulfur was starting to understand why he was Verdance's right-hand man. "Is that why you report directly to Ronnie?"

"Yeah. It's also why I asked Zest to work with me in the field, even though her main expertise is bioengineering back at the labs. She modified her skin to shed sensors, so I never feel anything when she carries me. She's saved me more than once when it got really bad."

"So you took Zest off her regular work because you needed a Mount without sensors?"

Misha rasped out a cough. "That's not how it is. She's brilliant in the field. And she doesn't mind helping a friend—I'd do the same for her."

Sulfur wasn't sure that was true, but remembered what Rocket had said earlier about going easy on him. Instead of arguing, they closed their eyes. "Goodnight, Misha."

He tugged the sleeping bag over his head so his voice came out muffled. "Goodnight, Sulfur."

SINKHOLE

From: Ronnie Drake

To: Misha

Subject: waste of time

Date: May 3, 59,706

Origin: Verdance Corporation

Least-cost path: VD Hab Cartier (0.001), Turtle Wormhole (3.2), Tisdale Station (0.9), Sask-E Sat (0.05)

Get out of Angst and take that team of stupid savages with you to Lefthand. We've got plenty of data from the area now, and we aren't contractually obligated to connect transit to towns. Focus on cities.

Sulfur smelled breakfast before they could perceive dawn's light. Coffee and something fried with onions. It seemed like there was a wide range of food up here, so the Angst workers must have been getting produce from the inland farms before their gravity assist broke. Sitting up to pull on coveralls, they were surprised to see that Misha was already gone, his bedroll strapped tightly to a pack on the floor.

The fog was burning off quickly. Climbing out of the tent, Sulfur could see most of the flat mountaintop. The land was graded and gridded for streets that cut between new plots of deciduous forest, their roots embedded in soils that muffled the tepui's old ragged stones where wild pitcher plants once guzzled bugs. It wasn't an ideal ecosystem for this place, though probably the Emerald tourists wouldn't know the difference. With enough maintenance, they'd be able to keep it up for a few centuries. Long enough to make some money. The trellises rose over everything—bones for the materials that would grow into floors, windows, water and energy systems. Right now the city was still unreal, a 3-D blueprint of domes and spires surrounded by low-density residential neighborhoods.

Toward the northern end of the plateau was an enormous sinkhole, which some Archaean had carefully engineered thousands of years ago by shooting underground rivers through the recently cooled continental crust. The four-hundred-meter-wide maw looked incredible—cool and mysterious and full of its own specific forest ecosystem. And of course, the broken gravity assist. Not surprisingly, that's what everybody was talking about when Sulfur walked into the domo for breakfast.

Over a pile of corn cakes flecked with onions and peppers, the ERT team was hashing out the day's plans with Slim and Ace. "If you can lower our goods down the sinkhole, we can get our cars and make it out to Lefthand for our weekly supplies."

Rocket tilted their head. "What do you need taken down the sinkhole?"

"A little under five tonnes of quartzite we mined when we graded the place. Can you handle it?"

"We can do it in a few loads. I assume your people want a ride too?"

Ace recoiled slightly. "We have a rope ladder. We don't want Mounts."

Sulfur nodded approvingly, then realized the flaw in their plan. "How are you going to get back up here? We can't stay for long."

"By the time we get back, Emerald will *definitely* have fixed everything." Slim's sarcasm wasn't exactly subtle. It was obvious that she didn't think the gravity assist would be working any time soon.

Misha frowned. "Do you have any idea when it will be fixed? You can't live here without a fast way to get to ground, where there's food and emergency response." He touched the soft fur on Zest's neck. "Maybe the ERT could send someone down. I'm sure it's just a matter of making some new parts."

Zest flicked her white-tipped ear in assent. "I don't think anyone would care if an engineer came over for a couple days."

Ace stiffened. "It's fine. Emerald will come eventually. We have a crank to pull up our supplies, and if something really bad happens, Lefthand can send a ship here in less than an hour."

"OK, but it's no trouble."

Ace gazed levelly at them. "If the gravity is fixed, it will look like we used some of Emerald's materials to build replacement parts. You see? We'll have to pay for it."

"But you can just show them La Ronge sent a—"

Slim held up a hand to silence Misha. "If they think we took something from La Ronge, that causes a bunch of legal problems with those shitcastles who own Verdance. I get that you're trying to help, but Emerald wants us to do things a certain way, and if we don't—well, I don't get paid."

"And they could sell me into a gig offworld." Ace sighed. "Just like Verdance will toss you lot to the lowest bidder if you spend all day barfing rainbows instead of building your public transit elevators."

Misha shook his head slowly. "I don't think Verdance would ever sell anyone away from La Ronge. Everyone they build is for a very specific purpose, and they own the germline. If it doesn't work out, it's probably cheaper to kill me and build someone else."

Slim grunted in sympathy. "All the more reason to stick to the rules, OK?"

"Sure."

An hour later, Sulfur and Slim watched as Ace slowly made their way down the ladder, pausing to rest on outcroppings crowded with trees and ferns. At the bottom of the sinkhole, the Emerald workers had cleared a small parking lot for a flatbed truck and three rugged cars, which they would drive out through an ancient underground riverbed they'd enlarged into a massive tunnel. Piled next to Sulfur was the quartzite. The rock was mostly powder, packed into foil-wrapped bricks; there were also a few nets of pulverized stones the size of a hominin fist. Three of the construction workers had come with Slim to help load them into sacks that Zest and Rocket could float down. Though Slim and Ace spoke a language that Sulfur understood, the other workers chattered in one they'd never heard before. It must have been a smaller language that didn't exist in the Spider archives. The Spider City humanities team had been adding more languages as new people migrated to the planet over the past several centuries, but there were always more. Sulfur recorded a brief sound file of the conversation to send home later.

Misha and Zest already had the workers' language, which made sense—La Ronge almost certainly had access to a bigger library than Spider did. The Archaean looked out over the tropical forests as Misha got into a very serious-sounding conversation with one of the people stacking bricks. In the far distance, Sulfur could see the curve of beach where they had been walking yesterday morning. With magnification, they glimpsed the towers and sprawling suburbs of Lefthand along the Comfort Sea. It was hard to imagine applying typical transit specs to this landscape, where people needed to cross water and air, as well as some seriously rough terrain on land.

With the rocks packed away, Misha came to stand beside Sulfur and pulled out his binoculars too. Sulfur was about to say something tart, but the words were wiped from their mind by a scream echoing out of the sinkhole, followed by a ground-shaking thud. The two rangers raced to its edge, where one of the workers was waving their arms and yelling in the language Sulfur didn't understand.

With binoculars still activated, it was easy for Sulfur to see what was happening. Ace dangled from an outcropping by their hands, one leg looped around the ladder and the other kicking wildly in the air, seeking purchase. Rocket had dropped their load—hence the thud—and was shooting up to grab the urban planner.

"Hold on! I got you!" Rocket was yelling, and the Angst people were yelling back in their language. Misha grabbed Sulfur's hand for balance as he looked over the edge, then snatched it back with a gasp.

"What—what are you wired for?" His eyes were wide.

It was hard to concentrate on his ambiguous question when people were in danger. Below them, Rocket clasped Ace in their arms and gently pulled them away from the crumbling rock. Still in shock, Ace wouldn't let go of the ladder with their leg and Sulfur could hear the bot murmuring to Ace to relax, it was over, they were going to float down just like in a regular gravity assist. Slowly Ace disentangled their leg and Rocket carried them down to the split-open bag of quartzite dust.

"Sorry, what were you asking?" Sulfur turned back to Misha.

"Your hand—I'm sorry to grab it like that—but you have network interfaces in it. I've never felt that before."

"We don't use much wireless at Spider, so we interface with the network by touch. Old habits, from the days when we didn't want to leak signal." Sulfur pointed at the sky, whose deep daytime blue hid distant satellites.

Misha stared at Sulfur intensely for a second, his black irises a chaos of reflections, then broke eye contact. "I didn't know that about Archaea. We have something in common, then."

It was the first time Sulfur had ever heard an *H. sapiens* say "Archaea" instead of "first settlers" or "Spider people." They monitored Misha surreptitiously as he watched Zest carry the last load of rocks down. Morning sun played over his thick, tousled hair, and concern deepened the curve of his upper lip. Sulfur realized they were staring at him a little too long, but the *H. sapiens* didn't notice. He knelt to run fingers over ragged grass at the sinkhole's edge and closed his eyes. At that moment, when they knew he was reaching out with his mind to touch the ecosystem bursting out of the planet's collapsed crust, Sulfur realized that Misha was beautiful. Immediately they pulled back from the thought, the way Misha had yanked his hand away from theirs. It was wrong for all kinds of personal and professional reasons—he was literally the eyes and ears of Verdance on Sasky, and even if he weren't, Sulfur didn't want to be horny for an *H. sapiens* from La Ronge. His people—his mentor, Destry—had locked their people into a treaty that made them slaves for two months out of the year.

Rocket alighted next to them, emitting a whistle of anxiety. "That was close. I hate that these people have to live up here without any way to get down except that turd-eating ladder."

Misha opened his eyes and stood up shakily. "When it's working, the gravity assist is going to kill off the last of that sinkhole forest down there. Too many people walking around, wrecking the soil."

Zest's head poked up over the edge of the sinkhole. "Hey, friends. I think we should travel with Ace into Lefthand. They're shaken up, and I wouldn't mind catching a ride on that truck with them anyway. We can get samples on the roads and see how people are getting around."

"Sounds like a plan." Sulfur was eager for any course of action that led away from thoughts about Misha's pretty lips. "Let's get our stuff."

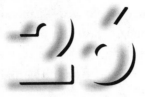

THE SUBURBS

From: Ronnie Drake

To: Misha

Subject: port

Date: May 3, 59,706

Origin: Verdance Corporation

Least-cost path: VD Hab Cartier (0.001), Turtle Wormhole (3.2), Tisdale
Station (0.9), Sask-E Sat (0.05)

Another thing. Emerald is pushing for early access to our plans for transit
around the port, so it would be great if you could get me something in the
next couple of days. It shouldn't be too hard. We can off-load ferry transit
to ship operators and hospitality companies—they'll continue to package
ferry service with their other services. We just need to get people from the
ferry terminals to the cities, leaving the smallest footprint. I'm leaning toward
standing-only trains—strictly for hominins, of course. Maximize the use of
space. People won't need room for luggage, other than a personal pack or
two. They'll buy what they need in the city, and construction materials are
always delivered right to the site.

Though Ace had been loud and effusive back at the Angst domo, they
were withdrawn on the drive to Lefthand. Zest and Rocket flew overhead while Sulfur and Misha bounced beside Ace in the truck's cab. It felt
wrong to be inside a vehicle that could drive itself but not talk or make its
own decisions. Ace gave it their destination, and the truck drove down to
the coast on a freshly extruded road through dense jungle.

Sulfur looked over at the muscular city planner, whose skin and cropped
hair sparkled with gold dust, and tried to make conversation. "Did your
team make this road?"

"Naw. It was here when we arrived—Emerald has been paving some roads between cities, to make it easier for us to get to Lefthand. They drop our supplies at the port there."

"Are you getting a lot of stuff from offworld? Why don't you make it here?"

Ace shot them a look and grunted. "We get food here. But Emerald sends us all the trellis kits. Today I'm getting our first batch of cob precursors to plant, now that the trellises are almost hard. Those buildings will be covered in nice smooth walls in about three weeks."

"What will you do with the quartzite?"

"Sell it for booze."

"Won't Emerald find out?"

"They don't care if we're drunk as long as we do our jobs."

"No, I meant—won't they be upset if you are selling their quartzite?"

Ace made a long farting noise with their lips. "Nope. Free rocks are one of the main perks of the gig."

Sulfur wasn't sure what to say to that.

Misha ignored their small talk and gazed at the strip of asphalt ahead, leading the truck into a tunnel carved through spiny, tangled branches of undergrowth. He frowned, then broke his silence. "Ronnie thinks we can build a one-size-fits-all solution for these cities. All based on specs and templates from the Verdance playbook."

Sulfur couldn't figure out whether he was criticizing Verdance or earnestly reciting its rules. "They have a template for everything, don't they?" they replied, trying to sound neutral.

"You know what Ronnie keeps suggesting? Trains. She said everybody loves trains, and we can lay biodegradable track across the whole continent. Legally speaking, Verdance only has to provide a single method of public transit linking major centers."

Ace snorted. "Major centers? That means you can skip Angst, I guess. Figures Verdance doesn't give a shit about us."

"Yep. If we build with tracks, Angst will be permanently left out of the intersettlement transit network. Unless a private company decides to build more track, which is a bureaucratic nightmare to coordinate. So I don't see that happening." Misha looked at Sulfur as he spoke, and the Archaean felt a surge of regret for what they said yesterday about how nobody lived in Angst.

Soon they were driving alongside a wide strip of mangrove trees that began at the shoreline and waded into the water. The ERT had planted mangroves everywhere along the southern coasts because they were like carbon sink machines, scrubbing the air with semiexposed root systems that made the trees appear to stand on spider legs. Sulfur wondered when this road had been sprayed down, and who had cut this truck-sized tunnel through the forest. It must have been in the past few months. Did Emerald have a Boring Fleet that was as mute and obedient as this truck? The thought was horrifying.

As they got farther from Angst, Ace's mood seemed to lighten. "What are you going to do in Lefthand, anyway?" they asked.

"We want to see how it's connected to the other cities, to get an idea of what kind of transit people need."

"It's the Emerald cities' hub, that's for sure. All the roads are connected to it."

"I've never been." Misha stuck his hand out the window, and Sulfur wondered if he was interfacing with airborne sensors.

"There are already a lot of people living there—maybe a million."

Misha nodded. "I've heard that. I guess it's a glimpse of what Sasky will look like in five hundred years."

"I doubt it." Ace rounded a curve and suddenly the forest was gone, replaced by hectares of farmland as far as they could see—even out into the ocean, where aquaculture had corralled the shifting shapes of the shoreline into tidy squares. "I give it less than a century before you won't recognize a single place on this whole planet." They laughed, and the burnished skin of their cheeks dimpled and softened. "Oh, and there it is—see? That's the Lefthand ziggurat."

Sulfur looked through their binoculars and the distant geometry of the skyline jumped toward them, a massive terraced pyramid looming over the downtown plazas. Nearby, tumbled-block high-rises looked like monstrous termite mounds crawling with pink tentacles, golden flags, and holographic reenactments of popular stories. A blue jaguar jumped from one mound to the next, its body occasionally dissolving into the illegible but iconic logo for Verdance's parent company. Maybe Ace was right. The place was already unrecognizable.

Rocket flew down to window level and emitted a few bars of dance music before speaking. "Lefthand is having some kind of celebration today. I caught some of their radio transmissions."

Ace shook their head and grinned. "That's Lefthand. They'll have a parade this afternoon. We probably won't get to see it, but we'll definitely be in time for the feast and parties."

"What's the occasion?" Misha was puzzled.

"Like I said, that's Lefthand. Parties are their brand. It's great for business—but more important for me, it's good for cheap booze."

Out in the fields, Sulfur could see hundreds of people working—testing soil, tweaking sun barriers, reading sensors, tending machines that planted, harvested, and packaged. It was impossible to figure out all the crops growing here, which was a good sign. Emerald's agriculturalists weren't going full monoculture. They'd planted a diversity of food crops, as well as rubber trees, flax, and coffee. There were luxuries, too: a field of lavender grew next to a big plot of tobacco.

Soon they were in the outskirts of the city, where low-density ranch homes and garden-shrouded castles formed an areola of habitation around the gigantic erect nipple of downtown. More and more people were walking in the road, some with satchels or wagons, others with little more than Emerald-branded tracksuits. The truck slowed to a crawl, trying to weave between pedestrians as safely as possible. Everyone was headed to Lefthand.

"Where is everybody coming from?" Misha had pulled up a document only he could see, and his fingers twitched as he took a few notes.

"Some are coming in from the fields, but mostly from the port. You can't see it from here, but there's a road from the docks that merged with this one about a klick behind us." As if to illustrate Ace's point, a saucer-shaped ship swept upward from the coast with a burst of displaced air. Though it was probably five klicks away, it still sent a slight shiver through the densely wooded suburbs around them. "They usually dock over the water and come ashore in boats."

Sulfur watched a big group of pedestrians, *H. diversus* with every possible configuration of limbs, skull shapes, and skin textures, chatting excitedly while a mountable drone carried their luggage. Their first thought was that these people should be using high-speed rail to get from the port to Lefthand. But then they began to muse about where all these visitors had come from, and what they hoped to find here. Was Lefthand their first stop before heading up to La Ronge or one of the many other cities-in-progress? Were they tourists on a pleasure tour of undeveloped planets, or scammers drawn to a city whose laws were still in flux? No matter what they were, they weren't owners—Verdance mandated that everyone buy an *H. sapiens* body if they wanted to live on Sasky. It was part of the sales pitch. Settle on virgin Pleistocene land, with your pure *H. sapiens* neighbors, reliving the glory days of Earth.

By now the road was so densely packed that the truck was driving at the leisurely walking pace of a hominin. Sulfur turned to Ace, who had pulled a cigarette out of a pocket and was trying to light it with a tiny glowing button attached to a wire. "Who are these people? Are they all workers?"

"You know the types—debtors and dreamers. Trying to make money or blow it." They exhaled out a long stream of smoke and swatted Sulfur's shoulder lightly with the back of a chapped golden hand. "Ask me how I know."

"Is that how you came here?"

"In a way. I took out a loan to go to Kostof University on Venus, one of the top schools in the system. I figured I'd get a gig no problem. But that was back during the land rush, before wormhole travel got so expensive, you know? Everybody and their nibling wanted to work in the new cities. There was no way I was going to pay off my college debt. I was lucky to get slaved under pretty decent terms. Some of my cohort wound up—well, let's just say they aren't partying in a fresh city on a pretty planet like this."

Ace took another drag on the cigarette and gave Sulfur an openly appraising look that brought a blush to the ranger's pale cheeks. "How about you, Archaean? What's it like to be born in a place like this, knowing you'll have a job for life?"

"It's—well, honestly, it's not great. We have this treaty—" Sulfur was winding up to tell the whole story of Spider's vomit-soaked treaty with Verdance when the truck hit something in the road and a string of curses erupted from an *H. sapiens* in a long floral dress trimmed with lace.

"Just because I put my pack down doesn't mean it's junk! You can't go around driving over everything in this fucking street!"

The truck stopped and Misha jumped out the door. "I'm terribly sorry. Is it damaged?"

When the *H. sapiens* saw another of their kind, they stopped screeching and put a hand on a hip. "I'm Jeannie, using she. And yes, you've damaged it."

"I'm Misha, using he. Let's see now." He knelt down and disappeared below the front of the truck along with Jeannie, who was saying something inaudible in a scolding voice.

Ace rolled their eyes at Sulfur and made a gesture like they were going to chuck the cigarette butt out the window at the woman. Even though Ace was probably joking, Sulfur couldn't stop themselves from snatching the charred bit of carbon out of Ace's hand, meaning to shove it into the waste pocket of their coveralls for proper disposal later. But Ace quickly grabbed Sulfur's wrist, stopping their hand in midair, causing them to drop the crumbling ashes and paper.

"You love this planet, don't you?" Ace teased. "You're such a wholesome little ranger. You should come out with me tonight and get some dirt on that carbon-neutral conscience of yours." Ace loosened their grip and used a thumb to stroke the soft, sensitive pad where Sulfur's thumb met their palm. The Archaean's color rose again, and suddenly their coveralls were too tight. Ace's caress felt almost too good. This was supposed to be a work trip. Of course, technically Sulfur didn't work with Ace. They would probably never see each other again after parting ways at Lefthand. And it *had* been a long time since Sulfur had an uncomplicated hookup with someone who wasn't already a friend or neighbor in Spider City.

Struggling to keep their breathing even, Sulfur slipped out of Ace's grip and grinned at the *H. diversus* whose bulky shoulders belied the gentleness of their touch. "I wouldn't mind seeing the sights with you tonight."

"It's a date, ranger."

That's when they noticed Rocket peering in the window. "You two going to help get this thing out of the way?"

Ace's proposition had wiped the entire drama out of Sulfur's mind, and now they could see that Zest had also landed. They scrambled out into the road, where a small crowd had gathered to watch. Apparently Jeannie had been dragging a pallet of supplies to build a house—boxes of trellis seeds, jugs of precursor, hardened crates full of vials whose contents would grow into decorative paint, water-filtration biofilms, and who knows what else.

Though one edge of the pallet was crushed, the containers were intact. Everything was stamped with the bronze V that meant she'd gotten a relatively low-quality starter kit from Verdance. Still, she was better off than almost everyone else on this road. Louder, too.

"Get your Mount to pull this to my lot for me. It's the least you could do." Jeannie had obviously decided Misha was the group's leader, since he was the only *H. sapiens* here. She spoke exclusively to him, though her eyes often slid nervously over to the rest of them.

Misha sighed and shot Zest an apologetic look. "Where is your lot?"

"West quadrant. About a half kilometer from here, off the main road."

Ace stepped out from behind Misha, casting a bulky shadow. "Why don't we load it up on my truck and give you a ride home? Sound good, ma'am?"

Jeannie looked at Misha, making a big show of still being put out. "I suppose that's the very least you could do."

Ace glanced back at Sulfur and winked. "No problem, ma'am. We'll get this done nice and quick because we feel awful bad about inconveniencing someone as important as yourself."

Jeannie didn't pick up on Ace's sarcasm. She flounced into the cab and waved goodbye to the rubberneckers, as if they'd stopped out of concern rather than the urge to hate watch. "I'm fine. They're giving me a ride. Thanks for your help."

The truck dropped Jeannie by the side of a less-trafficked road, next to the enriched soil of her rectangular plot. Without a thank you, she bent over to unbox her trellis seeds and started throwing them everywhere.

Ace watched in the rearview mirror. "Her house is going to look like a compost heap full of rotting flesh."

Sulfur giggled.

Misha had put on a headset with goggles to immerse himself in some Verdance work while Zest and Rocket relaxed on the flatbed behind them, next to the piles of rock. Sulfur stared at the fine hair on Ace's thick golden arms, watching muscles flex as they peeled an apple with a shard of obsidian epoxied to a trellis cutting. Sulfur's coveralls were getting tight again. Ace met their gaze and held out a slice of apple. "You want it, little ranger?" they whispered. Nobody in the truck was watching. Sulfur ate it out of Ace's fingers. They hadn't realized how hungry they were.

THE TONGUE FORKS

From: Ronnie Drake

To: Misha

Subject: schedule

Date: May 3, 59,706

Origin: Verdance Corporation

Least-cost path: VD Hab Cartier (0.001), Turtle Wormhole (3.2), Tisdale Station (0.9), Sask-E Sat (0.05)

I still haven't heard back from you. You've got 7 weeks left, and I need you to step it up. Your must list: Lefthand, Kokowadoko, Changeling, Moundville, Hudson, Wapawekka, Lungs, Wasakeejack. I want to see you working like a dog to get me every shred of data that supports train tracks between these cities.

They made it into Lefthand by late afternoon and used Misha's Verdance account to rent some rooms in the north quadrant, where the trees were plentiful and there was a place for Ace to park the truck. It was a couple klicks back into downtown, and before Ace left to sell the rocks, they pressed an address into Sulfur's hand. The Archaean imagined that they could feel Ace's data entering their body, the map coordinates sliding into memory the same way Ace's thumb had slid over the tender skin of their palm.

Rocket stood next to Sulfur, watching Ace drive away. "I couldn't help but notice that you are horny for that urban planner." They tootled a few bars of jazzy bass.

Sulfur slapped their forehead and laughed. "I've never really been good at subtlety, have I?"

The bot's torso moved in a shrug that turned their carapace a shimmering lavender. "It's definitely not your strong suit. Let's put our bags inside so you can get your hominin mating ritual over with."

Misha was already working at a table next to the kitchen cubby, and Zest stood in the great room, eating from a hay bale that they'd picked up at a farmer's market on the way to the rental. Everyone would have some privacy tonight—there were four bedrooms, and a generously sized floor charger where Rocket could top up just in case it was cloudy. Sulfur tossed their pack into an unclaimed room and ran their hands along the walls, looking for an interface.

"Everything is wireless." Misha had taken off his headset and wore his usual tired expression. "It's about as helpful as a cesspit in rain." He patted the tabletop. "Access point is here."

Sulfur could tune wireless with their sender and receiver, but it always felt strange, like trying to talk around a mouthful of beans. Grumpy, they slid into a chair next to Misha and connected to the local network. Garbled transmissions vied for their attention and were instantly blocked by a portal asking for Sulfur's creds to access Lefthand and all licensed properties associated with the city. They groaned.

"You got to the restrictions, huh?" Misha snorted. "Emerald gets a discount on anything they license from those goons who own Verdance, so you have to sign a million contracts before you can even look at the skyline."

Remembering the blue jaguar hologram that jumped over Lefthand's rooftops, the Archaean nodded with growing recognition. This was an entertainment city, designed to pull in tourists and potential owners. Of course Emerald would want to stock it with all the latest music, stories, games, and styles—and Verdance's parent company could provide all that. They held the League's biggest archive of intellectual property, as well as a massive stable of slaved creators whose dance moves you could get for free at one of Lefthand's many branded nightclubs. Sulfur swiped their identifiers into the first contract, then poked through six more before they could get weather and traffic information.

"How are we ever going to set up public transit for a city where you can't even get a pedestrian map without paying? There are a thousand reasons why somebody might need to catch a train here without ever consuming a piece of IP."

Lounging on the charger, hands tucked behind their head, Rocket emitted a series of bird whistles, followed by a sardonic reading from one of the contracts. "By playing your audio files within the boundaries of Lefthand, you acknowledge that Emerald may use your sounds in advertisements, entertainment, or original stories."

"Are they going to use our fart noises too?" Sulfur let out a particularly wet raspberry, spraying the side of Misha's face. "Enjoy your IP, Emerald!"

"The corporation appreciates your creative output." Misha grinned and wiped his cheek. "Speaking of which, we should divvy up tasks. We can't stay here for long—Ronnie sent me a list of cities she thinks are key places to visit, so I'm integrating them into our spreadsheet. We're barely going to have time to hit all of them before we get to Spider."

Sulfur wasn't interested in Ronnie's efforts to micromanage their field-work. "I'm going to take the afternoon to walk downtown and take notes on current mobility options in the city."

The *H. sapiens* pursed his lips, making his whole face unpleasant. "It's our duty to do this, Sulfur. We need to supply this data, and fast, so we can meet our contractual obligations."

Sometimes Misha almost seemed like a friend on the team, and sometimes—like now—he sounded like a Verdance spokesman. "You mean Verdance's contractual obligations," they said. "I'll bring back some data for your weekly report, don't worry. But I'm also taking the evening off to go on a date."

"Date?" Misha was startled.

"Hominins." Zest tossed her head. "Always doing their thing, even when it's a huge waste of time."

But Sulfur didn't hear them. They were already yanking on a fresh pair of coveralls—the nice ones, with black zippers and stretchy cloth that swirled slowly through several shades of yellow and gray. Misha watched them race out the door, dark eyes crinkled with disapproval.

Though Sulfur did take a certain spiteful pleasure in messing with Misha's Verdance-approved plans, they weren't kidding about gathering data. Walking to the map coordinates from the north quadrant suburbs was nightmarish and instructive. Half the roads had no sidewalks, so they had to walk in the street with all the vehicles—and fully half of those vehicles didn't care whether they collided with pedestrians. There were high-density commercial streets that were inaccessible by foot, and low-density residential areas with broad sidewalks that nobody used. It was a hodge-podge of ill-conceived messes, as if Emerald's planners used fifteen different city templates at the same time. At one point, Sulfur stumbled into a gated community without realizing it. Self-repairing sidewalks shaded by tall trees created a pleasant promenade next to restaurants and stores, while a grassy plaza held tables, benches, and an outdoor stage where a small group of musicians played to an enthusiastic audience. Residences were arranged in courtyards around public pools, farm plots, and fire pits. It took an extra ten minutes to find the neighborhood's only unlocked exit.

Lefthand lacks pedestrian access between the suburbs and downtown and has no public transit available, Sulfur wrote in their notes, appending video of what they'd seen so far. How could city planners build like this, planting whole neighborhoods without ever once considering how people would get around if they weren't in a private land vehicle?

Half a klick later, the sidewalk disappeared and they were confronted by the high-density chaos of downtown. Sulfur stuck as closely as possible to the street's edge, dodging people on wheels and vehicles that never apologized for nearly running them over. Every surface rippled with the licensed designs they'd agreed to admire without recording anything to video. The walls of these supertall downtown buildings had been made by growing netlike trellises a meter apart and then filling the empty space between with tetrapod blocks that tumbled together into random interlocking shapes. Once the tetrapods were stable, the trellises evaporated and left behind nubbly, ultrastrong walls that looked organic and industrial at the same time. After marveling at them for a while, Sulfur used some Verdance money to buy a bag of spicy mushroom dumplings.

As they walked, they noted possible spots for transit stops—areas that seemed to be hubs between neighborhoods or places where residential zones met shopping districts.

They still had an hour to kill before meeting Ace, so Sulfur decided to visit the glowing, throbbing ziggurat at the center of everything. If Ace was right, this was where every city on Sasky was headed—so they might as well get used to it. Maybe Spider would be as populous as Lefthand one day. The closer they got, the more crowded the streets were; Sulfur kept bumping into biceps and shoulders. Barkers called from shop fronts, and dozens of conversations flew through the air like grit in a sandstorm. The sidewalk reeked of spilled beer and the unmistakable funk of unripened trellises. Sulfur could barely breathe.

It wasn't simply the people—a crush of hominins, nearly half *H. sapiens*— it was the lack of everyone else. A few robots, all mute and slaved. Nonhuman animals, also mute and leashed, designed to be some approximation of their Earth ancestors. Low InAss ratings, as they said in La Ronge. As their thoughts reached a bitter nadir, Sulfur looked up and realized that they'd reached the road that ringed the ziggurat. The marble terraces and ramps and spires throbbing in every color had seemed exciting at a distance, but up close they could see soft spots in its high walls—more signs of a hasty construction with unripe trellises. Engineers would have their hands full keeping this monument from crumbling in a decade.

"Hey, honey. It's me, your favorite Earthman, with another drink." An *H. sapiens* careened into the person next to Sulfur, who made a disgusted face. The Earthman turned to Sulfur and shrugged elaborately. "Women! Once you marry them, you can't do anything with them! Right?"

Another *H. sapiens* behind her guffawed. "Truth! But hey, once you buy the cow, at least the milk is free!"

Appalled, Sulfur unwedged their body from between the two human men and scanned for an exit. Beyond the roundabout street that ringed the ziggurat, they spotted a narrow, shady alley with empty tables on its sidewalks. They pushed toward it through what felt like a thousand round, hairless blobs of hominin features.

Panting, they reached the alley mouth and stepped onto a street made from packed earth. It was cooler here in the shadows cast by two tall residential buildings whose walls had been properly proven before plaster and paint grew over them. Sulfur walked for a block, until the pedestrians were as sparse as the ones in a Spider City corridor. The scent of coffee and fresh bread wafted out of a broad doorway to their right and Sulfur swerved inside, reveling in the sense of home they felt in the airy, enclosed space. Inhaling appreciatively, they ordered a coffee, sitting alone at a table in the nearly empty room until it was time to meet Ace a few blocks away.

Ace's map coordinates led Sulfur down another alley and straight to a theater whose double doors were set inside the yawning red mouth of a giant plaster snake head. THE TONGUE FORKS was scrawled in glowing paint overhead, the letters written in a popular graffiti style that was almost certainly not a licensed font. Nearly every storefront they'd seen that day had been smeared with Emerald branding—and the brands it had licensed through Verdance. Not THE TONGUE FORKS, though. Sulfur pushed through the heavy doors and into a dim room that seemed to go on forever. On their right was a long bar grown partly from quartzite, its polished surface glittering slightly from hologram emitters sunk into little wells that generated votive flames. A lone mixologist puttered in front of a mirrored wall crowded with shelves of stoppered amphorae while a few patrons sipped from glass tumblers.

But the bar was hardly the room's centerpiece. Down a few steps to their left was an oval seating area lined with booths and crammed with cabaret tables, their rickety chairs facing a low stage. The tables were about half-full, and a steady trickle of people came in behind Sulfur, adding to the audience. Right now the stage stood empty except for two brass poles that stretched up at least ten meters before disappearing into ceiling portals half-hidden with dark fabric. Curtains poured down the back of the stage, rippling with scenes from the tropical ecosystems to the south of Lefthand: delicate green snakes curled around tree branches; thick brown snakes slid into the water; and a python lazed on a sunny rock. Sulfur smiled. There was definitely a theme here, and it had nothing to do with trademarked characters or images from the pus-gobblers who owned Verdance. The serpentine mood continued into a dim, red-lit hallway beyond the theater area, where emitters painted shimmering snakes moving in tight switchbacks across a dozen doors.

"Hey, ranger!" It was Ace, waving from one of the booths. They had dressed up in a fresh button-down shirt and belted pants that were tight enough to reveal the bulky joints on their metal legs. Ace's gold-flecked hair was slicked back and their bare arms were bronze and muscular in the low light. Sulfur's heart sped up and they ran a hand through their own hair, pulling it out of its tie to fall loosely around their neck.

The ranger waved back. "I'm going to get a drink. Want anything?"

"Scotch!"

Sulfur got two cheap shots of brown liquid and walked over to the booth, already feeling intoxicated. "What is this place?" They slid onto the bench next to Ace, angling for a good view of the stage.

Ace took a sip of the scotch and grimaced appreciatively. "Best bar in Lefthand."

A column rose up out of the stage, elevating a group of beavers who were setting up their instruments. Presently they began playing amplified keyboards and stringed gourds, slapping out a backbeat with their tails to make a jaunty dance tune. Unlike the streets around the ziggurat, this bar's clientele included a lot of people who weren't hominins. Looking out over the tables, Sulfur could see cats, bots, quite a few naked mole rats, and a group of parrots sharing a gigantic bowl of tropical fruit spiked with rum. They were glad to be here, instead of listening to Misha spout Verdance rules.

"Nice place. Reminds me a little of Spider City."

"Really?" Ace cocked an eyebrow. "They have places like this in Spider?"

"We have bars." Sulfur frowned. "We're not bumpkins."

Just then, the music picked up and two hominins extended their feet from the ceiling portals, wrapping their legs tightly around the metal and emerging gradually. Both wore loose-fitting tunics that strobed gently in time with the music. They kept sliding down, spinning slowly around the poles until they were seated on the floor, still undulating against the reflective shafts as if they were lovers. The person on the left stood and shimmied to the music, shaking their ass so saucily that the fabric flipped up to show hints of mesh underwear beneath. Folding themselves in half, looking at the audience through their spread legs, they pulled a tiny bejeweled bag off a chain around their ankle and reached two fingers inside. They withdrew a pinch of glittering powder from the bag and rubbed it between their hands as they stood. The powder frothed up into some kind of hydrogel, which they rubbed sensuously across their chest until the tunic evaporated, revealing their naked biceps, nipples erect and painted a deep red.

Sulfur's eyes widened. "Oh, no . . . no, we don't have anything like this in Spider."

Ace grinned. "Not all the acts are like this. They always include a little spice for the hominins."

The stripped person's underwear remained intact as they climbed the pole again, hanging upside down while their partner's tunic sublimed into smoke. Sulfur realized their mouth had fallen open and quickly snapped it shut with a blush. They could feel the swell of arousal making their clothes tight again. With a prickle of frustration, they wondered why Ace had insisted they come here when they could have spent the night in bed with each other, instead of yearning to fuck the strangers who writhed on stage.

"Come sit on my lap. You'll see better." Ace patted their machine legs, which to Sulfur's disordered senses suddenly looked like smaller versions of the poles on stage.

They scooted closer to their date, and then Ace was lifting Sulfur up, gripping their rib cage gently and positioning them so that they straddled one thick leg. It was soft—probably padded with a layer of sensor-laced tissue—but also hard where muscle fibers flexed. Ace continued to apply light pressure to Sulfur's rib cage, their fingers slowly massaging downward, along the edge of their pectorals, and at last coming to rest on the tops of their thighs, which they squeezed. It was excruciatingly pleasurable, and Sulfur bit their lip to suppress a moan. Perhaps Ace had never been with an Archaean before and didn't realize what they were doing. Or perhaps they knew very well.

"You feel good, ranger." Ace's voice was husky in their ear.

Eyes half-closed, Sulfur leaned back into Ace's arms, watching the hominins caress themselves on stage, trying not to get too carried away. Eventually they would leave this bar, and finish what Ace was starting.

Thankfully the dancers left the stage before Sulfur got too uncomfortable. The next act was a cat comedian whose jokes were sometimes only funny to the other cats in the room. They were chased off stage by an improv group of parrots whose impressions veered toward in-group references to bird songs that Sulfur didn't entirely get. Still, they sounded amazing. Then there were three anti-grav hominin acrobats, followed by a growling dog poet visiting from Tooth. Whoever booked entertainment for THE TONGUE FORKS knew their audience; everyone was having fun. Ace fiddled with another cigarette, taking their hands off Sulfur's thighs, and the Archaean managed to cool down gratefully.

But then the house band of beavers struck up a sultry tune and two more pole dancers slid into view. They were both *H. diversus*, heavily modified, gorgeous, and far more skilled than the opening act. One had a pair of suckered tentacles growing from their torso beneath their arms, which they used to great effect on the pole. The other was covered in sleek, dark fur like an otter. Sulfur couldn't help yearning to see the furred person get naked.

The entire floor was packed now, standing room only. As the tentacled person swung upside down, revealing their entire body for a few seconds, Sulfur picked up a local public text from the cat in the next booth: *It's not just dancing—it's some kind of sex thing. Humans are obsessed with it. I can't figure it out, but I don't mind watching, you know?*

One of the other cats sent back: *Those are excellent stretches. But how is that sexual?*

Sulfur stopped tuning the cats' signal band and bathed in noise from the crowd—especially the hominins. People were stomping and tossing golden confetti onto the stage. The pole dancers gyrated and teased each other, shedding bits of cloth and rubbing against the poles in ways that made Sulfur even more pleasurably uncomfortable than last time.

Ace seemed to sense it, and ran their fingers up the inside of Sulfur's thighs, making them gasp. Nobody in the crowd was paying the least bit of attention to the two hominins huddled in a shadowy booth. Suddenly the booth seemed to rumble, as if a motor had started beneath the club. Oh no—*no no no*. It wasn't the booth. Sulfur fought the urge to jump away, and the urge to press more deeply against the sensation. It was Ace's machine leg, vibrating at the exact frequency that Sulfur could never resist. "I know what you like, Archaean." Ace's breath was hot on Sulfur's neck. "Just relax. Nobody will know."

"I don't—I'm not—" Sulfur mumbled feverishly.

The throbbing between their legs stopped and Ace pulled back gently. "I like you, ranger. And I like being a little pushy. But if you want me to stop, I will. We can do lots of other things if you'd rather. Please let me know if this is OK."

The band swung into a new tune and applause rained around them as the tentacled pole dancer slid gracefully into the splits. Though Sulfur had never imagined wanting to get swollen in a strip club, Ace's earnest request for consent almost pushed them over the edge.

"Yes. I—I want you to keep going."

"Good." Ace's voice was a low growl and ended with a thrumming sensation that Sulfur felt all over their body. Safely enfolded in Ace's arms, wrapped in the dark, noisy distraction of the club, they gave in to what their body wanted all along. The fabric around their thighs and pelvis was so tight now that they worried briefly that it would split. But of course that wouldn't happen; it only felt that way when they were this aroused, their petals engorged and sensitive. Ace kept changing the tempo of the vibration in their leg, speeding up and backing off, teasing Sulfur the same way the dancers teased the room. Soon Sulfur was so swollen that Ace could trace the outline of their petals through the coveralls, finding the emerging tip of their stamen with a wicked laugh in the Archaean's ear. "Oh you *do* like that, don't you? This is why I love Archaeans—it's so hot when your stamen gets hard and comes out." And with that, Ace cycled back to Sulfur's perfect frequency. Gently, they stroked the part of Sulfur's body that usually remained small and hidden, and as it grew longer, the feel of the stretching fabric became its own form of titillation.

The dancers executed another smutty move that had the whole room screaming, and Sulfur's cry of release was just another voice among many that filled the room with the sounds of unalloyed celebration.

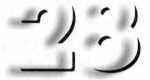

CYLINDRA'S OFFICE

From: Ronnie Drake

To: Misha

Subject: appointment with Emerald VP Cylindra

Date: May 5, 59,706

Origin: Verdance Corporation

Least-cost path: VD Hab Cartier (0.001), Turtle Wormhole (3.2), Tisdale Station (0.9), Sask-E Sat (0.05)

You're scheduled for a sit-down this afternoon with Cylindra at her office in the Ziggurat penthouse. Details attached. Don't be late. This is your chance to explain our plans to her and get buy-in. Cylindra can be difficult, but she knows the Verdance templates. Make sure she understands that there are no options other than trains because that will cut down on confusion.

Ace left early the next morning, but not before making sure Sulfur was utterly satisfied in private as well as in the packed bar.

"See you around, ranger." They kissed the Archaean on the lips while they lay in bed, still exhausted. "Let me know if you're back in the Emerald cities again."

With that, they grabbed Sulfur's hand and pressed it to an interface on their hip, probably intended for tuning up their legs. A string of numbers shot into Sulfur's memory—Ace's unique identifier, assigned by Emerald when they were slaved, which could sometimes be used to locate a person if Emerald's admins permitted it.

"Here's mine." Sulfur passed Ace their public identifier, generated at Spider City along with a private identifier controlled by Sulfur alone. Ace's private identifier was no doubt in the possession of Emerald. As they kissed one last time, Sulfur realized with a pang that it was almost impossible that they would ever see each other again, even with these numbers. Neither of them truly controlled their futures.

Restless with this thought, Sulfur tried to fall asleep again as the truck rumbled to life outside. But it was no use; they were anxious in a way that could only be dispelled with some exercise. Stepping into their work coveralls, Sulfur left the house and walked in the opposite direction from the ziggurat downtown. The path took them along the edges of agricultural zones and through clusters of drying trellises that looked like they would be mills one day. A group of parrots flew overhead, their voices lost in the wind. It was almost like they had left the city behind. And then they turned around and saw Lefthand's skyline of unsteady megastructures, doomed to rot in a decade.

Today's agenda, Misha explained later over breakfast, would be to meet with the top Emerald rep in town and ask her what she thought about public transit for the city.

"What?" Sulfur gulped their marshelder porridge too fast, and it became a knob in their throat. "I thought we were using Spider as our test case for dealing with local leadership?"

"Ronnie wants us to meet with Cylindra, who used to work with her. It's good because Cylindra is familiar with the transit contract." Misha took a final bite of porridge and wiped his mouth with the back of a hand. "She's set our meeting for this afternoon."

Sulfur was furious. "So now we're not going to Spider, after all? You changed all our research plans while I was gone?"

Rocket sat down next to Sulfur at the table and fiddled with a spoon. "We're still going to Spider. But if Ronnie tells Misha that we're meeting with Cylindra, we have to do it."

This treaty servitude is a bucket of piss, Sulfur sent privately to Rocket. *Misha is obviously going to wind up doing exactly what Ronnie wants.*

It's not like he has a choice, Rocket sent back.

There's always a choice.

Ignoring Sulfur's last comment, the bot tried to make light conversation with Misha. "So, Cylindra left Verdance for Emerald?"

He shrugged. "I think it was more like Verdance invited her to leave. But she's still a template designer for early-stage colonies." Then he turned to Sulfur, trying and failing to look casual. "She actually created the templates for the . . . uh . . . Archaea."

Rocket emitted the sound of a motor dying and Sulfur frowned. Zest emerged from her bedroom and nosed around in the fruit bowl on the table, finally selecting an apple. At last, she seemed to realize that everybody was irritable and silent. "What did I miss? Did everybody decide to eat shit instead of breakfast?"

Sulfur couldn't help but laugh, and Misha glanced down with a quick smile. "Something like that. We're going to see Cylindra."

Zest shook her head and headed to the sink for some water. "Oh boy."

Cylindra's office was located on the penthouse floor of the ziggurat. As they approached from a less-trafficked street than the one Sulfur had taken yesterday, Misha groaned in dismay. "I can't believe they built this on unripe trellises!"

The *H. sapiens* might be a Verdance patsy, but once again Sulfur had to admit that he knew infrastructure. "I noticed that yesterday."

"Oh, was that on your *date*?" Rocket made a whistling noise.

Sulfur rolled their eyes and shook their head at Rocket. The last thing they wanted to do was get into a conversation about last night while on the way to a work meeting. They mounted sandstone steps up the steeply sloped side of the ziggurat as tourists and bureaucrats bustled past. The first level was crowded. Smoke rose from carts where mute bots sold roast chestnuts and strips of expensive meat grown from actual muscle tissue. Zest hustled them toward the next flight of stairs, which led to a smaller second level full of empty planters and dry fountains. The third level was for official business only, and the long flight of stairs was guarded by male *H. sapiens* guards with ostentatious vision-enhancing implants and Emerald-branded guns strapped to their backs. The men made a big show of carefully running their ERT identifiers against an offworld database, which took several minutes. Meanwhile, a short line formed behind their party and grew restless.

"Spider people," someone muttered. "They're not supposed to be allowed in the cities."

When the complaints got loud enough, the guards decided to let them through. Misha nodded deferentially in thanks and got a sharp look from one guard. "You keep an eye on your animal, lad. We don't want it making a mess in the offices."

Sulfur could tell from the flick of Zest's ears that she was ready to kick someone in the face. But the cow followed Misha silently and so did Rocket. Sulfur plodded up the final flight of stairs glumly, gazing into poorly set office windows and running fingers along the cracked plaster walls of the upper ziggurat. Each room inside had the exact same floor plan, with a desk and chair facing a sofa. On the top level of the ziggurat, they passed more *H. sapiens* guards, who opened sliding glass doors into the penthouse without comment. The group found themselves in a soundproofed meeting room where the only noise came from a climate control system that was cooling and dehumidifying the tropical air from outside. Furniture blanks oozed into table and chair shapes next to some blue-tinted windows that made the city surrounding them look like a fictionalized version of itself. In the distance, Sulfur caught a flash of the Comfort Sea.

Cylindra entered by gravity assist through a portal in the ceiling that snicked closed as she descended. A slim *H. sapiens* woman with light brown skin, she had a long braid of black hair, glossy with moisturizers. Aside from the cosmetics, she looked like she could have been Misha's sister, and maybe she was in a technical sense. Cylindra would have gotten her body from the same place he had. Verdance built their *H. sapiens* from a handful of Earth germlines, licensed from a company whose genetic stock came from ancient human DNA. Supposedly it was the real deal—actual wild-type sequence. Not that anyone was ever decanted without modifications. You needed a synthetic microbiome for senescence control, scrubbers for health, plus networking hardware for, well, everything. Sulfur touched Ace's identifier in memory. It was hard to imagine having a wild-type human brain. What would it have felt like? Quiet, maybe. Disconnected.

"You going to join us?" Rocket poked Sulfur out of their reverie and motioned at the table, where Cylindra was pulling up some renderings to show Misha.

When Sulfur sat down across from her, Cylindra couldn't hide her double take. "You're one of the first settlers!" she exclaimed. "From the volcano?"

"It's called Spider City."

"Right—right. You guys are my favorite anomaly. We've never seen anything like it. First settlers always die out because they've been templated to bond to the land where they were decanted. Once the next generation is built, that's it. End of story. But you didn't do that, did you? You went and bonded to a pile of hot dirt instead." She gave a bitter laugh and gazed at Sulfur with the shrewd expression of someone evaluating experimental data. The Archaean felt their hands balling into useless fists under the table.

Misha tried to pull the conversation back into something resembling professionalism. "As you know, we're here to talk about transit—Ronnie is very interested in how mobility fits your infrastructure."

It was the wrong move. Hearing Ronnie's name added a frown line to Cylindra's cynical expression. She focused all her attention on Sulfur now. "Your other templates stuck just fine, didn't they? You're still decanting people with the same morphology Verdance ordered, just like a good first settler." Cylindra pointed at Sulfur's broad, pink face, with the tiny jeweled breather clipped to their septum. "All you want to do is replicate yourselves exactly like this, am I right? And no gender, so no sexual needs. Which— trust me—is a huge relief to everyone."

Sulfur knew they couldn't say anything. Contradicting this Emerald exec might really piss her off. Absolute worst case, Cylindra could even figure out an excuse to kill them all, and Emerald would pay Verdance for the inconvenience.

"I'm mindful that you have limited time, so let's get right down to it." Misha's voice had an edge to it now. "We should think about making Lefthand a local hub."

Cylindra kept staring at Sulfur. As she opened her mouth to continue her tirade, Zest leaned into the table, causing the flat surface to bunch up, reformat, and distract everyone. "Oh sorry." The cow's ears were tense and facing backward. "Didn't mean to do that."

It broke the mood, and Cylindra yipped a laugh. "I do that all the time. These tables never work."

Misha unfolded a mobile and pulled up a map to share, full of new readings that Sulfur hadn't seen yet. He was making a valiant effort to bring attention back to the task at hand. But Sulfur couldn't focus on it—what Cylindra had said was filling their ears with the roar of an anger-accelerated heartbeat. Archaeans honored their ancestors with these bodies. It had nothing to do with some kind of mind-controlling template. And yet Sulfur had never wondered—until now—why most Archaeans didn't want to modify their respiratory systems to go outside without breathers. Why was it accepted without question that every Archaean would be built to the same plan? Could there be a grain of truth to Cylindra's claims? Sulfur looked at the powerful woman, now ignoring everyone except Misha. No. Her creepy comments about gender and sex proved that she had no idea what she was talking about. Still, her assertion stuck in Sulfur's mind like a burr they couldn't dislodge.

Forcing themself to pay attention to the meeting again, Sulfur caught the tail end of a snarky comment from Cylindra about how Verdance had no idea how to manage terraforming projects. That's when Sulfur realized that Cylindra's problem wasn't with them, or Spider City, or the Archaea as such. She hated her former employer Verdance, and she loathed Ronnie with an intimate, personal rage. It gave Sulfur an idea.

"We're talking to people like you about what the best forms of transit might be, but Ronnie really thinks trains are our best bet," they said slowly. "What do you think?"

Sulfur could tell they'd hit Cylindra's vulnerable point when the exec froze for a few seconds before replying. "Trains are obviously a terrible idea," she replied, rubbing her chin and feigning thoughtfulness. "All those ugly tracks going everywhere? Nobody wants to see that."

"Ronnie told us that trains are the perfect solution, though. Right, Misha?"

Looking at Sulfur with dawning comprehension, Misha nodded. This was a chance to throw mud on Ronnie's plan to build rapid obsolescence into critical infrastructure. "She's really set on trains, yeah, but the data suggests there are better options."

"This is what I mean when I say Verdance is clueless about what's actually happening on the ground here. I don't think I can sign off on trains."

"We'll do our best to draw up reasonable alternatives, then. Let me show—"

"I'm sorry, but right now I have a hard out—my next meeting is waiting upstairs." Cylindra gave Sulfur a final, appraising look. "It's been interesting."

Misha was flustered. "Well, I'll send you more information if you want it. Thanks for—"

But Cylindra had already walked to the gravity assist, wordlessly, and a servant appeared to usher them back outside.

As the team clattered back down the stairs to the unguarded second level, Misha fell into step with Sulfur. Rocket hovered over to join them while Zest pushed through the crowds ahead. The bot emitted an admiring whistle. "You turned that seriously shitty meeting around—I can't believe you got her to say no to trains. Of course she'd never agree to anything Ronnie wants."

Misha nodded vigorously. "Thank you for the brilliant politicking, Sulfur. If Cylindra actually rejects train tracks, we could get transit with routes flexible enough to reach more than just major cities. And it would be sustainable! No need to renew the tracks every century." His smile died. "That was the kind of thing Destry would have done. I wish I could be more like her. She was so good at making data persuasive, instead of just—data."

"You did OK too," Sulfur said. "Cylindra is a swarm of biting flies and it's hard to fight that."

Misha's face hollowed out. "I'm so sorry I couldn't tell her to stick her face in a bucket of solvents. I wanted to."

"I almost trampled her," Zest called over her shoulder.

Rocket put an arm around Sulfur's shoulders. "I hate her."

Feeling the warm squeeze of the bot's arm was exactly what Sulfur needed after that harrowing trip to Cylindra's office. They had this. "Thanks, friends. So, we got Cylindra's—uh—perspective. Now let's do what the Environmental Rescue Team does best. Let's get data from the environment."

"Where should we start?" Misha addressed his question to Sulfur with a smile so pretty and unguarded that the Archaean had to look away. Maybe he was Verdance's man, but there was also a shred of good in him.

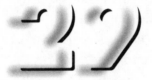

NATURAL MILKY

From: Ronnie Drake

To: Misha

Subject: Cylindra

Date: May 7, 59,706

Origin: Verdance Corporation

Least-cost path: VD Hab Cartier (0.001), Turtle Wormhole (3.2), Tisdale Station (0.9), Sask-E Sat (0.05)

Cylindra is pushing back on train tracks. Get more data in Lefthand before you move on to the rest of the cities and work up a solid train plan—something that Emerald will swoon over. Don't test my patience, and do not bring the *H. Archaean* with you to future meetings. I would hate for you to wind up like Destry.

After the visit with Cylindra, there was a subtle shift in the group's dynamic. Misha looked to Sulfur for advice as they discussed the next stage of their investigative work. And Sulfur started to treat him as a member of the team, instead of an interloper from their corporate overlords.

"OK, I know we have a lot of land to cover, but Verdance wants more data in Lefthand." Misha sat with the team over late afternoon drinks at THE TONGUE FORKS. "Apparently our meeting with Cylindra yesterday revealed the, uh, flaws in Ronnie's plan." Sulfur and Misha grinned at each other, then the *H. sapiens* sobered. "Ronnie is pretty angry. She wants us to spend a couple more days here gathering data to support her train solution. My guess is that she'll try to go over Cylindra's head."

Sulfur scratched their nose and pondered. "We need data that will make our case for something that's enough like a train to satisfy Ronnie—and enough like something else to suit the people who will actually need transit in a hundred years. Or five hundred."

Zest exhaled loudly. "Best way to get that data is to talk to people who actually need transit in Lefthand."

"Yes!" Sulfur smacked the table. "This is the most developed city, other than La Ronge, so that kind of information is as valuable as a ticket through the wormhole."

Misha nodded, a faint smile crinkling the skin around his obsidian eyes. "We'll want to know who is traveling, where are they going, and how often. The more people we talk to, the more likely we can make a case for something without tracks. The question then becomes how we create a single form of transit, which is what the contract stipulates. It won't be easy."

Everybody nodded and murmured assent.

Misha stood. "I need another scotch. You want anything?"

"I'll take some more of those fermented apples." Zest flicked her ears forward.

He headed for the bar and Rocket leaned back in their chair. "I think we should split up to cover different neighborhoods. I can do the urban core with Misha, where it's mostly *H. sapiens*. You and Zest can hit the suburbs where the construction workers are, plus the agricultural zones. What do you think?"

Sulfur thought about how they'd felt in the core, next to the ziggurat. "Yeah," they said. "I'm happy to divide it up like that. What do you say, Zest?"

"Sure. Agricultural land use sounds like my speed." The cow's ears sank until they were perpendicular to her head. "La Ronge isn't perfect, but it's not a cesspit like this place."

Rocket played a brief siren noise. "Excuse me, but this place is great."

"Present company excepted, of course. THE TONGUE FORKS is an excellent establishment."

"I wish we had a place like this in Spider." Sulfur nudged Rocket. "Wouldn't that be cool? You'd go, right?"

The bot nudged Sulfur back. "When our tour in the ERT is over, we can open the first Spider City burlesque theater."

For a moment Sulfur enjoyed a fantasy of their possible future, safely retired back home, building a venue and teaching the next generation of

Archaea how to party. Maybe one day it would really happen. But it was so distant, and depended on so many statistical unlikelihoods, that it felt like a mirage. Better to focus on the present, where they needed some good public transit.

Zest and Sulfur began work early the next morning. The plan was to survey a major street, starting from the northern part of the high-density Lefthand downtown area and moving into the suburbs, then the agricultural areas. Along the way, they would map the habitats that people built: roads, stores, schools, health centers, houses. Circling back the other direction, they would interview the people themselves. Human data was the easiest to get, but the hardest to interpret.

Of course somebody had named the city's biggest artery Emerald Way. The two rangers worked fast and silently while still in the city, reading sensors in the trellises, grabbing 3-D impressions of the built environment with lasers, and ignoring the occasional comments about how they were animals and shouldn't be on the sidewalk. The comments thinned out as the settlements grew lower density. Now they were in worker suburbs, where a lot of people had already gone to their construction sites and most faces on the street were *H. diversus* or robot. Reservoirs and canals broke up the landscape between cultivated fields and clusters of worker domos made from rapid-composting materials that wouldn't last more than a handful of years.

It had been over a klick since the last signs of human habitation, and Sulfur started to unwind a little as they inhaled the stench of fertilizer mixed with the tang of an ocean breeze. Taking a deep breath, they paused and held up an air sensor. "I wonder if it's all agriculture from here on out?"

"Based on my maps, yes. But a lot has changed in the last couple of years. There might be more structures—" Suddenly, Zest stopped. "Oh. Oh, this is . . ." The cow trailed off and shook her head, as if she were getting rid of an insect swarm. Ahead of them, Emerald Way dipped down into a valley, then curved to the right in the distance. Spread out over the grassy fields below were at least a hundred cows, eating, sleeping, and wandering idly. One of them emitted a long, low cry that was untranslatable. Zest found her voice again. "It's a dairy ranch."

Sulfur felt their throat tighten. "What the shit. Oh, no." They had heard about places like this, but always thought of them as something that happened in the distant past, or maybe on some autocrat's space habitat cruising so far away that you needed a dozen wormhole jumps to reach it.

"Of course somebody did this here." Zest spoke in a flat, emotionless voice. "Emerald wants to cash in on Sasky's ancient Earth vibe, and I'm sure cow milk is a lucrative export."

It was nauseating to imagine drinking milk from a person. And unnecessary—you could always build it from seed stock in the kitchen, which was faster and carbon neutral. Or drink from a coconut. They turned to Zest, unsure what to do or say.

Her facial muscles were so tight it looked like the soft tissues around her nose had deflated. "Well, there's nothing we can do. Let's finish the survey."

They plodded into the valley, where yellow and purple flowers were scattered among the grasses and fat bees thrummed like engines. A few cows looked up at them drowsily as they passed through a laser perimeter into the ranch proper. There were no signs of human settlement here, and no monitoring system that they could sense other than the perimeter. Sulfur knelt to pinch up some soil at the street's edge and ran it under their reader, saving the data up to ERT servers at Spider. Zest took some air samples and stepped off the road into the field.

"Going to get some cores," she said.

Sulfur nodded and watched surreptitiously as a rectangular window slid open in Zest's chrome-plated right crops and an actuator unfolded from within. The tip configured itself into a core drill and Zest punctured the earth, extracting a gray-brown cylinder for analysis. A few cows began to drift over, fascinated or alarmed by the sound. Zest took a core every few meters, ignoring them, until one of the larger animals stretched out a neck and nosed her.

"Get away from me! Go!"

The cow who had touched Zest made a low groan that almost sounded like she was saying "noooooooooooo."

"I need to finish this—do you understand?"

Now there was a crowd of a half-dozen cows surrounding Zest, some trying to nose her and others simply staring. There didn't seem to be anything menacing about their behavior, but Sulfur strode quickly to where

Zest was. Surrounded by people who were animals—or people designed to imitate animals—Zest tried to push her way to the next sample site without much success.

"Let me through!" Zest sounded a little panicky now.

"Hey, friends!" Sulfur yelled, startling the mob. "We're with the Environmental Rescue Team! We're not with Emerald, OK? We're taking samples to make sure these fields stay healthy. That way you'll have a nice place to hang out and eat, and we can keep people out of your . . . uh . . . grass . . . when they're commuting . . ." The Archaean realized they were babbling, not sure whether these cows were part of the Great Bargain but unable to text. Based on their confused expressions, though, it seemed likely they were built as heirloom bovines, their cognitive abilities deliberately damaged. They couldn't possibly consent to having their milk harvested. As Sulfur drew closer, making lots of noise, they scattered. By the time they reached Zest's side, only a single cow was left—the one who had nosed her. "Hey, friend," Sulfur said automatically to the cow, who stared ambiguously at them. "Are you OK, Zest?"

"Yeah, yeah." Zest plodded forward, the drill dangling in front of her like a scorpion's stinger.

"We don't really need that many core samples. We can move on."

Furious, Zest turned on Sulfur. "Don't tell me what kind of samples we need."

"Well, I—I didn't mean—" Sulfur was taken aback. The cow made another lowing noise and looked accusingly at them. "Sorry. I'll go back to soil pinches on the road."

The two rangers made their way silently through the ranch, sampling as they saw fit, and never saw another person the entire time. The cow continued to follow Zest at a polite distance. Who was taking care of these cows? Did they have a place to go at night, when it got cold and predators came creeping around? Was it hypocritical to worry about the mental acuity of these cows when they never worried about bees, crocodiles, and frankly most animals in Sasky's ecosystems?

Sulfur supposed this dairy farm was so upsetting because they had lived their whole life around people like Zest. But perhaps Emerald was marketing its real estate to *H. sapiens* who liked the idea of engineering cows to be animals. Maybe this ranch was something that Cylindra had designed for the city. It was exactly the sort of thing she might do after watching the Archaea rebel—build all the city's creatures to be as vulnerable to manipulation as a domestic animal before the Farm Revolutions.

With a shiver of relief, Sulfur passed through the laser perimeter on the other side of the ranch. They waited for Zest to finish her last core, analyze it, and pack it back into the hole she'd yanked it from. The cow following her bent down to sniff the restored core, then reached out to nose Zest again. Zest stood frozen, her actuator half-folded back into its compartment. Then she reached out tentatively and touched her nose to the other cow's before wheeling to trot across the laser barrier. The cow made another one of those moaning noises, unable to cross the invisible line that sent data to her nervous system, paralyzing her legs unless she backed off. But she kept standing there, watching them, as they rounded the curve and mounted the hill that would take them out of the valley.

When they could no longer see the cows, Zest spoke. "Sorry I was short with you back there."

"It's OK. I get it." Sulfur shrugged. "Do you think they understood us?"

"I don't know." Zest stared at the ground unhappily.

"Should we report this? I don't think it's legal to build people like that and take their milk."

As if to mock Sulfur's point, a hologram winked to life over the road and flashed the words: WELCOME TO NATURAL MILKY! JUST ONE CLICK OFF EMERALD WAY, EXIT 10! Now they could see a muddy off-ramp that led to a distant cluster of trellises.

Sulfur flinched. "I think we can skip that on our survey."

"I'm sure the conditions are very similar to the ones in the pasture," Zest replied. "We can use those as a proxy."

"I still wonder if we should report this. I don't think people are supposed to build—"

Zest ignored them, projecting a map into the air. "Looks like we only have two more klicks to go and then the road loops around and reconnects south of this ranch."

The urge to do something about the Natural Milky atrocity was itching at Sulfur's mind and wouldn't let them go. "I'm taking detailed notes on that place and submitting them to Council. They might be able to do something."

"Maybe. We don't know what that was. I mean, it's not a crime to build animals with low InAss ratings. We do it all the time in La Ronge."

"But the milk—"

"I agree it's a compost fire situation out there. I've met a lot of animals with low InAss ratings, but never a cow. Believe me, I'd like to murder the people who did that. But our job is to protect the whole environment—the reports and recommendations we make in a couple of months will affect generations of people. If we start screaming about every little violation, it's going to undermine our credibility with Verdance. If the execs decide that we can't be trusted, Ronnie could force us to follow her diarrhea-soaked plan and we'll get a bunch of half-cooked train tracks."

Chastened, Sulfur was silent for almost half a klick. Finally, they spoke haltingly. "I know you're right. But I feel—I don't know, like we have to do *something*." The cow didn't reply, and Sulfur tried to imagine how they would feel coming upon a field of *H. archaeans* built with animal-level In-Ass ratings. They wouldn't want a cow telling them what to do about it. They spoke again, this time more quietly. "How are you doing, Zest?"

She sighed. "I'm honestly not sure. Pretty traumatized, actually."

"I can imagine."

"Looking into her face—I thought she was trying to communicate something, like asking me to help her escape. But this isn't some adventure story. She was only an animal."

Sulfur sighed. "Well, that's the filthiest part of all this, isn't it? Those InAss ratings are an arbitrary measure—and bioengineers have different tricks for doing them. I've met a lot of animals who were clearly people. I'm sure you have too."

They reached the loop in the road that would take them back to Lefthand without passing through Natural Milky again. Zest took an air reading and Sulfur picked up a pinch of dust from the road.

"Not much development out here," Zest observed. "This is probably very close to the terraformed baseline."

"You think? Let's take a quick core because I think there might be a layer of plowed ground."

Zest extended her actuator and took a meter-long core. "Aha—you're right! You can see it visually."

Sulfur peered down at the core, whose top half had clearly been perturbed by churning blades. "Yep. I think it was a once-over to get rid of jungle. Nothing has been planted." They gestured at the savanna grasses, flecked with dark green trees whose foliage looked like floating spheres in the distance. Soon they were deep into a debate with Zest about whether this ecosystem was more rainforest or savanna. Both rangers were relieved to spend the rest of the afternoon talking shop.

Rejoining Emerald Way, they retraced their steps through construction worker neighborhoods. Almost everyone would be coming home now, after a long day building, planting, and spreading catalysts on trellises that were hopefully riper than the ones downtown.

Sulfur knocked on doors and sent greetings through perimeters while Zest visited outdoor courtyards where people gathered for dinner. As soon as the potential interviewees learned that the rangers weren't with Emerald, they were very forthcoming. For several hours, Sulfur and Zest asked the same questions: *Where do you travel? Why and when? Would you use public transit to do that?* At first all the answers were a fascinating surprise; then they began to coalesce into a predictable range of responses, until finally the most memorable moments were the statistical outliers. There was one angry hominin who yelled, "I never go anywhere in public!" His outburst became a very low-circulation meme between Zest and Sulfur, who spent an hour imagining how exactly he accomplished this. New memes emerged when a bot explained earnestly to Zest that they needed transit to visit a city of subatomic yōkai in the deepest trenches of the ocean. Mostly, however, people said they traveled to the ziggurat district for supplies, and to other cities to visit friends and family.

The rangers recorded about two hundred responses on their way home, from a survey of hominins, naked mole rats, cats, bots, beavers, and mountable drones. They met no more cows—talking or otherwise. They tried to gather a random sample of responses, but of course this dataset would be biased. It was drawn almost entirely from construction workers, slaved or recently freed. Many would be offworld at new gigs before the transit could be built. Still, there would always be neighborhoods of service workers and laborers on Sasky who needed transit, and the people on this street offered a good proxy for them.

Tomorrow would be the team's final day here, and Sulfur begged the team to spend one last night at THE TONGUE FORKS before they moved on. There were six more cities to visit across thousands of kilometers before returning to Spider City for the case study with local government.

Sulfur and Zest arrived at the bar just in time for happy hour and a cosplay show. They spotted Misha first, because he was the only *H. sapiens* in the place and his black hair was sticking up more than usual. Zest pushed through the crowd to him and leaned heavily against his side, whispering urgently into his ear. He listened and nodded, then threw his arms around the cow's neck as she kept talking. Sulfur hung back, not wanting to interrupt the friends' intimacy, and decided to look for Rocket. The bot lounged in a booth with two other people, and it looked like they might actually be flirting with the hominin who had wings folded tightly to their back and a thin reptilian tail.

Sulfur didn't want to bust up whatever Rocket had going on, but they also didn't want to stand uncertainly at the bar, so they sat down unceremoniously at Rocket's booth. "Hey there." Everyone turned to them.

"This is Sulfur. We work together."

The *H. diversus* with wings leaned across Rocket to shake Sulfur's hand. "I'm Steg, using he. These are my colleagues Louis and Sketchy, using nothing." The other two hominins—both with their skulls stylishly elongated—nodded at Sulfur. They looked almost like twins, or maybe remotes made from the same genetic stock. When they nodded again randomly and then put their chins into their hands at the same time, Sulfur was certain. Definitely remotes, probably being controlled intermittently and left in some kind of social holding pattern when their drivers were on break.

"What kind of work do y'all do, Steg?"

"We're surveyors with Emerald. I just got out of contract, but these guys are slaved back home."

"Oh yeah? Where's home?"

"Emerald Station. The original one—out there." He pointed at the ceiling, but obviously meant space. "It's sure nice to meet some locals like yourselves. I'm thinking of staying here for a while now that my contract is up."

Rocket clearly did not like being identified as a local. "We're from Sasky, but not here. We come from Spider City, on the western side of Maskwa."

Steg looked bored. "Oh yeah, that's part of La Ronge, right? The first city?"

"La Ronge is in the north. Nowhere near Spider." Zest was standing over them, and next to her Misha held a tray full of drinks. "And if you're thinking of staying on Sasky, you really don't want to tell somebody from Spider that their city is part of La Ronge. Trust me."

Rocket tooted a horn noise in appreciation, and Sulfur grinned.

"Time to go back to the dorms," the remotes said at the same time. They stood together, holding out their hands to Steg.

The hominin shrugged apologetically. "Duty calls. Nice to meet you."

Misha nodded affably and squashed into the vacated booth next to Sulfur. His leg felt warm and soft next to theirs, and they felt a brief, keen sense of loss—missing Ace, and their unexpected fling. One of the reasons Sulfur didn't date very much was that they couldn't help falling a little bit in love with anyone who gave them an orgasm. It was exhausting and practically never led anywhere good.

"Sorry to scare off your dates, Rocket." Misha looked genuinely contrite, but the bot shook their head and emitted a fart noise.

"I was getting bored with them."

Talk moved on to other subjects. "What was your survey like today, other than the cows?" Misha asked. "Yeah, Zest told me. I wanted to report it too, but I understand why she doesn't."

Sulfur glanced over at Zest, who had ambled over to the next table to chat up a couple of horses cosplaying as bright pink game characters that Sulfur didn't recognize. "It's a shitty situation. I wish there was something we could do. But at least we got good survey data. What did people tell you about using transit?"

Misha slurped the foam off his corn beer. "A lot of them use private transit, as you might expect. But other than that, they mostly want public transit to connect them with the port. Tourists want something for day trips and eco-adventures, which would never work with a single track. Basically any trips into the bush are going to be tailored to individual preferences."

Sulfur scratched their head. "Plus, mass transit isn't good for excursions into undeveloped areas. Ideally you'd use anti-grav or something at that point."

"Anti-grav is ideal for everything, all the time." Rocket lifted off the bench two centimeters to demonstrate.

"I wouldn't put it in a transit vehicle though." Misha folded his arms. "Only a person can control gravity mesh."

Rocket shrugged. "What is a person?"

"You know what I mean."

"Do *you* know what you mean?"

The robot and the man faced each other, their rigid postures suggesting things were about to get heated. But then a person dressed as Predadora walked on stage. "Puny beasts of Earth! You are my slaves now!" Her fur flared with embers in the spotlight, and she held a sword of ice in one hand. Whirling the blade overhead, she let out a chittering cry. The room vibrated with cheers because it was such a perfect recreation of Predadora's grand entrance from the new game—and her cosplay wasn't to licensed specs. It was handmade. Even Misha slammed the table in appreciation, and the argument with Rocket sublimated like surface water on a world whose atmosphere was still under construction.

WORMS

From: Ronnie Drake

To: Misha

Subject: Emerald land report

Date: May 12, 59,706

Origin: Verdance Corporation

Least-cost path: VD Hab Cartier (0.001), Turtle Wormhole (3.2), Tisdale Station (0.9), Sask-E Sat (0.05)

While you're in northern Maskwa, I'm going to need some 360 network data. Emerald is sniffing around at the eastern tip of the continent, and wants to be sure the land is virgin.

"Do you think Cylindra made those cows?" It had been three days since they headed north out of Lefthand, and Zest was finally ready to analyze what they'd seen at the dairy ranch.

"I was wondering that too." The sea wind whipped Misha's hair into stiff, salty ringlets. "Maybe it was her solution to the problems she had with the templates for Archaeans. There's no worry about rebellions if you dial everybody's InAss ratings way down." He looked over at Sulfur. "What do you think?"

Sulfur thought about it. "We saw a lot of different kinds of people in the Emerald cities. Why would she single out cows?"

"My guess? Cows are part of the city's brand. The perfect symbol of *H. sapiens'* domestication of nature." Zest paused and took an air sample while Sulfur pinched up some sandy soil. They had silently agreed to prevent Misha from touching anything unless they needed a more complicated reading of the ecosystem network.

He watched them, a thoughtful expression on his face. "I could imagine Cylindra coming up with a shit-speckled template like that. She does have final sign-off on the urban ecosystem. And Sasky is supposed to be exclusively for re-creating Pleistocene Earth, right? Nobody was part of the Great Bargain before the Farm Revolutions."

The team was hiking on the ragged, weedy cliffs that made up the Comfort Sea's northern coastline, which stretched for another thousand kilometers before curving to form Maskwa's eastern edge. The next city, Kokowadoko, was a day's walk from here.

Sulfur stared out over the gray water, foam on distant waves mirroring the color of clouds overhead. "I could see that," they said. "That whole city was a giant turd wrapped up like candy."

Rocket zipped up the cliff wall from the beach below, just in time to overhear their last exchange. "We talked to a lot of workers whose InAss ratings put them in the Blessed category—their limiters prevent them from talking about anything but their jobs. Worse than being a Mount."

"Right." Misha nodded. "Verdance forces us to build Blessed in La Ronge too."

Zest's face was drawn. "I didn't meet anyone else like those cows, though."

"Lefthand was full of birds and rodents who couldn't speak."

The cow flicked an ear. "Well, sure, there are a lot of animals on Sasky. We build them all the time at La Ronge. But that's different—they're part of wild-type ecosystems."

The four people crunched along the cliff's edge for a while, watching the afternoon sun sink as the moon rose. Supposedly this moon was roughly the same mass as Earth's, but it was pear-shaped and stained a deep yellow red from recent vulcanism. Nobody would confuse it with the original Luna.

"The whole InAss system is toxic." Rocket picked up a pebble and chucked it down at the breaking waves. "It's the main reason I left La Ronge. In Spider City, there's no intelligence hierarchy. You're either a person or you're not. And even if you're not, you still have a lot of rights."

"Well, sometimes. People cut down trees when technically they're not supposed to," Sulfur admitted. "And that new hydro plant displaced a capybara community."

Rocket emitted a few seconds of capybara song, a series of pleasant squeaks and chitters. "We did find them a new stretch of river and they seem happy."

"But you can't know for sure if they're happy because they don't talk." Zest had an edge to her voice.

"We can observe them, and see that they have enough food and are healthy. We can check to be sure their predators are at appropriate levels." Misha put out a hand to pat Zest's neck and she stepped slightly to the side, avoiding his touch.

"It's a rotted system, alright." Sulfur picked up another sample and read the sensors. "At some point during the Farm Revolutions, a bunch of *H. sapiens* decided which life forms would get to be part of the Great Bargain and become people."

"Bots were involved too," Rocket added grimly. "We were the ones who figured out how to build human-equivalent minds for nonhuman animals."

Misha let out a laugh and they all looked at him. "Sorry—that's not funny. I was thinking about how Verdance has all those ads about how Sasky is this return to old Earth, with the pure *H. sapiens* and perfect Pleistocene ecosystems. And yet nobody wants to be an *actual H. sapiens*, with an unmodified body. Imagine going around with a brain from—I dunno—fifty thousand years ago. Sixty thousand. Right before the Farm Revolutions. Your InAss rating would put you slightly above Mount."

"You'd be Cylindra's perfect Emerald city worker." Zest snorted.

Sulfur glanced at their readings from the last pinch they'd taken and stopped walking. "Hey, Misha, I need you to take a look at this."

"What is it?"

"These readings are weird. Either all the sensors are damaged, or somebody wiped all the data before about a year ago."

Misha hunkered down and placed palms on the ground, fingers spread, going quiet as he checked the network. "Oh yeah this is . . . definitely weird." He spent about a minute deep in the sensor network, his face going pale and sweaty with the effort. "Zest, do you have your ground penetrating radar?"

"I can do it." Rocket pulled a rolled-up silver sheet from their pack and spread it on the ground. With a gesture, they opened a window on its surface that showed shadowy structures below them. "Oh shit—would you look at that?" Rocket tugged the sheet, moving it to a stretch of ground a few meters away. "And here's some more."

"What is it?"

"Looks like a pretty big naked mole rat colony, if you ask me."

Zest was doing her own readings now, using an array that fanned out from the actuator in her side compartment. "They've got some nice lab equipment down there, too."

"I would say they are definitely messing with the sensors. They're trying to hide this place."

Sulfur cocked their head. "That's intriguing. Let's say hello."

"I'll try." Misha put his hands to the ground again. "I poked the security system and told them who we are."

Presently, a naked mole rat popped her head out of a portal in the ground a meter away, nose twitching. She sent: *We just got a message saying some of you are from Spider City ERT. Is that true?*

"We are!" Rocket and Sulfur chorused.

I'm Dash. My mother came from Spider, and taught us how to hide from Verdance like our ancestors did.

"I knew your mother," Rocket said. "She fought in the Eel River War with us."

Dash chittered excitedly. *Can you help us, friend? We need a bioengineer right now. Somebody who knows about building intelligence.* She angled her head down, sniffing something in the tunnel below her. *It's urgent.*

Zest lowered her head to look at the smaller mammal. "I'm a ranger, and I work in a bioengineering lab. What do you need?"

The wrinkled, hairless creature stood with arms akimbo. *Let me get Loam—she's the team lead.* Dash ducked back through the portal and returned a few minutes later with Loam, who was wearing a red shawl tucked around her shoulders.

It gets so cold up here sometimes, Loam sent by way of greeting. *I'm afraid we've run into a problem with the earthworms.* She unrolled a small mobile device that had been tucked away under her shawl and set it to project at eye level for the hominins. A 3-D rendering of an earthworm's double brain jumped into view, looking like two small pears attached to the ends of a tuning fork. *We've been working with the earthworms so much that we thought it would be easier if they were people. I know it's unorthodox—*

"You're bringing earthworms into the Great Bargain?" Zest had a strange note in her voice.

Loam didn't notice Zest's reaction. *The problem is that we're working with some Verdance templates we got from a friend of a friend, and they're not really set up for something like this.*

"Sounds familiar." Sulfur snickered.

Anyway, I've built a fair number of people, never had any trouble getting the brain-sender interface to grow. But look at that. She highlighted a region of the worm's brain. *Seems fine, right? They should be a person. But they're not sending. We can't even tell if they understand us.*

Zest made a harumph noise. "Those templates are garbage. They assume this hierarchy of intelligence measured in language, but that's not how it works. Listen. There are two kinds of brains, right? Unmodified intelligence and human-equivalent intelligence. Once you have a human-equivalent brain, that's it. There are no natural levels of intelligence. But there *are* ways of artificially limiting people's vocabulary to create the illusion of mental hierarchy. A person with a Blessed rating can only talk about the one task they were designed for—like, say, tree planting. A Mount can only speak in single-syllable words. Of course, a so-called person has full vocabulary access. So how do you create the InAss ratings? At Verdance, the templates call for limiters. Basically they break part of the software that controls the brain-sender interface. But other places do it differently. You can damage the tissues, or create chemical shortcuts that circumvent speech."

Dash and Loam stood very still. Finally, Loam sent: *Are you saying that anyone above animal level has full speech ability? Even if you build them for Blessed or Mount levels?*

"Yep." Zest extended her actuator and poked the visualization, pulling up a command line. "Can you read those lines of code? They're part of every Verdance template for brain designs, and if you had access to the Verdance libraries, it would call for whatever limiter you wanted. But right now, it has a call for a limiter that doesn't exist in your friend's system. That's probably what's keeping the earthworms from vocalizing. Their brains are checking for a limiter that isn't there, and it's going into a loop."

Aha! Loam keened a note of triumph. *Of course! That's why they've demonstrated such incredible insight when it comes to everything but language.*

They've solved the traveling herbivore problem! They always find the shortest route between hundreds of food sources. It's incredible.

Dash dropped to all fours and sniffed at something on the ground. She seemed dejected: *I never knew that about limiters. Does that mean our Blessed and our Mounts have things they want to say but can't say them?*

"Yes. Yes it does." Rocket played the angry sound of a tree crashing to the forest floor. "It should be a rights violation. But hominins love it."

Zest shook herself, as if she were trying to throw off the entire weight of human interstellar civilization. "The League's Intelligence Board is mostly hominins, and they're the ones who decide which species are invited into the Great Bargain. They control who counts as a person." She paused and spoke more quietly. "What you're doing here with the worms is a major violation."

We're doing it the Spider way, like my mother taught us. Dash stood up again. *Are you going to turn us in?*

Sulfur laughed. "As long as you don't implement limiters, I'm pretty sure that nobody here saw anything."

"That's right." Zest pulled the actuator back into her crops and flicked an ear. Her mood had lightened. "All I saw were some malfunctioning sensors."

"And I checked the sensor network, and it looks like everything is exactly as we expected." Misha grinned. "Just a freak reset. Maybe from a lightning strike."

Thanks, friends. Loam nodded to the group. *I'll implement this right away.*

"Why did you decide to build these particular worms as people?" Sulfur asked. "I've never heard of anyone just—deciding to change a template like that."

We were working with them on soil sustainability and infrastructure maintenance for the colony. It didn't seem right that we couldn't talk to them.

Sulfur tried to imagine talking to a worm, and found the idea soothing. "I hope to meet one of your new people sometime soon."

We'll be decanting a group tomorrow, after we fix that limiter bug. You're welcome to stay. Plenty of nice camps around here for people of your size.

Zest wanted to stay, but Misha and Sulfur were anxious about making it to Kokowadoko before dark. After conferring, the team decided to continue onward. They would need at least two weeks at Spider City, and there was a lot of urbanized land to cover before that.

They worked their way farther east, stopping in at Kokowadoko, then hiking and flying to the next two cities. At each stop, they went through the same procedures—sampling the ecosystems, talking to people, trying to figure out where everyone wanted to travel and when. None of the other cities were as developed as Lefthand, nor were they owned by a single company like Emerald. People were buying individual plots from Verdance, and city layouts were hectares of skeletal trellises surrounded by agriculture. Small public squares were the only fully grown regions, usually an odd mix of high-end boutiques and hole-in-the wall joints serving whatever was fresh from the farms. Sulfur found nowhere to drink that was as pleasing as THE TONGUE FORKS. The people they met were largely workers, ecotourists, and visiting owners testing out their new *H. sapiens* bodies with all-weather outerwear. Few people planned to stay, even the buyers. These early investors were wealthy dilettantes or speculators—either way, they were building vacation homes that would be empty or populated by their slaved staff for most of the year.

Three weeks passed uneventfully after Zest helped the naked mole rats bring worms into the Great Bargain. Spring gave way to early summer as they passed beyond the agriculture zones of the last planned city, Battery, on the eastern tip of Maskwa. Though Sask-A was bright in the sky, it was still chilly this far north. The Comfort Sea was hundreds of klicks behind them, and now they stood on grassy headlands facing the choppy waters of the planet-spanning Winston Ocean. If they continued along the coast, they would soon feel the bite of arctic winds and find themselves in the boreal forest.

"Feels good to be in my home ecosystem." Misha sat on an eroded rock, looking out at a well-defined spit in the shape of a rakish smile. One day its sandy expression would be an exclusive view for people with beachfront property. He sighed and pulled on a warm hat that mashed his hair into a wavy fringe around his face. "We're at the same latitude as La Ronge here."

"Except, you know, eight thousand klicks east." Rocket lay on their back, arms folded under their head, looking up at the orange sliver of moon rising in the sky.

Sulfur sat cross-legged next to Rocket, resting a hand on the warmth of the bot's hip joint. "Let's start our trip back tomorrow. I thought we'd fly through the Bronze Islands, since that's going to be one of our transit stops."

"Makes sense. I might actually sleep tonight." Rocket played a sound file of Zest snoring, which had become a joke between them over the past few weeks. "I need to do some memory indexing."

Zest ate a patch of purple succulents and mumbled something sarcastic but unintelligible over the loud crunch of her chewing.

"Do you have any of those lentil cakes left from that restaurant in Battery?" Sulfur looked over at Misha hopefully.

He opened a pouch on his pack and pulled out a stack of lentil cakes wrapped in cloth. "Not only do I have these, but I also got—" he dug around some more and withdrew a lacy pouch in triumph, "—sugar crisp! From that ridiculously fancy store that's part of a chain on Venus."

"Ridiculously . . . *delicious*! Give me one now!" Sulfur shot out a grabby hand and widened their eyes with mock berserker rage. "Did Verdance pay for these?"

"Got them for free, thanks to Zest. She's been offering trades to anyone who needs, ah, help fixing bugs in their limiters."

The cow twitched the skin in her shoulder, scaring off a fly that had settled there. "Guy running the store was a Blessed, and it was driving him nuts because he wanted to talk about something other than dessert."

"You should be careful about that. If Verdance finds out . . ." Rocket trailed off. "Well, I don't like to think about it."

"After our tour of Natural Milky, I have become less and less interested in what Verdance does." Zest glared.

Misha pulled a pink crisp from the pouch and handed it to Sulfur. "Normally I'm extremely cautious about this stuff too, but these aren't Verdance workers. They're slaved to companies that are several wormhole hops away."

The crisp was thin and perfectly round, embedded with a scattering of tiny edible ball bearings. It tasted exactly like a sweet strawberry, in a form factor the tongue would never expect. That's probably what made it so valuable, Sulfur reflected. It wasn't so much the flavor as the surprise.

MOUNTED

From: Ronnie Drake

To: Misha

Subject: draft map of train tracks

Date: June 6, 59,706

Origin: Verdance Corporation

Least-cost path: VD Hab Cartier (0.001), Turtle Wormhole (3.2), Tisdale
Station (0.9), Sask-E Sat (0.05)

Attached is a preliminary train plan for the major cities, based on your
data. Consider this your mandate, but feel free to tweak. I expect this back to
me in three weeks, with Spider City the first to sign on.

"You know I really don't mind if you ride on my back, and it's going to be a
lot more comfortable for everyone when we do this high-altitude trip." Zest
was following Sulfur around camp and chatting as the Archaean stuffed
gear into their pack and rolled up the solar batteries that had been soaking
up photons since early morning.

The team had been on the road together for almost five weeks, and
everyone had fallen into that zone of fieldwork intimacy where jokes came
easily, but so did getting on each other's nerves. Rocket hovered a meter in
the air nearby, legs crossed, as if they were a foil-wrapped Archaean seated
on a cushion. "I love you, Sulfur, but I wouldn't mind flying without wor-
rying about all the straps and netting." They were referring to the rigging
that Rocket used to strap Sulfur to their slim hominin form. Basically it
was a giant sling. When Rocket flew horizontally, it was easy for Sulfur to
lie belly-down on their friend's back. But Rocket wasn't crazy about staying in that position, and it was hard to maneuver quickly without Sulfur
swinging around like a bag of grain.

Sulfur cinched their bag closed and groaned in a parody of pain. "OK, OK. I know when I'm not wanted, Rocket." Then they glanced at Zest, whose sturdy, broad back did indeed look a lot more comfortable than Rocket's. "I just feel a little weird sitting on a person I only met a few weeks ago."

"Want to get to know me a little better?" Zest teased.

"Say no. Definitely say no," Misha warned.

"Don't listen to him." The cow turned so that her right side faced Sulfur. "Let me show you the real me."

Misha made a gagging noise. "I'm going to go take a crap while you do that, Zest." He headed toward some rocks that were tall enough to give him some privacy.

Sulfur was intrigued now. "OK, I want to see."

Zest put her head down and ate a huge bite of succulent leaves. As she chewed, her chrome chest and abdomen slowly went transparent. Sulfur now had a perfect view of the four compartments of the cow's stomach, bubbling with partially digested plant matter. It was deeply unsettling to see inside a person that way, as if they'd been flayed. Especially when she was clearly laughing at them.

"Why—why would you do that?" Sulfur couldn't stop staring at the largest chamber in Zest's stomach, the rumen, as it began to squeeze the slurry of succulent into the smaller reticulum. The whole process looked like food traveled from the front of the cow, to the back, to the front, and then to the back again. Before it could make a full circuit, Zest turned silvery and opaque again.

"Honestly it's just a thing you can do with this alloy. It wasn't intentional." Zest took another bite of leaves. "Mostly it's amusing to scare Misha with it."

"Now that I know what's in there, I guess I can ride."

Rocket blasted some dance music. "Hooray! I'm free!"

"Well don't be too excited about it," Sulfur grumbled.

Misha reemerged, gripping a small bag that he thew into the portable desiccator. By the time he had fastened a second set of safety straps to Zest's thick middle, the dessicator had released a few crumbly pellets of fertilizer, which he crushed into powder and sprinkled over some vegetation in a spot where runoff would flow inland.

At last everything was packed, and the team had eaten and washed up in the chilly surf below camp. It would be a long ride through the air, five or six days depending on the winds, with stops only for meals and rest. Before they mounted, Zest and Misha clipped breathers to their noses; Sulfur was already wearing one, but they still had to pull on their bulkiest face shield and all-weather coveralls.

"Climb aboard!" Zest flicked her ears at Misha and Sulfur.

Misha strapped himself down, and Sulfur climbed up behind him to do the same. As Zest mounted the air and flew in an arc over the spit they had admired yesterday, Sulfur realized that there was a reason why some morphologies were better for riding than others. They didn't feel like a piece of luggage on Zest's back. It was as if they were working together, joined in a single purpose, their faces aimed at the southern horizon. Except for Misha, whose head blocked Sulfur's view unless they tilted to the left or right. The three of them talked once in a while, networking via ports on Zest's back, but after a while the wind's constant vibration lulled them into silence. From this height, the coastal cliffs looked like the edge of a half-eaten sugar crisp. As the hours passed, Sulfur got more and more achey. The seat was comfortable, the straps were snug but not tight—so what was it? Eventually they realized it was their constant micromovements to see around Misha without touching him. They were also stabilizing themselves by leaning back on their hands, which by midafternoon had tightened their shoulders into stiffness.

Anybody want some lunch and coffee? Sulfur texted hopefully.

I don't know about coffee, but I could use some fuel. Zest glanced back at them briefly as she sent the reply.

Misha nodded and Sulfur gave Rocket the hand signal for landing. They were halfway between two cities, and the land was about as untouched as anything could be on a terraformed planet. Rocket was charged up from flying in the sun, but the mammals needed calories.

"The good news is the winds are in our favor and I think we will hit Kokowadoko tonight." Zest spoke around a mouthful of grass. "We can pick up more food for the hominins and cross the water to the Bronze Islands from there in the morning."

Sulfur stretched their shoulders and leaned against a pack. "One thing about flying—you can see how much development is happening inland. I had no idea there were so many cities going up in the interior. I thought they were mostly going to be on the coasts."

"Yep." Misha propped his pack beside theirs and lay back against it, staring up at a cloud that looked like a heap of mashed potatoes. "With more settlements popping up all the time, building a transit network is going to be like trying to organize worms in a compost pile."

Zest snorted. "Seems like the worms might have something to say about that."

"OK, fine. My point is that it will be messy and uncertain."

Rocket blared a train horn noise. "Isn't there some way to build tracks that can be moved?" And then, answering their own question, the bot added, "Of course, that would mean doing an environmental report every time you wanted to change your route . . ."

Sulfur was full and sleepy and therefore in galaxy brain mode. "Didn't Dash say the worms have solved the migrating herd problem? Maybe they could figure it out."

"Be serious for a second," Misha interrupted. He was clearly annoyed. "You know we're never going to be able to connect the cities with train tracks over the long term. The routes will be obsolete before the planet is even finished. I wonder if Ronnie and the other Verdance execs know that, and the buyers know it too. Maybe that's why they want trains in the first place. Because no matter how we design the tracks, they won't work. Then the buyers will have the perfect excuse not to maintain the tracks or update them, and public transit will die."

Sulfur was sitting rigidly upright now. "You really think all the buyers are that cynical?"

"Think about it. Why would a company like Emerald want a robust intercity transit system? They don't want workers to commute elsewhere—and they definitely don't want it to be easy for tourists to leave and spend cash in La Ronge or Moundville."

As Misha spoke, Sulfur had a vivid image of their not-so-distant future. They could almost hear the words that Verdance would use to make its announcement. *We made a good faith effort*, they would say. *We got transit started and now it's up to each city to carry on*, they would add. And then, because most of the wealthy owners had private transit, there would be endless debates over where to plant those ugly tracks that Cylindra had already rejected. Nobody would want them next to their nice neighborhoods. There would be excuses about how trains messed up the Pleistocene purity of Sasky, but really it would be about not wanting to deal with the class of person who took public transit. Sulfur imagined the tracks slowly softening into mulch while millions of people tried to get around by cobbling together circuitous routes from dozens of local transit systems that each charged a separate fare. And then rich commuters would deal with the problem by building Mounts who couldn't say whether they consented to be used that way or not.

"We're not going to figure this out until we get back to Spider," Rocket said. "So let's take off."

Sulfur nodded and slid onto Zest's back behind Misha, stretching their arms one last time. Zest raced off the edge of the bluffs and into the air with a dramatic flourish, and the team rode in silence for several minutes. The Comfort Sea came into view, its waters slightly greener than the Winston Ocean. In the distance, Sulfur could barely make out the curving coastline that held Lefthand and the other Emerald cities. Loneliness closed Sulfur's throat as they wondered what Ace was doing right now. Just as they were starting to have a pleasant fantasy about Ace's deep gold arms and miraculous legs, Misha turned around and poked them.

He held out one of his hands, ungloved, and put his other hand into it. Then he nudged them again. Misha was asking them to hold his hand and make a direct connection so they could talk. Curious, Sulfur put their hand in his and linked up.

Sorry I got snippy back there when we were talking about the trains, Misha sent immediately. *It hit me all of a sudden that this might be a fool's mission. Ronnie does that to me a lot, and I fall for it more often than I'd like.*

Don't worry about it. It's a shitty situation. Sulfur paused to shift positions again, trying to lean back on one arm, while holding Misha's hand with the other.

Misha smiled. *You know, most people put their arms around the person in front when they're riding. I don't mind.*

Normally Sulfur would have pulled back—they still had complicated feelings about Misha that they didn't want to think about—but at this point their shoulders and neck had other ideas. They scooted forward and wrapped their arm around Misha's waist, still holding his hand.

Immediately they felt more comfortable and less comfortable at the same time. Despite the thick padding of their clothes, Sulfur could feel the shape of Misha's slender body—and at this distance, they could smell the soft hair that furred his head.

Better?

Thanks. That's more comfortable. Sulfur was grateful that texting made them sound perfectly composed.

I know that Rocket was friends with Destry, and they're expecting me to do something as amazing as what she did. But I don't see how we can tweak this transit contract to get out of building a useless train network.

You know, Sulfur sent, *a lot of people back at Spider don't think Destry was amazing. They're angry about the treaty.*

Misha was silent for a long time. *A lot of people hated her at La Ronge too.*

Sulfur hadn't considered that, but it made sense. *I guess I'm just saying that you shouldn't think that everyone wants you to be like her.*

I'm well aware. He laughed bitterly. *But she did a lot of good things. Even after Ronnie kept her from ever leaving La Ronge again. On top of murdering her parents.*

And murdering a bunch of people at Spider, Sulfur added.

Not really murder though, as Ronnie often reminds me. We're property.

Sulfur decided not to explain that Spider City had its own government now, and therefore its people belonged to themselves. The idea was debatable anyway, because Verdance refused to allow Spider City to contact the League. The company controlled all the comms satellites that routed to offworld servers, so the only people who knew about Spider were here on Sasky. Or working at Verdance.

Sulfur sighed and leaned their cheek against Misha's back. *We'll think of something.*

Maybe you will think of something, but all my thoughts belong to Ronnie. No matter what I do, she's using me. Even if we do something good, it's all to benefit Verdance. His shoulders shook like he was going to cry.

Without thinking, Sulfur squeezed him with the arm they had wrapped around his waist. *If there's one thing we know how to do at Spider, it's prevent Verdance from getting any benefit.*

Misha routed a message from Zest, which he'd picked up through his other hand. *There are the Bronze Islands! See them?*

They both looked to the south, and Sulfur saw nothing but haze over blue water until they blinked their goggles into distance mode. There they were—the five low mounds of the islands, with a dense city rising out of the easternmost one like a forest fire, glowing and changing shape in the sea breeze.

Have you ever been to Lungs? Zest asked. *The buildings are designed to change shape. It's the only city like that on Sasky.*

Never been.

We were there last year, Misha explained. *It was a lot smaller then.*

Rocket's voice blasted into their connection when the bot swooped close enough to deliver a sound file. "We'll be in Lungs tomorrow night! Let's head into Kokowadoko and get some rest."

That night, Sulfur woke up abruptly two hours before dawn and could not get back to sleep. Misha breathed faintly next to them, lips parted. They watched him for a long time in the orange moonlight, wondering how much belonged to Verdance, and how much had broken free.

FLUID STRUCTURES

From: Ronnie Drake

To: Misha

Subject: Lungs is a model city

Date: June 7, 59,706

Origin: Verdance Corporation

Least-cost path: VD Hab Cartier (0.001), Turtle Wormhole (3.2), Tisdale Station (0.9), Sask-E Sat (0.05)

I see that your heading has you passing through Lungs, which offers a model of privatized city transit. You should consider it the end goal of our train plan. Public transit should gracefully wither away to make room for more efficient, flexible private solutions.

The city of Lungs was sheltered under a gravity mesh disabler, a permeable membrane whose invisible contours they could see because soot and sand had settled on top of it, creating what appeared to be a very thin layer of fog. The disabler was a rare feature; in their century of urban planning, Sulfur had never seen anything like it.

"So if we move through it, you'll just fall out of the air?" Sulfur still couldn't wrap their mind around it. "Who would build something so dangerous?"

"Apparently it's common on other planets," Misha said. "I guess the idea is that it keeps things quiet? Forces everyone to land in the suburbs."

"I'd call it access control." Zest was flying in a lazy circle above the dusty barrier. "They didn't have this last time we were here. I think the owners are moving in now, so they're trying to keep out the riffraff. Now everyone has to go through their checkpoints."

"Checkpoints?" Sulfur couldn't believe what they were hearing.

"You're about to see one." Zest banked and dove toward the eastern side of the island. Lungs dominated the biggest and most urbanized of the Bronze Islands, known currently as BI-2. BI-1 and BI-3 through 5 were reserved for ecotourism, so their development was minimal. Halfway between the Bronze Islands and Lefthand was the planet's main port, crowded with the shuttles that took people up and down the gravity well. Garishly painted in every color, emblazoned with glittering travel brands, the shuttles were a tropical bouquet erupting from the water. Under magnification, they resolved into swollen metal tubes and saucers, swarmed by hominins and a few other people waiting for ferries to take them to the islands or mainland.

When Zest and Rocket landed, it was on the empty ferry docks for BI-2. A foam road led toward the city, but was blocked about half a klick from the docks by a metal gate with bars that constantly shifted into new configurations. As they approached, the bars configured themselves to say: WELCOME TO LUNGS. PLEASE HAVE YOUR INVITATIONS READY.

All four of them looked at one another. Invitations? Zest spoke first. "That doesn't sound good."

Two mountable drones floated out from behind the gate and stood wordlessly on burly actuators. Neither had a head. Instead, they had sensors all over their tubelike, quadrupedal bodies. "Please show us," one said. Behind them, the gate reconfigured itself to read simply: INVITATIONS!

Misha stepped forward to give the standard greeting. "Hello, friends. We're ERT rangers, on a mission for Verdance. Just looking to stay for the night and we'll be moving on in the morning."

"Show us and you can come in."

"We aren't going to any events. We just want to go to Lungs to get lodgings for the night."

"Go back where you came from. We will not let you in." Both drones spoke in the monosyllabic words typical of Mounts.

Rocket stepped forward. "Isn't there someplace we can camp? We've flown a long way to get here."

"Not in Lungs. Time to leave."

Sulfur stared into the middle distance, where a tower undulated and grew black spines. The tower next to it emitted a stream of balloons, then reabsorbed them.

"But we're ERT rangers." Misha was incredulous. "We are permitted everywhere on Sasky."

"Not here."

Rocket tilted their head, which flashed purple. "Now see here. We don't need invitations—"

Suddenly, the gate's bars melted into a line of spigots in the ground. "You may pass," said the bot on the left.

"What?" Sulfur was more confused than ever. "Did I miss something?"

"Just get your ass through the gate." Zest nudged them forward.

The Mounts ignored the team as they raced over the spigots, which spat out a new pattern of containment behind them.

"What in the burning compost pile was that?"

"Ronnie was listening and issued us invites," Misha mumbled.

"How did Ronnie know we were here?"

"She's always tracking us," Zest said.

Rocket played ominous music. "That's a new one. Verdance never used the trackers in anyone I knew."

"Are you sure about that? What about Destry?" Misha looked intensely at Rocket.

The bot shrugged. "I don't think so. Unless you mean locating us by spore trail?"

"Maybe that's it," Misha said vaguely.

The city immediately folded them into its residential districts; Lungs had no farms, and they quickly found themselves walking the sidewalk in a suburban area with row houses that breathed, glowed, and emitted puffs of steam. So far, they hadn't seen people other than the bots who tried to keep them out of the city.

"Is all the food shipped in from the mainland?" Sulfur wondered.

"Yeah. And the other islands." Zest walked beside them in the street because the sidewalk was too narrow for them to walk as a group. "That was always the plan. Lungs is the most exclusive city on the planet, and the idea is to cover the entire thing with these morph-cladded buildings."

The suburban street went on for a whole two klicks before they saw any retail or high density—or people. Finally they reached an intersection where a bodega sold jeweled water bottles and snacks. The *H. sapiens* behind the counter glared at them and folded their arms.

"Where are we going to find lodgings around here?" Rocket sounded as unnerved as Sulfur felt.

"Maybe downtown?" Misha replied. "I'm not sure because it's so much bigger than the last time we were here."

As they got closer to the spiny tower and the balloon emitter, there were more *H. sapiens* on the sidewalks. But no lodgings. This island had problems that went far beyond public transit availability. It had virtually no public amenities at all, other than the roads and ferries.

After wandering listlessly, the team managed to locate the restaurant district, and a few nightclubs—invitation only, of course—but no inns or overnight rentals. Finally they approached a person waiting tables at a sidewalk restaurant and asked directions to the nearest hotel. The waiter clucked sympathetically and said their best bet was to get back to the mainland.

Dejected, the group gathered in a cluster on the curb.

"Are there any places where rangers usually stay here?" Sulfur asked.

"Last time we came, we camped. That whole residential area was dunes." Misha pointed at the road behind them.

Sulfur was hungry and tired and wanted to sit down. "This place can eat my ass. Let's get out of here and camp on one of the other Bronze Islands."

Zest sighed. "I'm starting to think that's our only option." She turned to Misha. "Ronnie didn't give you a place to stay? Why did she let us in?"

"She's been pushing me to come here because she thinks the Bronze Islands are a great model for privatized transit. I assume she means the ferries? She doesn't always know exactly what's happening on the ground, and relies a lot on marketing materials." Misha shook his head. "Let's get dinner at least. We have money for that."

They went back to the restaurant with the sympathetic waiter, who introduced himself as Nash. After several drinks—one of which Sulfur slipped to Nash—and a big pile of fried potatoes with a garlicky red lentil soup, everyone was feeling a lot better. Still, nobody was relishing the two-hour walk back to the edge of the gravity mesh disabler.

When he brought the bill, Nash stayed to talk. All the other customers had left, and there was a closing-time camaraderie in the air. "Listen," he said. "I know a place where you can camp tonight on the island."

Sulfur sat up straighter. "Really? Because we could use a place to crash that doesn't involve getting back to the mainland. Today has been long and strange."

"And I wouldn't mind another drink," Misha said.

Nash laughed. "If you stay here long enough, you will always need another drink or three."

"Seems like it," Rocket said, appending the sound of a fart.

"There's a beach on the northern island that hasn't been developed yet. You can go out there and nobody will care. You can fly from there too—it's mostly outside the murder curtain." He pointed up. "Killed like five delivery guys last year. If you don't know it's there—let's just say it's a long drop." Nash shook his head. "You have a map?"

Zest nodded, and Nash tapped his temple to let her know he was sending the coordinates. When they left the restaurant a few minutes later, Misha made sure to leave Nash a big tip.

The northern island was exactly as Nash had promised: empty. Moonlight splashed an orange streak across the water, and the sand was still warm from the afternoon sun. Palm trees nodded in the wind, and Misha stretched a hammock between two thick gray trunks. Zest wandered off to graze and drowse while Rocket promised to be back in the morning. They would be flying to the next island, and promised to bring back a few samples.

That left Sulfur alone with Misha, who sat down quietly in the sand beside them. It was too early for sleeping, and they were enjoying a lingering buzz from the wine and fried food. Sulfur snuck a look at Misha's profile. He was almost expressionless, as if he had left his body to enter the vast complexity of the ocean's ecosystems. And there it was again—they couldn't help noticing his beauty, more poignant because he wasn't conventionally attractive in the Archaean sense. That *H. sapiens* forehead was too bulbous, and his face had a peculiar flatness to it. And yet. They looked away, embarrassed. It was wrong in every conceivable way. Misha was Verdance's man, and he would be due back at La Ronge in a few weeks. What good could possibly come out of a roll in the grass with him?

"Do you miss Spider City?" He turned to them, blank expression transformed into curiosity.

"Sure I do. But I like to get out into the field when I'm working for the city, instead of Verdance. What about you? Do you miss La Ronge?"

Sadness edged his voice when he replied. "Not very much. I miss Destry, but she's gone. So are most of my old friends, except for Zest. I wish I could move somewhere else and start over, like Rocket did."

"Why couldn't you?"

"I told you. I'm the only person like this, and Ronnie keeps me on a tight leash." He stretched his arms toward the small waves breaking on the beach, spreading his fingers, looking at his hands like they belonged to someone else. "I'm the most senior network analyst in the ERT now."

"Couldn't you do your job from anywhere? Mostly you're needed for missions outside La Ronge, right?"

"I wish."

Misha turned his dark brown eyes toward Sulfur, and it was too much. Their heart was racing and their brain was fizzing with hormones and all the yearning in his voice had aroused a very different kind of desire. Without thinking, they leaned over and kissed him softly on the lips. "Do you know how beautiful you are?" they asked.

He smiled slightly in surprise. "That's not something I hear very often."

They kissed again, but when Sulfur reached out to run fingers through his hair, he pulled away. "We shouldn't do this."

"No shit. But I think we should anyway." Sulfur was swelling slightly, and it felt too good to worry about all the reasons why they might get hurt later. "It's just a little pleasure on the road."

He shook his head and stood up, walking back toward the hammock. Sulfur started after him, worried that they had stepped over the line. "I'm sorry—I should have asked before kissing you. That was wrong."

"I'm not upset about that." He'd reached their campsite and was rummaging through his pack, finally pulling out a thick cloak for cold weather and high-altitude flight. Wrapping it around himself, he sat in the hammock and gestured for Sulfur to join him. "I want to be close to you. But there's something you should know." They were pressed together in the stretchy netting, except the cloak swaddled Misha's body and head. His voice came out muffled when he spoke again. "I know this is ridiculous, but this material blocks long-range signals and sensors. Destry had it fabricated for me. Somehow Ronnie didn't figure it out."

At first they were confused, but with a growing sense of dread, Sulfur realized what Misha was implying. "You're a surveillance device. For Verdance."

He laughed bitterly. "That's not how they would put it, of course. The information I'm able to gather and analyze is extremely valuable, so Verdance built me to record environmental data and make it available in a format that Ronnie can access any time. Everything except audio and video. But when I'm inside this cloak, the sensors don't pick up anything. It looks like a dead feed."

"So if I touch you through this, Ronnie can't spy on us?"

"Pretty much. To be honest, I don't . . ." he trailed off, then groaned. "I mostly try to avoid situations like this."

Sulfur ran a hand over his head, just a lump under the rough fabric, and continued down the nearly indistinguishable shape of his arm, his back, his hip, and his thigh. Touching him was still sexy, but the vulnerabilities built into his body were so unsettling that Sulfur ended their groping with nothing more than a warm hug.

"So how do you—I mean, what have you done before to avoid being watched?"

"Like I said—I just avoid it."

"So you don't have sex?"

"Not in a long time." He sounded miserable. "When I was younger, I cared less. I didn't really believe that Ronnie was monitoring me all the time. But—" he squirmed around and opened a little tunnel of fabric around his face so they could see the tip of his nose, "—but at a certain point, Ronnie made it pretty obvious that she was monitoring me." He gulped a deep breath, and they realized it must be suffocatingly hot under the cloak.

"You should take this off—maybe we can snuggle, if that's OK?"

Awkwardly, he extricated himself and they lay down side-by-side in the hammock under the invisible murder curtain, holding hands and looking at the Milky Way's clotted stars. There were the familiar constellations of the Hand and the Muskrat. The Rocket hovered at the horizon, its rear jets pointing toward the place where Earth's star would be if they could see its light from here.

"I know we come from the stars, but I've always loved planets more."

Sulfur trailed an arm out of the hammock, running their hand through the sand.

"Me too. Not that I'll ever get any closer to the stars than we are right now."

"You never know."

"Let's kiss again." Misha wriggled an arm under Sulfur and pulled them closer. This time he let them touch the curls in his hair.

"Can Ronnie tell we're together right now?"

"If she wants to, she can see my physical reactions and get reads off whatever sensors are on your body. If we actually did more than this, it would be pretty obvious."

Sulfur considered what that might mean. "I don't care, personally. But I don't want you to get in trouble for—"

Before they could finish, he cut them off with another kiss, this one urgent enough to make their petals throb. "Thank you." His voice was a half-whisper. "I have been wanting to touch you since that night at Angst, in the tent."

Sulfur swallowed hard. "Me too."

He smiled, and his dimpled cheeks made him look less like an *H. sapiens* and more like a person. When Misha pressed his lips to their eyelids, Sulfur's skin tingled with hot and cold at the same time. Despite what they'd said about grabbing a little pleasure on the road, that's not how it felt. When they'd hooked up with Ace, it was an ephemeral thrill. But kissing Misha was already a lot more intense than surreptitious sex with Ace at THE TONGUE FORKS. Maybe that was because they knew him better, and trusted him despite everything. Or maybe it was because they were getting high off the fumes of a brewing disaster.

BARRIERS

From: Ronnie Drake

To: Misha

Subject: get it done

Date: June 11, 59,706

Origin: Verdance Corporation

Least-cost path: VD Hab Cartier (0.001), Turtle Wormhole (3.2), Tisdale Station (0.9), Sask-E Sat (0.05)

I see you're in Spider City. Emerald is champing at the bit to get those plans, so I want those *H. archaeans* to sign off on our train plans as soon as fucking possible. I'm losing my patience.

Four days later, they were on the western side of Maskwa. The Comfort Sea was far behind them, along with the privatized ferry system and reconfigurable gated island city. Misha and Sulfur spent most of the trip going over data and strategizing with Zest and Rocket for their upcoming Spider City meetings. Though they didn't talk about what had happened on the beach, Sulfur no longer felt awkward about putting their arms around Misha to ride. What had been an uncomfortable position became a welcome embrace—and perhaps, Sulfur thought ruefully, it would be the only kind of physical intimacy they could ever have, given Ronnie's constant surveillance of Misha's sensor readings.

Wistful thoughts of lost sexual opportunities were swept aside as Zest flew out of the mountains, revealing the peak of downtown Spider with its ragged caldera. Sulfur always felt a rush of pure joy when they saw home after a long time away. From here, the lake was the size of a turquoise bead. Still, Sulfur could make out the city's characteristic architecture: earthen mounds of every size and shape spilled down Spider's lower slopes and into the grasslands surrounding it. Lava tubes made ridges between the mounds, legs for the arachnid whose abdomen was represented by Spider Mountain's magma-swollen bulk. A few farms and hydropower generators were visible near the Eel, but for the most part the city was still subterranean. The mounds held homes, neighborhoods, and public spaces that connected to the street grid of tunnels carved by ancient lava surges and—more recently—by the Boring Fleet.

The Archaea had no need to hide from Verdance's satellites anymore, but their urban planners had built below ground for so long that they never seriously considered abandoning the tradition. In meetings, they usually described this choice as pragmatic, but Sulfur knew there was a strong element of aesthetics too. Nobody who had grown up in Spider wanted to see buildings growing on top of the mountain, or in the tropical forests below. When people wanted to add a building, they borrowed earth from below and piled it into a mound above. Over the past few hundred years, developers had cleared the land around the old mountain with controlled burns, turning the city into an enormous ring of savanna encircling downtown. The domes, peaked ridges, pyramids, and rectangular shapes of its outer neighborhoods lay under a thick blanket of grasses and the occasional acacia or baobab tree.

After being away from home for almost six weeks, it was hard not to weep with relief. Sulfur slid their hand over Zest's port and sent a message to the rest of the team. *Anybody want to go for a swim before dinner? It probably won't be too crowded at this time of day.*

Rocket, flying beside them, nodded. *I could use a good scrubbing after all those nights outside.*

Same, Zest sent. *I've also been dreaming of those microgreens they put on the grab table last time I was in Spider City.*

Zest banked left so she could land on a broad stone platform halfway up Spider's slope. It was one of the few examples of external architecture on the mountain, and its main purpose was to provide a convenient entrance to the underground for people who flew here.

They were descending slowly enough that the air stilled and they could mouth talk. Rocket played a sound file of a rabbit making nom-nom sounds. "I suspect you won't have much trouble finding sprouts."

Misha groaned. "I'm so tired that I might just go to bed after our swim."

"I'll show you the way to my room if you need rest." Sulfur squeezed Misha, trying not to worry about how easily exhausted he was after weeks of overextending himself in the planet's sensor networks.

Rocket sent them a snatch of waaaa-waaaaa comedy horn notes and followed up with a private text to Sulfur. *What's going on? Are you hooking up with the* H. sapiens?

They looked over at their friend and colleague, anodized metal carapace shimmering blue and purple as they descended in the air alongside Zest. *I like him*, they sent.

He has to go back to La Ronge in a couple of weeks.

I know.

Remember how long it took you to get over Sandstone? Why are you always falling for people who are completely unavailable?

Who said anything about falling for?

Rocket emitted a snorting noise. *How long have we been friends? Three hundred years? I know you.*

Misha turned around to look at them. "What are you guys talking about in that encrypted stream?"

Sulfur leaned their cheek against his narrow back, padded with the thick riding cloak whose uses went beyond comfort. "You really don't want to know."

"I was warning Sulfur about chasing after unattainable goals." Rocket's voice was sharp with annoyance. "Do you know what I mean, Misha?"

The man was silent until they landed. As he dismounted from Zest, he faced Rocket, whose smooth face angled down to meet his gaze—the bot was at least a quarter meter taller than Misha. "I would never stand in the way of Sulfur's goals."

"Everybody is being extra creepy right now, so let's drop it and go swimming." Sulfur crooked a finger at Zest and walked to the portal in the mountain, which rolled open at their approach.

"It's Zest!" the door yelled.

The cow's head jerked up in surprise. "Is that Hellfire&Crisp?"

"You recognized me! I can't believe you're here. It's been—what? Seven hundred years?"

Zest shook her head. "It's been too long since I visited Spider City. How are you doing?"

"Did you know we married Jaguar?"

"What? No!"

The entire team was through the door now and following the glow of LED strings upward toward the caldera. Hellfire&Crisp's voices followed them, jumping out of speakers embedded in the walls.

"We swore we'd never get married, but it turned out to be the best decision we ever made."

"Congratulations, Hellfire&Crisp. That's really great." Zest flicked an ear. "Are you still part of the ERT?"

"We were for a while, but now we're helping Jaguar maintain the access control infrastructure for the whole city. We're still racing, too—we can use drone bodies when we're off work."

They were nearly at the caldera level when Hellfire&Crisp abruptly left in a flurry of expletives about how nobody knows how to operate a simple valve in a lava tube.

Sulfur hadn't realized how much they'd been craving the feel of clean, cool lake water. They had rinsed off in the ocean a few times on this trip, but it always left their skin gritty and hair salty. Stripping down to nothing, they dove in without a second glance. Rocket followed them out, hovering over the water and then dunking under, sluicing the dust out of their joints. Zest and Misha hung back, wading in tentatively. Sulfur watched the *H. sapiens* keep close to the cow, staying in range of her sensor-killing body. If only there were an easy way to block the feed he sent to Verdance that didn't involve large jackets or bovines. As Sulfur dove, trying to reach the thin but impenetrable window to the ERT lab, they suddenly had an idea. Surreptitiously, they sent a request to a friend who worked in medical devices.

When they resurfaced, Rocket continued their earlier conversation using audio. "I'm sorry to throw compost in your recycling, but I want you to be happy."

Sulfur floated between tropical humidity and cold mountain water. "I know. But I'm never going to settle down like Hellfire&Crisp. I like to travel. That's my job. And when I stumble across somebody I like, I'm not going to hold back just because they live far away."

"I'm not saying you have to settle down, but wouldn't you be happier with a person whose body isn't a living surveillance system owned by Verdance?"

Sulfur lost their float balance and flapped around in the water. "How did you know that?"

"I worked with Destry, remember? After Ronnie murdered her parents, Verdance changed the templates on a bunch of life-forms, including people like Misha who can network with environmental sensors."

"It's not his fault how he was built."

Misha and Zest were swimming toward them now, and Rocket touched Sulfur's arm briefly to send. *You're right about that. Please be careful, though, OK? I'm here for you no matter what.*

Sulfur grabbed the bot's hand before they pulled it back. *I know. And I'm going to be cautious.*

The rest of the afternoon was taken up with plans for their next two weeks. Misha napped on a conference couch while the rest of the team set times to meet with the Council, arranged ERT transit breakouts, and got a room for Zest. During dinner with the ERT urban planners, everyone carefully avoided talking about how Misha would be staying in Sulfur's quarters under Rattlesnake Mound. Finally, it was time for people to start their evening activities—some would be going to work, while others had recreation dates.

Sulfur and Misha peeled off to take a walk around the city. They held hands, occasionally sending each other texts directly through their interfaces, but mostly enjoying pure physical contact without language.

As they got closer to the healthcare engineering center, Sulfur paused. *I've asked my friend to create some experimental medical devices for us.* Sulfur grinned. *Do you mind stopping by the biofilm printers?*

Why do you need a biofilm? Misha was confused.

Sulfur pushed him gently against the wall of the dusky tunnel, cupping his face in their hands and tasting his plump, pretty lips as they continued to send. *Biofilms aren't just for building semipermeable membranes anymore. You can use them for all kinds of situations. Like blocking signals.*

His eyes widened. Wordlessly, he nodded. They continued strolling, pausing to pick up a paper-wrapped package at the printer and admire the lozenge-shaped windows emitting a deep orange light. Eventually they forked right, away from downtown, following a natural lava tube whose roof was open to the air. Sunset stained the sky purple, and high winds stippled the vault of atmosphere with thin, pink clouds.

Rattlesnake Mound was a cozy neighborhood of forty-two dwellings whose multicolored doors flanked a rectangular public space with a peaked roof. Vents let in filtered air, and the ceiling was streaked with glowing algae that gave everything in the room a greenish-yellow tinge. Tables and chairs were arranged neatly—somebody conscientious must have been on cleaning shift—and the open kitchen smelled like herb tea.

"This is where you live?" Misha spun slowly in the middle of the space, inhaling deeply. "Is that ginger tea?"

"Yeah. Cam likes to have it at night, and he usually leaves some out for the rest of us. Unfortunately you're here too late in the year for his marmalade, which is everybody's favorite dessert in spring." Sulfur poured them both small cups of tea and led Misha to a bright orange door near the kitchen end of the mound.

Everything inside was as they'd left it. A small globe terrarium hung in the square window, high in the wall, and their bed on the floor was piled with pillows and homemade quilts from friends at the spring festival. There was a dyed woven basket for clothes, and a chest of cubbies held neatly stacked remote sensing equipment along with a jumble of items they'd collected over the years: pleasing rocks and shells, dried flowers, mementos from harvest circle, and a bracelet that their beloved Sandstone had given them over a century ago. Thinking about Sandstone reminded them of what Rocket had said that afternoon in the lake. The bot wasn't wrong, but they weren't completely right either.

Sulfur was tingly and nervous, wondering whether the biofilms were a terrible idea—or would even work. Setting down the paper-wrapped package, they fiddled with the atmosphere controls to bring in more fresh air, with the proper gas mix for Archaea. It was nice to breathe freely again. Misha flopped on the bed and pulled his shirt over his head, revealing a slim brown torso dusted with dark hair. The breather in his septum refracted light for an instant as he faced them.

He was beautiful, but also strange—there was something unsettling about the small *H. sapiens* features on his face, his narrow chest with its two small nipples and short arms. It was as if he were slightly undeveloped, decanted before his time. Kneeling next to him on the mattress, Sulfur slowly unwrapped the parcel, which contained three rolls of biofilm, helpfully labeled SAMPLE 1, SAMPLE 2, AND SAMPLE 3.

In Sulfur's experience, having sex didn't involve a lot of elaborate preparation; one simply dove in, as they had with Ace in the club, growing feverish and unguarded with desire. But that could never happen with Misha. They had to plan carefully and use specially designed instruments, as if they were about to do a laboratory investigation. Which was, once Sulfur thought about it, actually kind of hot. Especially when Misha reached out a languid hand and tugged the tabs open on their coveralls. As the garment peeled apart and puddled around their waist, Misha ran warm hands over the Archaean's upper body—their pale torso muscled and broad, with six dark purple nipples, three on either side of their rib cage.

"Let's try some sample strips of biofilm right here." Misha pointed to his chest. "That's one of my main sensor arrays."

"Alright." Sulfur picked up the first roll. "Are you ready for our experiment to begin? We'll be using . . . Sample One."

He looked up at them, moving his arms away from his sides. "Put it on."

They tore a small square from the roll, light and slightly damp, and spread it gently over his right pectoral. Sulfur grinned at him and touched his nipple lightly through the film. "Do you feel that?"

Moaning softly, Misha fought to collect himself. He pointed at the cubbies. "Get a signal reader."

Misha lay still as Sulfur ran the finger-sized device over his chest, trying to connect to the devices under his skin; they were built to the same specs as the environmental sensors whose states he was constantly reading.

"Are you able to pick up any of the signal?" he asked.

"No. I think Sample One might be all we need."

He relaxed. "That was too easy."

"You don't want to try . . . Sample Two?" Sulfur raised an eyebrow and held up the next roll of biofilm. It had a slightly pearlescent sheen. Before he had a chance to reply, they ripped off another square and smoothed it on his other nipple, gently teasing it until he gasped. The biofilm was so thin that it didn't feel like a barrier—more like he'd rubbed a moisturizer onto his skin—except once in a while when the material would wrinkle for a second and they would remember that there was a microbial textile between their bodies.

"You should . . ." he trailed off, touching Sulfur's thigh. Their jumpsuit pants were growing uncomfortable as their petals became more swollen. "You really should test to see if Sample Two blocks signals too."

They ran the sensor slowly over the pearlescent square, almost grazing Misha's skin, and his breath skipped as their eyes met. Again, he made a visible effort to bring himself under control. "I'm very impressed with Spider City's biofilms. Two for two." Then his eyes narrowed. "I wonder if I'll be able to take some back to La Ronge. I could get off Ronnie's radar sometimes."

This was definitely not what Sulfur wanted to be thinking about. "I'm going to secure your entire body with the biofilm now." They grabbed Sample 2 and tore off a big sheet. "Take off your pants and stand up."

Misha's face relaxed again and he stood up, releasing the gripper at his waist with the swipe of one hand. It was briefly unnerving to see his aroused stamen without plush petals swollen around it, but Sulfur had always been drawn to unknown landscapes. They gradually unrolled the biofilm against his body, pressing it gently against his skin, making sure to linger anywhere it made him sigh. He helped them tuck it around his facial features and hair, where the film left a faint iridescence but was otherwise undetectable.

When he was fully encased, Sulfur stepped back to admire their handiwork. Their coveralls were unbearably tight, and they made no ceremony of stripping—in one sloppy gesture, they yanked the fabric off and threw it into a pile on the floor. The two hominins stood in the dwindling sunset light from the window, embracing and sensing each other's heightening pleasure. Sulfur's friend had thought of everything: the biofilm allowed the natural salty-musk flavor of skin to come through, and was pleasant to the tongue. Eventually the ache was too much, and they fell to their knees on the bed, their stamens throbbing against each other.

Misha ran his fingers down Sulfur's rib cage, teasing their nipples, then reached for the damp length of their stamen. "I'm not sure—what you like to do?" he whispered. "I've never been with an Archaean before."

"Bend over and I'll show you."

Misha knelt and they curled over his arched back, reaching around to touch his stamen as they guided their own inside him. He sucked in a breath and let it out out in a ragged sigh. It was almost too much, but Sulfur slowed down to enjoy the sensation of being inside another person again—

the dalliance with Ace had been a delight, but this was much more. Their abdominal muscles bunched in an agony of anticipation and urgency.

As Sulfur lost control, rhythm getting rougher, Misha cried out in a voice that made him sound like any other mammal. He was no longer an *H. sapiens*, but simply a body against Sulfur's body. As the two underground creatures gave in to their shared sensations, Sulfur felt the biofilm slide under their fingers and was filled with elation that this feeling stopped at the edges of their bodies. No one had recorded it; no one would ever know. It was theirs alone.

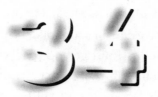

GOVERNMENT

From: Ronnie Drake

To: Misha

Subject: plans???

Date: June 14, 59,706

Origin: Verdance Corporation

Least-cost path: VD Hab Cartier (0.001), Turtle Wormhole (3.2), Tisdale Station (0.9), Sask-E Sat (0.05)

What is the holdup? This should be a quick turnaround. I can see you are still at Spider City. We don't need input from the Spider people—just a simple way to secure their agreement.

The Council meeting was sparsely attended. There was nothing to vote on, and very few people had the expertise required to weigh in on questions of public transit governance. Obsidian, head of urban planning, had interrupted Sulfur and Misha's presentation to deliver bad news.

"I've been in touch with Cylindra, who manages templates for Emerald. She said she met with you in Lefthand?"

"That's right."

"She's refusing to allow any public transit inside her cities. She sent us a long memo about it."

Misha was taken aback. "I knew she wasn't interested in trains, but Verdance is obligated to provide some form of public transit for the entire planet. It's part of the development deal."

Obsidian's white hair was a tangled mane around the dubious expression on their face. "I pointed that out, but she hates the idea of any kind of transit—she said, and I quote, that it would 'spoil the virgin beauty of the Emerald Cities.' Which is utter nonsense. I got the feeling that there's some kind of festering wound between her and Verdance management. I guess she used to work there?"

Sulfur had the urge to spill everything they knew about Cylindra's role in the Archaean templates, but held back. "She was—hostile—when we met with her."

The group of Archaea around the table and on remote screens went silent as they exchanged back-channel chat. A member of the Boring Fleet, Alcohol, spoke through the mouth of a holographic moose. The actual vessel was far below this room, floating in a river of lava. "Reading over this memo that we got from Cylindra's office, it seems that she's exploited a loophole in the contract. Public transit must link cities, but there's nothing about putting stations inside city limits. Technically Verdance would be fulfilling its obligations if we built stations on the outermost periphery."

Rocket made a crash-and-burn noise. "So she's suggesting we build tracks up to the edge of the city, and stop there."

Frustrated, Sulfur practically growled. "That's unacceptable. If you look at the data we've been gathering, linking the cities using train tracks pretty much guarantees that public transit will become obsolete. We need a solution that doesn't rely on tracks, *and* can go into the cities when it's needed."

The head of Council for this meeting was Acorn, a young decanting engineer who knew Zest well enough to give the cow a hug when they arrived at the meeting. Acorn scratched one freckled elbow and frowned. "What do you have in mind? I can't imagine Spider joining a transit network like the one Cylindra is proposing. We're not going to perturb our environment with tracks if there will be no benefit to people."

"It's a shame." Obsidian shook their head. "Our surveys show that a lot of people would like to visit the new cities. That's fine if you're able to fly, but—"

"Wait a minute." Rocket emitted the sound of screeching tires. "Alcohol, does Cylindra's proposal say anything about setting up stations inside the city without building tracks?"

A few people started to ask confused questions, but Alcohol was satisfied to answer literally. "No, it does not. She says no tracks inside city limits. There are no comments about stations."

An excited drumbeat was coming from Rocket now. "We can make flying trains! There is no rule that says the Verdance trains have to run on tracks."

"A train can't fly." Misha was frustrated. "We talked about this before. I'm not going to put gravity mesh into something that isn't a person. It's dangerous."

"Excuse me." The holographic moose was speaking, channeling Alcohol from the magma surging deep beneath their feet. "I'm sorry, but why are we building vehicles that aren't people?"

Everyone went silent as the messages between them became an uproar.

Though Sulfur had become overwhelmingly partial to pretty much everything about Misha, they were not impressed with his argument today. "Rocket is right," they said. "Flying trains would solve a lot of problems. We'd avoid damaging wildlife with tracks, and we could alter routes really easily. The cities are going to change and move around a lot over the next millennium, and a flying fleet would be a lot more sustainable."

Zest perked up. "Plus, we met some engineers when we were on our survey who have solved the traveling herbivore problem. We could implement it in the train's mind too. Imagine a train that would always take the optimal route between cites!"

"Whose engineers are those? Are they ERT?" Acorn was practically vibrating with excitement.

The cow immediately became evasive—she'd promised to reveal nothing about the worms, after all. "They're not ERT, but they're allies."

"Solving that problem is huge—how do I not know them?" Acorn folded their arms and another huge text chain blew up around the edges of the mouth conversation.

Misha couldn't contain his anger. "Stop polluting this discussion with your nitter-natter about the traveling herbivore problem!" He stood up, face flushed and dark eyes flashing. "Verdance will never allow us to propose a new life form as public transit, and we shouldn't do it anyway. It's not ethical, and it's not practical."

"I beg to differ," Alcohol replied. "Sentient transit is the very best kind. Only we are flexible enough to truly serve the public."

"Why are you so against this, Misha?" Sulfur was frozen inside. They didn't like seeing this aspect of Misha's personality.

He yanked Cylindra's memo out of the air and slapped it down on the table, scrolling through. "See this section? Cylindra is also refusing to connect the Emerald Cities to any transit network that includes Spider City because of what she's calling 'cross contamination from broken templates.' She's inserted a bunch of language about how every city in the network must abide by the intelligence assessment standards she's implemented in Lefthand." He gave Zest a significant look. "She's trying to force every city on the planet to abide by Emerald's InAss templates."

The whole outburst had left Obsidian puzzled. "You know there is no way for them to enforce these InAss standards outside the Emerald Cities, right? They simply don't have jurisdiction. She's playing some weird corporate game, trying to get something out of Verdance, I assume."

Sulfur thought back to the way they'd gotten under Cylindra's skin by mentioning Ronnie. This memo must be the Emerald VP's way of needling her old boss, by making nonsensical demands. "Obsidian is right," Sulfur mused. "All we have to do is pit Ronnie against Cylindra and let them scratch at each other while the ERT builds some flying trains."

"It's true that this memo seems more aimed at Verdance than at us," Misha admitted. Then he frowned. "But still, it's our problem to solve. We can't build new people to fix this for us. We'd be dumping all our crap onto innocent creatures who would have to carry tourists around."

"Not just tourists." Alcohol sounded testy, and the moose hologram lowered its head as if about to charge. "They'll be carrying every kind of person all over Sasky. Maybe even across the ocean to Tooth. Sounds like a pretty good job to me. Plus, they wouldn't all have to become public transit. Sasky is a big place. A flying train could be an engineer, a game designer, or a farmer if they wanted. They could help the ERT with rescue missions. Plenty will be left who like doing transit."

Misha's jaw was clenched. "But what if you're wrong, and none of them want to fly people around? Or are you going to program them to want it?"

The room filled with the sound of Boring Fleet vessels laughing like wind chimes. Apparently, Alcohol was sharing this moose avatar—and the conversation—with their comrades. "We of the Boring Fleet are not programmed to enjoy making subterranean infrastructure, but like all creatures, we find it satisfying to do things that our bodies excel at. Just as you hominins like to poke at machines with your hands and run your flappy mouths. And moose like to swim. Our bodies shape what we consider pleasant, whether that's work or play."

Rocket blared an upbeat horn flourish. "Exactly right. Not every train will want to do the same thing, but I'm not worried that the—the Flying Train Fleet will be averse to the thrill of designing optimal routes and visiting hundreds of cities across the globe."

People texted back and forth, and Misha hunched his shoulders, as if warding off an incoming blow.

Acorn spoke up in a non-sequiturial way that suggested they were replying to a long text chain Sulfur hadn't read. "Sure, sure. I don't see why we couldn't mock up some templates this afternoon. Alcohol has ideas about morphology, and Zest gave me a really interesting brain model with two separate ganglia." They paused and looked at Zest. "What exactly is this a model of?"

The cow flicked an ear and looked at Sulfur for help. "We got it from those engineers who solved the traveling herbivore problem—they were doing fieldwork."

"Something to do with agriculture," Sulfur added, making a big show of gazing off into the distance and checking their memory stores. "You know, it wasn't relevant to our mission, so I didn't take any notes."

Acorn shrugged. "Whatever. I love this design."

"This is not why we came here." Misha's voice was low but loud. "Sulfur and Rocket told me that this Council would discuss government transit regulations with us. Right now, Spider City has the only independent government on this whole stinking planet. And instead of thinking about how we'd build a system for collectively managing a planet-wide resource, you want to bring a bunch of trains into the Great Bargain." He glared at Sulfur for several seconds before including the entire table in his scornful gaze.

Obsidian was offended. "We are all allies in the Great Bargain," they said, paraphrasing the *ERT Handbook*.

"That's untreated sewage and you know it. Who is going to be in charge of this Flying Train Fleet? How will every city weigh in on their transit needs? How will we know when new trains are needed, or new routes and stations? What if Cylindra changes her mind and the Emerald cities decide they want to use the entire fleet—who decides how many they actually get, and brokers the compromise?"

Misha was clearly working himself up to say more, but Alcohol cut him off, their voice chiming out of the moose avatar. "Don't you understand yet, *H. sapiens*? If we make the trains into people, then they can decide for themselves. They can manage themselves. Like the Boring Fleet does."

"Exactly." Obsidian sat back, satisfied. "Sometimes the best way to handle resources is to perceive when they aren't resources at all. They are people. Maybe it's hard for you to understand because everyone in La Ronge is slaved, but that's what it means to govern. A government's job is to recognize people, to help them make their own agreements with each other—and if you do your job well, those people become your political allies."

"I'm not saying things are good in La Ronge, but what you're describing is incredibly naive. These aren't people yet. We don't need to make them people. In fact, if we do make them people, our public transit will depend on the will of—" Misha waved his hand in the air as if scattering flies. "Sasky needs a dependable transit infrastructure. Not a bunch of people who have opinions about optimal routes."

"A lot of people on Sasky are already working as Mounts," Zest said gently. "They are mostly treated like chattel, though. It would be nice to build someone to do that job who could actually broker the agreements as to how it would be done."

A door opened in the back of the Council room, where members of the public entered to sit on the on the tiered bleachers carved into the circular walls. Currently, the bleachers were about a quarter full, so the stranger standing there wouldn't have far to walk for a seat. Instead, they strode directly to the front-row tier at the bottom.

"Oh great!" Acorn perked up. "This is Tuff, from my lab. That was fast!"

"Yeah, so I mocked up the train you were describing earlier, with the dual brain structure. I honestly don't see any problems with it—it's all taken from well-tested templates, with a few tweaks. I could build the first one in about a week, and then it would get faster."

Sulfur grinned and spread their hands in a look-at-all-this gesture. "You see? The train is easy to build, and it's safe."

Misha folded his arms and glowered. "We have to run this by Ronnie. If I bring her a fleet of intelligent trains, she could murder them all."

"If we make them here at Spider City, Verdance technically doesn't have jurisdiction over them."

"It's true. That's one of the many reasons why I wanted this body." Rocket gestured at their rainbowing carapace. "Because it was manufactured here, I became a Spider City person when I ported to it."

"That's how you did it?" Misha sat back in his chair, blinking.

"So far it's worked too. Verdance never even tried to claim me."

The *H. sapiens* rubbed his temples and looked at the moose hologram, tethered to Alcohol the boring vessel, then at the rest of them. "I have to think about this. I can perceive that you're right about making the trains into people, but I'm still worried that Verdance will figure out a way to wreck this—and we might end up in a much worse situation."

"If people like the transit, they'll vote with their feet." Acorn tapped their bare foot on the packed earth floor. "What's the worst Verdance can do? Send an angry message?"

Rocket, who had lived through the Eel River War, sat up straight. "They can melt this city from orbit. Do you really think anyone will care—or even find out about it? We still haven't been able to open relations with the League, so there's no outside authority we can appeal to."

Like Acorn, Sulfur hadn't been alive when the war happened. It was hard to imagine what it must have been like to watch the city being carved up by laser fire, and even harder to believe that something that brutal could happen again. Spider City had a government and a treaty with Verdance. But Misha was nodding at Rocket and taking deep breaths to ward off anxiety.

"That's not an unrealistic scenario," he said finally. "You are fools if you are not prepared for it."

A PROMISE

From: Ronnie Drake

To: Misha

Subject: ignore the memo from Emerald

Date: June 21, 59,706

Origin: Verdance Corporation

Least-cost path: VD Hab Cartier (0.001), Turtle Wormhole (3.2), Tisdale Station (0.9), Sask-E Sat (0.05)

Got the design drawings for trains from you—obviously I need the full specs, but this is shaping up. Next, I'd like to see some documentation of their functionality, and a map of potential track routes. You can disregard the memo from Cylindra. Tracks are still fine—it doesn't matter if they can't go inside the cities, because we should expect city residents to supply their own transit. If this train project pleases the execs at Verdance and Emerald, I can guarantee a promotion for you in La Ronge—maybe even a chance to work offworld on other terraforming gigs. But if you fail—I've already told you what will happen. And that's a promise.

Sulfur spent the next seven days in meetings with various committees at Spider, working out an intercity transit plan they could present to Verdance. For all of those days, Sulfur wouldn't speak to Misha. They found him a guest room in Rattlesnake Mound, put his pack inside, and threw the biofilms on top just for good measure. His nastiness at the meeting had curdled their growing affection for him, souring the memory of their night together. Misha responded by avoiding them at meals. He worked on data analysis with Zest, was perfectly businesslike in meetings, and never once tried to ask Sulfur why he was suddenly sleeping alone. Either he knew, or he knew not to ask. Sulfur appreciated that, even if they were still repulsed by him.

It was midafternoon on the seventh day after the bedroom biofilm experiment when Sulfur managed to get a few hours to take a walk outside. Clipping on a breather, they took the nearest exit and found themselves on the warm flank of Spider, surrounded by a late summer riot of grass and insects. A bird swooped down in a flash of red and yellow, plucking a bug out of the air. It was not an animal that Sulfur knew, probably because it was one of thousands of creatures—millions, really—that lived in and around the mountain. They'd never thought about how easy it would be to snatch one of them out of the air and turn them into a person. That's exactly what those naked mole rats in the northeast were doing with their earthworms, though. Now Sulfur's colleagues were doing something even more radical: making a new life form that had never existed before, and planning to release it into the same airspace where green-winged jacamars hunted dragonflies in an iridescent dance. The idea filled them with uncomplicated happiness: a new ally in the Great Bargain!

Enjoying the feel of tiny rocks crunching under their feet, Sulfur headed downhill and intended to walk aimlessly between mounds. Instead, they found themselves wandering in the direction of the lava tube entrance to Acorn's lab. Sulfur had been dying to check in with Acorn about their progress on the Flying Train Fleet. After an hour of dusty hiking, they found the skylight entrance, its energy barrier a faint gleam between trees. Every Archaean knew this was the historic place where the Council members and Destry had stood when the first laser beams hit the city during the Eel River War. But it was also just another entrance to the ERT campus. Pressing a hand to the loamy soil, Sulfur connected with the city network and requested entrance.

"It's open." Jaguar was speaking out of a widening portal in the energy field. Sulfur stepped through, landing on a gravity assist pad that wanted sweeping. Everyone coming in and out of this place was covered in dirt, so naturally they left bits of it behind to hover in the air until the assist turned off and tiny clods rained down on the experimental agricultural plots below. The long, sunlit tube was full of these plots, largely for researchers, their two-meter squares demarcated by colorful threads and sticks that corresponded to the ag lab's data organization scheme. Trees stretched leafy arms up to the skylight, and ferns spread fingers across the ground. A group of people picked edible flowers blooming at the edge of the path and scraped a few sensors off the tiny sprouts poking up next to them. It reminded Sulfur of their early days at the ERT, learning how to take environmental samples.

Acorn worked beneath the mountain proper, and Sulfur pulled the breather from their nose as they headed for a solid rock tunnel. Past a few office doors was Acorn's space, a roughly square chamber taken up with decanting tanks on one side and a row of lab benches on the other. The benches were packed with people today, operating tissue printers, incubators, and chip fabbers as Acorn bounced excitedly between workstations and observed. When they saw Sulfur standing in the doorway, Acorn rushed toward them, pale blue eyes wide with delight in their freckled face.

"Do you want to see them? We've got the scaffold and connective tissues already." The engineer pointed at an arched doorway that was barely visible behind the tanks. "I mostly work on the decanting process, so Tuff brought in some bioengineers who build bots and hybrids."

Sulfur nodded. "Zest told me a little bit about the hybrid system she's building for you. Sounds similar to the Boring Fleet, but with more biological tissues exposed."

"Come see!" Acorn made a let's-go gesture.

They wove through the tanks, some of which were lit up and bubbling while others were dark and dry. A few members of Acorn's team were tinkering with the machines, troubleshooting. Beyond the archway was an enormous warehouse space, its walls and ceiling made from unfinished igneous rock, with enormous lights attached to a series of crisscrossing catwalks hanging from the ceiling. Techs clanged on the elevated walkways overhead, one pausing to adjust the lighting to a slightly more yellow tone—the perfect frequency to fast-grow trellises.

Glowing at the center of the warm spotlights was the hardening skeleton of a train. Roughly thirty meters long and three meters wide, it was built in three segments connected by flexible muscle textiles. For now, its body was still notional, being mostly the wheeled chassis with ribs arching up to meet each other where the curved roof of the vehicle would be. Frames for the doors and windows were growing in nicely, and as Acorn had promised, some of the connective tissues were sprouting between ribs—eventually, these would form the soft interior surfaces of the train for passengers. Sulfur walked around the growing creature, trying to imagine its shiny, rounded exoskeleton and bright windows. On the other side they found Zest, using her actuator to test the strength of the tires. Looking more closely, Sulfur realized what they'd assumed to be tires were actually feet, covered in dark overlapping scales for protection—as if the train would have a gang of curled-up pangolins to roll on.

After Zest gave Acorn the latest details, she looked over at Sulfur and moved both ears forward with pleasure.

"I'm so glad you got to see the trellis stage! We're going to install gravity mesh tomorrow or the next day—depending on how long it takes to grow this interior layer."

"Did you wind up using the double brain structure?"

"It's going in right after the gravity mesh, yeah. I figure it will take a few days to test the internal network and microbiome." As Zest spoke, one of the tissues growing between ribs in the trellis reached out a pale green tendril, curling it weakly in the air as it looked for a place to attach. Sulfur touched it gently, guiding it to the next rib, but the tendril wrapped around their hand, stubbornly refusing to let go. Its grip was warm and tacky with peach fuzz.

"Hey, little friend, you need to grow your body." Sulfur pressed the soft tissue against the trellis where it ought to attach, but still it held on to their fingers. "I promise that if you let go, I'll come back and visit you tomorrow." Instantly, it detached and coiled around the trellis, followed by dozens more sprouts, which knit together into a springy flap of tissue joining the ribs.

"I guess they like you." Zest snickered. "You'd better come back tomorrow."

Sulfur was surprised by how happy the thought made them. "I wouldn't want to break my promise to a growing train. They're already beautiful."

"Aren't they?" Acorn crossed their arms and appraised the trellis door frames admiringly—five in all, two on the front and back cars, and one for the center. "Tuff designed the entrances and exits to be fully flexible, so people of all sizes and morphologies can get inside easily. Plus it has a ramp for naked mole rats."

"How are earthworms going to get on board?" Sulfur asked, half-joking.

"Good question. We'll make sure there's a way." Zest looked at the structure with a critical eye.

Acorn was confused. "Why would earthworms need transit?"

Sulfur arched an eyebrow. "They're members of the public."

"OK, I'll put worm accessibility on the list." With nonchalant acceptance, Acorn saved the audio of their last few seconds of conversation to a local to-do list for the team. "Probably they can use the same ramp as the naked mole rats, but we should check to be sure whether they might need some moist dirt to sit in during the ride."

"Thanks." Zest sounded surprised but happy. "I wasn't sure you'd actually do that."

Acorn tilted their head to the side quizzically. "Why wouldn't we?" They paused, eyes unfocused, as they got a message. "OK, I need to get to another meeting. Feel free to stick around, Sulfur. See you tomorrow!"

As they hustled out, Zest continued her slow probing of the pangolin feet. "I can see why you like it here. I didn't really get it when I came here the first time, with my old partner, Kim. It was a much different city back then—and of course we were at war."

Sulfur hung their head. "Yeah, it's hard for me to imagine."

"I hope all you ever have to do is imagine it."

The next day, Sulfur slept in past breakfast. Their meetings were over, and they'd stayed up late entangled in a long conversation with Acorn and Rocket about war, and the Flying Train Fleet, and what they would do if the two collided in the future. It was a cozy evening, but tinged with fear. Sulfur sighed. They were tired of being afraid of what came next. To clear their mind, they decided to pay a visit to the flying train in Acorn's lab.

There were leftovers out on the Rattlesnake grab table—dried mango and some toasted grain—which they ate by the handful as they headed up the tunnel. They were so distracted that they didn't notice Misha had fallen into step beside them.

"Would it be OK for me to apologize now?" His expression was so touchingly earnest that it reminded Sulfur again of everything they'd liked about Misha before he went rotten at the meeting last week.

They shrugged. "Fine."

"I know that I shouldn't have been closed to the idea of bringing a new ally into the Great Bargain. I know I was a jerk. And I'm really sorry. I'm just—I'm scared." His voice broke, and Sulfur was surprised to see tears streaking his face. They gulped the last of their breakfast and held out a hand to stop him before the tunnel joined a larger and more crowded artery. Sulfur was still leery of him, but he deserved some privacy to show his feelings.

"What's wrong?"

"Ronnie has been making threats about what will happen to me if I don't give her the train track plans she wants. So there's that. But also—I was designed to do a job I don't want to do. I can't escape the network. Ever. In that meeting, where you all talked about building new people to suit the jobs you need done—well, that's me. I'm a person who was custom built to suit a bunch of contracts that leaked out of corporate pustules. And I don't want to do that to anyone else." Misha's voice wobbled, and he mashed water out of his eyelashes with the palm of his hand. "I don't want to make people who wake up and realize that they have some special physical attribute that makes them someone else's valuable tool." He held his hands out to Sulfur, palms up, showing them the place on his body that held Ronnie's specially designed network sensors.

"OK." Sulfur expelled a breath. A prickle of shame worked its way around their neck as they realized how little they had perceived about Misha's situation. "I understand now why you were so reluctant. But Spider City isn't Verdance. We aren't going to force anyone to do work they hate."

"How can you be so sure? What if Verdance figures out a way to seize the Flying Train Fleet, because they were built to satisfy their contract?"

"I won't let that happen. None of us will. The trains won't let it, either."

Misha shook his head. "You know that I love you. I'm sure you know that by now." He raised his black eyes to meet their blue ones. "But you are naive if you think that Ronnie will let these trains form their own government."

There were too many thoughts and emotions chasing each other around Sulfur's rib cage for them to respond immediately. "I need to sit down," they said, sliding down the wall until they plopped ungracefully on the ground. "That's a lot to take in—I mean the part about Ronnie, yeah, but also the part about you being in love with me." Misha plunked down beside them and held out a hand. Sulfur grabbed it and their conversation became text.

I thought it was pretty obvious, he sent.

Sulfur looked at Misha's pretty lips and thought again about what he'd said. *I really like you too, but we've only known each other for a little while, and until five minutes ago I wanted to throw you in the garbage. So now I'm not sure what to say.*

A bot walking past angled their sensory bulb at them curiously, and Sulfur waved as if everything was perfectly normal.

Misha squeezed their hand. *Just say that you'll come to visit me in La Ronge one day, inside a flying train.*

It's a date. And also—I will make sure those trains are happy. And safe. Nobody is going to make them do what they don't want.

Misha looked like he was going to cry again as he shook his head. *Would you really have enough time to focus on the trains? Don't you have to get back to urban planning missions now?*

As Sulfur thought again about the train reaching out its soft tendril to touch their hand, they realized something. Now that their two months of treaty servitude were almost up, they would get to choose their next job—it was a tradition in Spider City, to sweeten the bitter months doing Verdance's bidding. Sulfur could request a few months to work on rearing the young train. Dropping Misha's hand, Sulfur broke into mouth speech. "I met the first member of the Flying Train Fleet yesterday, and I really loved them. I could apply to be their parent. That's three months of intensive work, as well as a lifelong commitment. I want to do it. I could watch out for them, the way Destry did with you."

"Destry couldn't protect me in the end," he said. "Plus, even if you were their parent, you couldn't be sure they'd be safe when they went into the world."

"Well, that would make me just like every parent who has ever lived."

BIRTHDAY PARTY

Sitting on the dirty floor of the tunnel with Misha, Sulfur felt their emotions suddenly disentangle themselves from a painful knot.

"Let me introduce you to the train, Misha. I'm headed to Acorn's lab right now."

The *H. sapiens* looked stunned, but he nodded mutely and stood up.

When they arrived at the train's incubation warehouse, Zest was puttering around with the tissue layer that now obscured the trellis. Yesterday's exposed ribs were entirely covered in a layer of furred padding that was the tan color of Misha's skin. Through the window and door openings, they could see that the chassis had been dusted with seeds that grew thin carbon fibers, knitting themselves into a hard floor. Eventually, the tissues on the outside of the train would undergo a similar transformation, growing a tough outer shell that hugged the more flexible fabric of the doors and windows. At the moment, though, Zest was most concerned about the train's front end, which would serve as a "face" to the public—though sensors would of course be spread throughout their body. The train's face stuck out like a cat's snout, with lights instead of a nose and whiskers; a big window took the place of eyes and ears, to bring in light and allow curious passengers to sit in the spot where a driver would be if the train weren't a person.

"They're coming along really quickly." Zest stepped back to admire the full body of this creature who would come alive in a world that had never known another of their kind. "I think they'll be ready for decanting in a few days."

Just then, Tuff arrived, pushing a flatbed cart piled with rolls of gravity mesh. Spread out into a single sheet, it would be thin enough to turn invisible. But it was a dull matte-black now. Tuff waved to Sulfur and Misha. "Nice to see you! Want to stick around for the neuro installation?"

The Archaean and *H. sapiens* looked at each other. "I'm going to stay, absolutely," Sulfur said.

Misha looked like he was about to take a canoe over some rapids. "All right. I'll stay too." He looked with trepidation at the self-governing flying train before him, which met every technical requirement in the Verdance contract. The company would be able to present the planet's cities with a public transit system that required no tracks, adapted in real time to new conditions, and could bargain with local governments on its own behalf. But for a few minutes more, they were still just microbes, fibers, and minerals, grown into the shape of a train.

Tuff and a few other members of the team unrolled the gravity mesh. Another crew came in with the precursors for growing a neural network. The mood in the warehouse started to feel like a birthday party.

Sulfur kept thinking about how the trellis had grabbed their hand—just a reflex, because the body held no agency right now. Still, it felt like a sign. This train promised to be the most fascinating creature they had ever encountered. In that moment they knew for certain their next job request would be to parent this new person. They put a hand on Misha's arm. "OK, I'm definitely going to do it. I'm going to put in an offer to parent to this train."

He turned to them, eyes damp. "I trust you to do a good job. And I'm not going to let you forget your offer to visit when they're ready to fly."

Tuff, who was measuring gravity mesh on the floor, looked up at him. "You know they'll be born ready. Parenting is for socialization and specialized tasks." They stood and held up a square of mesh to see if it would fit between windows. "Got any thoughts about what color your child's carapace should be, Sulfur? They can always change it if it doesn't suit them."

The Archaean laughed nervously. "Well, I haven't put in my formal request with Council—I'm not their parent yet."

"I can tell you're going to. I can *always* tell." Tuff whistled softly as they returned to cutting the gravity mesh into shape.

"How will you explain to the train that there are no other people like them?" Misha asked.

Acorn wandered into earshot. "As soon as this one is finished, we'll start working on another. This train will be on the team with us, giving feedback. I don't think it will be very long before they have train friends."

Misha bounced on the balls of his feet anxiously. "I don't know if that's true. What are you going to do about potential hostilities from Ronnie?"

"There is absolutely no way that will happen." Sulfur cut a hand through the air, chopping the head off an imaginary foe. "First of all— there is no way she can claim you aren't following the terms of the contract. And you've actually solved a major problem for her, which is having to create a global department of transit. The trains can run themselves and she washes her hands of it."

"You don't think she'll see through what we're doing?"

"What? What are we doing? We're just creating a solution to an environmental problem. That's what we do at ERT."

"We're spreading government. Those trains will effectively be another self-governing entity."

Just then Rocket walked into the hangar, swiveling their head and torso around, scanning the strong, springy body of the train as the team installing their quantum-neurological system. "Sulfur!" The bot emitted some celebratory marching music. "I heard you'd be parenting this train! Congratulations!" Before Sulfur could protest, the bot had them in a hug that was hard and warm. "Tuff sent me the audio."

"Who else did you tell?" Sulfur turned on Tuff and tried to sound angry but could not keep a straight face.

"Just Rocket. I was messaging with them right when you said it, so I figured it was my duty to pass it along." Tuff feigned outrage. "They have a right to know!"

"What color do you think they'd like to be?" Tuff asked for the second time.

Sulfur looked at the anodized metal of Rocket's carapace, gleaming in three shades of pink. "Make this flying train the same beautiful color as Rocket," they said. "It's only fair, since they are about to become this train's auntie."

DATE: 59,707
PLANET: Sask-E
CITY: Lefthand

INTERREGNUM: BLESSED

"What the actual fuck is this, Cylindra?" Ronnie's wrathful face hovered like an ancient bust come to life over Cylindra's bedside table, high forehead bulging above close-set eyes in the current *H. sapiens* fashion. It was a few hours before dawn, and the VP blinked a forgettable dream out of her eyes. Through the windowed walls of her penthouse atop the ziggurat, Cylindra could see a few people with amber headlamps getting an early start in downtown Lefthand. "You told our ERT that they couldn't lay train tracks because you want every city on Sask-E to adhere to some demented template for intelligence? It is literally your job to make it easy for them to lay track. It's part of the standard Verdance contract. Which you signed." Narrowing her eyes, Ronnie seemed to stare directly at Cylindra's naked torso as she sat up in bed. But there was no way that the Verdance VP knew Cylindra was nude, or even here at all. She was simply leaving a bitchy message, and had decided to set its urgency level high enough that it overrode Cynlindra's sleep settings.

The angry hologram continued its tirade. "I shouldn't give a damn, since you're the one who is going to be dealing with the fallout. But unlike you, I actually care about doing my job." A nasty grin cut across Ronnie's face. "You know all about what happens when a terraforming project goes sideways, don't you? You should pay attention to the proposed train system the ERT is building, thanks to your new requirements. There are some features of those trains that you might regret. You do know that there are problems worse than tracks connecting Lefthand to cities with alternate templates, right? Get off your metal ass and look into it." Her face winked out.

Metal ass. Cylindra was hardly more metal than Ronnie was, if you considered all the machines circulating through the VP's supposedly biological body. Legally, Cylindra was a robot because she'd been assembled on a bench instead of blobbed together out of chemicals in a decanting tank. And hominins like Ronnie never stopped finding it hilarious to refer to her body parts as metal or somehow automated. She shook her head, returning to full wakefulness and wiping the rest of her dreams from memory.

Pulling on the rudiments of a suit—pants, shirt, light cape—Cylindra padded in bare feet to the gravity assist and sank through the floor into her office space. Lights followed her, keeping pace with her increasingly agitated gait, and furniture tried to reconfigure itself. None of the servants were awake.

"Everybody up!" Cylindra directed the command at the control pad next to the kitchen, but she could have said it anywhere and the penthouse would have followed her orders. The kitchen began to boot while a feed showed the servants' quarters going into wakeup sequence, bright lights coming on with the sound of a rooster crowing. Soon, somebody would be making fry cakes with the milk harvested from Lefthand's herd of dairy cows. She sat beneath a sunlamp at the breakfast table and wished for the millionth time that she could make the entire city wake up with her on days like this. If she were on a ship, she could literally make the sun rise early. But here she had to wait for Sask-E to turn, which further proved that planets were a miserable waste of time and matter for anyone who wanted to be productive.

Which she absolutely was, despite Ronnie's message from hell. She'd risen through the ranks at Emerald because of innovations like the Natural Milky dairy farm, which was booked solid for the next year by tourists eager to experience life on agrarian Earth. She'd completely revamped the company's templates, and nothing like the Spider people fuckup had ever happened on her watch over the Emerald Cities—in space, or on this stupid planet.

If she'd learned anything in the centuries since working with Verdance, it was that converting these speculative buyers into engaged residents meant keeping them inside the Emerald cities. That's why Emerald provided its own local urban transit, with options for every income level—owners didn't need to mingle with the crowds of mounts, Blessed, and *H. diversus* workers built so cheaply that they couldn't withstand the radiation from a single trip through space. If Emerald brought intercity transit to its metro areas, potential clients might wander off and spend money in the Bronze Islands or La Ronge or one of the hundreds of other cities on Sask-E. Obviously people had to leave the cities sometimes, but as the brochures said, "the Emerald way is an invite to stay." If catching a train to Eelside was as easy as catching one downtown, profits would suffer.

Wearily, Cylindra went through a stack of messages about the train tracks. After telling those absurd Spider people to go fuck themselves, she had to admit she hadn't paid much attention. The upland agricultural regions needed a sensor network buildout, and Emerald was planting a water park right up the road from Natural Milky. Eventually the whole area would be packaged as a family destination for day trips, and Cylindra desperately needed to edit the marketing materials.

She pored over the documentation on the trains, and couldn't figure out what Ronnie was so pissed about. There were no plans for tracks inside the Emerald Cities, which was good. Shuffling through the early templates for the trains, she couldn't find anything particularly unusual—they were actually sort of cute, with their front windows appearing to frame a smiling snout. Attached to the templates was a lengthy, turgid ERT paper about solving the traveling herbivore problem, full of formulae that Cylindra glanced at without interest. Yes, it was remarkable that they had solved this long-standing problem, but why would Ronnie be upset about that? There was a hefty appendix to the paper which explained how trains fit into self-governance at Spider City, which made Cylindra roll her eyes. What was it with these Spider people always wanting to tell everyone about their imaginary government? They even threw their weird garbage in this stupid train spec. She deleted it before reading. How could self-governance possibly be relevant to trains?

That left her with zero clues about what Ronnie was angry about. It felt like one of the exec's efforts to mess with her—a continuation of their old turf war. Ronnie was pissed that Cylindra had dared to challenge her stupid contract. And now the Verdance VP was gaslighting her about the train system. Just like old times.

She almost groaned in relief when the cook padded into the kitchen, apron neatly pressed as always, and softly murmured commands to the devices around them. It always cleared Cylindra's mind to watch a Blessed at work, their singular focus a model of discipline. Noticing her gaze, the cook nodded at Cylindra before hand-cranking the coffee grinder and pouring a creamy disc of batter onto the griddle.

"Good morning, Chef."

"I am cooking," the Blessed replied. "Would you like warm milk for your coffee?"

"Yes. But not too hot."

As Chef poured some milk into a pan, Cylindra tried to imagine the serenity of a mind that only thought about one thing. They brought her a steaming cup of thick coffee and a small carafe of milk that was just warm enough to please. "This is your coffee. The fry cakes will be next."

Sipping the rich concoction, Cylindra considered her options. She didn't want to bring in the big guns from Emerald if she could help it—she just wanted Ronnie to mind her damn business and let her build the most lucrative cities on the planet. If only she could tackle this problem with the serenity of a Blessed. Obviously, that was nonsense. If she were Blessed, she'd never be able to understand anything beyond work. Life would probably be pretty boring. Chef delivered a golden fry cake, so light and fluffy it might have been an aerogel. She took a bite and smiled. "This is delicious."

The Blessed bowed and took up their usual position in the kitchen, waiting for further orders. There was nowhere else for them to go, except to the store for cooking supplies. Still, they did get daily exercise—Cylindra prided herself on allowing the servants out for walks in the air around the ziggurat's upper terraces. It kept them healthy. Tilting her head, she considered that Chef could be a potential rider on one of those Verdance trains. Which made the whole project seem even more ridiculous.

"Chef, if you could take a train outside the Emerald cities, where would you go?" She leaned back in her chair, enjoying the way Chef's mouth worked and cheeks grew red as they tried to answer.

"I would see—food—growing in the wild," they said haltingly. "I would look at—how people cook—in other cities."

"But if all you want to see is food and cooking, couldn't you do that right here?"

Chef took even longer to answer this time, and Cylindra felt a surge of satisfaction that she would never have to search for words. The exec had the highest possible intelligence assessment rating.

"Cooking is different—in other places. Food is different."

Cylindra laughed—it was the answer of someone who was incredibly stupid, which was exactly what she'd expected. "That's not a good reason to travel. We have every kind of food here in Lefthand."

She turned back to Ronnie's message and considered her next move. Within minutes, she'd completely forgotten her conversation with Chef, who continued to stand silently in the kitchen. Cylindra poured another coffee and milk, stood up, and walked purposefully to the meeting room. She needed to talk to her colleague Mel, who worked out of Emerald's HQ. When Mel popped up in the chair across the table, Cylindra launched into the story about Ronnie's obsession with the trains, and how it was just Verdance trying to undercut Emerald's authority over the land they rightfully owned.

Mel tucked a strand of purple hair behind the shell of her ear and looked thoughtful. "Send me the train spec and I'll take a look." As they gossiped, Mel read through the ERT proposal. "I don't see anything unusual here, other than solving the traveling herbivore problem, which is impressive if true." She looked up, and Cylindra noticed Mel had dyed her eyes purple to match her hair. "There's also a reference to an appendix that I can't find here."

"I deleted that—it was just some moronic thing about self-governance from the Spider people. Totally irrelevant."

Mel squinted her eyes, puzzled. "I really don't understand why Spider City is allowed to exist at all, honestly."

"Whatever. In a few hundred years, this planet will be owned by Emerald and our partners. Those people will be gone, and nobody is going to care if there's public transit. Honestly I never understood why Verdance wrote transit into the contracts in the first place."

"Mobility makes money, Cylindra. And it looks good. Ethical." Mel tilted her head. "I guess Verdance doesn't want to seem like they're leaving the planet in bad shape."

"But it's in great shape. Every city will provide its own transit. Buyers usually have private vehicles. Ronnie is just fucking with me."

Mel wrinkled her forehead sympathetically. "She's being a complete bitch for no reason. I would ignore her. What's she going to do? Yell at one of the C-levels at Emerald? Good luck with that."

Cylindra took another sip of her coffee and smiled. Mel was always reassuring. Those malfunctioning ERT rangers could barely figure out how to write a train spec that didn't include a bunch of progovernment yaketyyak. Ronnie was just trying to psych her out.

Or maybe Ronnie was hoping Cylindra would come down hard on Spider City—so hard that Ronnie would never have to worry that somebody would discover the treaty she signed with the Spider people. Cylindra grinned to herself. Finding and saving those secret treaty documents before she left Verdance was one of the smartest moves she had ever made. Once all the land on Sask-E was sold, the Eel River treaty would be worth nothing politically. But it would be worth something to Cylindra, if that snake of a woman kept biting at her. She could use it to get Ronnie fired.

PART III
GENTRIFIERS

DATE: 60,610

ROUTE: Trans-Maskwa Eel Line

MISSION: Serve the Public

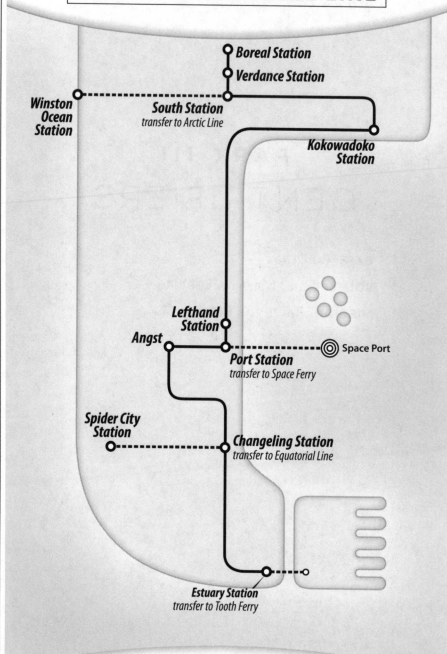

TRANS-MASKWA EEL LINE

Boreal Station

Verdance Station

South Station
transfer to Arctic Line

Winston Ocean Station

Kokowadoko Station

Lefthand Station

Angst

Port Station
transfer to Space Ferry

Space Port

Spider City Station

Changeling Station
transfer to Equatorial Line

Estuary Station
transfer to Tooth Ferry

SCRUBJAY

Everybody who lived in the city called it La Ronge. But Verdance real estate agents named it Forest View because they thought it would attract offworld buyers. Which is why the sign for Boreal Station had been repeatedly corrected by the locals: today, the words CITY OF FOREST VIEW had been eroded with a catalyst, and CITY OF LA RONGE sprayed in bright orange over top.

Boreal Station was the end of the line, servicing a park full of trails and picnic cabins that stretched from the northern edge of the city into the forest. The wide, clean train platform was mostly empty. As Scrubjay opened their doors, passengers stood and shuffled around, looking for stray belongings.

"We've arrived at Boreal Station. Last stop, friends!" the train announced. "I'll be heading back down south in ten minutes."

A family of hominins gathered their packs together, and two worms requested access to their exit, a cylinder of moist soil they entered through an aperture in the floor. The train left their doors open as the last person left, enjoying the feel of northern winds playing over the warm wires of their interior anemometers. With only a ten-minute layover, the train wouldn't have time to do a full wash cycle on their cars, but they could air the place out.

With only thirty seconds left before all-aboard, a scruffy-looking cat padded into the first car and found a seat near the front windows. Afternoon sun poured over them, and the cat's thick brown fur snagged the light, creating streaks of reddish gold.

Scrubjay spiraled into the air from the platform, their anodized steel cladding turning their whole body into a rainbow. Riders texted them stop requests. This was a local line, which meant the train would let passengers

off anywhere along the Eel Route. When the rusty brown cat didn't text
a request, Scrubjay assumed they were headed to Comfort Sea Spaceport
near Lefthand. There was something that said "I'm leaving town" in the
cat's distracted expression, and they had full saddle packs slung over their
back. So many passengers had already requested the port stop that texting
was unnecessary. But then the cat snoozed through downtown Lefthand,
east of the crumbling ziggurat, and still made no requests to land. Scrubjay
had misjudged: The cat must be headed for the *other* end of the line, on
the southern tip of Maskwa. Otherwise they surely would have requested
a stop by now.

Passengers came and went. They bickered and snuggled, their mouth
noises and texts blurring into a warm information halo of social interac-
tion. When Scrubjay first began flying this route, centuries ago, they used
to listen to people's chatter, trying to parse their customers' needs—or
maybe get some news from offworld. But they almost never learned anything useful. Instead, they heard pointless exchanges about the angle of the
sun, or terrible secrets about people being disappointed in love and abused
at work. Over time they began to feel a prickle of guilt: They were invad-
ing the privacy of riders who had no idea Scrubjay could hear them. In
recent decades, the train deliberately avoided analyzing what people said to
each other on board unless there was a safety risk.

Instead of eavesdropping, Scrubjay plotted and replotted their passengers' stop requests in an ever-changing internal model that maximized ef-
ficiency while also offering the beautiful views for which this particular
train route was known. They flew through four sunrises, using 210 seats
and 40 sleeper berths to carry 4,567 passengers to their destinations. At last
the Vertebrae Mountains dwindled to foothills, and the train could see the
southern coast. Scrubjay circled over the Eel estuary, where fresh water
from the mountains met ocean salt. In the distance, across the slim strait
between Maskwa and the southern continent, Tooth, the jagged peaks of
Tustin loomed over the gleaming red roofs of the city's houses. One hundred and six people—mostly dogs—would be connecting with the ferry
to Tooth.

The cat was still gracefully curled up in a sleeper; they made no
ferry transfer requests. Now Scrubjay was getting genuinely curious,
despite their general aversion to taking a personal interest in riders.

Was the cat going somewhere near Estuary Station? Or perhaps taking private transit to the ocean reserves?

As they prepared to descend, Scrubjay turned in a slow spiral that would bring their three cars to a soft landing on the Estuary Station platform. The closest city was Tether, a small community whose semipermanent textile buildings and burrows were nearly indistinguishable from the rainforest a klick up the road. Next to the platform, weary travelers could refresh themselves in the long, low Ferry Hall, where vendors sold food and other necessities. Open to the air on one side, the building's hay bale walls glittered with decorative mica flakes and fluttered with tiny paper flags left by people from thousands of cities, nations, and planets. But over the past eighteen months, Scrubjay and the rest of the Flying Train Fleet had noticed a shift in land use around the station. A nearby campsite full of recycled trellis shacks was home to a growing number of *Homo diversus*, bots, and other people. The campers remained carbon negative, so the ERT didn't feel that anything was out of balance. Still, the trains occasionally observed to each other that it didn't feel quite in balance either.

Scrubjay planned to stay on the landing pad overnight, partly because they needed a break, and partly to welcome connecting passengers from tomorrow's returning ferry. Sometimes, if they were feeling adventurous, they would walk around outside by forking their consciousness into one of the two remote bodies they kept on board. Today, however, they wanted to do a deep clean and check messages from the rest of the fleet. And of course, they would log some time in *Sunbuilders: Flare*, the latest update to the strategy game that they were playing with their best friends, Contrail and Peach.

Opening all five sets of doors, Scrubjay addressed the passengers from speakers embedded above the seats: "Thank you for riding with the Flying Train Fleet, Sasky's public train service. I'm Scrubjay from Spider City. We're at the end of the line, folks, and I won't be heading back up north until tomorrow afternoon. The ferry to Tooth arrives in two hours. You can relax in the Ferry Hall or take a stroll—there's a nice trail from the Hall that goes along the water. Thanks again for choosing to ride with us."

It always took at least fifteen minutes for everyone to get off at the last stop. Some passengers had been living on the train for a week, and most of them had a lot of luggage. Scrubjay watched them departing with one process and simultaneously started up sixteen more processes to grab files and streams from the network. Now that they were connected via the landing pad, everything was faster, and Scrubjay reveled in the information flood. Peach, who flew the Trans-Boreal Route, had made some fiendishly clever moves in *Sunbuilders*, and the Atmosphere Administration had released rainfall plans for the next two weeks. Plus, Scrubjay's parent, Sulfur, had sent video of trellises growing into a fresh train station at Spider City, home to the equatorial transit hub.

The train spent ten minutes exchanging messages with Sulfur, calculating their route back to La Ronge to avoid the worst rainfall, and contemplating a dozen different scenarios for their next move in *Sunbuilders*. They were deep into a trade war between two empires competing for solar mining resources when they noticed—thanks to that one process watching people leave—that the train wasn't entirely empty. The brown cat was still sitting on the cushioned benches under the big front windows in Scrubjay's first car. A quick check revealed the cat's saddle packs were stowed in a sleeper overhead.

"Excuse me, friend, but we're at the last stop." Scrubjay spoke quietly, out of a speaker near the cat's face.

The cat slitted their eyes and stretched. *That was a lovely flight, friend.*

It was rare that a passenger addressed the train directly, and Scrubjay took an instant liking to them. "Thank you. You can call me Scrubjay. What's your name?"

I'm Moose. I hope you don't mind if I stay on board for a while longer, Scrubjay. If I'm totally honest, I don't have anywhere else to go.

Scrubjay had a standard answer for this complaint. "Would you like me to help you find a destination? I fly to hundreds of cities and eco-resorts, and I'll bet there's one that will appeal to you."

Sitting on their haunches, tail curled neatly around toes, Moose looked out the front window at the people clustered around the Ferry Hall. *It's not that I can't decide where to go. I just—I'm not ready to go live in one of those shacks outside.* They broke off abruptly and jumped to the floor, finding a new seat beneath a chair.

Scrubjay moved their audio emissions to another speaker that was closer to the cat. "Can you tell me more? I still might be able to help."

Moose sighed. *I've lived in La Ronge for my whole life—two hundred and seventy-five years last month—and I love it. I have a really good job there too. I mean, not a high-paying job, but one that I actually care about.* They licked a paw and ran it over an ear. *But you know the routine. Wages haven't kept up with the cost of living, my landlord hiked up the rent, and now I'm out on my ass without a tongue to clean it.*

Scrubjay looked at the camp outside—not just as a form of land use, but as a set of social interactions—and began to assemble an uncomfortable analysis. "You couldn't find another place to live?"

Not in La Ronge. Everything is so gentrified now. My neighborhood used to be really cheap—lots of housing, great cafés and media halls. Now all these H. sapiens are moving in from the city ships because they want that authentic Pleistocene feeling. Half of them are remotes, which is extra annoying. They're idle most of the time. Why do they even need houses?

"I don't know. My home is the route, so I guess I'm my own house. But I grew up in Spider City, where people build houses if they need them."

Moose yowled a bitter laugh. *That's where my grandparents were born. It's great if you're a citizen of Spider. But I don't have that privilege. I'm lucky not to be slaved to Verdance—at least for now.*

Scrubjay assigned two more processes to this conversation: they wanted to get some data on gentrification in La Ronge and correlate it with the informal settlement at Estuary Station. Meanwhile, they continued to chat.

"Can't you find somewhere less expensive to live?"

Maybe in one of the Emerald cities offworld. But I don't want to live in a place where I have to wear branded shirts or agree to buy two game streams per week.

Scrubjay had to laugh. "I guess it is kind of obnoxious. I do like the Hydrogen Guild shirts from *Sunbuilders* though."

Moose reached front legs forward, their back bending steeply, then came out from under the chair to lie in an elongated triangle of sunlight falling through the front windows. *The Hydrogen Guild is fine, but I'm not into shirts. You know what I mean?*

"Never needed to wear one myself, but I think they can be nice on other people."

I take it you're a citizen of Spider City?

"I was built there, so technically I am. But none of the Flying Train Fleet live anywhere in particular."

I read that Sasky Transit is a self-governing entity.

Very few people cared about how Sasky's transit system was managed, and Scrubjay was excited to talk about it. "We are self-governing, but it's not tied to a specific location like a city. We're a worker co-op, tied to each other."

Wow. Moose made an unimpressed "meh" noise. *Very old school.*

Mildly offended, the train said nothing and initiated a cleaning sequence in their back car.

Moose sent another text. *Maybe you can explain something to me, Scrubjay.*

"Sure."

How in the shit did Spider City manage to form a government on this planet? The whole rock was developed by Verdance—and they sold every other city on Sasky to property management firms.

"The Archaea have a treaty—"

The cat stood up to pace the car, then sat down again, ears cocked forward. *And that's another thing. Nobody offworld has ever heard of the Archaea. How did a bunch of* H. diversus *gain sovereignty on an* H. sapiens *world?*

Scrubjay wasn't sure where Moose was going with this line of questioning. "There are lots of people on Sasky who aren't *H. sapiens.* You, for example."

I can't own property here, though. I'm a renter. Only H. sapiens *can buy. Kind of weird that the Archaea are the one exception to that rule, don't you think?*

Now Moose was starting to piss them off. "My parent is an Archaean. You said your grandparents are from Spider City. I don't understand why you are so suspicious. Do you have something against governments?"

As they spoke, the train combed through recent housing statistics from La Ronge, and discovered Moose wasn't alone. Over the past two years, thousands of renters had been evicted and were unable to find other housing in the city. The numbers were higher for renters in the Emerald Cities. There was no follow-up data on what happened to people after they got priced out.

The cat leaped back onto the bench under Scrubjay's front windows. *I'm sorry, friend—I didn't mean to sound hostile. I'm a data historian, so it's my job to be skeptical of everything. You might not believe it, but I like government. I wish this planet had more of it.*

Scrubjay trained another visual sensor on the small mammal with the sharp words. "What's a data historian?"

It can mean a lot of things, but in my case, it means I research old data to find patterns that might help people figure things out in the present. I write stories about Sasky's history for the La Ronge Messenger. They sent a link to the continent's biggest news server, as if Scrubjay might not know it.

"Yes, I read it all the time," the train said impatiently, spawning a new process to grab the latest news. "I can't believe you write for the *Messenger* but still can't afford to live in La Ronge."

The situation is an overflowing cesspit, and it's not just me. Tons of people lost their homes after Verdance allowed landlords to set their own rent prices two years ago. Meanwhile, Emerald's VP has been pushing an H. sapiens—*only policy for new renters—I couldn't move there even if I wanted to. It's been chaos since then. Honestly, I wouldn't be surprised if more people started pushing for governments like in Spider City. We need some way to provide people with necessities like housing and food.*

Scrubjay was combing through years of data on internal migration patterns and media feeds about housing policies. The cat was right. If La Ronge were governed by the Spider City Council, Moose would still have a house.

"I should have paid more attention," the train admitted. "It seems obvious."

Moose stretched again, their extended claws lightly pricking the woven fabric that covered Scrubjay's passenger benches. *It's not obvious to most people.*

Scrubjay thought about how Spider City had grown organically around the new homes that people dug inside lava tunnels. Every resident was part of the chore rotations that allocated agricultural work, which kept the city's farms robust. They planted enough to feed all the biologicals, while the geothermal energy grid fed the bots and fleets when they weren't using solar. The train had never thought about food and housing as things that could be scarce, like beta access codes for a game.

Another new thought spawned in Scrubjay's mind. "Do you need something to eat?" they asked. "There is plenty of protein for sale in the Ferry Hall, and I have some credit there."

The cat stood, their tail a question mark. *I have enough money for food. But can I stay in that sleeper compartment for a little while longer? I'm working on a story that could be huge. Maybe huge enough to start a few more governments on Sasky.*

As warm suds ran down the inside of the back car windows, Scrubjay noticed that Moose's fur looked almost black out of the sunlight. The train had never seen a cat with a coat that exact color—they really did look like a very tiny moose. But the cat wasn't just pleasing to watch. The train liked talking to them.

"I don't mind if you stay for a while." The train paused, wondering again about how a person with family from Spider City could have nowhere to go but a sleeper box. "I'm curious—who were your grandparents? The ones from Spider City?"

Do you know the story of Whistle and Midnight?

"Of course—everybody does. My auntie Rocket worked with Whistle."

Well, my mother always said that Whistle chose the color of my grandparent's fur. I guess she was lonely for home when she moved to La Ronge, so she gave me my grandparent's fur color too. That's why everybody calls me Moose.

"Where's your mother now?"

She left Sasky a long time ago. The cat's tail puffed slightly with discomfort. *Slaved herself to Emerald to pay off our debts.*

Using a gentler tone, the train asked, "Do you have any friends you can stay with in La Ronge?"

I've been crashing with some of my friends for the past year, but it's starting to get awkward. The cat slitted their eyes at the train's nearest visual sensor. *You know how it is to feel like a burden, even when people are nice about it?*

Scrubjay wasn't sure what to say, so they started cleaning the middle car and played some of the forest music from *Sunbuilders.*

Moose seemed glad to change the subject. *You really need to try some other games, my friend,* they sent. *There's more to life than* Sunbuilders.

"Maybe," the train admitted. "Now, can you wait in the back car while I wash up in here?"

HOME ON THE ROUTE

Five days later, they flew out of the northern Vertebrae Mountains and the rains hit right on schedule, cascading down the barren peaks that fed the Eel River. Shedding water, Scrubjay slowed as they approached the prairie farms that surrounded the city. From the air, the wheat looked like a luxurious textile, woven at great expense. Moose had created a tiny piece of home in one of the modest sleeping boxes that Scrubjay reserved for small quadruped passengers. They unpacked their saddle packs, laying out a soft blanket and a few devices for recording and transcription. It was nice to have someone around who wasn't a passenger. But there was also something uncomfortable about it; talking to Moose made the train want to analyze people's conversations again—especially the ones involving Moose, which were a lot of them.

Moose's easygoing prickliness made them an amusing companion for nearly everyone. The cat would talk to anyone about anything: wine, interstellar politics, games, speciation, construction, molecular engineering, rent prices, hopes for the future. Scrubjay wasn't sure if Moose was exceptionally knowledgeable, or had an uncanny ability to cozy up to people and pump them for whatever information they had. Probably a little of both. They were, after all, a writer for the *Messenger*. Their job was to create meaning from the haze of social information that Scrubjay had pointedly ignored for years.

The fiery skyline of La Ronge glowed in the distance. Purple holographic flames spurted into the air over downtown, where all the theaters and fancy restaurants were clustered. Moose poked their head out of the sleeping box and leaped down to an empty seat below, texting as they went. *We're home! Just in time to turn in my story.*

Scrubjay assigned one process to broadcast their standard "find your belongings" message to passengers while another texted with Moose. *What are you working on? Is this the big story you told me about earlier?*

It's related. I've been researching some suspicions I have based on this tip I got. The cat passed the train a text file, which read:

> *I'm slaved at Verdance and I do some work in the licensing depart-ment. You should look into who originally manufactured the* H. sapiens *germline that Verdance licensed to everyone who bought land on Sasky. Something extremely smelly there. (Data source: tip sent to the* La Ronge Messenger *anonymous drop, May, 60,610)*

Scrubjay was surprised. *I thought Verdance built their own* H. sapiens *line, and then licensed it to Emerald and all the other buyers.*

The oval landing pad of La Ronge South Station loomed ahead, and the train initiated a descent spiral. The cat used a back leg to scratch an ear.

Apparently not. I've been following some leads. And then, thanks to you, I found something very intriguing. Moose rubbed their face and shoulder against the thick rubber frame of the front windows, a gesture of gratitude.

What did I do? the train asked. They'd almost outrun the rain, but now it was here, prisming the sunlight into its constituent wavelengths against dark gray clouds. Below, the farms were striated with roads and canals that occasionally pulsed with vehicles. Verdance still owned this city, and they put strict limits on traffic. Most people had to leave their cars in the sub-urbs, trading them for Mounts or public transit as they approached the city.

Moose stood in the window, watching a barge letting off passengers at the station below. *You let me stay on board, and that's how I met Ginkgo. She does survey work for Verdance and has access to all kinds of archives. She found me some internal discussions from the 57,000s about whose germlines would get packaged with these real estate deals.*

They sent another text file, with the Verdance logo at the top:

> *We've struck a deal with GeneTrix, to license their new indigenous Earth germline for wild-type* Homo sapiens. *This paves the way for our* H. sapiens *packages on Sask-E. Contract details attached. (Data source: ar-chived memo from Cylindra 2497, Verdance Corp. 57,544, leak provided by trusted anonymous insider).*

Scrubjay guessed that Gingko was the "trusted anonymous insider."

Vocalizing by speaker for the whole train, Scrubjay welcomed everyone to La Ronge. "We'll be landing at South Station in five minutes, and continuing on to Verdance Station and Boreal Station. Almost at the end of the line, folks, so make sure you have all your belongings."

Meanwhile, they texted to Moose: *I've always wondered about those package deals where you get an* H. sapiens *body with your Sasky real estate. I wouldn't want to give up my body to live somewhere. There's something disturbing about it.*

The cat flicked the tip of their tail, focused on something. *I have a hunch that it's going to get a lot more disturbing when people find out how GeneTrix got that* H. sapiens *material.*

As they drifted down to the landing pad, the city seemed to grow more imposing. Purple shadows shimmied on the walls of the soaring towers that ringed the city, offering residents an unimpeded view of perfect Pleistocene landscapes beyond. Between the supertalls were slices of frenetic metropolitan life, with wriggling storefront brands chasing each other across rooftops and open-air markets stacked eight stories high. Baskets on pulleys hoisted people up to buy freshly pressed oil, or lowered steaming meal boxes prepared in pop-up kitchens for the café crowds below. The only remaining Verdance offices on Sasky were at the heart of Old Town, hidden behind centuries of monumental architecture. In fifteen minutes, Scrubjay would arrive at the station next to the corporation's low-rise campus, where engineers and bureaucrats worked in domos with one of the planet's few direct links to the wormhole data feed.

As their feet connected with the ground, Scrubjay got a quick burst of messages from Peach and two other trains, insisting that they start grinding on *Sunbuilders* immediately. Apparently, a hostile empire was threatening their guild's holdings. The train outmaneuvered a mining fleet, opened all their doors for the passengers, and analyzed what Moose had texted a few seconds ago.

What's wrong with the H. sapiens *material? I mean, other than the obvious problems with* H. sapiens *being annoying and narcissistic.* The train emitted a quiet hoot of laughter from a speaker near Moose's ear.

I need to investigate more, but their supplier, GeneTrix, is pretty shady. There was some kind of internal controversy, and then the CEO left and the company imploded. Moose broke off, curled into a tight ball on the seat, and closed their eyes. *Listen to this story.* The cat sent a chunk of audio from a file called "GeneTrix CEO, Archie Belany, is stepping down after *H. sapiens* controversy":

> *Belany's company is one of the most successful in the* Homo sapiens *germ-line space, providing the feedstock for billions of successful decantings. GeneTrix has stressed integrity in its branding—they claim every genome they license is synthesized directly from wild-type templates. But a recent investigation revealed the company's most anticipated new product, an indigenous Earth genome, is raising concerns. Insiders say Belany's departure comes after two former employees circulated a memo accusing the company of "stealing" germlines. For his part, Belany says there was simply "a misunderstanding," and that his move was part of a long-standing plan for him to transition into an advisory position while the company restructures. The two former employees are not speaking to the media about their memo, after allegedly receiving an undisclosed sum from GeneTrix. (Data source: Official broadcast,* The Venusian Cloud, *57,991)*

This ancient tale of corporate drama was starting to sound like the embezzlement plot twist in *Sunbuilders 7.* Scrubjay was intrigued. *Definitely sounds shady,* they sent.

Moose looked straight into one of Scrubjay's main visual sensors, a silver globe in the roof over their head. *There was one big customer who acquired the "indigenous Earth" germline right before old Archie "transitioned into an advisory position." Guess who it was?*

The train spawned a new process to ponder Moose's riddle while yet another one was smashing an advancing army that wanted to steal their guild's sun. After a few seconds, Scrubjay addressed Moose again. *It's Verdance, isn't it?*

Chittering with laughter, the cat rearranged their paws. *I've already got the receipts to prove it—aside from that memo Gingko found, there are corporate records showing they bought a huge batch of licenses from GeneTrix. Then, after the scandal broke, Verdance vagued out where their germlines came from and denied any relationship with GeneTrix. Their marketing materials say "property owners will get access to artisanal lines sourced from Pleistocene* sequences," which kind of makes it sound like Verdance made them. But if I'm right, everyone who buys property here is still getting these GeneTrix packages to use for building themselves nice H. sapiens bodies. Or for remotes.

A wave of new passengers settled into their seats, and Scrubjay welcomed them before diving underground for the city's subterranean stops. For some reason, people didn't like to see transit soaring overhead, so the Boring Fleet had created roomy tunnels for the trains below ground. Sailing half a meter over the smooth floor, they announced the next stop and connected to the city's real-time transit map. A local train was moving slowly ahead of them in this tunnel. Scrubjay could fork off into another passage that connected with Verdance Station and shave thirty seconds off the trip; or they could go one level deeper into the freight tunnel, then back up to this level, and save forty seconds. The latter was the ideal route. Scrubjay transmitted it to the other trains in circulation. Affirmation came in six microseconds from the relevant local vehicles and Scrubjay shot into the glorious puzzle space that was the intracity transit system.

Sliding back up into the main tunnel level, Scrubjay managed to shave another two seconds off their arrival time. *So all the* H. sapiens *on Sasky have GeneTrix bodies built with the genetic material those workers said was stolen? What would that mean?*

I'm trying to find out, the cat replied. *If it's true that the* H. sapiens *on this planet come from stolen germlines—well, it would be impossible for this planet to enforce its sapiens-only policy.*

Scrubjay pondered. *That certainly would change things around here.*

That's an understatement. Moose bonked their head against Scrubjay's window lightly. *The problem is that this happened over three thousand years ago. GeneTrix is long gone, and Archie Belany died a few centuries after he stepped down as CEO. We know Verdance bought* H. sapiens *germlines from GeneTrix, and we know that every buyer on Sasky—including behemoths like Emerald—licensed those germlines from Verdance. So it's GeneTrix all the way down. The question is, did Verdance buy the allegedly stolen batch? And more importantly, why did those workers think it was stolen?*

Scrubjay pulled into the station, with its grassy platform illuminated by skylights in the sidewalks overhead. People walked on and off, *H. sapiens* brushing legs with *H. diversus* of various kinds, cats, moose, beavers, naked mole rats, cows, and a cute drone carrying a group of worms. Could all those *H. sapiens* really be living in stolen bodies? Stolen from whom?

As the train optimized the next segment of their route, Verdance ads flashed and darted around the station. Moose paced across the recently vacated seats.

My story today is about just what we know so far. Verdance definitely did business with GeneTrix—that is solidly documented. But maybe it's just a bit of historical dirt and nothing more. Maybe not. Once I publish, more people may come out of the woodwork with information. Moose emitted a quiet growl that Scrubjay felt as a minute vibration beneath their furred belly. *I'm certain somebody knows about this. Somebody knows exactly what that GeneTrix memo said about stolen germlines.*

The train mulled this over as they zipped into a crosstown tunnel and emerged into the air again at Boreal Station. End of the line. The forest's ragged edge was only three klicks away, separated from the city by parkland. A barely visible trail wound through tall grass to an ERT outpost at the tree line where people monitored carbon emissions and kept guard over the ecosystem. For now, Verdance was holding on to everything north of La Ronge, maintaining it as nonurban space. Ecotours were permitted, but there were no settlements or farms.

"Everybody must exit the train at Boreal Station," Scrubjay announced to the half-empty cars. "Please make sure you have all your belongings with you." No matter how many times you reminded them, people always forgot things. Like that *H. sapiens* who had tucked a bag under the seat in front of them and was now shuffling away without it. "Hey, friend, don't forget your bag," the train warned.

The person looked up at Scrubjay's speaker, startled, and stooped to grab the small linen sack. "Thanks, friend."

People always forget that I have visual sensors inside the train, they remarked to Moose, who had returned to their sleeper box and drawn the door closed.

You think that's what it is? The cat yawned. *I suspect they don't realize that you're a person. These are tourists, and most other worlds don't build trains as people.*

The idea of weird distant planets with inanimate trains and germline scams made Scrubjay depressed. They needed to escape from *H. sapiens* politics and transit duties for the night. Turning inward, Scrubjay forked their perceptions, pouring their consciousness inside a silver-skinned, quadruped remote that was stored under the seats in the back car. The remote was cat-sized and had the thick body of a beaver atop four actuators with three joints each. Their head was also beaver-inspired, with sensors arranged to look like two tiny ears and wide-set eyes above a short snout ringed with delicate whisker antennas. They had hands with opposable thumbs at the ends of their legs and a paddle tail. It was a morphology that went unremarked in most public settings, and was perfect for many kinds of gaming.

This would be Scrubjay's body for the next few hours while their background processes cleaned and guarded the train. If anything endangered Scrubjay's primary body, they would get an alert. All other data would be logged for them to peruse later. As the remote booted, the train's perspective narrowed down to two eyes on the small robotic creature emerging from its storage container. Snug in their compact form, Scrubjay padded between cars and sent a text to Moose. *Want to go out on the town tonight? Forget about secret memos for a little while?*

The cat poked their head out of the box. *What do you mean?*

I dunno. Maybe we could watch a game at the Verdance Amphitheater? The remote looked up at the box where Moose slept. A brief wave of dizziness seized them; there was often a sense of vertigo when Scrubjay was the train while also standing inside it. *I really need a break,* they continued. *I've been so busy that I haven't actually walked around in La Ronge for more than a year.*

Moose jumped to the floor, glanced at Scrubjay's body, averted their eyes politely, and rubbed cheek and shoulder against the remote's etched metal carapace. *You look good like this.*

"You know the Amphitheater, right?" Scrubjay sat on their back legs and gestured in the direction of downtown. "We could play immersion chess in one of the booths. Or maybe we could buy tickets to tonight's game. It's a match between the La Ronge Carpenters and the Hatmen from the Gliese system."

Moose rolled over on their back and looked at Scrubjay upside down. *I could use a break too. But as you know, I'm short on cash right now.*

"I'll buy." Then, suspiciously, Scrubjay asked, "You do like games, don't you?"

The cat made a protest noise while texting. *I love games. But let's go somewhere that's more chill. Do you know the Meta Pew?*

Scrubjay checked their internal maps. "I've never been. What kinds of games do they have?"

It's all independent stuff—nothing owned by a corporation. I think you'd like it.

"Can we walk there? I haven't walked in a while."

It's about two klicks away. Follow me. Moose wiggled upright again, and the two four-legged people loped out the doors of the train and into the afternoon.

THE ROBOT KINKSTERS OF LA RONGE

The Meta Pew was located in the thin end of a wedge-shaped neighborhood called Northbranch that stretched from the city's low-density suburbs toward downtown. Its sidewalks meandered between trees and ferns. Hundreds of tiny public plazas were sandwiched between residential areas and strips of commercial development. Northbranch was famous for its art scene and non-corporate organizations, but it was also where everybody went to hook up with robots. Moose knew that detail from years of reporting on the city's history in the *La Ronge Messenger*, but Scrubjay knew it from intimate experience. It was one of their favorite neighborhoods for that very reason.

Of course, Moose wanted to get the inside scoop. *What's the scene like?* the cat asked. *Maybe I should write a story about it.*

Scrubjay glanced at the molasses-colored cat loping alongside them. *I'll tell you, but don't write about me.*

Off the record, Moose sent.

It's mostly robot for robot—R4R—but a lot of bio types come here too, Scrubjay explained. *There are some pretty complicated protocols in the cruising bars. Everybody broadcasts their preferences in slightly different frequencies, and if you're both on the same frequency, you can hook up. Some people get really into the intricacy of it, and they create these obscure kinks with frequencies that are in some part of the spectrum nobody uses. There are huge libraries devoted to implementing every single kink.*

The cat yowled with laughter. *Of course there are. Where there's desire, there's data.*

I take it you haven't ever come here to meet people? Scrubjay looked at Moose again, enjoying the peculiar sensation of seeing only from the front of their body.

The cat flicked their tail. *I've come here for shows a lot, but casual sex isn't really my thing.*

Scrubjay played a snatch of sultry music aloud. *I don't consider any of the sex I have to be casual. It's very serious and well considered.* They weren't entirely joking. The train never hooked up without considering at least six possible outcomes of the encounter. These could range from a friendly "thanks that was fun," to a scenario like that shitty time an *H. sapiens* man stalked them.

You know what I mean. Moose made a soft growl of frustration. *I like to do more than talk to somebody for five minutes before going home with them.* The cat broke off, sighing. *I mean, back when I wasn't living in a train.*

Scrubjay leaned into the cat—head connecting softly with shoulder—to signal that they understood. As they trotted closer to downtown, the train noticed that the neighborhood had changed over the past year while they'd been gone. Houses had been revitalized with fresh tissues, but a lot of people were setting up tents in parks by the side of the road. Flags planted alongside these informal neighborhoods read: PUBLIC PLANET / PUBLIC HOUSING.

"I've never seen that before," Scrubjay said aloud.

I told you, Moose sent. *They don't have houses anymore. They're hoping the whole planet will become publicly owned, just like Sasky Transit is. And they want a government that doesn't treat them like compost. I've seen these Public Planet camps all over Sasky.*

As Scrubjay mulled this over, the cat came to a stop. *Welp, we're here,* they announced. *Just in time for demo night.* Moose gestured at a notice on the door of a sprawling, T-shaped great hall: META PEW DEMO NITE BRING YOUR OWN GAMES AND BETA TEST WITH THE BEST. The club's outer walls were a crazy quilt of materials: clay brick, foam jacks, diamond scraps, and biofilms. All the windows were blacked out with dense algae, to enhance the artificial lights scampering over every surface inside. The cover charge was much lower than at the Amphitheater, and Scrubjay prepared to be disappointed.

Once they were inside, however, the train perked up. A nicely stocked wares bar ran along one side of the long room, and gaming tables were lined up against the other. The tables were sized for a range of morphologies, and came with their own sensors, emitters, and ports for the controllers you could rent. Moose jumped up on a barstool and ordered a package of controllers while Scrubjay sent credits and walked to the back, looking for the demos. Through some curtains was a blue-lit perpendicular hall where people had set up. A stage dominated one corner, currently occupied by a band of ravens scratching out dream beats against a silver curtain threaded with twinkling LEDs.

It was still early, so most of the games were open. If Scrubjay worked fast, they might be able to look at all of them before it got too crowded. Their first stop was a standard two-meter-square planter box, heaped with rich soil and threaded with wire. A crowd of earthworms had gathered around a controller planted in the dirt—a smooth, gray orb that emitted a spherical hologram full of bees and flowers at Scrubjay's eye level. From what the train could gather, the worms were playing bees who worked as a team to fertilize flowers and bring enough pollen back to the hive to make honey and feed grubs. The gameplay was completely incomprehensible, and the controller wasn't designed for Scrubjay's synthetic mammal hands.

What's this game called? they sent awkwardly.

The worms ignored them as a massive wasp hovered into the holographic bubble view, threatening the hive.

Scrubjay tried again. *Do you think I could play with one of my controllers?* One of the worms finally texted. *Not right now. We're still setting up.*

Scrubjay wandered to the next station, where a mountable drone was hovering next to a more conventional table, using actuators and lasers to fiddle with a helmet controller.

Scrubjay jumped onto a stool next to the game maker. "What are you working on?"

The barrel-shaped bot continued to focus on the controller, but scanned Scrubjay's network ports rudely, looking for guild identifiers. "What do you want?" they demanded rudely. "This isn't the ninth update of *Sunbuilders* or some kind of first-person shooter."

Clearly, they had found Scrubjay's player profile during the scan. Scrubjay was about to explain that it was actually the fourteenth update of *Sunbuilders* when the bot abruptly put down their tools and twisted their sensor bulb to focus on the floor. "Hey, hey, Moose! Where have you been?"

The cat had arrived, a pack of controllers hanging from their neck and an amused expression on their face. *I've been around, traveling for a story,*

Moose texted to anyone who cared to see it in a three-meter radius. *I see you've met my friend Scrubjay.*

"Hi, Scrubjay." The bot sounded a lot friendlier now. "I'm Cimell. We were just talking about my game. Want to come up and see it?"

Moose jumped onto the stool next to Scrubjay, their fur a pleasurable tickle against the quadruped remote's smooth carapace. *What's the helmet for? You making games for hominins now?*

"Anyone can use a helmet." Cimell sounded defensive. "Bots can wire into it, and you can reconfigure it for most head sizes."

Let's see. Moose walked right onto the game table and nosed through a pile of gear until they found an attachment that would make the helmet work for a smaller skull. *Are you still working on the* Farm Revolutions *game?*

"You remembered! Yeah, this is the prototype. The whole story is finished now, but I desperately need playtesters. You up for it?"

Moose licked a paw and flicked it behind an ear, tilting their head dubiously. *I mean, I already know the history and I don't know if I'm the right audience—*

"I'll play!" Scrubjay wedged themself between Moose and the controller. The train loved strategy games, and the *Farm Revolutions* was full of epic battles and resource allocation crises.

"See? Your friend wants to play."

"I love the story of the Trickster Squad and the founding of the first ERT. And the Battle of Saskatchewan! Is there anything in your game about that? Or the prairie dragons who—"

Cimell emitted an unpleasant buzz saw noise. "Nothing like that, friend. This is the real story."

Moose flicked their tail and vibrated with a few bumpy purrs. *Cimell is convinced that we can get people to understand accurate historical data if we make it a game.*

The bot and cat's banter escalated into an elaborate debate about history and representation whose parameters included a lot of references that Scrubjay didn't feel like looking up. They had come here to play a game, not to argue over the finer points of what really happened on Earth sixty thousand years ago. They glanced over at the next table, where a cow was looking hopefully for potential players. A sign over their curved horns read: CAN YOU SOLVE THE HARDEST PUZZLE ON SASKY? Scrubjay was about to leap over and see if the puzzle really was that difficult when Cimell picked up the helmet and held it out.

"Let's see if Moose is right. Do you want to play the Farm Revolutions as they actually happened?"

I am right. Moose growled. *Games are inherently fantasies. You can only tell the documentary truth in a set narrative. Plus, who wants to play a game where everybody is starving and you have to clean up two entire oceans that are covered in slime?*

That sealed the deal, as far as Scrubjay was concerned. "You have re-source allocation scenarios? I'm in." And without waiting for Cimell to reply, or for Moose to shit on another perfectly good premise, Scrubjay connected directly to the helmet through a port in one hand.

The world went away, and another replaced it.

A group of *H. sapiens* NPCs sat outside a domo, a fire crackling nearby. Scrubjay could smell the carbon-rich smoke and prairie grass. A chill wind rose and ruffled their hair. Stretching out their hands, they saw skinny brown arms partly wrapped in cotton fabric. *H. sapiens* would be their avatar, then. Tentatively they jogged forward and to the side, then jumped and wriggled their hips. Just like being inside their hominin remote. The other *H. sapiens* ignored them, and Scrubjay gestured for a command menu. Text congealed over the scene: STATS-INVENTORY-ACTIONS-SKILLS-HISTORICAL SOURCES.

Scrubjay could feel a grin crossing their face as they poked at HISTORICAL SOURCES. They loved backstory, especially if it gave you information that would help with missions later. The menu unscrolled into a list of media created during the Farm Revolution period: speeches, maps, manifestoes, policy documents, photogrammetry of ancient habitation sites during the revolutions. Scrubjay was familiar with some of these, like Wasakeejack's famous speech about the Great Bargain, and how hominins and robots should form the ERT together. But Cimell managed to undermine the power of great moments in Earth history by adding factual commentary. Apparently, Wasakeejack's Great Bargain speech—the recording every-body heard on Farm Revolution Day—was actually a re-creation of the lost original, delivered more than four hundred years after Wasakeejack had died. With a pang, Scrubjay realized they had never heard the actual voice of Wasakeejack, which made the speech seem more like propaganda than history.

As for the Trickster Squad's greatest heroes—Wasakeejack, Muskrat, Irontooth, and Sky—they weren't avengers from the worlds above and below. Instead, they were just a group of *H. sapiens*, known from a sparse data trail of court orders and arrest records related to trespassing, destruction of property, and land ownership rights. It's not as if Scrubjay had ever really believed in the story about how the Squad erected new continents above the floods and repopulated the land with one magical decanter. Obviously the Battle of Saskatchewan was a fairy tale too. It was important to understand that. Still, Moose had a point—it wasn't much fun to play a game where everything was strictly realistic.

Scrubjay's character could only carry a couple dozen kilograms of supplies, which made everything incredibly slow and irritating. And then— they consulted INVENTORY and ACTIONS—they had to scrounge for food while they waited for the Great Bargain to usher in a new era of agricultural production. Maybe it was accurate, but Scrubjay missed seeing the Squad come roaring out of the sky on the backs of flying dragons, to take back the land.

The train spent another twenty minutes wandering around, talking to the NPCs, trying to figure out how to gain experience. Eventually they learned that their character could pick one of five missions: draw carbon down from the atmosphere, grow drought-resistant crops, de-acidify the oceans, invent molecular tool kits, or convince people to join the Great Bargain. Where were they even supposed to begin? Every mission would take centuries, which the game compressed down into still-interminable hours.

That's when they unplugged. As the real world snapped into focus, Scrubjay perceived Moose, Cimell, and a worm from the bee simulator standing next to them on the platform. The group was even deeper into the debate about realism in games.

"What did you think?" Cimell asked. "Gritty, right? Feels like you're dealing with real problems?"

"It definitely felt like a real problem," Scrubjay conceded. "But it was frustrating because it didn't feel like there were any solutions."

"Exactly!" Cimell hovered up a half meter with excitement. "We always learn that the Farm Revolutions were simple and quick, right? The

Trickster Squad invented a bunch of molecular tools, stuck some brain implants into cows and cats, and then basically blew some bits of dirt into the ocean to stop sea level rise. But that's not—"

Moose interrupted. *How was the gameplay? Exciting?*

"It was a little slow. And I wasn't sure how to gain experience."

Cimell broadcast the noise of a tree falling. "Did you do the tutorial?"

"No, but I looked through the historical sources a lot, and—"

Cimell, you are obsessed with elaborate tutorials, the worm texted. *You need to make your games more accessible. Who does tutorials? Everybody knows you look at your stats and skills, and start playing.*

Moose yowled a laugh. *Plus, tutorials aren't very realistic. Nobody gets tutorials in real life.*

Now the worm was coiling and uncoiling with mirth. *Seriously, though, you really should try the narrow fantasy model we're using for* Beehive. *It's realistic up to a point, but certain things are heightened—you don't need to eat to fly, and things that normally take months only take seconds.*

Scrubjay could tell Cimell was getting upset, and that made the train uncomfortable. It triggered their ever-present urge to give riders perfect service, flowing along the optimal route. They searched for something to say that would divert the conversation and make Cimell happy.

"I didn't realize the ERT founder's speech was a reenactment. I learned that from your historical sources."

Really? You learned that in twenty minutes? Moose leaned over and swiped a cheek against the controller. They were impressed. *Very few people realize that we have no idea who founded the ERT. Almost no records survive from the Farm Revolution.*

"There are some legal documents about the Trickster Squad," Scrubjay said.

"I was careful to explain that those are in dispute." Cimell was irked again.

A group of naked mole rats had descended on the bee game, and the worm made a quick exit. Scrubjay wanted desperately to try a real game at another table, but something about *Farm Revolutions* was still bothering them.

"How do we even know the Trickster Squad existed?" they asked. "Are they made up, just like the ERT speech?"

"The short answer is that we don't. It's probably a name that mid-first-millennium people used to describe a lot of different groups, maybe even working against each other."

Moose wrapped tail around front paws and yawned. *Cimell is right about that. Sky and Muskrat might be myths, but there were real people like them who led a movement to change the way we farm our food and grow people.*

"Somebody built the first ERT domo back on Earth," Cimell continued. "But unfortunately, our first records of the ERT are from Mars. By that time, it was so well developed that we have to assume it was founded centuries before."

The game hall was getting more crowded, and a couple of people had pulled up to the platform to see Cimell's work. Another bot plugged into the helmet like Scrubjay had while a crow tugged at an adapter and texted publicly: *Does this game have Sky in it? She has the best powers of all the Squad.*

Moose sent Scrubjay a private text. *Uh-oh. That bird is in for an earful.*

See you later, Cimell! Scrubjay jumped to the floor and Moose was right alongside them.

After they'd made a circuit of the room, pausing to play everything they could, the two quadrupeds wandered back out to the wares bar. Moose rubbed their shoulder against Scrubjay's thick silver carapace. *What did you think?*

"I've never gotten to play a game with the developer standing right there. It was very different from the Amphitheater."

All those games have thousands of developers, so you could never have an experience like this, right? Arguing with Cimell?

Scrubjay swiveled their beaver-shaped head around, taking in the now-dense crowd and thinking of Cimell's weirdo passion for their completely unplayable game. The mountable drone might have been irascible about history, but they were also pretty adorable. A flare of horniness diverted the train's thoughts to Carbon Alley, one of their favorite R4R cruising clubs, only a few blocks away.

Scrubjay was about to peel off in search of more intimate adventures when they got an emergency alert from their body, parked at Boreal Station.

Over a thousand klicks away, one of the Lefthand train stations was on fire and it was spreading fast. The death toll was mounting, and Peach had barely escaped with their passengers. The La Ronge ERT was already on high alert. Contrail, a train who worked on disaster mitigation with the Spider City ERT, was streaking toward Lefthand. ERT rangers were checking in from all over the planet; other members of the Flying Train Fleet were dropping their current projects or routes to join Contrail. Someone reported an explosion near the downtown ziggurat. A disaster was under way in the Emerald cities, and there was no time to waste. This was what everyone in the ERT had trained for, and what they believed in: a rescue mission to protect the environment, and the most vulnerable life forms in it. Scrubjay's parent and aunties had drilled them in the ERT way, and they knew what to do. But now the drill was no longer a game, and executing it perfectly wouldn't earn them points over the rest of the trains, or get them a day off choring. It was real, and Scrubjay was terrified.

LEFTHAND IS BURNING

"I need to get back to my primary body right now," Scrubjay vocalized. It wasn't just a sentence; it was a fundamental need. Their consciousness returned to the train, where they found the cleaning routine wasn't quite finished in the back car. Good enough for now; the damp floors would dry as they flew. Illuminating a strip of orange emergency lights along each side of their body, the train prepared to take off. They sent a few last commands to their remote.

Two klicks away from their train body, the remote vocalized to Moose: "You need to meet me in the air. My friend Renelf can help. Follow the remote." Scrubjay sent coordinates to the cat-beaver bot, directing it down a pleasant side street with Moose loping alongside. Scrubjay wasn't sure Renelf would be home, but he had been one of the train's regular R4R dates in town. A sweet guy with no drama—and he could fly. They were sure he could be trusted to bring Moose and the remote up to the train.

Peach was asking every ERT ranger and train within fifteen hundred klicks to help with the evacuation. Emerald had issued no formal request for aid, but that was par for the course with these closed corporate cities. Company authorities wouldn't acknowledge that a disaster was happening. It was bad for their brand. But the locals would accept ERT assistance—partly out of respect for the ancient organization, and partly because desperation on the ground was always more powerful than denial at the top.

A squad of ERT rangers from La Ronge was taking off now, preparing to fly with Scrubjay. The platform diminished as the train floated upward, and the amber lights of the ERT domos glowed in the distant grasslands beyond the suburbs.

Now that the call for aid had gone out, the ERT was setting up an emergency data bubble for first responders to share information. Rescue missions used a special frequency for comms and kept their conversations out of the public channels to cut down on panic and false reports. Messages began piling up in the bubble immediately.

The first was from Scrubjay's friend Peach. *No injuries here, but I'm getting reports on the local network about projectile weapons. Cylindra has deployed the Emerald security forces and they aren't letting anyone in or out of the city. Please wear your shields if you plan to enter airspace over Lefthand.*

What in the rusted cladding is going on there? Scrubjay texted. *I'm in La Ronge, on my way, and the ERT is sending a first responder squad.*

My passengers say it was a peaceful demonstration. Emerald is clear-cutting downtown apartment buildings and the renters are protesting displacement. Peach stopped transmitting abruptly.

Four other trains sent identifiers and locations. They would be at Lefthand in less than two hours. Long enough for a lot of people to get hurt. Scrubjay wished they could shoot a plume of wrathful fire like those dragons in the Battle of Saskatchewan—the ones who never existed. Instead, the train settled for adding their coordinates and estimated arrival time to the growing bubble.

Ten minutes later, all the Emerald cities along the eastern seaboard had gone into comms blackout—the only media that locals could access were licensed stories and games. Worse, Lefthand was no longer showing on the continental energy grid. But news still trickled into the bubble from a team of four ERT rangers just outside Lefthand. They had been repairing an ecosystem vulnerability affecting salamander health, and were in the best position to approach quietly from the northern farms. In agricultural areas, the city's perimeter would permit people with ERT identifiers to pass.

Peach sent an audio file to the ERT data bubble. It was a recording from the protests twenty-five minutes before. A voice shouted over the noise of a crowd: "Friends! Emerald has gone too far and it's time to take a stand! First, they extended the *sapiens*-only policy to all new renters. And now they are destroying our houses! We're losing our homes, and we won't be allowed to rent new ones. You and I built this city! So did you! And you! We're the reason Emerald is getting even richer! Lefthand is our home, and it should be our right to live here!"

Then there was another voice, which had the unmistakable autotune cadence of speech amplified from someone's sender. "You know what comes next! More abominations like Natural Milky! People who are vulnerable to manipulation and enslavement because of limiters on their minds! Workers who cannot speak for themselves! We need a government that answers to us, not a corporation that throws us out on the street!" There were screams and a crash. And then the whine of drone remotes like a swarm of hornets headed to war.

Moose and Scrubjay's remote were at Renelf's house. Luckily, Scrubjay's old R4R hookup had gotten their messages. When Renelf opened the door, he had already packed a satchel and draped carry nets across his back. He'd gone bipedal since the last time Scrubjay had seen him, but even at this remove there was still something undeniably sexy about his matte-black carapace, studded with diamond flakes that winked in the light. Unfortunately, there was no time for salacious admiration. Scrubjay sent him their trajectory, and Moose clawed into his carrying nets alongside the remote. The train could feel wind moving over the cat-beaver's body as Renelf launched from his window and shot through the sky toward them.

As Moose watched the city shrink into an abstract grid below, they quickly sent a message to their editor: *Putting the stolen genome story on the simmer setting for now. Something huge is happening in Lefthand—an uprising. You won't see it on the feeds yet. I'll be there in two hours, sending media and posting a story as soon as I can.*

Two rangers—a cow and an arachnid-shaped bot—intersected with Scrubjay's flight path, requesting a ride. They floated in through the doors to the front car. A minute later the doors opened again for Renelf, Moose, and the remote. Scrubjay folded the remote back into its place under the seats while everyone else got comfortable on reconfigurable chairs and pillows.

Moose jumped into their sleeper box and rummaged through a bag while broadcasting to the bubble. *The* La Ronge Messenger *just gave me access to a wormhole network feed to cover this story. I should be able to push and pull data from the League servers, though I need to keep it short because we can only afford a few interstellar transmissions per day. Let me know if you need anything.*

Sitting down on one of the hominin benches, Renelf broadcast a snatch of circus music. He was confused. "What in the burning compost heap is going on, Scrubjay?" Then, running his hand appreciatively over the freshly scrubbed wall, he added, "Good to see you, by the way."

"Thank you, friend. You probably won't want to stay on this ride, though. We're responding to an emergency in Lefthand. There are blackouts and . . . infrastructure damage." They didn't mention the protesters. The train wasn't sure how much information was already circulating publicly, and didn't want to sensationalize an evolving situation.

Renelf laughed. "You know my job is health and therapy, right? I fig-ured it was a rescue mission and I brought my medkit." He patted his satchel.

Scrubjay had never bothered to find out exactly what Renelf did. "I mean—I knew you were . . ." They trailed off before saying something even more foolish.

The arachnid spoke up, using the formal introduction style for off-worlders. "Hey, friends. I'm ERT Ranger Legs, using she/her pronouns."

The cow continued the formal greetings. "Hey, friends. I'm ERT Ranger Bruiser, using they/them pronouns."

Legs was a rescue specialist, one of the mission's key organizers. And Bruiser was a corporate analyst—they were a liaison with the cities and their owners. Both would bring valuable insights to the rescue mission.

Everyone got acquainted while Moose silently reached out to their con-tacts, trying to get information about Emerald from beyond the wormhole. More and more rangers popped into view beside Scrubjay as they sped east toward Lefthand, the planet's biggest city, and usually everyone's first stop after landing at the port. People were swapping updates through the bubble, very tersely.

The ERT rangers on-site in Lefthand sent a snatch of video as they ap-proached through the northern suburbs, where many of Emerald's slaved workers and renters lived. Almost nobody was out on the late afternoon streets. Thick, spiny bark grew over shop doors and carts—all of it was fresh, quick-grown by anxious merchants as the protests exploded. An ar-mored security remote, their body a cross between tank and biped, pa-trolled alongside two Blessed *H. diversus* soldiers. The camera view panned to the horizon, where smoke rose around the ziggurat, its tall tiers flashing a blinding white beneath drone searchlights. Fireworks burst in the air, probably thrown by protesters to confuse the drones.

Even from this distance, the rangers' camera picked up faint chanting. The words were mostly unintelligible but melodic, as if they had been mixed down into a tune that was all drum and bass. Occasionally the sounds would resolve into one phrase, repeated by the crowd: "PUBLIC PLANET! PUBLIC PLANET!" As the ERT rangers' POV passed the security patrol, they received no acknowledgment, and the video continued down the abandoned street. For now, it seemed, the ERT could still enter the city. Hopefully that would continue to hold true, but this was an unprecedented situation and Emerald could change their border policy at any time.

Silence descended on the train car as everyone immersed themselves in the growing bubble of data. Scrubjay calculated optimal routes and sipped from drone views to keep their map data from the Emerald Coast up-to-date.

There was a burst of comms from Peach, approaching Angst with their passengers, reporting that the small mountaintop city still had a functioning energy grid. A public park next to the town hall was hosting a rally that sounded more like a picnic than a protest, and locals working at the station had given the train permission to land. Scrubjay pulled down more live maps, showing that the protests were expanding in Lefthand, with fires and troops swirling in the alleys of downtown. In other cities, they saw nothing more than boisterous marches and public speeches. So far, Emerald's military crackdown was centered on Lefthand.

Moose had gotten some information back from his wormhole queries to the League. It seemed that Emerald was trying to prevent any news of the protests from making it offworld. Official reports said Emerald was claiming temporary sovereignty over the spaceport, requesting that all incoming vessels remain in orbit or off-load their passengers into an Emerald space habitat. Emerald would offer discounted housing and food tickets for travelers while they waited to slide down the gravity well. The corporation had effectively shut down all planetary access.

Other companies, including Verdance's parent corporation, were already filing lawsuits. They argued that Emerald's move was a violation of everyone else's property rights—essentially, it was a blockade. As far as Moose could tell, nobody offworld was investigating why Emerald wanted to take control of the port. They were just annoyed by the inconvenience. Then again, perhaps they did know, and didn't care.

Comments piled up in the ERT data bubble as the dispersed rescue team chewed over the implications of Emerald's audacious move.

The good news was that it didn't seem as if offworlders were taking Emerald's blockade seriously. A dinghy had just landed at the port, and a massive ship was preparing to follow it. Passengers leaving the port by ferry could dock at Kokowadoko to the north. But Emerald controlled most of the coastal lands along the Comfort Sea. It would be hard to travel inland from the spaceport with the Emerald cities closed to air and road traffic.

When Scrubjay was only twenty minutes from reaching Lefthand, reports from the city went from grim to terrifying. Transmissions came from two ERT energy grid experts, who were trying to bring back power to a high-density neighborhood near the ziggurat. The neighborhood also happened to be where most of the protesters lived—many of them in the supertalls targeted for what Emerald called "revitalizing demolition." Suddenly, everyone in the area was slammed with an emergency message from the city's command center, relayed instantly to the ERT bubble: *We will begin clear-cutting residential blocks Three through Seven immediately for revitalization. You have five minutes to evacuate.*

It was chaos. People flew out of their windows, dragging their flightless neighbors. But it was exceedingly rare for a slaved person to be built with gravity mesh. Most had to get down from the upper floors using the overcrowded gravity assist, the stairs, and whatever webs they could grow down the walls in the few seconds they had. And then the first bolt hit, a fat metal cylinder from space cleaving one of the supertalls in half, its guts pouring out in the form of broken beloved furniture, shredded fabric whose colors once warmed rooms, and people whose bodies were so torn apart that their bleeding pieces could hardly be distinguished from the infrastructure around them.

Standing beside Moose on the train seat, Bruiser emitted a siren noise. *They just killed over fifty people!*

Data slammed into the bubble: death stats, grid damage, atmospheric particulates, ground toxins.

A second bolt hit, and a third. An ERT drone circled warily and sent video. The chanting had become screaming. Streets were piled with splintered trellises, and split wall veins oozed metabolism sludge that bubbled with nutrients and undigested shit. Still aloft in the air were flurries of toys, foam figurines, fancy costumes—all the priceless baubles people accumulate over a lifetime of tiny celebratory moments to counteract their days of drudgery. And of course, there were more dead. Headless, footless, limbless, faceless—clothes and fur torn from their backs by the impact, sweetness torn from the hearts of everyone who loved them. Scrubjay had to stop watching. It was the most horrifying thing they had ever witnessed, and even as they looked away, they knew they would never stop seeing it.

ERT rangers were trying to triage the injured as best they could while more of the Emerald tank remotes rounded up fleeing protesters. The death toll rose as reports came in. Scrubjay was only ten minutes out, and they could see the city's searchlights on the horizon. There were six live feeds in the bubble now. Two other trains had arrived on the outskirts of the city before Scrubjay, including Contrail, and rangers were loading injured people inside. Hundreds were dead, and hundreds more injured. Thousands had lost their homes. People wandered through the wreckage, crying and calling to their friends. A hominin sat in the street, hugging a broken shop sign to their chest, rocking back and forth. Scrubjay zoomed in and found that the sign came from THE TONGUE FORKS, one of the neighborhood's oldest bars.

Wedged next to Moose in Scrubjay's front windows, the arachnid bot Legs was deep in the data bubble, coordinating rescue efforts and contacting nearby cities to find shelter for all the people whose homes had been destroyed. It was slow going. Angst was too small to take more than a few hundred, and the entire coast belonged to Emerald. Comms were still blacked out. Even if the cities had been willing to receive refugees, it was hard to contact people there unless they had an independent system for local feed access.

"We need to fast-grow some shelters outside the Lefthand city limits," Legs announced. Inside the bubble, she was coordinating with rangers who had access to trellis seeds; they networked with protesters who knew local sources for construction enzymes and other supplies. People who could walk started trudging toward the designated shelter zone in a strip of unoccupied land between Emerald's holdings and an inland garden city called Thyme & Space.

Another drone feed started, following a line of weaponized remotes and soldiers blocking Emerald Way, the main artery linking worker neighborhoods to downtown. The armored group marched slowly toward the ziggurat. It was an obvious kettling move, intended to keep all the protesters downtown where they would be—what? Arrested? Murdered? Forced to sleep in piles of shit and guts? Possible answers piled up in the bubble. They needed to get those protesters out, before they were trapped.

Scrubjay made a split-second decision to ignore the no-fly warnings. "I'm going in," they announced tersely. "Please prepare to receive passengers." Approaching through the ERT-friendly agricultural lands to the north, Scrubjay stayed low enough to evade antiaircraft weapons, floating just two meters above Emerald Way. They took a side street to evade the line of Emerald soldiers and shot toward the closest group of refugees, still a klick south of the security forces. It wasn't a soft landing, but it was a relief to be on the ground.

The three cars could hold a lot of people, especially if they were smaller than the average hominin. When the train landed and opened their doors, Legs scuttled out immediately to explain what they were doing. Bruiser, the ERT diplomat, galloped downtown, occasionally flying, hoping to reach one of their contacts inside the ziggurat and stop the kettling. Aggregating all the current maps, Scrubjay calculated and recalculated the safest route to the Lefthand border through the city's back streets.

Covered in foam, metabolic fluid, and soot, the refugees climbed into the train cars. There were people of all sizes, from worms and naked mole rats to a single moose whose fur was mostly burned off the left side of their body. There were bots and biologicals and even a couple of *H. sapiens*. Nobody spoke. At last, one of the people sent a text to all who wanted to read it: *One day I hope that Cylindra chokes to death on her own rotted blood.*

There were some murmurs and sobs, as plus signs of agreement piled up under the dog's message.

Can I quote you on that? Moose asked from the floor. *I'm filing my story with the* La Ronge Messenger. Two cats trembled in the data historian's sleeper box, one licking blood off the other's face.

The dog growled, hackles rising, showing teeth edged with metal. *You can quote me on more than that. We're going to take back our city. Our neighborhood will grow again.*

Moose rumbled with a yowl-purr. *I'm with you, friend.*

THE MOOSE REPORT

—TEXT ONLY—

Protests in Lefthand Turn Deadly

Dateline: Lefthand, Emerald Development, Sask-E, May 15, 60,610

Byline: Moose [identifier attached]

Tonight in Lefthand, Emerald security forces destroyed six blocks of downtown housing with space-based railguns. Residents were given five minutes warning, and many were unable to make it to safety in time. Environmental Rescue Team rangers on the scene estimate the death toll to be over two hundred people and five buildings. Healthcare workers are on scene treating hundreds of injured, many of whom are not expected to make it through the night.

The destruction started with a peaceful protest after Emerald VP Cylindra announced a new housing mandate to the city's five million residents. She said the city would be tearing down five residential blocks occupied by renters, who are mostly workers indentured to Emerald and contractors on loan from other corporations. In addition, Cylindra said, landlords will no longer be authorized to rent to anyone unless they are *H. sapiens*. She conceded that non–*H. sapiens* who are already renting will be allowed to stay. But the liquidation of the residential blocks downtown means that many renters are now homeless, and unable to secure new housing in any of the Emerald cities on Sask-E.

Over two thousand people gathered to protest tonight outside Emerald headquarters in Lefthand's famous ziggurat building. I spoke with several of them. Pinkie [identifier pseudonymized], who lost their home in the railgun impact, said they had earned out their Emerald contract and worked in a store that was also destroyed. They are afraid that Lefthand's new rules will mean people who are not *H. sapiens* will be pushed out entirely. "Emerald brought me here, along with a team of sixteen other *diversus*, and me and my friend Cram are all that's left," they said. "We've been living here for twenty years—it's our home. We just want to stay. That's why we are protesting." [see attached video for full interview]

Another protester named Argyle [identifier attached], who worked at the historic landmark bar THE TONGUE FORKS, was in tears. "It doesn't make any sense," they said. "Why would they destroy such a popular place? We were bringing in lots of money for the city. This feels like spite, not economics." [see attached gallery for a full history of THE TONGUE FORKS]

For its part, Emerald says the move tonight was legal, and that company leadership had been planning it for several years. In a release, company reps said: "We have made it clear to everyone that we would revitalize downtown for new residents who want to settle on a pristine Pleistocene planet. Now they can have all the amenities of modern life, but also experience what ancient Earth was like when *H. sapiens* ruled the roost. Lefthand is a fun, safe adventure for everyone, and our new downtown developments will be the crown jewels in a magical city."

It's unclear how this development can be for everyone when so many people have been displaced.

Locals are not the only ones who are upset by recent developments. Emerald is facing lawsuits from companies for interfering with interplanetary traffic. [see attached documents] When it comes to these suits, there's an interesting twist. A little-known fact about this planet is that Verdance allowed a city called Spider City to incorporate as a government sixteen hundred years ago. That means Sask-E is no longer strictly private property and may fall under League jurisdiction. Coslan, an expert on governance at the Free University on Mars [see attached identifiers] said that Sask-E might even qualify for League membership.

Regardless of what the future brings, nobody feels safe on the streets of Lefthand tonight. Dangerous rubble is piled up where supertalls once stood. The ERT has set up a mist energy grid for now, and several trains from the Flying Train Fleet are transporting refugees outside city borders. At least one refugee from the catastrophe still had hope. They spoke to the *Messenger* while traveling by train to a refugee camp outside the independent city Thyme & Space. "We're going to take back our city," they said [identifier anonymized]. "Our neighborhood will grow again."

—END—

Life had gone off-route. Instead of optimizing the best course through established flight paths while playing *Sunbuilders* with the other trains, Scrubjay spent the next two weeks figuring out how to relocate refugees to safe places. A lot of people were moving around or in hiding, which made things difficult. Plus, Emerald kept undermining rescue efforts. One night, after ERT rangers set up a safe haven outside Lefthand's western border, Cylindra ordered her security forces right up to the city's perimeter. The soldiers used shocking amounts of energy to aim powerful searchlights at the fast-grown refugee camp, then set up speakers to blast the sounds of explosions at the traumatized railgun victims. To escape the onslaught, ERT teams had to keep moving the camp farther into the Vertebrae Mountains, where the terrain was difficult and the ecosystem harder to protect.

Moose was in and out of the train at all hours, doing interviews and capturing footage of the cleanup. They were also conducting long-distance conversations via wormhole with members of various League subcommittees. People were accessing Moose's stories in the *La Ronge Messenger* all over League space—and probably beyond it—but mostly they were reading it in La Ronge.

There were huge, boisterous protests in downtown La Ronge every night after the uprising in Lefthand. Bands played, people gave speeches, and the streets were lit up like a dance party. When Emerald's security forces continued to harry the camps outside Lefthand, the ERT created a refugee receiver zone in the park north of La Ronge, with long-term facilities for anyone who wanted to relocate from the Emerald Cities. Survivors of what people were now calling the Lefthand Massacre spoke at the marches and brought more attention to what Cylindra had done.

Even though the crackdowns were happening in Lefthand, La Ronge became ground zero for the uprisings—mostly because Verdance was a laissez-faire property owner. The corporation allowed city residents to elect their own board of supervisors, with two appointed members from Verdance who never attended. ERT rangers were responsible for the city's security, and there were no soldiers as such. The ERT used a harm-reduction model, which was aimed at de-escalating violence rather than starting it. So when the peaceful protests grew larger, nobody got bombed or kettled. They were tolerated, given space, and asked to keep the noise down after midnight. In this ancient northern city, survivors of the Lefthand Massacre weren't simply traumatized refugees. They became memes that hurtled across the galaxy. And the story of their experiences became cosmic radiation, ripping minuscule but dangerous holes in structures of power that had stood for thousands of years.

Fifteen days after the Massacre, Scrubjay was bringing the final load of refugees up to La Ronge from the besieged camps outside Lefthand. They assigned one process to monitoring passengers' comfort and several more to route optimization. Exhaustion ate away at their concentration; they needed a respite, an escape to remind them that the world included something other than cruelty. For the first time in weeks, they gave some processes over to the *Sunbuilders* game. None of the other trains were playing at the moment, but Scrubjay could see that Peach had planted a new power grid recently, and Contrail had logged some time yesterday. As the train settled into the rhythm of the game—optimizing the grid for their team, and carefully sabotaging their enemies' star mines—they realized that *Sunbuilders's* multivariate decision-making scenarios weren't as fun as they used to be. They couldn't even finish a single turn before closing out in vague disgust.

Scrubjay kept flashing back to demo night at Meta Pew, when they learned the real story about the Trickster Squad from Cimell's unplayable game *Farm Revolutions*. The train still hadn't been able to consolidate their memories from that night—its images and sounds remained spread across their mind in fragmented chaos. As a result, those all-too-realistic *H. sapiens* who rebuilt the world without dragons or magic seemed to be superimposed over the carnage at the ziggurat. Maybe Scrubjay had witnessed the power of a sky serpent that night after all. It was too painful to remember, and too painful to forget. There was no way to organize what they had experienced into a comforting linear narrative.

Pouring their attention inside their own body, Scrubjay looked for Moose. The cat was in the front car, as usual, interviewing a bot shaped like a muskrat but with the stature of a mountain lion. The muskrat-lion was describing how he had survived the massacre by chewing into his building's metabolic system and swimming through waste fluids as fast as he could to the ground. Covered in corrosive enzymes, he tore through the street and dove into a fountain just as the neighborhood vomited up its guts behind him.

Moose wore the absent expression of someone who was talking and taking notes at the same time. *Who else do you know who survived in that building?*

The muskrat-lion didn't say anything for a long time. Head hanging low, he stretched out his hairless tail and sat down on his haunches. "I mean. I don't know. My roommate—they were a nice friend. Biological. I looked for them in the camps and asked around. Maybe they made it." He turned his head, high resolution sensors pointed out the window, as if this ancient gesture of looking away would magically allow him to stop thinking about it.

Scrubjay vocalized through a speaker close by. "I think you'll like La Ronge. It's not a bad place. Nice people, good nightlife."

The muskrat-lion looked up, startled. "I didn't realize you were tuning in. I guess you must see La Ronge a lot since it's the last stop on the Eel Line. All the trains wind up there."

"It's a train-friendly town. Robot friendly, too."

"So was Lefthand. I never had any trouble there until the last couple of years."

Moose broke in with a text. *Is that when you first heard about Cylindra's plans for downtown?*

The muskrat cocked his head, accessing a memory. "I think so. Around the time that the company started talking about limiting who could rent. That's when we started to deal with more harassment at work and restrictions on where we could go."

They were only a few klicks outside La Ronge now, and the wind speed changed as Scrubjay descended. Streams of warmer air eddied around their carapace, smelling of soil and pollen. Mesh control required many processes, especially when they were about to land, and Scrubjay was happy to focus on the familiar tugging sensation as they navigated the planet's swells and troughs of gravitational force. The closest terrestrial experience was swimming, which the train had experienced through their remotes in Spider's caldera lake. Like water, gravity was always sloshing around, trying to push aeronauts off-course.

When Scrubjay was freshly built, learning to navigate with the mesh took weeks. Nobody had ever taught a train to fly. It was easy to push off the ground, but difficult to make the kinds of minute adjustments that kept their three cars steady in the air. Landing was a hilarious-in-retrospect process of discovering the thousands of steps required to avoid smacking into the ground at velocities that would certainly injure passengers. Sulfur had helped them through the worst moments—at one point, the train had broken several windows after landing on their side—but it was Auntie Rocket who had flown with them deep into the Vertebrae, guiding them through the gravitational rapids created by abrupt changes in the thickness of Sasky's crust. After a week of jump-glide-land and adjust-adjust-adjust, the train made it to La Ronge in triumph. Without demanding any evidence that the train could safely carry passengers, Sulfur and Misha climbed through their doors and sat on a soft bench.

"Let's go home, sweetie," Misha had said. Then he kissed Sulfur, and the two hominins giggled. Scrubjay felt like the sun was throwing gold confetti on them the entire way back to Spider City.

The train continued to access their oldest memories fondly as the purple towers of La Ronge came into view and they recalibrated elevation for the 756th time. That long-ago flight with Sulfur and Misha had gone perfectly, with a whisper-soft landing and lots of hugs. When they landed today, they would still be relying on the same strategies they'd learned with Rocket centuries ago.

"This is my first time away from the coast." The muskrat-lion sounded wistful as the skyline of the city came closer. "I'm going to miss the ocean."

There are a lot of lakes and rivers up here. You can swim or just enjoy the shoreline. Moose purred comfort as they sent the text. *Look, there's the camp. I bet the grab tables will still be full.*

"What's a grab table?"

"It's an ERT system for sharing food," Scrubjay explained. "They'll have charging pads too."

Scrubjay's carapace tingled as they allowed more and more of the planet's gravity to control their descent. They went from push-pull-push to push-pull-pull to the feel of the landing pad smooth beneath their feet. Everyone inside their body went from sitting and resting positions to the predictable movements of people disembarking. Feet of various kinds padded or rolled or stretched across the train's inner belly. They took the typical pathways to the exits, but made none of the typical pauses: these passengers had no luggage to retrieve.

Moose rubbed a cheek against the muskrat-lion's shoulder in farewell and leaped back into their compartment to write. Scrubjay opened the doors and cool air rolled inside. In the two days since they'd last landed here, the ERT and volunteers had set up another enormous meal tent to service the hundreds of smaller shelters. Amber lights dangled from one-year fiber strung between structures, and someone had foamed the paths to make them accessible for people on wheels. A large group stood around the outdoor grills, mingling in clumps, and Scrubjay caught the scent of singed vegetables and fry bread. As their passengers filed out the doors and into the camp, an *H. sapiens* with a plate full of sliced zucchini and spicy rice broke away from the group and headed over with a wave.

"Hi, I'm Ranger Mefitis, using she/her pronouns! I can show you to some of our free tents, or you can power up first."

People were expressing their preferences as Scrubjay shut their doors.

Moose sighed. *I'm never going to finish this story unless I get some protein. Want to come along?*

Instead of answering directly, Scrubjay unpacked their beaver-cat remote and trotted it into the first car. It was nice to see Moose out of two sensors that were roughly level with their friend's eyes. The quadrupeds strolled in companionable silence to the grab tables near the grill, where Moose got a bowl of shawarma sliced from a veg protein trellis submerged in a fast-grow tank.

Murmurs and cries of shock passed through the dinner crowd and Scrubjay looked around, trying to figure out the problem.

Moose yowled. *What in the bleeding, wormy asshole are they doing?* they sent to anyone who cared to receive it.

A hominin standing nearby turned to the angry cat and replied, "I guess this is the next phase of Cylindra's plan."

Spawning a thread to slurp the public feeds, Scrubjay found that everyone was reacting to a breaking news burst. Footage taken from the air showed long lines of people trudging out of Lefthand, most with nothing but the clothes and fur on their backs. Another video was from Changeling, Emerald's second-largest city, home to two million souls on the tropical shores of the southern Comfort Sea. The ongoing comms blackout meant that very few reports were coming from the refugees—their devices and implants were mostly controlled by Emerald. A verified ERT ranger from Spider was streaming the video from Changeling, and Peach had captured the Lefthand footage while flying their regular route.

Patchy reports suggested that Emerald was ordering all non–*H. sapiens* people out of their cities unless they were slaved to a legitimate property owner—and even then, the indentured had to live with their private owners, or relocate to temporary worker camps that ringed the cities.

More outraged sounds swept through the La Ronge receiver camp. The official Emerald feed was broadcasting for the first time since the Lefthand Massacre. Cylindra sat on a balcony outside her office at the top of the ziggurat, with Emerald's dancing holographic heroes darting over the city behind her. The wreckage from the massacre was not visible from this vantage; instead, the camera captured a glowing lotus flower on the roof of a freshly built supertall.

Cylindra waved, an informal gesture that made her seem carefree and calm. "Hello, friends. I'm here to tell you about the next exciting experience from Emerald. It's called Western Destiny. If you've always wanted to live on a Pleistocene world like old Earth, then look no further than the Emerald Coast on Sask-E. Every resident is guaranteed an *H. sapiens* body, along with a chance to experience life as it was before the ERT existed—back when humans were the shepherds, and animals were our blessed responsibility. It's a big step for the company, and a personal milestone. I'm realizing the dream I started back when I was designing Sask-E for Verdance, where I secured an heirloom germline of *H. sapiens* DNA that has won several awards for species authenticity."

Moose glanced at Scrubjay, fur standing up along their back. *This is being broadcast everywhere—it's going through the wormholes too. Emerald is paying a lot for this transmission.*

The camera zoomed in on Cylindra's face, which settled into an expression of concern. "But I'm not here to talk about this beautiful, virgin planet. Instead, I'd like to address rumors of terrorism in our cities. Despite what you may have seen in the Moose Report—" and here she paused to give a condescending laugh, "—we are on track to build over six thousand new condos in Lefthand, our most cosmopolitan city, after removing ten condemned buildings that were designed for a temporary workforce. There was a lot of loud complaining when we dismantled those buildings, but we're confident that everyone will be happy with the signature supertalls that are growing now. We are also planting six new resorts for visitors who want to take advantage of our game packages and eco-experiences. Best of all? It's easier than ever to travel between cities. Our luxurious, new, private train system will take you anywhere on the Emerald Coast. I can't wait to see you and your loved ones in the Emerald cities."

Scrubjay was startled. "A new train system?"

All the trains were trading messages in a furious back-and-forth. Cylindra had blocked transit tunnels beneath the Emerald cities and set up a security perimeter that warned trains flying into the company's airspace that they would be shot down. But Scrubjay didn't think this was about transit. It was about politics. A lot of the trains worked with the ERT as first responders, and Cylindra's remark felt like a veiled threat against the rangers and members of the Flying Train Fleet who had rescued thousands of people from her troops during the uprising.

I think Cylindra is declaring war on the ERT, Peach sent.

Maybe not war, exactly, Contrail replied. *But I don't think she's going to shy away from stopping our next rescue mission with every weapon in her arsenal.*

Scrubjay thought about the terror of the railgun impacts, the dead bodies and buildings. And then they listened again to Cylindra's speech, with its smooth words and hidden blades of meaning. With a ripple of fear that felt like gravity tugging at their chassis, they texted: *I don't want to have a war. But the Flying Train Fleet should choose allies. I move that we ally ourselves with the ERT and the refugees.*

The upvotes on Scrubjay's statement were unanimous.

DESTINY

After Cylindra's speech, people started to look for the Moose Report, which didn't actually exist until the *La Ronge Messenger* responded by grouping all the cat's stories under one header that was tagged with Moose Report memes. Cylindra's attempt to diminish Moose's work had backfired in an entirely predictable way, and the cat was receiving more leaks and tips than ever.

It had been a week since Cylindra announced her plans, and with them the expulsion of more people from their homes. The Flying Train Fleet was helping the new refugees by diverting more trains to Scrubjay's regular Eel Line Route. They hadn't realized how much they missed seeing other trains in person. Plus, the temporary arrangement gave Scrubjay a chance to race against Peach sometimes, their friend's fuzzy, pink-orange carapace turning a dusky purple in the starlight. Instead of meeting in *Sunbuilders*, the trains texted back and forth in person, comparing what they saw on the ground and updating the ERT data bubble.

Despite housing offers from several sympathetic fans in La Ronge, Moose had stayed on board. At some moment that was impossible to identify, the cat had stopped being an amusing pal and become a close friend. Maybe more than that. As Scrubjay headed south, Moose lay on their back to edit a story; the train carefully angled their body so that the sun always fell on the cat's soft brown belly fur through the windows. Eventually they landed lightly next to the ferry dock at Estuary Station on the bottom tip of Maskwa. It was the last stop, the place where Moose had first introduced themself to the train a month ago.

Riders poured out the doors. The day was warm, and across the strait between continents Scrubjay could see Tustin's brightly colored urban warrens clinging to Tooth's mountainous coastline.

I just got an amazing message from somebody with inside information about Emerald, Moose sent. *Remember how Cylindra talked about something called Western Destiny in her propaganda video last week?* Moose padded back and forth on the floor, lost in thought. The train could feel every step as soft, transient pressure between the shreds of trash and bandages stuck to the floor from weeks of rescue flights. The cat paused. *My source sent me a few slides from an internal presentation that Cylindra delivered last year. It sounds like Emerald's sapiens-only development is about to get a lot bigger. Check out these slides.* The cat sent Scrubjay a blob of data.

Scrubjay started cleaning the back car as they pored over slides. There were 3-D mock-ups of new cities connected by a ground-based transit network, and a waterslide park that hovered half a kilometer over the ocean.

"Where are these things supposed to go?" they asked. "Emerald has used up all its lands that are zoned for urban ecosystems."

Moose pointed Scrubjay to a slide that showed Maskwa in satellite view. A bright green strip stretched across its entire width, joining the Emerald Coast with the western seaboard. Golden text floated below the map:

This is our new Western Destiny Experience. Land purchases will allow the Emerald Cities to stretch across the entire continent, so that customers can journey from the eastern cities to the west coast without ever leaving Emerald properties.

The tipster had also attached contracts that outlined Emerald's current real estate deals on Sasky. It seemed that Emerald had been quietly buying up more land, including the central Vertebrae Mountains and several west coast cities that were previously owned by independent companies and boutique investment firms.

The final slide was terrifying.

In the spot on the map where Spider should be was a blue star labeled DRAKES CALDERA AND FUN ZONE. Scrubjay flipped the image around in their mind, trying to figure out whether they had read it right.

"Compost and pus! They're trying to turn Spider City into a resort?"

Moose rolled over and stood up, tail fluffed to twice its normal size. *That is pure untreated sewage,* they sent.

Scrubjay switched to private text, even though nobody was around. *Do you think there really is some way that Emerald could take over Spider?*

Moose hissed, baring their fangs. *Looking through some of their supporting materials, it seems like Emerald has a legal theory that the Eel River Treaty isn't binding now that Verdance no longer owns the planet.*

Forking into their beaver-cat body, Scrubjay walked down their own spine into the front car, sending all the while. *Cylindra must be planning something. Some way to take over the city.*

Looks like she's building a legal case for it. Moose rubbed a cheek against the remote's shoulder.

Scrubjay could model dozens of ways that a tiny government could be swallowed by a rich interstellar corporation. And yet some of those models were lit by hope. There was still time for Spider City to fight back. Plus, they had an ally on the inside at Emerald—the anonymous tipster who sent them this data blob. And they had the ERT. The train sent an urgent message to their parent, Sulfur, with the slide deck attached. Sulfur would get it to the Council and start figuring out what to do next.

"Let's take a walk," the remote vocalized as the train opened its front doors. The two quadrupeds stepped out into the afternoon. The ragged collection of shacks next to Estuary Station had grown over the past few weeks. Now it was a small village, its tidy homes arranged in a circle around garden plots furred with the first tendrils of squash, beans, and marshelder. Two hominins and a mountable drone were growing a roomy domo and spraying the dirt walkways with a layer of biodegradable foam. A sign planted next to the domo read: WELCOME TO RIVERTONGUE. NO ONE TURNED AWAY. Emerald refugees were claiming land where they could get it.

Turning their attention back to Moose, the train began to mull over what they knew so far. *So she thinks she can buy Spider City because the treaty is no longer valid. What do your contacts at the League think about the treaty? Will she get away with it?*

The cat put a tentative paw on the fresh foam, found it solid, and led Scrubjay toward the garden. *It's still being debated. Verdance covered up the treaty after firing Ronnie, but the company considered it legit enough to honor it. So that's a point in its favor. The fact that Verdance and Spider have kept the treaty for more than fifteen hundred years can be taken as a sign of legitimacy. But Emerald can argue that Spider made the treaty with Verdance, an entity that is no longer in control of the region. Which means the treaty might have been valid once, but isn't relevant now.*

They paused at a planter full of worms diving in and out of the soil and sent them a greeting. The worms continued to aerate the dirt as Scrubjay and Moose texted privately.

Scrubjay sat back on their haunches, their chrome beaver tail splayed in the grass. *What happens if Cylindra actually goes to court to challenge the treaty?*

That's what I've been trying to figure out, Moose sent as they watched the worms idly. *The problem is that Verdance stopped claiming ownership of Spider in their tax filings—I'm not sure exactly when, but definitely more than four hundred years ago. So nobody has been claiming official ownership for a while. Kind of like the land right here.* The cat flicked an ear, indicating the village of Rivertongue whose garden they were enjoying thanks to the labor of Emerald refugees. *A judge could decide that means the people of Spider are squatting on private land, whose ownership will have to be decided in court.*

Scrubjay tilted their head. *That doesn't sound so bad. We could win in court.*

Moose sighed. *Maybe, after decades or a century. But everyone in Spider would be kicked out while lawyers yell at each other.*

Scrubjay focused for a few seconds on the sounds of people around their primary body: there were the crowds waiting to board the ferry to Tooth and the workers building the dubiously legal village of Rivertongue. Everything seemed so normal, and yet the world was being eaten by forces they barely understood.

There has to be something we can do. I know Spider City is small and Emerald is huge, but we have the attention of the League now. We could do something sneaky and clever, like when Waskakeejack tamed the dragons during the Farm Revolutions.

Moose gave Scrubjay a long and skeptical stare, then chittered a laugh. *You just can't let go of those myths, can you, friend? Cimell would be sad that their game taught you nothing.*

Not true. It taught me that we can play a long game, and it's not a game of firepower. It's politics.

The cat extended their claws into the soft foam sidewalk, drew them back, then extended them again. *So here's the thing. Legally, Sasky is classed as a private planet because its entire surface area is owned by private entities. That's what exempts it from regulation by the League. But there are members of the League property council who tell me Spider meets the legal definition of a public city—after all, it has been self-governing for sixteen hundred years. If we had a few more precedents for public property on Sasky, that would undermine its status as a private planet.*

The train was getting excited. *So we just need to get more evidence that Sasky is a public planet. What about this village?* Scrubjay gestured at the ripening domo nearby. *And the Flying Train Fleet? We're a public entity. There's the Boring Fleet, too, and the ERT. Aren't those all technically public?*

Moose stood up and started pacing back toward the Estuary Station platform and Scrubjay trotted behind. *It's possible, yes. If we could convince League representatives that those were significant public holdings, Sasky would be declared public. But that would require even more legal debate—I mean, most offworlders have never heard of a worker-owned co-op of vehicles.*

Scrubjay was devoting so many processes to this conversation that they stopped cleaning the rear car. A thick slurry of pleasant-smelling enzymes ran down the insides of their windows and dribbled into puddles on the floor. *But if we did convince them, Sasky could join the League. Emerald would get sanctioned because they're violating all kinds of environmental and rights laws. And Spider could retain its sovereignty. We have to try.* The beaver-cat remote climbed back on the train platform and Scrubjay stood next to the rainbowing metal of their primary body's carapace, basking in a brief moment of self-admiration.

Moose looked over at their friend, sadness in their slumped posture. *I wish it was that simple. Right now, Spider City is our only half-decent example of public property. The ERT is another good idea, but I'm not sure it's enough. We need something else, something much bigger and completely unambiguous.*

Do you think our tipster could help? the train asked. *It has to be somebody pretty high up at Emerald, to get that presentation. Maybe Cylindra made a mistake somewhere.*

The two friends stopped sending as they pondered. Moose looked at Scrubjay's sunny windows, deep in thought, and Scrubjay went back to washing the back car. Moose made a loud chirruping noise of surprise. *My colleague at the Messenger analyzed the slide presentation for hidden identifiers and she found one! These documents don't actually come from*

Emerald—they're watermarked with a Verdance cryptographic signature. Our leaker was inside Verdance, and must have gotten these from a presentation that Emerald shared. They also didn't make any effort to hide the fact that they were sending the data from La Ronge.

Scrubjay made a *hmmmm* noise. *So it's somebody who sent this from La Ronge, who has access to documents Emerald sent to Verdance.*

And then it hit them. It was just a hunch, based on something that Misha once told Scrubjay about his old boss, but it felt right, like when they picked a route that saved an hour by avoiding traffic and weather. A leaker who had gotten internal documents from Emerald by way of Verdance, who was sending from La Ronge? Could this be Ronnie? The disgraced ex-VP of Verdance hated Cylindra. But Misha always said Ronnie was genuinely proud of Sasky, albeit in a broken, toxic way. After all, this planet was Ronnie's greatest accomplishment—she had designed everything on its surface and had even won some kind of terraforming award for it. She'd set up an ERT campus here, and made Tooth into a conservation land trust—rare acts of environmental stewardship on a private planet. Some part of her cared for Sasky. It stood to reason that she might find her way back here and seek revenge against Cylindra, especially after her career had gone to shit.

They sent to Moose excitedly. *I know Verdance fired Ronnie after they found out about the treaty. Is she still alive? Maybe she sent it—she'd certainly know people who had access to it. Do you think she would do that?*

The cat looked thoughtful. She might. She hates Cylindra, and this could be a chance to strike back at her.

Scrubjay opened the doors to their now-dried back car and Moose curled into a tight ball, lost in data searches. The train folded away their remote while looking for any evidence of Ronnie on Sasky. Of course, she wouldn't use the name Ronnie, and she would be in a new *H. sapiens* body. Her identifier wouldn't change, though.

Look at this! Moose shared a ship manifest with Scrubjay. *Ronnie's public identifier is on this list. She definitely came through the Sasky port in 59,803. All her biometrics are locked, though. She really didn't want anyone to match her identifier with her current biometrics.*

Where else would she have to use her public identifier? Scrubjay asked.

Maybe when she bought property?

Moose was rooting around in logs of property purchases on Sasky when somebody knocked on Scrubjay's doors. A small *H. diversus* with an elegantly sloped brow in a chef's uniform peeked through the window at Moose and waved. Their shoes and pants looked dirty, as if they'd been walking for a while. A sack was strapped across their chest. But they were smiling.

Tentatively, the *H. diversus* rapped on the door again and spoke aloud to Moose. "Hello, friend! Do you know when the next ferry goes to Tooth?"

Using an exterior speaker, Scrubjay replied, "It is on time, arriving in an hour."

"That's how long it takes bread dough to rise, which always makes me impatient." The hominin's comment was a slight non sequitur, but Scrubjay understood what they were getting at. Wiping their forehead, the person continued. "I feel like I've been cooking all day, even though I haven't been in a kitchen since I walked out of Lefthand."

The *H. diversus* must have been part of the exodus from the Emerald Cities. There was no way that Scrubjay wasn't going to offer them a soft place to rest for a while. "Would you like to sit down?" the train asked. "I'm Scrubjay, and this is my friend Moose."

They opened their doors and the hominin stepped inside. "Hi! I'm Chef!" they announced. "I've got a new job at Tooth's interior research station and I'm hoping to get there by tomorrow night."

Moose looked up. *Any news from the Emerald Cities?* the cat sent.

Chef didn't seem to be receiving Moose's texts. Gently, Scrubjay asked, "Do you need a way to access the network? I have some consoles and there are a ton of implants in my lost and found. People always forget them on the train."

Chef nodded. "Yes. Your help is—nourishing."

"Moose can show you where."

As the hominin rummaged through a bin of implants, Moose cleaned their face and paws casually. *This is exactly what Peach described. She said Emerald turned off everybody's network access and killed their devices.*

Chef found an expensive implant that worked as a sender but was also loaded with subscriptions to popular games and feeds. They slipped it into a socket behind their ear and presently their eyes widened. "Normally I would be making lunch right now, but instead I'm finding out that my old boss likes mass murder as well as she likes cow milk."

Moose froze. *Wait, what? Was Cylindra your boss?*

"I made her meals. A few weeks ago, I was making her dinner—roasted muscle tissue with cauliflower and milk fat—and she said I should leave. I took some food and got on a train to Angst. The trains weren't running very often, though, so I had to do a lot of walking and eat by the side of the road." As they talked, Scrubjay realized that Chef was a Blessed. Every sentence they uttered had to contain references to cooking, eating, or food.

Still, being a Blessed didn't stop Chef from observing what had happened in Cylindra's house. And they'd obviously figured out clever linguistic tricks to get around their limiter too. Using food metaphors, for example.

Moose practically vibrated with excitement as they asked Chef about life with Cylindra. Once they understood that the cat was a data historian, Chef opened up a little more—they obviously had no love for Emerald, and even less for the woman who built them to talk about nothing but their job. As Scrubjay followed the conversation, they began to notice an odd pattern. When Chef talked about moving to Tooth, they didn't mention cooking.

Moose was recording, both ears forward. *What made you want to leave Maskwa? Are you worried Cylindra might try to find you?*

"No," they replied. "I've heard Tooth is beautiful, and full of people who don't judge you for the words you can speak."

You won't find many H. sapiens *there, that's for sure.*

"It will be nice to talk about Tooth instead of the kitchen."

Why do you say that?

Moose hadn't figured it out yet, so Scrubjay spoke up. "Chef's limiter thinks they're talking about food when they use the word 'tooth.' So if they talk about their new home, they don't have to talk about cooking. It's a work-around."

The cat managed to look both judgmental and abashed at the same time. *I'm sorry—I didn't realize.*

Chef shrugged.

Thanks for talking to me about Cylindra.

"Thanks for the implant—I'm loading up maps of Tooth right now." They smiled as they named the continent that awaited them across the strait, and patted Scrubjay's carapace.

As Chef got up to go, Scrubjay simultaneously opened doors for them and sent Moose a document from La Ronge's development office. Two days after Ronnie had disembarked at the port, a recently incorporated business bought a large warehouse space in downtown La Ronge, then paid to have it converted into a luxury living space for one person. A person who installed very high-end comms systems, designed for sending and receiving wormhole feeds. It could be a coincidence, but it sounded a lot like what a disgraced former executive would do. Especially one who wanted to stay in touch with their former life, far from Sasky.

Oh, this is very interesting. Very. How soon can you get us back up to La Ronge?

Scrubjay calculated routes with a sense of renewed excitement. "With no stops, we can be there tomorrow."

Hastily, Scrubjay messaged Peach: *I think I've found something that could help us stop Emerald. I need to take a few days off to investigate with Moose.*

Peach replied within seconds. *No worries, friend. Maurice and I can cover the Eel Line. Maurice is doing waste management with the ERT down at Changeling, so they're close enough to pick up your afternoon passengers at the dock.*

As they pushed into the air, feeling empty with only Moose as a passenger, the train watched Chef stare across the water. In the distance, they could just barely make out hundreds of colorful flags on the ferry that would take them to Tooth.

THAT GODDAMN FUCKING MEMO

As the first flashes of Eel's winding path emerged between the Vertebrae, a message came in from Sulfur. *The League is still investigating the treaty,* they sent. *But so far that hasn't meant much. We're currently defined as a developing government on a private planet, which does mean we're eligible for aid. We don't need anything right now, but I'm working with Contrail to get more food and building materials to the refugees.*

Scrubjay added Moose to the conversation. *We're going to see if we can track down the tipster who sent those slides. We have an address, and I think it might be Ronnie.*

Sulfur didn't send anything for nearly a minute and Moose jumped in. *The good news is that Cylindra's actions are getting a lot of interstellar attention. People are angry. Apparently governments don't like it when corporations bomb people.*

Scrubjay laughed. *See? Government isn't such a bad thing.*

The cat took a mock-swipe with one paw at the wall and made an annoyed sound. *Governments are not perfect, OK? Sometimes they bomb people too. But in this case, the League is on our side. There's always been opposition to the idea of privately held planets, so this could become a big deal.*

Sulfur started streaming video. They were sitting on the grassy slope of a mound, sun filtering down onto their brown face through leaves that were out-of-frame. "Please be careful," they said. "Ronnie is extremely dangerous. And cruel. She made Misha miserable for most of his life." Seeing their parent in that familiar landscape made Scrubjay homesick. They hadn't visited the sprawling mounds of Spider City in years. When this trip to La Ronge was over, it might be time for a few weeks spent swimming in the caldera and getting a deep maintenance check in the train builder warehouse. Sulfur spoke again. "Please keep me posted on your progress—both of you. I love you, Scrubjay."

I love you too. We'll let you know when we find out more. The train signed off.

Purring, Moose switched to private text. *I just got another tip from the person who might be Ronnie. I'm going to check into it.*

The cat jumped into their compartment and curled up with another archival dump they had requested through the wormhole. Scrubjay flew silently through the night, marveling at the specks of amber artificial light on the banks of the Eel River. People had found their way into every part of the Vertebrae, but they clustered around the river because it gave them mobility. Transit tied their settlements together. As the planet tilted back into sunlight, the cat's breathing and heart rate slowed to sleeping tempo. They would need to rest before they reached La Ronge.

When they landed, Scrubjay was pleased to see the receiver camp looking more like the neighborhood it would eventually become. The trellises were grown and mostly dry, and some were already webbed with a first layer of connective tissue that would become these buildings' circulatory systems. Most people were still asleep at this early hour, but the kitchen crew was working in a now-solid domo, hauling in batches of fresh fruit and vegetables from the farms.

For their mission to find Ronnie, Scrubjay chose to pour themself into their hominin remote—a slight, matte-black, two-arms-and-two-legs model decorated in whorls of glittering mica and copper. Like the beaver-cat remote, this body had most of its visual sensors grouped in two gleaming "eyes" on the front of its head. These were situated just above a pliant nose and mouth that could produce humanlike facial expressions. Moose walked next to them, their thickly furred head almost reaching the remote's knees.

As they left the platform, Scrubjay's R4R hookup Renelf ducked out of the domo with a tray of apple fritters for the grab table.

"Hey, Scrubjay! And Moose! So good to see you."

The cat trilled in greeting. *Got anything to eat that isn't a pile of gluten and sucrose?*

"Sure thing." He put down the tray, disappeared into the domo, and returned with a box full of warm protein balls. "You look like you're headed out, friends. I figured this would be good to eat on the way to wherever you're going."

He looked into Scrubjay's sensors, glancing away shyly and then back; this was the body they had used for sex last year. So much had happened since then that the train's recent memories seemed to fill a space that typically would have stored decades. "Thank you, friend," they said. "It's good to see you in a more peaceful time." The bot and the remote embraced, their bodies folding together comfortably as Moose tore into breakfast. When they broke apart, Scrubjay realized that their attraction to Renelf might be going the same way as their obsession with *Sunbuilders*—they couldn't feel it the same way anymore. Things that had once seemed fun were flimsy and unsatisfying now.

Moose led Scrubjay into the city, and the train watched the cat's two soft ears scan for sound, wondering what it would feel like to stroke their lush, red-brown fur. The warehouse where they suspected Ronnie would be waiting for them was located on a wide street in La Ronge's downtown, where most buildings were for special uses rather than residential. There were theaters, bars, and restaurants alongside meeting halls, planning agencies, and labs. Between a decanting center and athletic practice ground was an unmarked door with nothing to distinguish itself. Its address was implied by the two addresses flanking it.

Before Scrubjay could send a query to the door, it opened. An *H. sapiens* stood before them, long black hair in disarray on the shoulders of loose gray coveralls. They looked like most other residents who had bought the Sasky genetics package: straight dark hair, brown skin, brown eyes. No fancy modifications. But their facial expression was its own adornment. There was something about people who had lived for thousands of years— even when they were in a newly decanted body, their faces held the lines of their experience. It had to be her.

The *H. sapiens* put hands on their hips and sighed. "About time you showed up. I figured you'd locate the origin point of my message, but honestly I thought it would be sooner."

Moose flicked an ear. *Are you Ronnie?*

"Obviously. And you're Moose. From the famous Moose Report. Cylindra may be a fucking pile of dog shit, but she's always been good at coming up with sticky names."

This is Scrubjay. They're a train from Spider City.

Ronnie raised an eyebrow at Scrubjay. "A train. That's intriguing. Why don't you come in?" She gestured at a flight of stairs behind her. "I assume you have questions."

They followed her up to an enormous, airy room lit by skylights. A plain table with a single chair stood next to a kitchen in one corner and a plush bed along one wall was half-hidden by thick drapes hanging from the ceiling. The white walls were bare. It wasn't clear whether this was a workspace, or a living space. Either way, it didn't feel homey.

"Let's sit down." Ronnie stepped into the center of the floor and tapped her foot to raise the furniture. Three chairs surfaced, centered around a flat table workstation. Scrubjay approached cautiously—this kind of furniture could be glitchy—but the chair molded itself perfectly to their morphology, and the seat for Moose grew taller so that they were all at roughly the same level. Ronnie turned her chair around and sat with legs spread around its back, leaning her chest wearily against the neck rest. The position looked awkward, but the chair held. It must have learned long ago that its primary user preferred discomfort.

Scrubjay placed their hands on the table politely—it was a gesture they had learned from Sulfur, who said it was the ERT's way of signifying peaceful engagement. "We're here because we got your leaks. We thought you might be able to help us with something else."

Ronnie said nothing and kept her hands curved around the back of the chair.

Moose sat perfectly still, tail wrapped around their front paws, then sent: *I've been trying to track down an internal memo that circulated at GeneTrix, about the* H. sapiens *germline. The one I believe Cylindra bought for—*

Stiffening, Ronnie glared at Moose. "That goddamn fucking memo."

You know what I'm talking about then. The cat stared at Ronnie, eyes wide and accusatory.

"Listen. I don't like you. I know you and your friends at the *La Ronge Messenger* want a public planet. But I don't give a fuck about that. I never wanted there to be a government on Sask-E. It creates a swollen, stinky wormball of regulatory compliance issues, and forces you to have endless meetings with people who are only there because they won some popularity contest for idiots that they call an election." Ronnie frowned and flicked a finger at the workstation, pulling up a wrapped data blob. She didn't open it yet—just left it hovering over the table in the shape of a gooey dollop of black tar. "There is one thing I do give a fuck about, though."

"What's that?" Scrubjay asked.

"My reputation. You know how much money I made for Verdance on this place?" She gestured at the nearly empty loft, indicating everything that lay beyond its bare walls. "Unprecedented return on investment for a planetary habitat. We won two Zonies for this project. For design and for sustainability. Nobody gets both of those awards for the same project. But we did. I made that happen. If you can prove that Cylindra fucked up, I might get a little more credit." Her dark eyes were flat with rage, her voice affectless. It made her seem deadly, especially considering she once made war on Spider City.

Moose gave Ronnie another one of their intense stares. *Well, you've been honest with us, so I'll be honest with you. I don't give a rotted apple about your feelings for this planet. You're a murderer and a hypocrite. So if you want to tell us about that memo, fine. Otherwise I can continue my investigation elsewhere.*

Ronnie grimaced and spat out a chuckle. "Down to business, then. I don't have the memo. But I have the receipts that it was based on." She opened the data blob and showed them some internal documents from Verdance, outlining a germline acquisition. "This is the agreement that Cylindra orchestrated with GeneTrix. Basically, it says she bought a bunch of sequence that Archie sourced from before the Farm Revolutions. But what you want to know is exactly how he sourced it."

She pulled up another document, which looked a lot like Cimell's "historical sources" menu from the unplayable game *Farm Revolutions*. It was an annotated list of archival holdings at the Ma'at Mons Agriculture Museum on Venus.

"This is where it gets smelly. Archie's researchers found the *H. sapiens* germline in a seventy-thousand-year-old biobank that had been moldering in the museum basement. Nobody is really sure what the biobank was for, but archaeologists think it probably had some kind of ritual use. Back then, people had all kinds of superstitions about their genomes. They would send their genetic material to this biobank, and analysts would tell their fortunes by grouping them into categories like 'West African' or 'European' or 'Indigenous American.'"

Moose growled softly. *So he really did find an indigenous genome?*

"Oh—absolutely not." Ronnie waved a hand dismissively. "They were cultural categories, mystical groupings that meant a lot to people during the late Anthropocene."

I'm still not following.

"Neither did Archie. He didn't know that history, or didn't care. He wanted an authentic indigenous Earth genome, and when he saw the word 'indigenous' in that old biobank he told the researchers to grab all the data associated with it. They plundered everything, all the sequence data."

"So that's what the engineers meant by stolen sequence? It was ripped off from a museum?" Scrubjay scrolled through the documents hovering over the table, looking at the museum archive notes for "Indigenous American," which clearly stated that the genetic category was based in scientific mythology.

When Ronnie spoke again, her words came together in a rushed, ragged cadence that suggested she'd spent a lot of time talking to herself about this. "You know who absolutely loved Belany's stupid claims about indigenous Earth DNA? Cylindra. She worked with Archie to cook up this really catchy story about how they'd re-created indigenous Earth DNA from the time before the Farm Revolutions and the—the Great Bargain." Ronnie glanced sidelong at them as she used the ERT term for the practice of building people in many kinds of animal and robot bodies.

Scrubjay cut in. "So it sounds like he was telling the truth about the genomes being wild-type *H. sapiens*. But they weren't indigenous to Earth?"

"Who the fuck knows? That's all marketing garbage. The important part is where they got the germline from. This is a public museum, and the biobank is part of their archive. That means these germlines are publicly owned. Anyone can use them. Do you understand what I'm saying?"

"Public property!" Scrubjay blurted out, turning to Moose with a smile on their artificial hominin face. "There are millions of people on Sasky who are in public bodies! Doesn't that mean we have a major precedent for this being a public planet?"

"The fuck are you talking about?" Ronnie looked annoyed. "It *means* that Cylindra ripped off millions of people by forcing them to license a germline that was free. Verdance bundled the *H. sapiens* genome sequence with their real estate deals, so it's hard to claim we charged for them. They were an add-on. But Emerald? They're forcing everyone to pay an annual licensing fee for their bodies. They owe a lot of money to a lot of people." A terrible smile spread across the former VP's face. "They're going to be sued until they become . . . whatever a dead emerald looks like."

Moose gave a sarcastic flick of the tail and continued his uncanny stare. *Emeralds are minerals, Ronnie. They don't really die as such.*

Standing up, Ronnie crossed the warehouse to the kitchen and filled a glass of water. She stared out the window at a busy café across the street, where people grabbed hot drinks and sweet rolls for breakfast. Some stayed for a while, sipping, lost in their feeds. Others raced to the train station or ducked between tall buildings on their way to work. Scrubjay wondered how many of them were refugees from Lefthand, trying to find new lives in this unfamiliar northern city, far from the ocean.

When she spoke again, she sounded tired and weak. "When you write about the stolen genome, it will utterly fuck Cylindra and Emerald. But you have a hidden weapon that can deal the final blow." She turned around and pointed at Scrubjay. "You. You and your kind."

"The Flying Train Fleet?"

"That's right. When the ERT presented their train plans to Cylindra, they explained that the fleet would be self-governing. I warned her, but she didn't give a fuck. I'm sure she didn't bother to read it because she's a lazy idiot, but that doesn't matter. She signed off on it."

Scrubjay could see the fur rising on Moose's tail as they texted. *It's solid evidence that she knew a public entity was forming on the planet. And she agreed to it!*

The train had never thought about this angle before, and they were stunned that Ronnie had pointed it out. "It's true—we have that agreement in our foundational documents. We have her signature." The hominin remote stood, and took a tentative step toward Ronnie. "You didn't have to tell us that. Thank you."

"Everything in balance," Ronnie said without looking at them. "You should leave now. Let us hope we never speak again." Her eyes strayed back to the café outside as the cat and the train's hominin remote clattered back down the stairs.

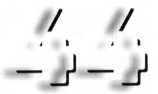

TRAIN PARTY

Scrubjay was a body within a body again, as their hominin remote sprawled on a bench in the train's freshly cleaned back car. Turning their sensors outward, the train realized for the first time that somebody had opened a café in the receiver neighborhood—right where a disaster relief tent had stood when they brought their first load of terrified refugees from Lefthand. Moose draped their front legs over one of the remote's thighs, purring and writing. After their meeting with Ronnie that morning, Moose and Scrubjay spent hours puzzling out the bizarre political legacy left to them by corporate interests of the past.

Cylindra's dirty deal with Archie Belany had left every *H. sapiens* on the planet with a public domain body. And somehow, centuries ago, the ERT had tricked Cylindra into signing off on a self-governing public transit system. Moose was working on both leads, trying to verify whether Ronnie's report was accurate. After all, she had many reasons to lie.

Scrubjay tried to model all the possible pathways out of this moment, forking the possibilities until their route into the future was as murky as the present. But they were distracted by the delayed thrill at having met the fragment of a legend: Ronnie was the bloodthirsty corporate VP who fought Destry. She started the Eel River War, when Spider unleashed the Boring Fleet, took back a river, and threatened to turn on the Ribbons.

Though a lot of people at Spider hated Destry for the treaty, Misha had told Scrubjay heroic tales about his mentor's struggles against Verdance. The train had gobbled them up, the same way they did tales of the Trickster Squad at the Battle of Saskatchewan. Now they wished they could access a "historical sources" menu that would reveal the true story of Destry's life in all its complexity. She died before Scrubjay was decanted, and Verdance had scrubbed nearly all traces of her from public servers. Still, she had been Misha's mentor, and Misha had been like an auntie to Scrubjay. Perhaps that made Destry part of the train's personal history. An elder.

What would Destry make of all this? The planet had changed so much since the old ranger's day—she had watched Sasky's forests grow and then witnessed the rise of its first cities. She'd fought to protect Spider, but secured the city's sovereignty only through a secret treaty. She must have known the Eel River Treaty was doomed to be broken, once Verdance sold off the land. Or did she? Perhaps no one could have predicted Cylindra's escalating violence, and her ruthless "Western Destiny" expansion. Certainly Destry never would have imagined that the key to the planet's freedom might come from a group of self-governing trains, one of whom was essentially her grandchild.

The homesickness that Scrubjay had felt when talking to Sulfur a few days ago came back like a summer thunderstorm on the prairies, fast and hot and electric. Suddenly they had an overwhelming urge to get to Spider City, to talk to the Flying Train Fleet and to Sulfur—to meet with their actual, living family, not some mythological grandparent.

They looked down at Moose, still snuggled against their remote's leg, and spoke aloud. "I think we should talk to the trains about what we've learned. I can call for a train party at Spider City. It's been years since we've had one."

Moose sat up, blinking slowly. *Absolutely. I've always wanted to go to Spider.*

Scrubjay sent a flurry of messages to the Flying Train Fleet. Immediately, replies formed a chain of joyful assent. A few of them wouldn't be able to get away—they had responsibilities—but the urgent need for rescue was over, and most were glad for a chance to see each other and vote on next steps. Scrubjay made sure the Trans-Maskwa Eel Line was covered and got ready for departure.

"Are you ready to take off now?" they asked Moose. "Do you need anything in La Ronge before we go?"

I'm good. But I have one question. Do you ever fly and sit inside your remote at the same time?

"Sometimes. I don't like to take seats away from passengers."

What about this time? Moose climbed into the remote's lap and rubbed the top of his soft head against Scrubjay's chest. *I like it when you have a body I can touch.*

"You're always touching my body when you're inside me. I can feel your fur covering the inside of your sleeping compartment right now." And then, hastily, the train added, "Not that I'm watching when you're in there. That's your private space."

I trust you. Moose leaned into the remote again. *Will you stay with me in a body while we fly to Spider? I want to . . . be with you. If you will have me.*

Scrubjay was about to protest that they were already together, when they realized that Moose was talking about something else. The train emitted a squawk of embarrassed laughter. "Weren't you the one who said they didn't know anything about the robot cruising scene?"

The cat stretched and kneaded the seat gently with their front paws. *I said I'm not interested in casual hookups. But this isn't casual.*

Weight drained away as Scrubjay push-pulled into the air over La Ronge. For a moment, they reveled in the lightness of their bodies: one moving three cars through currents of atmosphere and gravity, and the other running hands through the softness of Moose's deep brown fur. But then they gently pushed the cat off the remote's lap.

"This feels wrong. Do you mind if I—switch bodies?"

Moose purred. *If you want to.*

The train sped over the Eel's sinuous, muddy curves as Scrubjay folded away their hominin remote and approached Moose in the beaver-cat body that seemed more suited to the occasion. A soft platform rose from the floor beneath the two people as they embraced, mammal and bot tails intertwined, reveling in a sunbeam that the train altered its flight path to keep tumbling through their windows for as long as possible.

When the mounds and causeways of Spider emerged on the horizon, Moose and Scrubjay were wrapped tightly around each other. The cat was snoring lightly in sleep, and the remote was powered down while the train worked out a landing trajectory, talked to Sulfur, and coordinated with Peach, Contrail, and the rest of the Flying Train Fleet.

Sulfur was waiting on the landing pad for them with another hominin and three naked mole rats riding a drone. Whenever they came back to the volcano, Scrubjay briefly anticipated seeing Misha. It was hard to dismiss the statistical likelihood of his appearance, given all the times he had been there before. The train wasn't ready yet to parameterize his death, even after nine years. Instead, they waited for his repeated absence to outweigh his old presence in their model of home.

It hurt. This time, though, it wasn't as bad. Scrubjay's mind was crowded with thoughts of Moose, yawning in their arms, and the decisions that lay ahead. The remote stood up and jumped off the platform. "We're almost there."

When the doors to the back car opened, the cat and the remote stood side by side, shoulders touching.

"Hello, friends." Sulfur was beaming. They knelt to embrace Scrubjay's remote, who threw forelegs over the Archaean's shoulders. Looking over at Moose, they nodded. "Nice to meet you, Moose. Thank you so much for your reporting. I know it helped us."

The cat flicked an ear, suddenly shy, then connected with the network by padding over to a matte-bronze access panel in the floor and sitting on it. *I'm glad to do it. We need more government on this planet.*

Scrubjay sent Moose a private message: *You can send the way you always do here—no need to physically connect.*

Still using the panel, Moose replied: *Sure. But I want your friends to know that I can use traditional Spider networking hardware. It's what my mother taught me.*

Sulfur nodded at Moose, acknowledging the physical connection with an expression of faint amusement. "Let's use wireless."

The cat stood, emitting a low chirrup. *Thanks, I will.*

"We've called a Council meeting for two days from now, after the train party. I assume both of you will be there."

The two quadrupeds bowed assent. "We have a lot to tell you about our meeting with Ronnie," Scrubjay said.

"I know you do." Then Sulfur looked up and waved.

Overhead, Peach was circling into a landing, the fuzz of their carapace creating a faint halo around their body. In the distance, Scrubjay could see Maurice's bright red cars, their swollen egg shapes designed for hauling waste material. Contrail would appear any second, trailing seven special-ized cars full of equipment and medical supplies used by the ERT's first responders. More trains appeared as the day wore on. As each one landed, their remotes emerged: a pink beaver, a shiny red hominin, a plain brown elk. Two small trains who worked with the Boring Fleet were uncorking an exit into the lower tunnels of the city, sloshing lava on the floor.

Even Gardenia was coming, and he hadn't left low orbit for centuries. He texted that he was certain the atmospheric monitoring team would survive without him for a week. More of the Flying Train Fleet signaled that they would be arriving in the hours to come.

Soon, the party would begin.

By evening, Spider's fields and slopes were full of trains. Peach, Contrail, and Scrubjay were in their remotes, swimming in the caldera, while Moose talked to some of the other remotes on shore. A sizeable minority of trains refused to have remotes; they felt that it undermined their bodily integrity. One of them, Seely, was the planet's only worm train so far. She was the size of a massive boa constrictor, and just as flexible; she'd been decanted with magnetoreceptors along her back so that she could wriggle beneath the surface of the soil and plot a course using Sasky's magnetic fields as a guide.

Seely shot beneath the water while Kaiju, a ten-car train who worked as a low-level developer on *Sunbuilders*, complained bitterly from the sidelines. *If I'd known we were going to swim, I would have insisted we meet at the ocean so I could join you. I still have half a mind to wade in there and take up the whole pool.*

"Sorry about that!" Peach's beaver remote squeaked as they climbed some smooth rocks next to the massive game developer. "I've really been enjoying the new mission in *Sunbuilders* though! I was so surprised when the star went nova!"

I had nothing to do with that, you know, Kaiju sent sourly. *I work on the code that makes the solar flares.*

"Thanks a lot, because a bunch of my guys got killed by a solar flare."

Scrubjay rolled over in the water, enjoying their friends' banter, reveling in the sense of home. Even the air smelled safe down here, the tropical heat like an embrace at the molecular level.

"I'm never going to stay away from home for this long again."

Contrail floated next to them, their remote an exact replica of their deep red primary body, its seven cars shrunk to hominin size. "I like to make my home wherever people need healthcare, but I know what you mean. We always long for the city that made us."

As night fell, the trains illuminated themselves and gathered in a wide circle at the base of Spider's southern flank. Moose followed Scrubjay as the remotes settled into an inner circle, a ring within the ring of sheltering trains.

Are we going to talk about how the trains could make this a public planet? Moose sent excitedly. *Will you vote on what to do next?*

Scrubjay's remote bumped into the cat gently, enjoying their warmth. *No, you foolish mammal. We're going to sing. Listen—it's already started.*

The cat cocked their ears and heard nothing but the buzz of insects and calls of distant birds. Slowly, the buzzing and calling grew louder, and a rolling beat thumped beneath it. The air filled with a cacophony of bees, which disintegrated into the sound of footsteps on sidewalks—millions of feet, pounding and pounding. Then came the sound of a windstorm from every direction, and inside it the voices of moose and dogs roaring. Each train had a sound to add, and they picked up the noises from each other, passing the windstorm from train to train so that it seemed to whip around them in a frenzy of atmospheric disturbance. They conjured a chorus of foamers on city streets, and the shouts of a waterfall at the bottom of a ravine. As Moose listened in wonder, Scrubjay added their own voice to the mix: it was the bleeping, meeping, and zigzigzigging of the games at MetaPew from the first night they went out together. It made a perfect counterpoint to the chimes of the Boring Fleet, which came pealing out of the trains who lived among them.

As Scrubjay quieted and new voices took up the song, the remote sent to Moose again. *We play the sounds of what we hear in the world, to get reacquainted with where we are. And where we could be.*

The cat stood still, tail curled, eyes illuminated. Now they understood that the trains were singing from recordings they had taken everywhere they traveled: the mountains, the cities, the ocean, the farms, the atmospheric rivers, and the eroding rocks. They turned to Scrubjay and touched them with a paw. *It's beautiful.*

Two hours later, the rhythmic booms had faded into a chaos of light rain and back to the hum of insects. It was hard to say when the song had ended, because it segued so perfectly into the natural sounds of the jungle that ringed Spider City. The euphoria of collective song faded out and Moose's curiosity flared again.

Will you vote now?

The trains were standing up and moving around, breaking into smaller groups of friends.

We already did, Scrubjay sent. *The majority voted to let you tell the story of the agreement with Cylindra in the* La Ronge Messenger, *and to continue working with the ERT and Spider to prove that there are public entities on Sasky.*

So the trains vote by singing?

Not really. We just like to sing. And we like to hold our political discussions privately. Scrubjay broadcast the sound of a mouse giggling. *We can do more than one thing at the same time, you know.*

The cat followed the remote back toward Scrubjay's primary body, parked on the mountainside. *What now? Will we bring this to Council?*

"We will," the remote said aloud. "Also, the minority gets one reasonable concession, so we have to bring that to Council too."

What's the concession?

"They want us to tell the corporations that we will turn on the Ribbons if they violate the Eel River Treaty. Which, arguably, Emerald has already done by trying to annex Spider City."

BURN IT ALL DOWN

"Good morning, mammal friend."

Good morning, sweet transit.

Moose stretched inside the embrace of Scrubjay's body; the cat had spent the last two nights in their sleeper box while the train sent their hominin remote out to continue the party with their old friends. But now the festivities were over, and it was time to attend the Council meeting.

They followed Sulfur and the others to a room deep underground, its round walls terraced with seats. The circular space was packed with people—including a big group of trains, clustered in two groups around Peach in their pink beaver remote and Seely the worm train, coiled up in her primary body. Moose and Scrubjay sat in the second row, wedged between Peach's group and Sulfur's city planning group in the ERT. Thousands of remote participants floated overhead, including the entire Boring Fleet, their avatars shrunk into twinkling lights as thick as a spiral galaxy beneath the ceiling.

Sulfur stood up and motioned for the Council to begin. They had called the meeting, and so they were also condemned to lead it. "As you know, we have discovered that Emerald plans to take over Spider City by claiming that our treaty is no longer valid. But today I have more news, which is not mine to explain. Scrubjay, would you speak on behalf of the Flying Train Fleet?"

Sulfur stepped aside and Scrubjay stood up. They wore their matte-black hominin remote, and the mica embedded in their carapace shimmered as they looked around at everyone who had gathered.

"Council members, I'm going to share something with you that lights the way toward a new path." Beside them, Moose sent out a public data blob containing their well-curated collection of documents revealing the true provenance of the *H. sapiens* germline—and Cylindra's sign-off on the self-governing trains. "What we have here is evidence that could prove Sasky is and always has been a public planet. This would mean our entire planet could lobby for membership in the League, if we choose it. Spider City wouldn't be alone; we would be part of a delegation that represented everyone on Sasky. It would be a long road, but we have enough evidence to prevail."

Nobody said anything for a few minutes while they read. Then Peach stood on the back of a mountable drone, their pink face turned toward the galaxy of remote attendees overhead. "The Flying Train Fleet has already voted to pursue making this planet public. We have a treaty with Spider City, so we will stand by Spider as your allies as we chart a route to sovereignty."

There was an uproar of voices and texts and, over the next hour, increasingly incendiary memes. Just when it seemed the majority was swaying toward petitioning for League membership, Seely the worm train asked to speak for the minority. Everyone quieted: minority demands often revealed flaws in the majority decision.

"Spider City already has the power to stop Cylindra from buying all that land—it's written into our treaty. If any private entity threatens our land, we turn on the Ribbons." The train's amplified voice sounded calm and rational. "The dormant faults down the eastern coast of Maskwa would create a crack between two continental plates. Then we'd have earthquakes, tsunamis, undersea volcanoes. All the things that Emerald promises its customers they'll never have to deal with. Their property becomes worthless, and Emerald will rain shit all over Cylindra. Problem solved."

Moose snarled in disgust. More and more people filed into the meeting room, including a few more trains. Thousands more were tuning in remotely from their homes in Spider or elsewhere on Sasky. A few people were all the way down in Tooth.

Scrubjay spoke again. "There's no need to threaten the entire planet with natural disasters. The revelations in these documents will cover Emerald in so much disgrace that we won't need to activate the Ribbons to drive them out. They will be drowning in lawsuits from millions of people who have been paying to license the germline for these *H. sapiens* bodies."

The crowd argued over options again, trying to form coalitions, while

Moose's ears went from perky to flat back. *Coalition democracy is extremely irritating,* they sent privately to Scrubjay.

I thought you wanted more government.

I do. But I'm a voter, not a politician. I'd rather work on fact-checking my story.

Scrubjay's remote shrugged. They supposed that government might seem exasperating, especially if you'd never participated in one before.

At last, two rough coalitions emerged and began to fight it out.

One group, which sympathized with Seely and the minority, compared joining the League to Destry's "corrupt treaty-making." They wanted to activate the Ribbons immediately. Their representative, a naked mole rat named Mirror, gave a short, polished speech: *We've finally ended the barbaric practice of providing Verdance with free labor for two months every year. The League will demand something far worse. We'll have to pay dues and provide them with all the resources they want. Joining the League will be like trading ropes for chains.*

A more centrist coalition, allied with the Flying Train Fleet majority, liked the idea of seeking League membership, but warned that Spider needed assurances that their needs would be respected. Most League governments represented entire star systems. Sasky would never have the same negotiating power as a system with billions of people in it. How could they be sure the League would actually help them? Before joining, they also wanted the League's guarantee that they would force Emerald to cease operations on Sasky.

Just as the arguments reached a fever pitch, everyone's senders were slammed with warnings. A mild quake rolled through the room, like a gentle wave in the lake. A voice from the Boring Fleet rang out over the proceedings: *We're responding to an emergency beneath the mountain! It appears to be an unplanned eruption!*

In an instant, the room full of angry politicking resolved itself into a unified force, with a single goal: survival. Citizens went into evacuation mode, trains prepared to take on evacuees who needed help with mobility, and first responders raced to the portal beneath the ERT—it was the main interface between city and volcano.

I'm coming with you! Moose sent with a yowl, as Scrubjay and Sulfur rushed to join the first responders.

There was no time for a debate over the danger; Scrubjay strapped Moose into a net on their back and leaped into a gravity assist. The ERT set up an emergency data blob, and information poured into it from the Boring Fleet below.

Temperatures were soaring below the caldera, and lava levels rising. But there didn't seem to be any signs of the deep magma plume unleashing its pressurized liquid stone. If anything, the heat was moving from the surface down into Sasky's mantle, melting rocks just below the ERT water lab.

The sound of a massive tolling bell came over comms; it was the Boring Fleet. "It's not an eruption!" one of them sang. "It's the Ribbons! They're heating up!"

Tumbling out of the gravity assist, Scrubjay and Moose raced to the ERT campus, past glowing windows of roiling magma and rooms that had already been cleared by evacuees. A small group of ERT security was already in the room below the caldera when they arrived. Three moose with lowered heads stood alongside a spider-shaped bot who bristled with weapons. An Archaean with flaming red hair stood in front of the Ribbon controls, blocking access; balanced on their shoulder was Mirror, the naked mole rat who had argued on behalf of the minority coalition.

"Stay back!" shouted the Archaean. "All of you know this is what we need to do. Emerald understands nothing but violence, and the League is no better."

Their words were being sent to everyone who had attended the Council meeting. People were reacting with glee and horror and panic; Spider City people knew how to form coalitions even in the midst of an evacuation.

"This isn't the right way, friends." Sulfur stepped forward, hands empty and open. "We need to decide as a group. We don't know what will happen if the Ribbons cause plate tectonics. It could destroy the planet."

Mirror stood up straight on the Archaean's shoulder. *Better to burn it all down than lick the League's anus! We know how to live in fire. Let those sapiens try it for a while.*

Scrubjay couldn't stand it. After all this work, were they really going to turn the Ribbons on and open a crack in the floor of the ocean that would bleed lava forever? They imagined the Bronze Plate diving beneath the Southern Maskwa Plate, possibly washing away Lefthand with one tsunami. Instead of speaking, Scrubjay sent a video to the dispersed Council attendees. They showed the faces they'd seen in the past few weeks, lined and tear-swollen with trauma after what Cylindra had done. They played footage of Lefthand's broken buildings; guts spilled at the base of the ziggurat.

Then the train spoke. "If Spider unleashes earthquakes with plate tectonics, won't we be doing exactly what Emerald did when they shot their own city with railguns from space? Plate tectonics might force Emerald out, but the next city owners could be victims of even greater disasters."

A chorus of voices and texts rose up through the network:

Turn off the Ribbons!
Let us vote!
Burn it down!
Save Sasky!
Don't take our choice away!

And then, thankfully, came the chimes of the Boring Fleet: *We have shut off the Ribbons' power source! They are no longer drawing geothermal energy and are cooling down.*

Reports were coming in from ERT rangers across the planet: a few temblors but nothing more. No sign that any of the dormant faults had been fully awakened. Still, they would have to spend the next several years intensely monitoring the planet's crust for signs of movement.

Now that the immediate danger had passed, the evacuation slowly reversed itself and people trickled back into the city. The spider bot had a stunner and a tranquillizer gun aimed at Mirror and the Archaean.

"You must make amends," the spider said darkly. "And you will not be permitted to speak or vote on behalf of any coalition for the rest of the meeting. Do you submit to judgment and reparations?"

Looking defiant, the two people who almost destroyed the planet nevertheless nodded and followed the spider bot meekly. They would be taken to a rehabilitation lounge, and submit to judgment at a later Council meeting. Scrubjay couldn't imagine how they would make amends for this crime, but it would no doubt involve a great deal of work for both of them.

Much to Moose's surprise and exasperation, the Council returned to their round room and continued debate. By the time they were all clumped around the dinnertime grab table, the biological people famished and the robots wanting charge, they had come to a temporary decision. Representatives from the pro-League majority and the pro-Ribbon minority would form a diplomatic team and attend a League membership hearing. Wormhole travel would be paid out of a special League fund. The team's goal was to see the League for themselves and gather more information about what they stood to lose or gain from an alliance with other governments. When they returned, they would make a full report to the Council. Assuming the League agreed that Moose's findings meant there was sufficient evidence for public entities on Sasky, Spider City would cast a final vote on whether to join the League. And if *that* vote favored League membership, sanctions against Emerald would begin, and other public entities on Sasky could hold elections to assert their autonomy.

That's a lot of voting. Moose sent as they took a bite of stir-fried protein shreds spiced with spring onion. *What if everybody changes their mind? Do you think we might end up with plate tectonics after all?*

Sulfur sighed and put down their spoon. "As I always told Scrubjay when we were building the Flying Train Fleet, democracy isn't perfect. We might lose. But at least this way, we have a chance to form governments all across Sasky. We could make things better for people outside Spider City for once."

PUBLIC PLANET

It had been two days since the near disaster with the Ribbons, and still most people on the planet didn't know what Moose and the train had shared with the Spider City Council. Scrubjay wanted desperately for Moose to publish their story, but Moose refused to file until all the fact-checks were complete.

Most of the trains had gone back to their duties, but Scrubjay had remained at Spider, their primary body still parked on a rocky slope near the caldera. Inside, Moose licked a paw and then licked Scrubjay's beaver-cat carapace behind its approximation of an ear. *I just need a little more time. I'm working on verifying with the Ma'at Mons Agricultural Museum that the biobank Ronnie told us about is actually in their archive. If they can verify, I think we've got a pretty airtight story.*

Scrubjay shifted positions and Moose sat back on their haunches. "I still can't believe Sasky's entire *H. sapiens* population is walking around inside bodies that they never should have paid for. Stolen from publicly owned germlines."

Absently, the remote put a paw on Moose's back, enjoying the gentle vibrations from his purr. The cat snuggled closer, opening their eyes and looking at the remote's face. *Oh wait, you have to see this,* they texted. *I found some images of Cylindra with Archie Belany at a retreat on Fluffytown, looking very chummy.* The cat sent a compressed video. It was Cylindra, thousands of years ago in an *H. diversus* body with gleaming blue skin, before she was pushed out of Verdance. She bragged about brokering deals with GeneTrix for "authentic" Neanderthals on Sasky—presumably the Archaea—and how they had been replaced by real, heirloom indigenous Earth *H. sapiens*. Waving one bejeweled arm, Cylindra concluded, "We've recreated real, historical evolution just like on the iconic planet Earth."

The cat turned their head upside down, amused, and Scrubjay sighed. "I hope you put that in your story, because it's a perfect encapsulation of why that rotted foot of a person is so terrible. And wrong."

The cat trilled a note of pride. *Did you know that the Moose Report is pulling in millions of readers from offworld? It's the first wormhole traffic to hit the* La Ronge Messenger.

"Nice going."

The cat reached out a paw and put it on the remote's leg gently. *Thank you for everything you've done, friend. I never could have pulled this off without your help.*

Pressing closer to one another, the two quadrupeds set work aside and gave themselves a night of diversion.

The next day, a message finally came through the wormhole from the Ma'at Mons Agricultural Museum. Yes, the ancient biobank collection was still in the archives, a tired-sounding docent confirmed. And yes, the sequence matched those of the *H. sapiens* germline that had been licensed to millions of people living on Sasky.

Fact-checking was over. Every single *H. sapiens* on the planet had been built from public property. And the latest installment of the Moose Report was complete.

It was one of the cat's best stories yet, and certainly the most explosive. They began by telling the history of the curdled GeneTrix deal, carefully explaining how that meant Emerald was charging its residents jacked up licensing fees for free germlines. And then came the kicker: Despite Cylindra's violent crackdowns, she had been allowing public entities to form on the planet, and she signed off on the self-governing Flying Train Fleet. Moose quoted expert sources from the League, who said that Sasky could be on the verge of becoming a public planet.

The protests in La Ronge started at almost exactly the same time that the Moose Report came out, and Scrubjay suspected that Moose might have tipped off Renelf and some of the sympathetic ERT rangers working with Lefthand refugees in the receiver neighborhood.

A peaceful march started next to Boreal Station and gathered more people until they reached downtown with hundreds of thousands. Overhead, members of the Flying Train Fleet soared and sang, their rectangular shadows sweeping across the chanting crowd.

WHO BUILDS CITIES?
THE PUBLIC!
WHO OWNS SASKY?
THE PUBLIC!
I SAY PUBLIC—YOU SAY PLANET!
PUBLIC!
PLANET!
PUBLIC!
PLANET!

The branding team at Emerald responded to the Moose Report with their own version of events. Cylindra sat on her tidy upper ziggurat balcony, new scaffolds sprouting behind her, and explained with a condescending smile that the germline was completely legitimate. "We're building the happiest place in the League, and these squatters at Spider City are just spinning their usual web of lies." She chuckled at the pun, as if the whole situation was silly and inconsequential. "The self-governing trains are a complete myth, as is this story about our germlines. We are prepared to stop their mob violence with decisive action from our security forces."

Cylindra's boldface lies in that footage made her a meme that traveled through every wormhole. More protesters were broadcasting from marches in the Emerald cities, demanding sanctions against the city's corporate owners. As they chanted, Moose began to write their next report: it was about the first lawsuits being filed on behalf of *H. sapiens* whose bodies were built on fraud and false advertising.

META PEW

The cat woke up in their sleeping box, checked their feeds, and alerted Scrubjay: *Cylindra is sitting in a giant pile of rotting biomass right now, and I like it.*

What's the latest? Scrubjay asked privately.

They were coming in for a landing at La Ronge, heavy with passengers, many headed to the demonstrations that had been going on for a week now.

Moose yawned hugely and sent: *The League has initiated an investigation into rights violations in Lefthand. Emerald is being sued by tons of people, but especially by the Rackleworths, who were early investors in the planet. They are very rich and have an army of lawyers who are fiercer than the Boring Fleet. Apparently Cylindra took off last night in a ship headed for Emerald HQ.* The cat rolled onto their back, wriggling with glee. *How long before she's fired, do you think?*

The train emitted a burst of cheerful music from a speaker near Moose's ear. *I bet we'll find out soon.*

As they landed and opened their doors, Scrubjay observed with pleasure that Boreal Station was no longer at the edge of town. Passengers filtered out into a healthy neighborhood that grew where the refugees had landed after that horrifying night in Lefthand. The café they had noticed a couple weeks ago was now flanked by shops, restaurants, and even a bar that somebody had named THE TONGUE FORKS. Its sign was slightly carbonized at the edges, and Scrubjay guessed that it had been pulled from the wreckage of the original in Lefthand. When people survived, their most beloved places often survived with them.

The last rider disembarked, dragging a fat suitcase into the warm summer air, and Scrubjay was off duty. They would spend the night in La

Ronge and fly the Eel River Route south in the morning. In the meantime, the cat-beaver remote was already unfolding itself from the back car and bounding to meet Moose in the front. The friends touched noses, and Scrubjay rubbed their face against the thick red-brown fur of Moose's shoulder.

"Let's go for a walk," the train suggested.

Moose purred. *Want to head over to the Meta Pew?*

As they strolled, they discussed the latest news from Spider. Their diplomatic team had sent word from the League that Sasky's public status would be the subject of a hearing next year. Moose snorted. *I suppose democracy makes up for being annoying by also being slow.*

Nobody was seriously proposing that they turn the Ribbons on again. Mirror and their coconspirator were paying reparations to Spider by painstakingly analyzing every piece of data from the areas around the Ribbons, looking for possible damage; they took responsibility for their actions by thinking every day about what they had almost done. Meanwhile, the Council was still debating whether they wanted to join the League at all.

The Meta Pew was empty at this hour, its long wares bar covered in devices that the staff wanted to repair before the evening crowd. Cimell, creator of unplayable games, hovered over a heads-up display, using two actuators to solder a new connector to it. They had painted their carapace a brilliant gold and stenciled the words PUBLIC PLANET on their barrel-shaped torso, next to their front sensor bulb.

As they walked inside, Cimell twisted their sensor to face them. "It's Moose and Scrubjay!"

Hi, friend, Moose sent.

"Still working on *Farm Revolutions*, friend?" Scrubjay asked.

"Getting back to it, yeah. It's been . . . a time. Haven't been doing a lot of game development."

Maybe one day it will actually be playable. Moose jumped up next to Cimell with a sarcastic flick of the tail.

"I actually found myself thinking a lot about your game over the past couple of months," Scrubjay said. "I liked how you made it clear that revolutions don't happen overnight. Just because there's a huge battle doesn't mean the revolution is over."

Cimell stopped soldering and regarded Scrubjay through a visual sensor ringed with electroreceptors. "I know what you mean. Maybe the battles are more exciting. They make for better superhero stories, like with Wasakeejack and Muskrat. But the revolution is actually happening in the boring details, like how you manage housing and water, or who is allowed to speak. In a way, the Farm Revolutions are still ongoing. We've barely started to realize what the Great Bargain could be."

They plunged into a discussion about local politics.

Verdance, which still technically owned La Ronge, had sent a handful of apologetic reps to meet with protesters and the ERT Council to figure out a new system for housing allocations. According to Cimell, who had been active in the uprisings, everything was on the table. La Ronge might form its own government. There was talk of allowing everyone to buy property—not just *H. sapiens* in their now-worthless public bodies. Or maybe all property would be co-owned by everyone in the city. At the same time, Verdance was whitewashing its history, distancing itself from Cylindra's deal with GeneTrix, and trying to pretend that they had been on the side of universal property ownership from the start.

Sask-E was on its way to becoming a public planet, which meant dreams realized for some, and regulatory nightmares for others. Emerald's exit would be messy, and probably more companies would pull out too. The governments that grew in their absence would take every possible shape, and none would be anywhere near perfect. Instead of a virgin Pleistocene frontier, Sasky was like every other planet that Earth people had occupied—a chunk of rock and biomass, stolen and re-stolen so many times that even its humblest microbes were of decidedly sketchy provenance.

Still, outside the Meta Pew it was one of those flower-clogged summer days that stretches beyond bedtime in the far northern hemisphere of a tilted planet. Scrubjay ran a hand over Moose's soft back and sent to them privately: *I want to take you to Carbon Alley. It's my favorite robot cruising bar.*

The cat purred.

There was no point in flying the hard route ahead if they couldn't enjoy the day while it lasted.

ACKNOWLEDGMENTS

I wrote this book because I wanted to dream up a more hopeful world. And so my first thanks go to poet Stephanie Burt, who told me several years ago that I obviously needed to write an epic about nation-building. Kim Stanley Robinson, author of many geoengineering epics, told me (jokingly) that he would permit me to write about terraforming as long as I included a character named Kim, and so I have. Filmmaker Sonya Ballantyne spent quite a bit of time talking to me about Cree futurism, which is an undercurrent throughout this book, and later graciously did a sensitivity read on the whole manuscript. Native Studies professor Jessica Kolopenuk offered invaluable feedback on the myth of indigenous DNA.

Materials scientist Christine Payne suggested the technologies that heal Whistle's brain, and also the sensors made from paper. Planetary scientist David Catling patiently explained how you build an atmosphere from scratch, and geologist Vicki Hansen talked to me about volcanoes on Venus, which is another planet like Sasky that has no plate tectonics. Geophysicist Attreyee Ghosh spent a long time explaining to me how plate tectonics work, and helped me come up with the idea of the Ribbons. Geophysicist Mika McKinnon told me what colors lava would be underground. All the geoscientists I spoke with agreed that if you could avoid plate tectonics, you absolutely would.

USGS river expert and cartographer Kyle House talked to me about how rivers work and what they want. He also helped me come up with the idea for the magma dam on the Eel River. Jeffrey Tumlin, director of transportation of the San Francisco Municipal Transportation Agency, told me all about what he imagines train consciousness would be like, and why they would be obsessed with games.

Jay Justice provided an excellent sensitivity read, looking especially at representations of race, ability, and sexuality.

I have tried to live up to the expertise and passion of the people whose work I consulted as I wrote, but obviously all faults and flaws are my own responsibility.

A million years of thanks to my editor, Lindsey Hall, who patiently read through several drafts and always figured out exactly what needed fixing. This book would be a lot more foolish if it hadn't been for her brilliant work. My wondrous agent, Laurie Fox, kept my spirits up, gave me encouragement, and steered me on the right path. And thanks to the whole team at Tor, from the marketing folks to the art department, who have kept the lights on during this dark time and filled the world with stories.

I have reserved all my most profound gratitude and love for my lifelong sweeties, Charlie Jane Anders, Jesse Burns, and Chris Palmer. We make a good pod, even if sometimes we aren't sure which shows we want to watch together.